# When You
# Come Home

a novel

Nora Eisenberg

Curbstone Press

First Edition, 2008
Copyright © 2008 by Nora Eisenberg
All rights reserved.

Cover design: Susan Shapiro
cover photo: courtesy of Magnum Photos, New York, NY.

This book was published with the support of the
Connecticut Commission on Culture and Tourism
and donations from many individuals. We are very
grateful for this support.

Connecticut Commission
on Culture & Tourism

Library of Congress Cataloging-in-Publication Data

Library of Congress Cataloging-in-Publication Data

Eisenberg, Nora
    When you come home : a novel / Nora Eisenberg. -- 1st ed.
        p. cm.
    ISBN 978-1-931896-47-4 (pbk. : alk. paper)
    1. Persian Gulf War, 1991--Veterans--Fiction. 2. Persian Gulf
syndrome--Fiction. 3. Marines--Fiction. 4. Homecoming--Fiction.
5. Political fiction. I. Title.
    PS3605.I83W48 2008
    813'.6--dc22

                                        2008036982

CURBSTONE PRESS   321 Jackson Street   Willimantic, CT 06226
        phone: 860-423-5110    e-mail: info@curbstone.org
                        www.curbstone.org

*to the memory of*
*Sandy Taylor,*
*warrior for peace*

*On January 16, 1991 the United States launched Operation Desert Storm, attacking Iraqi forces occupying neighboring Kuwait. Forty-three days later, the U.S. and its allies had defeated the Iraqi military, leaving an estimated 100,000 Iraqi soldiers and 10,000 civilians dead. Only 148 U.S. troops died in battle in that first Gulf War, the remaining half a million returning home unharmed. Or so it seemed.*

# When You Come Home

## April 1991

## Mimi

*She's on her back, her eyes fixed on the dimmed ceiling light, so I can't catch her gaze to slow her down.*

*Hold off, I say. Not yet, darling.*

*How long...Mimi? How long...baby?*

*Her call is loud, as if I'm rooms away, and not on my knees on the floor at the foot of her bed, looking inside her, probing her with my hand.*

*Just a little longer...a little longer. I stroke her long legs.*

*She moans, and I moan with her, Soon, darling, soon. She's purple and pulsing and ready to go.*

*Then she's thrashing, writhing. Fuck soon, she cries. Now. Right fucking now! You fucking hear me?*

*I see the dark dome, shiny and slick.*

*Yes, I say. Now.*

*One push does the trick, and he's out of her and in my hands. He has a cap of black curls, cocoa skin, shell pink palms and soles. I survey him from head to toe, toe to head, and back again.*

*Is everything okay? she says.*

*Better than okay, I say. He's perfect!*

*You sure? she says. All the parts are there?*

*Every last one, I laugh as his baby penis showers us with pee.*

*Then we cut the cord together, and I lay him on her chest.*

*Say hello to your mama, I say, slipping her nipple into his wild, starving mouth.*

*Lily is warming up the van when I pull into the driveway,*

1

*clearly pissed. I climb in beside her, and she lets me kiss her cheek, but she doesn't kiss me back or even try to smile. Impatient by nature, she always wants what she wants when she wants it. Today, though, she is a crimson-faced troll. She wants my son, Tony, and nothing else. Not my explanation about the midnight call from a mother in the thick of labor, not my assurance that we have three hours to make it the ninety miles to the base. Only when I describe the baby and his helmet of black hair does she pay me any mind.*

*Black as Tony's was? she says.*

*Not quite, I tell her. It's family lore that my son was born with black hair, which he shed at a year for golden curls. Oh, no one's like our Tony, I laugh.*

*And then her face assumes its natural peachy blush and she laughs. She's our Lily again.*

*The rest of the ride it's, What will he look like? Will he be wearing his jeans or his uniform? Will he be pooped from it all or hopped because he's back? What's the first thing he will say, do? What will he want to eat?*

*I am as excited as Lily, but her intensity—and the early morning delivery—leave me drained, and I sleep lightly as she chatters and cackles imagining my son and our reunion. At the exit from the Interstate, she wakes me.*

*Madam, she announces like she's my tour guide. Ten minutes to your destination, Madam.*

*And I pull myself from a dream, a standard I haven't produced in years—the same drive down the same road to the same destination.*

*Earth to Mimi, she calls.*

*Earth to Mimi. It's her phrase of the week and she says it with pride. Lily is a cliché artist, and I mean artist or at least pioneer, a cliché pioneer, if not creating then discovering expressions in their infancy. From Lily's lips I have heard first such basics as, Have a nice one. Any-hew. Duh. With words, and most anything, she's an open, eager pup. And as loyal as a spaniel. New phrases come, old phrases stay. And old friends, or whatever I am to her. Whatever. Sometimes she calls me that. Hi, Whatever, she'll say on the message machine. Don't wait up for me, Whatever. Not a shred of anxiety hides behind the joke. She knows she is as important to me as Tony is. As important as Henry, his father, was. We pass a sign for Peabody Base. Where Tony is waiting. Where with baby Tony in my arms, I waited for Henry, for Henry in a box.*

*Lily's eyes are on the road, but she reads my mind.*

*Don't go there, she says. Don't even think of going there! He's coming home. This one's coming home. A no-brainer, if I ever saw one.*


*The parking lot is jammed but we find a spot for the van. Then like we ourselves are marines, we all march—a battalion of worried family and friends—up the hill, past the Quonset huts, the officers' club, the mess hall, around the barracks to the parade field. It's April but the field is still a mess, icy here, muddy there. And again I feel myself sink. What if he doesn't come? Around me, I catch the grim faces of other mothers and fathers, too afraid to tempt fate with a smile. March, two, three, four. Please, two, three, four. At the bleachers, a woman sergeant points the way—you left, you right. She is all business, but her eyes smile, and I guess that she's a mother too, and I smile back, grateful, as if she's a crossing guard, protecting our kids this last leg of their journey.*

*They're in the mess hall, she announces. Secretary of Defense Cheney is welcoming them home via satellite. It won't be long.*

*Then suddenly they're there, the long green line of them, marching onto the field of sludge.*

*Lily sees him first and calls his name. Maybe Tony hears*

3

*her. His big white smile explodes from his thin worried lips. But he stares ahead—eyes on the jarhead before him—and marches straight.*

*I guess they're still on duty, I say.*

*Well, I'm not, Lily laughs. I'm a free agent.*

*And then, like the lizard-bird they invented for one of their childhood plays, she swoops down the steps, slithers under the barriers, flies across the field, then jumps him, clasping her arms around his neck.*

*She laughs and cries, calling, You're home, home sweet home! Oh my God, oh my God!*

*Then the rest of us follow, escaping the bleachers, running and crying.*

*A bugle band plays behind us. It's been playing all along, I guess. But finding him and holding him tight now, I feel calm enough to hear the medley. From the halls of Montezuma to the shores of Tripoli....God bless America....The home of the brave....*

*I drive us home. The kids sit in the back—a holdover from when they were little, when I'd belt them in, side by side. In recent years, I've sometimes growled, What am I, a chauffeur? But today I'm pumped with joy. Tony naps in Lily's lap, Lily hums, and my eyes fill with joyous tears as I think, My son is back. My kids are safely in the back. The earth is back on course.*

*I exit the Interstate as soon as I can and take the Commonwealth Expressway. I want to see the dogwood and magnolia, the pear and peach, their buds preparing to pop. When Tony was away, I hadn't noticed trees or sky or rain or snow, just the Gulf and the desert on the TV screen, the fiery burst of bombs. I turn on the radio to hear the local weather.*

*Maybe a cold spell tomorrow, maybe a storm, I call into the back. I want my son to be assured that his scorching desert days are over. At our exit, it begins to rain that cold piercing rain that our part of the Appalachians features in April, and I'm grateful.*

*"Ice or snow?" he mumbles from his sleep. "Or sleet or hail?"*

*Nothing with my son is simple, even the smallest detail offering an occasion for tormenting indecision. Should he fill up at the Exxon or the Gulf station? Should he pick up pizza or Chinese take-out? Should he wear his sneakers or his moccasins? Going to the war was not a decision but the outgrowth of indecision: Should he work in healthcare like his mother or be a jarhead like his father? Confused, and low on cash, he decided to study biology and history at the state college and join the marine reserves, the latter paying for the former and providing him with the sense that he was keeping his options open. The only thing he was ever sure of, I think, was Lily. That he needed her—to tell him what to do, and make him laugh.*

*It was Lily who would prick their pinkies, the first time wrapping the wounds in a single bow of gauze so that for a full day and night like Siamese twins he was joined to her and she to him. "Blood children," she anointed them, not yet knowing the word "siblings" but knowing blood brothers wouldn't do.*

*Who Lily was to him he couldn't decide—despite her frequently executed blood ritual. To Tony, she was not family—not sister or cousin, later on not girlfriend or lover. The year before he went to the desert, a course in the modern novel suggested the possibility that Lily was his double. A psychology course the year before that made him think she might be his alter-ego. The college's requirement to keep a personal "learning log" that "applied studies to life" and my son's constitutional tendency to be a slob who put nothing away—because the right place involved choices and decisions—conspired to provide me with more information*

5

*than a mother should have. So more than once, I was face to face with an open notebook. With scrawls about girls. And about Lily. What she was to him. Was she this? Was she that?*

*Tony was two when Lily was born. I remember the day she came home from the hospital, how patiently he waited in our front yard for Connie's car to turn the corner, how carefully he scrubbed his hands so he could hold her, how tiny and delicate and clearly beautiful she was, her hair the color of lemon, her eyes black as olives. Back then, we all lived on the other side of the highway, on the valley road behind the ski school, in the saddest little ranch homes ever built, twin two-bedroom houses, one white with red trim, one red with white trim, both with pitiful bay windows affording a view of the other alone. Everything about us seemed to coordinate. One with only a father, one with only a mother. Lily's father, Ronnie, back from Vietnam dead to all but drugs, her mother running off early on to escape his drug-fueled blows. Me dead to all but Life with a capital L, as Lily would say—trading the misery of my boy-husband's death in Vietnam for the joy of catching babies—and caring for my son, and then Lily those days, then months, then years, when Ronnie took off to shoot up and fight, and then die. I would have adopted Lily. We all knew Ronnie's plans to get clean and come back for her would never materialize, but Lily said it would hurt him too much to sign her over for good. And so we managed with bi-annual continuing orders from a good-hearted county magistrate. Once Lily makes a decision, it's wise not to fight.*

*Evidently someone down the road has been posted to watch. For by the time we pull into the driveway, neighbors are gathered in the front yard bearing covered dishes. When Tony emerges from the van, they cheer. The Edwards girl from down the street plays "It's a Grand Old Flag" on her recorder, and then her brother toddles over. Marie Edwards snaps a Polaroid of her son giving my son a flag. Two kids from the cul-de-sac unfurl a computer printout: OUR HERO. Luisa Molto from across the street holds a basket of daffodils and crocuses from her back yard. Then everyone follows us inside to set down their offerings.*

*Someone produces a case of cold Budweiser and the toasts begin. When Henry came back, or didn't, when Henry's body came back and the neighbors were waiting for us back in our little house the other side of the highway, it was quieter, but the same words circle the air: True hero. You showed them. Kick ass. God bless.*

*Now in our noisy kitchen, Lily reads my mind again. Give it a rest, she whispers. This one's back for real. Alive and kicking.*

*Then seeing that "this one" has laid his head on the kitchen table, like a kindergartner at nap time, his shrill snore challenging the din, we both begin to laugh. And the neighbors, blowing kisses and hi-fiving the air, tiptoe out.*

*Tony won't be budged. Lily and I settle beside him, nursing our beers and watching, in silent joy, his strong, even breath. The worries that have tormented me for the interminable days of the five-week war—that he'd been killed, maimed, lost in the desert—seem years away.*

*From his sleep, he says, The fucking sand. It's everywhere. He coughs and says, It's really hard to breathe.*

*A dream, I croon. You're home, you're safe.*

*Home sweet home, Lily croons.*

*Sweet, he says. You're sweet. Your letter. What you said....* *His eyes are closed but his hand finds her hand, then her pinky, linking his with hers, like when they were children, little blood children joined as one.*

*Then Lily is lifting him to his feet, leaning him on her shoulder, walking him down the hall to his room.*

*One foot, then the other.... One arm, then the other.... Very good. I hear her coaxing him out of his boots and uniform.*

## Lily

*I wasn't mad at Mimi, just edgy. I hadn't had a real night's sleep in weeks. For forty-three days and nights we watched CNN every chance we got, and I don't think we made it to bed before two any night and I leave for the Shenandoah Animal Clinic at seven. And sleep was shitty. When we shut off the TV, shut our eyes, stopped paying attention, it felt like that's when disaster could strike. Like from ten thousand miles away we'd been keeping guard, like the TV was our command station from which we issued our orders: Bring him back safe. Or else.*

*Then there was the delivery. Did she really have to catch a baby that morning? I know she said the lady was early, but wasn't there another midwife in the entire Shenandoah County to step in? And would it be so terrible if a regular old doctor delivered one of her babies now and then? Would the sky fall in without her coconut milk massages and Enya tapes? We weren't late, but we could have been. I hate even thinking of being late while Mimi seems to love these Superwoman shows starring herself. Watch me bring a new life into the world, run a conference on pre-natal care in Appalachia, raise an orphan girl, bring my son home from war without a scratch. As if all that praying she did—and don't think I didn't hear her calling upon God, God-Henry that is, every morning in the shower—would make everything work out.*

*I'm not being fair. Mimi's good people. And mostly I was just scared, mad scared—to see Tony again. And you know you can go really far with Mimi before she'll get angry. So I was all huffy and silent like it was something Mim had done that morning, when it was really something I had done that made me so afraid.*

*Would he remember what I wrote?*

*How we should be together, in every way, when he came home. How I couldn't imagine living without him. That when he was away and in danger, it all became crystal clear.*

*I guess you could call it a dirty letter, that letter where I laid it out, laid myself out. I didn't exactly say, When you come home, I want you to do you know what to my you know what and I will do the same to you and yours. But I was definitely thinking along those lines when I wrote, When you come home, let's really be together. Forever. I think I did write, I miss you so much and think of you all the time in a whole new way. I wrote so many versions, so I can't remember if the one I sent said that I was still a virgin and something along the lines of, When I think of doing with anyone else the things I've started thinking about doing with you, I get nauseous, which tells me a lot. I know I wrote, When you come home from the war/operation/whatever they want to call it, I'll be there in every way. And I ended my letter: What do you think about these ideas of mine? So he'd have to answer.*

*He wrote back and said, You're right. They call it an operation but this is an all-out war. Like I was that Christiane Amapoo lady on CNN interviewing him for the news. And like he's telling her and the viewing public, You're right. That's how I see it, too, Ms. Amapoo. Not one word about the other stuff. He's naturally shy, but I know he's had sexual relationships; when he was on the phone with his ex-girlfriend Kim once, I heard him say the word suck. Okay, I'm a risk-taker and he's not. But he'd been at war, which was pretty risky, so why couldn't he just close his eyes and open his heart and write? I wasn't expecting suck or fuck at all, and maybe not even, I'm all yours, forevermore. But a teensy response to my gigantic personal revelation.*

*After I wrote that letter and he wrote back his war correspondent spiel, I let it go—in my letters but not in my heart. And all morning as I got ready to go to Peabody, then in the van, I am going nuts thinking, What will he say? Will he do his regular routine, his this or that, or maybe and could it be one day, this way or that way routine? Or would he pretend I never wrote those things? Just give me a hug and say, Hi, there, Pits, which is one of his names for me 'cause the top of my head reaches just below his armpits. Like nothing had changed when for me the world had changed 1000 %. Pits! I used to sniff his armpits and tell him he had BO, which he never did. He had a beautiful smell, like brown mustard, which seemed perfect given the color of his skin.*

*I had to calm down before we got there. So I just kept my eyes on the car ahead of us and tried to empty my mind of all thoughts about him. But then images started floating in, not exactly thoughts but pictures of him. Like his skin, that gorgeous gleaming bronze Cuban skin, from his father. His eyes, tree-frog green from Mimi. Then his long arms and legs, and then the private part of him I hadn't seen since I was little.*

*Mimi was snoozing but suddenly she's talking about Tony's black hair, when he first came out, and I could hardly breathe from all the love racing through me. Then we were there and he was just marching onto the parade field, looking straight ahead, like he didn't see me. I know he was just following orders, but I couldn't take being apart from him one more minute, and I rushed him. Then everyone followed, and even though I was sobbing like crazy I started to laugh, too, because it was like I was a captain or some other military hotshot leading everyone to action. They'd been traveling for three days and were beat and, just as I'd hoped, their goodbyes were short and sweet. And we were on our way!*

*In the van, I had him right where I wanted him, beside me in the back. I settled his head on my lap, and then a few minutes later I pried his paws off his rucksack and put them on my boobs, and I swear he was smiling up at me from his sleep the rest of the ride, as happy and tingly as I was, I like to think.*

*At home, he fell asleep at the table, and I just sat there watching him. He started talking about the desert and his voice sounded so deserty, so dry and lonely. I never wanted him to feel that way again and I wished I could pour myself down him, to be inside him, soaking him. I was seeing that creek we used to catch minnows in, the one that gushes through Mt. Hope cemetery, keeping it green and wet, way into the winter most years. Then I was getting wet, which had never happened to me before. Not even when I wrote him that letter.*

*I wanted to hear about the desert. But I wanted to know about the other stuff. Him and me. And then with his eyes still closed, he's saying, Your letter. What you said. Sweet...so sweet. Then he opened his eyes and looked at me, not hard like, Hey babe, but like, Hey there you are...hey I missed you! I took that look as his answer, and my cue. I said, You're very tired....Let me help you take your things to your bedroom, help you get to bed. Yada yada. The rest is history.*

### Tony

*I saw my mother first. I'm marching onto the field, but I glimpse her in the bleachers, with her Mother-Teresa, long-suffering face. Jesus Christ, crack a smile, I think. I'm coming back from the fucking war and she's suffering. I almost died. I almost lost my left eye and my right hand. And my mind. And there she is like she's gone through the Battle of the Bulge. I know why, of course, but still it's a drag, and I don't want to look. Besides we're still in formation and not allowed to look any way except ahead.*

*From the corner of my eye, I see Lily too. She is jumping up and down. Tony, over here! she calls. Then like we're little kids again, playing tag or something, she shouts, Hey, you, Ready or not. Here I come. And she flies from the bleachers down to the field and onto my back, leading the way for a full-scale charge.*

11

*Everyone's running onto the field now, and shouting, Welcome home. You made it back. You're home. And everyone was crying. Everyone.*

*There was a field of food, balloons, two bands, and squads of clowns handing out snacks and drinks. My whole unit was wasted—from three months in the sand and the last week in beer and travel—and only Barr, our leading alcoholic, could have managed a party at that point. The rest of us just grabbed a hotdog and a coke and said some fast goodbyes. And besides, we'd pissed and shit our pants together, and were glad not to have to look at each other for a while.*

*In the back of the van, Lily had me practically on top of her. She had written me in Kuwait City that she wanted us to stop being so brother-and sister-like. I thought if I wrote back anything about it—Okay or Maybe or Let's talk—I'd be tempting fate, like I was sure I'd come out on the other side of the desert alive, and for my presumptuousness I'd be punished with instant death by Scud. But still, some nights on the desert, I'd feel so scared and lonely, and I'd start thinking of Lily. I mean I was always thinking of Lily but I mean in the way she said she wanted.*

*A couple of times I put my hand down my shorts as I thought of her. I whispered, Oh, baby, Oh, my sweet baby. But then I'd stop. I could never imagine not having Lily in my life but had never thought of this, which is surprising because I'm generally horny as hell and couldn't get enough of Kim, my girlfriend at college. But Kim wasn't Lily. With Kim, the sex was easy but everything else felt hard, and no matter how much I tried, I'd feel torn in two. On one side was my soul, which is to say Lily, on the other side other girls and sex. Your soul or sex, sex or your soul, I'd debate. Then leave it to Lily—coming up with a new plan, which is, I guess, the oldest plan in the world, or the oldest non-plan. Be natural. Let's be together naturally and fully, she wrote. Body and soul. But would it work?*

*After supper, Lily helped me carry my bags to my room while mom washed up. I was falling asleep on my feet, and she started undressing me, like you're too tired to do this yourself. Then she's stripping me, and I'm like, Are you sure? And she's saying nothing, just working off my pants and shorts. She's touching me everywhere, and I'm still going, Is this the right thing? She licks me like our old cat Lemon used to. Delicately, here, there. And I'm feeling with every lick like a ton of sand is lifting. I'm crying, Lily, Lily, and touching **her** and licking **her** and she loves it. Then out of nowhere, I start telling her about the land mine that I thought was a rock, how it started sizzling in my hand, burning a hole before it fizzled, about the oil falling from the sky that blinded me in one eye for one full week. How I pissed my pants every day and shit them twice that I could remember. Not exactly romantic talk but our bodies were naked and maybe I figured why not our insides? She starts licking my dick and my ass, like I'd done something great. I do the same to her, and then we're going off together like twin fucking bombs. Then I say, You sure you like that way? Maybe we should do it the other way. She says, What other way? Show me. Which she always used to say to me because I'm older. Show me how to skate a figure 8, show me how to draw an ape, show me this, show me that. And I show her.*

# Spring

# 1. Their Place inside the Mountain

There was no storm in the night, but a soft steady rain, and by morning the sky is clear and everything beneath it glistening. Mimi wakes early to drive up the mountain road to talk to Henry. She wants to tell him that everything is okay—their son has come home. She drives quickly, feeling what she hasn't felt in ages, that thrilling belief in every inch of her body, that anything is possible, like she felt the first days here up on the mountain, when she first met Henry.

They'd come to the Shenandoah Valley from very different places—Henry from Miami, Mimi from D.C., he from a family of Cuban cigar rollers that made good by opening a cigar store on Collins Avenue, she from an Italian family that came to Washington, like so much of its white population, to do something "official." Her great-grandpa, just back to Philadelphia from the First World War and penniless, knew someone who knew someone who landed him a job sweeping floors in the main post office, where he quickly discovered he had no aptitude for indoor life and with his first month's wages opened a produce stall in the old North Market at the end of Georgia Avenue. For three generations, tobacco on Henry's side and fruits and vegetables on hers, had kept their families afloat, or at least bobbing. Just enough was different in their backgrounds to fascinate the other, but their families' similar struggles—to become American, to shed accents, to get by on modest incomes, from products of the earth, no less—made them feel instantly at home with each other.

They'd come in the winter, to be counselors at the ritzy kids camp that Monuten Lodge used to run on school breaks, the only two people on the entire mountain, it had seemed, who couldn't ski. He loved her the first time he saw her, falling before she ever hit the slopes, as she made her way up the kiddy hill holding on to a rope. He had wanted to pick her up, but she righted herself quickly, smiled embarrassedly, though no one was around except him and he was in his car, and hobbled back inside. He followed her into the lobby, watching as she wrestled off the cumbersome skis. Then she went into the gift shop, and he watched through the window as she studied bottles of *avant* and *apres* lotions, hand-knit turtlenecks patterned with giant snowflakes and pines, angora and tartan throws. She had smooth olive skin, wine colored lips and cheeks, jade eyes and blue-black hair, but it was the lingering pain in her face, struggling for dignity after the humiliating fall, that got him. He had never stolen before, but he wanted to give her something to make her happy, and since he would not be paid till the end of the week, he grabbed the violet lap blanket she'd been stroking like it was a cat, draped it over his shoulders ostentatiously like a frat boy with a crew neck, and brazenly pushed through the door. Here, he said catching up with her in the lobby. Later, he told her he'd pinched it. But by then they were inseparable and the blanket, those first days of passion, too soiled to return, which, because she came from a family of honest vendors, was her first impulse.

He had been born Enrique, but to her he was always Henry. And this morning, with their son safely home, she calls out his name as soon as she turns onto the crumbling asphalt road that climbs the mountain.

"Henry, Henry," she calls, "he's back, he's back."

She laughs because she loves her son so, because the war didn't destroy his beautiful skin and hair, like Henry's all the same tawny brown, catching the sun like copper. How amazing that she should laugh, she thinks, as she parks the car on the shoulder of the road, for she always cries when she comes here, missing Henry.

There is a place on Monuten Mountain that she and

17

Henry thought of as theirs, a place *inside* the mountain is how they'd thought of it. To get to the dark secret spot they had to find the path off the mountain road, then find a small hole in a thick swath of fir, and feel their way with their hands to the small clearing. From the road, no one could see in. But inside the green tent, they could peek out across the whole valley. That first winter, hiking while the others skied, they'd discovered the place, trekking there again and again, to make love and survey their lives, the immense vista encouraging them to do both grandly. Long sex sessions in the snow on the top of the mountain alternated with long talks. No tobacco and produce for them. She wanted to be a surgeon. Yes, yes, he thought that was perfect for her. He wasn't sure what he wanted. Just to be with her, watching her. He couldn't bear to be away from her. A perfect plan would be for him to work at anything and then come home to look at her. She'd laugh in delight because he loved her so, but she'd tell him he'd tire of that, and what about when they had children? Then I'll stay home and look at all of you, he'd say. Look out for all of you.

Today, she makes her way down the path quickly, eager to talk to him.

Inside the circle of trees, she says, "I don't know what I'd have done if he hadn't come back. He looks so handsome and healthy, tired but so handsome and healthy."

She tells him how Lily ran across the field and how the whole crowd followed. She tells him it's a very different war than Vietnam. It had been quick and ended happily. "At least for our side," she says.

She's watched too much CNN not to know that lots of Iraqis have died. The footage of the nonstop bombings has shaken her, many nights making it impossible to sleep. But this morning she can think only of herself and her family. "Henry," she says. "Everything's okay again, baby."

When Henry didn't come back, when she was nuts with grief around the clock, she'd keep up his end of the conversation too, which scared her, making her worry for her sanity. But his voice and words were the only ones she wanted, the only ones that gave her any comfort. Today, for the first time in a long time, she feels his words bubble inside her again, but today she's not afraid. She's happy. With Tony back, it feels like Henry is back. Life is taking off where it had stalled twenty years before.

"I looked out for you good," she hears him say. "You and our boy." He says, "Give my boy a kiss. Tell him his pop's so glad that he made it back. Celebrate for me, baby. Buy him our cake!"

The double seven-layer from Stoehmer's. Of course! she thinks. "Of course!" she says. "What a good idea, my angel."

"Yum-yum-yum," she hears him say, his chant for sweets or sex.


At Stoehmer's, she asks for their cake—a tower of dark fudge, the richest and best cake they make. She picks out some candles because her son has passed his twenty-first birthday on the desert. As soon as she hears Tony stirring, she'll light the candles and march the cake to his room, like she used to do on their birthdays. All day they'd nibble away at it, always leaving a little wedge, to relight at bedtime for an extra wish.

Beth Stoehmer refuses to let her pay. She points to the banner. WELCOME HOME BOYS AND GIRLS.

"Today's on me for all our heroes. Back before we knew it! That's the way to win a war."

She takes her decorating bag and shoots sun yellow cream on the earth brown fudge: WELCOME HOME HERO.


Back home, Mimi heads off to Lily's room. Most days, she knows, Lily is up early, reading books on pet care for her job at the local vet. In their home, Lily is the mistress of all ceremonies, and she'll want to view the cake and give it her

OK. Welcome home hero! Dumbo, is more like it, she can imagine Lily teasing. For both of them had begged him not to join the reserves. You never knew when a war would start up, and their families had had enough of war. But he was back—whole, healthy. Dumbo, hero—let the celebration start!

"Ta-da," Mimi calls, poking her head into her room.

But Lily is not there. She was going to take a few days off, but probably her boss called and begged her to come in. Mimi can't resist showing the cake to someone. She will leave it by Tony's bed, to surprise him when he wakes.

Opening the door, she sees them, asleep in each other's arms. She tiptoes to the kitchen, flushed with shock and confusion.

Had it ever passed through her mind—the two of them together? Once when a sitter had cancelled at the last minute, she'd sat them in back of the lecture hall at Lawson College, where she was teaching a course on reproductive biology. She'd hauled a stack of books to keep them busy, but when she went to retrieve them, the books were unopened. Tell us more about reproduction, they clamored. How old did you have to be to reproduce? Who could do it? Could they do it together? Was it fun? She answered badly, she knows, for just getting through the days back then was hard, and she favored simple solutions. She said something along the lines of, You are not brother and sister, but just about and so you can't reproduce!

It must have been a good ten years ago, because she remembers now consulting with Henry, in one of those private conversations she still indulged in when she was feeling clueless and forlorn. She remembers Henry saying, What the hell. And her getting mad. Easy for you to say. You don't have to bring them up!

But he was right. What was the big deal? In a way, she thinks today, it simplified things. The two people she loved most in the world would be together, forever. As she and Henry had only dreamed of.

When they wake and appear in the kitchen, they rush to the cake, fingers out like children.

"To celebrate," Mimi says, "coming home," she says. And the two of you? she thinks. But of course says nothing. She feels her face flush again. Will her blush give away that she knows?

"How'd you know?" Tony says, blushing, too, a bright mix of embarrassment and pride.

Lily crawls into her arms. "You just had a feeling, right? In your bones, right? A light just went off, my darling Whatever?"

# 2. The Quilt

Lily is the "human service director" of the Shenandoah Animal Clinic. Hearing her title, people often take her for a personnel director, but it is human service not human services that Doc Juarez, the vet whose clinic Lily has been working at since junior high school, uses to describe Lily's work to distinguish it from what he calls "direct animal service." Lily works with the humans, not with the animals. She tells the staff which cages to clean, which dogs to groom, which dressings to change on which neutered cat or dog or occasional potbelly pig; she tells the teary or testy owners whom to see and where, in the warren of animal service suites in the back. It's there in the back, though, that Lily believes she belongs, and she often regrets that her organizational skills have moved her up the ladder, which is to say, down the hall to the front desk, where the human arrangements get made. Sitting at her desk, most days, she wants only to be with the beasts, feeding, bathing, petting, cooing, administering drops and tonics, wrapping bandages, and when all else fails holding them in her arms and kissing them goodbye. Doc Juarez acknowledges her animal talent, but for now there's no one else he trusts to run things right, up front. Lily consoles herself with the fact that the pay is excellent for someone with only a high school diploma, and in two years, she will begin the vet assistant program at Western State Community College, and then, when she's saved up enough, study to be a full-fledged vet like Doc, who says he could see her in charge of the whole place, when he gets old.

Lily arranged for a week off when Tony came home, but after a few days Doc is overwhelmed and she returns to work.

The office is crowded her first day back, and Jessie, the birth technician, is out sick. This means that Lily gets to spend most of the day in the back, helping two Siamese cats and one mournful mutt birth their large litters. Between the births, she organizes the back, which is a mess, resupplying the cabinets and kits with gauze and ointments, needles and blood tubes. When Tony was away, she reorganized the front, making it more efficient than ever. Designing flow charts for the staff and satisfaction forms for the pet owners helped her stay calm. And somehow it also helped her feel close to Tony—like she was a little marine herself, marching around with her forms and supplies. Today, she knows that up front all is running per new procedure: People take numbers and wait for Wanda, the receptionist at the desk beside hers, to call them. The vending machines have been serviced and hold a full array of waters and juices and snacks for people and pets alike. Magazines and books on the care of animals are arranged by species and then breed on the racks along the front wall, and in baskets on the floor, flannel balls and leather bones are available for animal use.

At home, before she left, she'd laid out drinks and snacks and Tylenol by Tony's bed so he would have everything he needed, which, she thought, included her gone. At five or so, the phone had rung and she heard Mimi's litany: how long? how often? how intense? Then her boots on the stairs, the van revving up then pulling out. I could stay with him, she thought—all day, just the two of us. But if she stayed at home, she knew, they'd paw each other nonstop, and he needed to rest. Not that they've touched much the last few days. Mimi's been around and even though Mimi knew about her and Tony, Lily was shy about leaving her own bed at night, only in the morning coming to him, settling herself on the foot of the bed to study him, like Roco, the dog, liked to. She loves watching Tony's chest rise and fall, his nostrils—triangular like a colt's—flare, the breath, sounding like a baby parrot's whistle as it blows it in and out. But with Mimi gone, she might be tempted to crawl up the bed and under the covers, which she did the day Mimi brought home the double seven-layer and then went out to check on a cervix. Tony had gone back to sleep and Lily had brought slices of the cake to his bed and then one thing led to another and it ended up not better than the first time, of course, but more fun due to the chocolate frosting involvement. She will never regret one second of either of their times together, but after the second time, he looked so tired that she was afraid to interrupt his sleep. He needed a few more days to restore fully and then they'd have it all.

She wishes Roco were better company for Tony. She had found the stray spaniel mutt in her yard years ago, when her father was still home and her mother was still coming to visit now and then. She had named him Roco for them—a combination of Ronnie and Connie, to remind them of how it should be—the two of them together, loving each other and her. When Lily came to live with Mimi and Tony, Roco came too. Now the dog is fifteen years old with a collapsed bladder and rotting teeth. He sleeps all day, at the foot of the bed, too tired to open his eyes to give Tony the solacing doggy look she knows he loves.

The mutt bitch who is birthing today is at least half retriever. Tony's hair now is in its wintry tan phase but in the summer it turns the exact same gold as Cleo's fur, Lily thinks. How fun is it to find Tony everywhere she looks!

"Good girl, Cleo," Lily says as the first pup appears. It's a boy, and even with the slick still on, it's clear he's golden too. "Good boy," she whispers as she helps him find a teat.


Tony's sliding into a ditch at the side of a makeshift desert road. Everything is sand, and the more he tries to climb out, the more he's sucked in. He snorts sand, swallows sand. Then Lily appears and screams at the sand, Get off him…or else! And then everything is fine. The first nights home, Tony has this same dream, drowning in sand until Lily shows up, and then, like in a rewinding film, the sand flies up, taking him with it. Then in the dream, and then in his actual room, he finds himself safe in bed, sitting up in his bed, rubbing sleep, not sand, from his eyes. Lily. In dreams and life, she made everything better.

After a few days, when Lily returns to work, even when he's fully awake, Tony sometimes is certain that he's still in the desert, and he breaks into cold sweats. When Roco sees that, or rather smells that—for the dog's eyes, even when open, hardly work any more—he slithers up the bed, like a seal, and licks his salty skin. Some days, except for going to the bathroom, Tony gets out of bed only to let Roco out in the yard to go. The dog touches him, but scares him. They seem like an old couple, lying there all day, producing their secretions and excretions, smelling up the joint.

He knows he has to get his act together. And at the end of the second week, charmed by the pear tree outside his window, decorated with small green buds, he makes a private deal: before the buds burst open, he'll stop crashing and be on the move.

The third week back, he manages to read. He has always been a news-hound, reading the *Washington Post* whenever he can. But now the prospect of world capitals, world leaders, foreign conflicts makes him weak, and he picks up the Blue Ridge Herald or the freebee Shenandoah Shopper, charging to the home sections to survey all the things they can buy when they marry. They haven't decided exactly when or even if they will marry. But it's clear that at some point it will happen. He doesn't know when they will decide: will he ask her, will she ask him, will they just decide the same thing the same second? Like when they come? Both times in bed their timing was perfect. But from one of his mother's human sexuality and reproduction books, which he'd pick up when he was bored or horny or both, he's learned that men had to learn sexual patience. They were very clinical books with only black and white anatomical drawings at best, and they always disappointed him. But that phrase—sexual patience— intrigued him, then and now. He doesn't actually wish for the magic to end, but maybe a little part of him does? So he can show her how he'd do anything for her?

Who ever thought he'd enjoy reading the home section of the paper! The pages and pages of ads seem like an atlas to him, with maps of unfamiliar regions. Apartments— furnished and unfurnished. Furniture—finished and unfinished. Styles—contemporary or country or traditional. Surfaces for walls—paint or paneling or wallpaper, for the floor—wood or tile or carpet. Each day, he circles the possibilities, each red mark seeming a welcome stoplight, halting his mind, which, when he least expects, flies back to the desert. It had started on the plane home, where he hardly slept because as soon as he closed his eyes he was back in country, engulfed in blazing heat and burning fear. It was only in the van riding home, his head in her lap, his hands on her breasts, that he knew, for sure, where he was and could close his eyes and doze. When she's at work, he studies the ads and when she comes home, he shows her what he's marked and the decisions that await them. And then, he can sleep.

Finally, the fourth week, some of his energy returns. During the day, while Mimi and Lily are at work, he takes care of the house. He likes dusting, sweeping, shopping, cooking. He has never been religious, but after the months of sand and dirt, sirens and Scuds, the domestic tasks feel what he can only call sacred, like they are rituals for cleansing his soul, or diverting future disaster, or giving thanks that his life has been spared. Only the vacuum with its awful motor booming like an Abrams tank throws him back to the desert, so he sticks to brooms and mops.

Every morning he rides his bike down the blossoming roads. One day, in a sudden burst of adrenaline, he rides the twenty miles down the old quarry road to his college. After a few summer school courses, he will graduate, and now that he's here, he thinks, he should seize the moment to register early. But by the time he reaches the registrar's office, he doesn't have the energy for the long line and just prints out the forms and his transcript at one of the computer kiosks that have sprouted all over while he was gone.

One afternoon, he rides the car two exits down the highway to the Southern Skies complex, where on weekends, except for the one weekend a month that he had to go to Peabody, he used to work, Saturdays as a laborer, Sunday mornings as a guard. Taking the exit, he sees Southern Skies shooting twenty stories into the sky, having doubled its height in the five months he's been away. He honks hello to two older guys he used to joke with, eating their lunch near the road. They point to a sign on the tool hut, WE SALUTE OUR BRAVE TROOPS, and wave him over. Just reading the words "war" and "troops" exhausts him, and when he waves back it doesn't feel like he's lifted his hand but a hundred pounds of bricks. Should he stop to be polite and stay? Should he go home while he still has the energy to drive? If the foreman doesn't appear by the time he counts to three, that will be a sign he should leave. One-two-three. No foreman. So he just blows his horn again, opens his window, calls out, "Great to see you," and, "I'll be back," and loops back to the highway.

He thought he had left the hocus-pocus of looking for signs in numbers/colors/anything back in the Gulf, where it had begun. An odd number of sirens is a bad sign, Scud reports in threes are better than in pairs. But he has no time for these games—there is so much to do! Besides arranging his job and summer school schedule, he has to drive down to John Adams High to talk to the principal about his transcript, which was missing eight credits for student teaching. In the middle of the fall semester, when he knew he was going to the desert, he doubled his time at the school, working the morning session too, so he could get credit for the whole term and graduate on time.

You have nothing to worry about! That's what the principal had said when Tony explained he had to leave the second week in November. He was a giant of a man and when he seized Tony's hand, Tony felt relieved, not only about his credits, his graduation, but about the looming war. Dr. Moser's hand seemed twice the size of his own, and for a long, calm moment, the first in days, he stopped worrying. It felt like his own hand was him and he was a baby, and Dr. Moser's hand was a cradle, which he fit into perfectly. You help us, we'll help you…you and us…us and you…, Dr. Moser said, and Tony felt the rhythms soothe him, like a lullaby. Rest assured, young man, Dr. Moser said, and he could swear he was hearing one of the lullabies his mother would concoct to ease his nighttime fretting. How did it go? Rest and dream, my boy, and may tomorrow bring you joy…?

Some joy! Without those credits, he was screwed. Totally screwed. Without those credits, he couldn't finish up this summer! And then next year, he'd be stuck in school again and broke. And then how could he and Lily get on with their life?

Before they flew home from Kuwait, his captain gave them his hero-for-a-day pep talk. The welcome home party's over fast, he said. It's, Have a beer, hero! And then you're on your own, staggering through your life alone. Tony tries to stay calm. As soon as he has some energy he would meet with Dr. Moser and remind him of their arrangement. He would never feel that same goo-goo-ga-ga baby trust again, but man to man, he'd talk to him. Man to man, he'd shake his hand as hard as he could. To remind him that they'd made a deal.

Every day, since he's come home, he's felt stronger in both body and spirit, but there's no doubt that the transcript has been a downer. Since the Gulf, he's felt less significant than ever, a wimp among marines, a small body in a vast desert of sand and death. Now the feeling has returned, the sense that he is insignificant degrading, some days, into the

conviction that he is invisible. For several days, when he goes
to the store to buy the paper or groceries, he doesn't speak
when spoken to, assuming, until stares tell him otherwise,
that he can't be seen. And then he waits for Lily to come
home, to see his face reflected in her eyes, which assures
him he still exists. One day you're a hero, the captain had
said, and the next day you're a nobody. It was a roller coaster
ride, he said, and all you could do was hold on tight and ride
it through. Tony closes his eyes and imagines himself in a
little roller coaster car, with Lily beside him. With her to
hold onto, he'd ride it through and get where he wanted to
be. Days at Southern Skies, nights at the college or home
hitting the books, one weekend a month down at the base,
then the base one last time for the month of August, and then
he'd be done with both college and the reserves! That is, if
the foreman hires him back and if his credits come through.

Make it happen, Lily tells him one night, and he promises
her he will. The next morning, he puts on his best chinos and
his least frayed flannel shirt and drives down the highway.
John Adams or Southern Skies—which should he go to first?
Maybe the job first because it was less stressful talking to
the foreman? Or maybe get the harder task of talking to the
principal over with and then the job? But, again, he feels
insignificant and incapable of decisions, and again he finds
himself looking for something that will decide for him. Three
kids in the car in front are looking out the back window. If all
three wave, he'll drive to the school. But suddenly he can't
see the car, only dark shadows creeping from the borders of
his mind. Another highway, and then a burning smell, which
makes it hard to breathe and sends him to the shoulder to
catch his breath and clear his mind.

Thoughts can't kill you—that was the point of another
of his captain's talks. Disturbing thoughts would attack from
time to time, but they could defeat them, just like they'd
defeated the enemy. He told them a trick: Imagine your mind
is your weapon, and just blast them away. Tony drove a light

armored vehicle—with a 25 mm weapon. *Booooom, booom, boom,* he tries. It works. And then there's no other highway, just this one that hugs the Shenandoah, and he drives on.

But, again, where to go? Magnolias peek over the concrete fence. Their sweet scent floats through the open window and reminds him of Lily. Now he imagines she's there in the car, saying, It's Dr. Moser not Dr. Monster! Don't be afraid, silly! And suddenly, he's not.

At John Adams High, he takes the steps two by two and marches to the principal's office. But Dr. Moser is not in. The secretary doesn't look up, and, again, the thought crosses his mind that he can't be seen. He turns to leave, but then again imagines Lily is with him, as tiny as a Smurf, sitting in his shirt pocket. She's calling up to him—dictating a note to leave for Dr. Moser: *I'm back and would be ever so grateful for the chance to talk to you about the matter of credits. My telephone number is....* He scribbles his number. And: *Thank you, now as ever for your generosity and understanding.* He laughs. On his own, what would he have written? *Dear Dr. You-Have-Nothing-To-Worry-About, I'm really worried. Or: Dear Dr. We-Help-You, Help! Or: Hey, Shithead. How could you be such a shithead!*

At home he feels so relieved that he's taken care of something.

"Well done," Lily says when she calls to check on his morning. "You made it happen...start to happen, all by yourself!"

He wishes she weren't so sensitive about her size so he could tell her how he imagined she was with him in his pocket all day.

"And tomorrow I'm going to register for that quickie June summer school session," he says. If the line is long and he's bored, he'll open his jacket and play with his Smurf. He laughs.

"Good job," she says. "Way to go!"

Lily thinks of this first phase of their life together as their R and R, not the usual Rest and Recreation, but a serious healing time, in which to *Repair* and *Restore*. On bookcases in each of their old houses perched photos of their respective parents tanned and smiling on white tropical sands, toasting their futures with tall icy drinks. She and Tony were both conceived in drunken collapses, Lily imagines, on these Pacific R and Rs, reckless binges from which a new life came without anyone thinking about what they've done and their responsibilities to others. In the Repair and Restore kind of R and R, a service person and his/her mate build their solid future.

Phase Two, F the F (Facing the Future), Lily believes, will grow from their R and R as it never had a chance to with Ronnie and Connie. Ronnie was slated for home, and Connie came to meet him in Fiji; but at the end of the week, he decided he couldn't live without the heroin he'd fallen in love with in the jungle. And he signed up for a second tour and a third after that, even though Lily was born by then and had cried that she would never forgive him—even if he came back. She knows year-old children are not supposed to understand ideas like forgiveness, let alone express them in full sentences. But she is sure she remembers that, then him flinging her in the air to cheer her up, her feeling only belly dread that by the time she started her descent he'd be gone.

During her R and R with Tony, for the first time in her life, Lily feels something like forgiveness for Ronnie. She used to think that there would never be a time when her father's war would be behind her, Vietnam and then all the conflict and craziness that followed it—her father's drugs and screaming tattooed buddies, her mother's desperate tears and exits, her own freakish, orphaned state. Vietnam somehow had claimed her life as surely as it had claimed her father's and Henry's. But Tony came back. Tony's war was over in a few weeks, with everyone back, healthy and sane. And her life and the whole world around her, the whole United States of America, it seemed, was back. *Repaired and Restored*. She doesn't tell even Tony about her phases and phrases, because she knows they are corny. But they help her comprehend and plan.

Lily firmly believes that *Facing the Future*, her future, will depend first and foremost on building a good relationship with the man she loves. Marriage should be the foundation of that relationship and she wants the day they pour that slab to be perfect. She buys *Modern Bride* and *Bride Today* and *American Wedding* and any other magazine she can find with "Bride" or "Wedding" in its name and stashes them all over so that no free moment will be wasted. Waiting for bread to toast, or the bath to fill, or the car to warm, or a pet to settle down—she reaches for a magazine and researches options. "The Wedding Cycle—from Proposal to Honeymoon," "Developing a Seating Plan for Your Big Day," "Balancing the Scale of His Side and Your side," "Choosing a Gown to Express the You Underneath."

Before now, most of her free time has gone to understanding the habits and needs of animals. But the same joyful attention she has brought to animal bathing and feeding, breeding and healing, she now brings to the subject of her wedding. Mimi and Henry married the week before he left for basic training, a municipal lunchtime wedding followed by wine and pizza back home with their buddies, then Henry's departure for Vietnam, then the brief R and R, and then his death a week later and nine months before the birth of the son he never saw. And then there were her own parents' dreams blown to pieces. But with the right invitation, music, food, flowers, on top of the special feelings, of course, her wedding will mend that train of misery. Like the white coat she proudly wears at Doc's, her white dress will announce, I am a healer. A healer of my past!

Now, for the first time ever, happy memories of her

parents spin in her mind. Her parents as childhood sweethearts. They'd shown her pictures of themselves arm in arm in junior high. And on rare quiet days they'd tell her how they met at gymnastics club, how he sweated when she'd walk on the high bar, how they'd spot each other day after day, planning to become a performing duo one day, appearing at county fairs and community events. Some days they'd perform for her, flipping, jumping, twisting together into a perfect tower—Steeple to the Stars, they called it—where you couldn't tell whose body part was whose, or where one of them ended and the other one began.

After a performance, she'd beg them to marry, which they said they would when Ronnie's nerves calmed down and work got steady and they'd saved enough to do it right. Among the fantasies that supported Lily through those years was being her parents' flower girl, and some days she'd bring them bouquets of whatever she could find—dandelions and clover from the front yard, goldenrod and loosestrife from the bottom of the road—to show them how helpful she would be not only as a flower girl but as an all-around aide, at the wedding and well beyond. She wanted her parents to see how they could count on her, and, knowing this, to give up their post-war habits and resume their old capable and coordinated ways. She remembers now telling them that they were a "terrific team"; and if they could manage the "Steeple," they could manage anything.

Engagement party, shower, wedding, then baby, then baby parties, theme birthday parties, etc.—every article in her growing magazine collection reveals and revives those old buried hopes. Some days, she even pictures Ronnie and Connie beside her at her marriage ceremony. You're great! they call to her like she used to call to them when they did their routines. She feels so happy then, and looking up from these daydreams, she sometimes feels a momentary shock that they're not there.

The engagement party section of her favorite wedding

cycle article offers different options for different personality types. If organization and efficiency define you, then you need to honor that and use it to your best advantage. Consider "packaging" your proposal and your engagement celebration into a single event. If you've linked up with your opposite—which this type often does—this is especially advised. "Particularly for procrastinating, indecisive men, the 2-in-1, double-whammy approach makes sense. *He'll* never surprise *you*, so you utilize all your organizer skills and surprise *him*!"

Double-whammy. Her declaration to him in the letter, followed up later in his room his first night back, was surely one of those. It wasn't the first time she surprised him—and herself—with special feelings, though she's hardly thought about it since it happened. She was eleven, and her Aunt Sally had dragged her to her Baltimore house to live. There wasn't a single thing about that time that wasn't hateful to her—her tormenting cousins; her condescending, cliquish schoolmates; her cruel and totally unnatural aunt, who made her sleep on a folding cot in the living room despite a perfectly nice, unused extra bedroom with a real bed. Lily cried every day that she had to go home. And twice a state trooper found her walking south toward Virginia on I 95 and drove her back to Baltimore.

Finally Mimi came to get her, and that's when it happened. Tony was in the front seat, totally changed in the six long months of her Baltimore exile. His Adam's apple wiggled in his neck, his chin glistened with new gold fuzz, and she had to control herself from stroking him. Not B.O. but a scent equally pungent and manly like car wax floated off him, making her woozy. My guy, she found herself chanting silently, imagining she was Connie with Ronnie at Virginia Beach in 1968, getting pinned. For a month she kept a diary in which she confessed daily, *Dear diary, I can't help myself, I'm crazy about the guy.* Then Tony found the diary and told her she was a dork. He got busy with real girlfriends, she with the animals down at Doc's. She stopped thinking

about stroking him—she was busy fondling her beasties—
and the feeling passed. Until he went to the desert and she
was afraid he might never return, the feeling had never
reappeared. But she thinks she knows which pile of boxes in
the garage the diary is in. How funny will that be when she
shows it to him!

A centerpiece for both engagement and wedding parties
can have special meaning, one of the articles says. For each
celebration, a centerpiece built around a sentimental object
with special significance guarantees special memories to last
a lifetime. Her diary could be the *star* of her engagement
gala! She could place it in the middle of her ma's old blue
milk glass mixing bowl and surround it with roses. She could
invite people to a party, a barbecue probably for she imagines
it in summer; and no one would know the barbecue party had
a purpose—to announce that their life had a purpose now!
Not even Tony would know what was up. But she'd call him
aside, present him with the diary, ask him to marry her. She'd
get down on her knees. "Acknowledging that your man is a
little goofy doesn't mean you love him any less. In today's
world, the organized, energetic woman can take charge of
popping the question," the article on individual wedding
styles says. She laughed when she read that, because it was
so right: if it was left to Tony, the question would never be
popped. Ask her today or tomorrow? This week or next? Give
her a ring or a pin? That was Tony. So why not just move
ahead and double-whammy him. With the little diary and
maybe a little pinky ring to remind him of the old pinky
pricks. She'd write a note, something like, *Blood children
once, and now conscious adults making adult commitments.
I am totally committed to you for life. Are you to me?* She
imagined them in the kitchen. And then when Tony said yes,
they'd walk out the kitchen door into the yard, where
everyone would be waiting, with the grill going, and they'd
place the diary in the centerpiece on the table, then walk onto
the grass and make their announcement and kiss before their

community. Getting engaged was both an intensely private and an intensely communal event, the article said.

In the wedding cycle story, there's a how-to side-bar on the wedding quilt, which the author believes is making its comeback in the American wedding. "It's a tradition that we have sorely missed in the do-your-own-thing era, which is happily drawing to an end," the author writes. And it's easy to start. "Ask each guest invited to the engagement party to bring a piece of old clothing or household linen to contribute to the quilt." Lily loves the idea of old scraps making something new. Mimi's wedding dress, a long batik of periwinkle plumes—she thinks she knows where it is and is sure that Mimi would be glad for the dress to play a role in her quilt. Her grandma's tablecloths were in a trunk somewhere—how special would it be to go to sleep each night under patches of those lively cherries and strawberries and daisies! Plus cloth contributions from other family members: on behalf of Ronnie, she might have to buy a yard of the camouflage cotton they carry at Walmart's; but she could find an old T shirt and tie-dye it for her mother's contribution; and look for a madras plaid something at the Goodwill so that Aunt Sally could be involved even though she was a major bitch. And then all the other guests with their own beautiful materials! Though, of course, if she "packaged" the marriage proposal and the engagement party, no one would know to bring anything, and the quilt launch would have to wait for another community occasion or begin with just the textiles already in her possession.

# 3. The Team

Tony has no idea what Lily is planning. But his own plans begin to fall into place. He hasn't gotten a call back from Dr. Moser but the foreman at Southern Skies has called back and he will begin next week. And he has gotten all the courses he wanted for summer school session and placed out of one! Early mornings he runs with Lily along the Blue Ridge Trail, feeling as they climb the blue hills that they are running through heaven. How crazy is this world! One day you're sure you're going to die, and the next day you feel like you never ever will. He is dying to ask his best friend, Homer, if he felt this way with his wife, Nancy. Of being blessed or actually turned into a god yourself, like with this person at your side forever you have such super powers that nothing bad could ever happen again! He won't tell Homer who it is, just the feeling inside him, and see if he guesses on his own that it's Lil'. That's what Homer called her: *That's Lil' for Little not Lily, because you're so tiny and cute*, he'd say. Homer will be his best man. And Lily will probably want Nancy, as her best woman or first bridesmaid or whatever they call it.

For years, his life and Homer's have run together. When he wasn't with Lily, and often when he was, Homer was there. He imagines those days a lot, the two of them on their bikes, riding side by side on the wide looping path that follows the valley all the way from Monuten up to the old Blue Ridge Post Road. *Riders through peace and strife, riders through death and life*—that was the cheer they composed for themselves, and well into their teens they'd shout it at the top of their lungs as soon as they hit the trail.

When Homer found Nancy, he took Tony out for a bike

ride to tell him. He said, There's another member on our team, buddy. He showed him a picture of a cocoa-colored girl with yellow eyes. She was clearly gorgeous, but for a second Tony thought her truly heinous and hateful. He imagined the two of them, Homer and the girl, on bikes side by side, each with an arm out touching the other, hogging every last inch of path, squeezing him out, making him fall, riding off oblivious. She's heinous and her eyes are weird and witchy, he told Homer. He laughs now when he thinks back. He's crazy about Nancy. And Homer has always been crazy about Lily though he is absolutely clueless about the new developments.

For by the time Tony got Lily's letter laying things out, Homer's company had moved out into the desert. It was just crazy fate that had put them on the same plane out—an American Airlines commercial flight, where they got plastered on free rum and cokes that the stewardesses kept giving them, along with worried smiles—and then in adjacent tent cities in Al Jubayl, waiting for the war to begin. But even if Homer had been there, he doubts he would have told him while they were still in country.

He had joined the marine reserves, in part, because of Homer, admiring his discipline and courage. And he believed that if he was to come back alive, he needed every bit of marine wisdom and spirit that his big bud could spare. So the few letters he wrote Homer were all about Apache helicopters, cluster bombs, bunker busters, friendly fire, Scuds. What did Home know about these? What had he seen? Did he have any advice? Would there be a ground war too?

He remembers their last night together in Al Jubayl, sitting on the wharf, watching a gaggle of kids combing the tent city trash for food. USA, USA, George Bush, George Bush, they chanted, smiling up at him and Homer.

Palestinians, Homer said. They're smiling. But they hate us. Because we're here defending the Saudis and Kuwaitis who hate them and treat them like shit.

Not too long before, Tony had read a book about the war in Lebanon and a few on the Israeli-Palestinian conflict. But, here, in country, he couldn't remember a thing. The Saudis and Kuwaitis are our friends? The Palestinians are our enemies?

He studied the boys' eyes for something hateful—some jagged flashes of rage and deceit. But he saw only pools of fear and hunger. Our friends' enemy—a bunch of scared starving kids.

His heart began to pound. His hand began to shake. Jesus, Homer, what are we doing here? he asked. His voice came out squeaky and childish.

Devils don't ask, Homer said. Ask too many questions and you lose your edge. Devils are here to kill, not question!

Then Homer stood up, stretched his long legs, and marched down the pier and back. Ever since he was a kid, when he was restless for action, which was often, Homer would stretch his legs and start to march. Sometimes in a circle in the yard. Sometimes back and forth in Mimi's kitchen. It meant it was time to act. Go to the arcade. Get the bikes. Go to the library or hobby shop…. Get this war going. Then the sun set and it was time to make their way back to their tents.

The next morning he heard that Homer's regiment had left. But Homer's words stayed in his mind the rest of the time in country. The sirens, the Scuds, the smoke, the bodies. What for! he'd think, and his heart would pound. He'd hear Homer then: Devil dogs don't doubt! Devils don't question! And his panic would subside for a while.

Devils. Devil dogs. Leathernecks. Jarheads. Greens. They went by many names but they were a single people, a creed, even a race. When Tony joined the marine reserves, Homer said they were no longer a black guy and a white guy but now both green, Homer dark green and Tony light green according to corps parlance. In the language of the corps, he, Homer, was a "lifer," a career Devil, while Tony, a reservist, was a "camper." How good it was to have his big bro welcome him to Green Land and guide him through rough patches.

It had always been that way, though in the very beginning it was he and Lily who had welcomed Homer. Homer had moved to Monuten from Norfolk when he was ten and Tony was eight. Both of Homer's parents worked at the Western Virginia Historic Village, where they played the part of eighteenth century slaves, his father in bib overalls and straw hat, making baskets, or shoeing horses, or planting tobacco; his mother in long muslin dresses and aprons and bright bandanas cooking or serving or sewing in the big house. It was part of the "Roots Project" of the Western Virginia Historic Foundation, whose purpose was to celebrate the contribution of the African slave to the American colonies. On a class trip, a couple of local kids had recognized Mr. and Mrs. Joyce, and back in Monuten they refused the new kid on the block admission to a game of Red Rover being played in Mimi's front yard. There was a red team and a white team but no black team, no slave team, the main bully declared.

Interesting, Homer had said, marching back and forth at the edge of the yard, like a general contemplating strategy. Very interesting. Then he stopped marching and turned, charging one team and then the other, breaking the taunting child chains into pyres of whimpering bodies. Inspired, Tony shouted, Learned your lesson? Don't ever try that again. Or else. He'd picked up that last phrase from Lily, who compensated for her small size with the portentous words, which left the enemy to imagine their big, awful punishment. *Or else.* Tony followed it with a Chinese menu of possibilities. Or else I'll break all your knees. Or I'll punch in all your noses. Or I'll crash all your bikes. While he was shouting, Lily said, Scram or I'll call the cops. You're trespassing on private property. And everyone dispersed to the other side of the street. She dragged a blanket to the front lawn, laid out Oreos and chips and Cokes, so everyone could see what special fun they were having with their new best friend. It was perfect. In one stunning moment of retaliation, Homer had transformed from neighborhood scapegoat to neighborhood hero—and they, defiant comrades, basked in his glory.

Over the years, though, when Homer would claim Tony alone for "boy stuff"—shooting beebees, skipping stones in the creek, trapping rabbits, biking down the Blue Ridge trail—all of which, besides the hateful trapping, she did as well as them, Lily would shout that she wished the neighborhood kids had kicked their asses good that day. Sometimes, when she was super lonely and super mad at them, she would follow them on her bike. How good would that be—all the blood flowing from your stupid orifices! she'd call to them. If he looked back, Tony knew, her face would be puffy and red from crying and shouting. She was a troll, an adorable troll. Tony thought that back then and he thinks it now. How had he ever left her behind like that? He'd never leave her again.

As soon as Homer came back, they'd be a foursome, their own little unit. He imagines them riding into the future—on bicycles. Built for two, or maybe four. Did they have them for four? he muses. If so, were they all in a single row one behind the other, or two by two?


Nancy Jackson Joyce, Homer's wife, calls to say that Homer's regiment is back. She's driving down to Peabody the next morning to get him.

Lily has answered the phone and asks if she wants them to drive her.

"You're soooo nice, Lil'," Nancy says. "But it's a long drive and you just made it. I wouldn't think of dragging you there again. You or your bro."

He's not my bro anymore, Lily wants to say. And I'm not so nice. The truth is that ever since Tony had been called up, old childhood resentments toward Homer have been creeping back. She can't wait to let Homer Joyce know that *he*'s not in charge any more. If they went with Nancy, Lily would hold Tony's hand the whole time, which would let Homer know that *she* was his partner now. She could tell Homer when it was good to join them, when it was time to clear out. She feels so mean. But it's not just the old beef but a new one. Manhood. Honor. Obedience. If Homer hadn't talked that crap day and night, maybe Tony would never have joined up. It wasn't just Homer, she knows—it was Henry too, the ghost of Henry the Hero egging him on. But Homer's rap was half of it.

To be fair, though, Homer was more than a he-man talking macho clichés. *Right the wrong. We stand for something. Stand up for the underdog. All men are created equal....* Even now, when she remembers those lines from Homer's riffs, she tingles with pride, as she had in the yard when he broke down those chains of shitty kids who'd said he was a slave and couldn't be on the team. For Homer, being a marine had to do with never being anyone's slave again, no one ever being anyone's slave, or master. That was the whole idea of America, the American team, he'd say.

She agreed. And if America were ever attacked, she has often thought, she'd join up in a heartbeat, maybe using her animal care skills to treat the wounded.... But what did loving your country have to do with marching to the other side of the globe! Whenever possible, she liked to talk out problems. Words not fists, she used to tell Ronnie when he'd come home cut up from a fight.

Homer could have gotten Tony killed! she thinks now. She pecks a quick kiss into the phone and hangs up, before she can say anything she regrets. She loves Nancy and loves to talk to her. Lately, though, she hasn't had a chance.

Last week, when Nancy called, Lily wasn't home. It was Tony she wanted to talk to anyway. Lucky you were out, he laughed, when he reported the conversation to Lily.

What's going on, Tony? Nancy had demanded. He hasn't found time to write to me in two weeks. The war's over…so what's occupying him! You need to tell me what's going on right now, Anthony!

Nancy is a third-grade teacher and Tony had to struggle not to laugh. You need to! Right now, Anthony!

He's probably been sleeping round the clock, Tony said.

Sleeping with whores, Nancy said. Pardon my French, but I've had it. This is not acceptable behavior.

The truth was that Homer's behavior had Tony worried, but for other reasons. A few weeks before, when Tony was first home, Homer had written to tell him that he suspected that *Nancy* was running around. He wanted Tony to trail her though he already had proof: She had written him, confessing, "I can't wait till you're back!"

"The bitch couldn't wait for me. And is fucking all over the fucking place. Fuck her," Homer wrote. Tony had to investigate the specifics and get back to him!

"Nothing to investigate. You've misinterpreted big time," Tony wrote back. "Can't wait as in so excited." He'd run into Nancy at the mall and Homer was all she'd talked about. She was tutoring every day after school—to surprise him with a down payment for a house. Tony told him all but that last part.

"If you say so, I believe it," Homer wrote back. The men in the squad had also said he was way off base, but he hadn't believed them. So he'd pinned her photo and letter on the Wall of Shame, where the men hung pictures of women who'd once been wives and girlfriends but had turned into shameful, cheating whores. Homer wrote, "But I always believe you, bro, and I have taken down her photo and put it back in the sole of my boot under my dog tag. I don't know what's got into me."

There's no one else, Tony had assured Nancy. He wasn't sure why Homer hadn't written, but he knew for sure that there was no one else.

Since he'd met Nancy in high school, there had never been anyone else for Homer. Homer was a toughy, but Nancy tenderized him, and he loved it. She was the student government secretary, tall, beautiful, and capable. Her parents were both teachers, her mother from Virginia for generations; her father half Panamanian, half New Orleans Creole. Nancy was golden-skinned, golden-eyed, with a golden voice, as fluid and fluent in French and Spanish as in English. Homer was a good student but inept in languages, and Nancy, who was also head of the service society, became his Spanish tutor. As society president, she no longer tutored, but he impressed her at his "diagnostic" session at the "Spanish Clinic," speaking the worst Spanish she'd ever heard. Every sentence was studded with the errors in vocabulary, verb form, noun number, gender. But he spoke quickly as if he were fluent. He was on a mission, she thought. He couldn't stop to listen.

He understood her perfectly, when she asked him questions in Spanish, but he answered in his haywire patois.

She said, Adónde vas? (Where are you going?)

He answered, Joino las marinos, which she gathered meant, I'm joining the Marines.

She asked, Quando?

He answered, Quanto yo graduaro, by which he must have meant, When I graduate.

You have to stop and listen to people, she said in Spanish. You can't learn a language without listening. And if you don't pass Spanish you'll never graduate.

Escuchar con tu! Solo con tu.

He'd listen to her. Only to her. His fate was in her hands.

She began at the beginning. I am. I sing. I love. He hung on every word. If it came from her lips, he'd hear it—its form, its sound, its shape. He learned to speak slowly, so he'd have more time with her—and correctly, so she'd think well of him and give him a chance.

Tony, I'd like you to answer that question for me, right now, Nancy had said. Why would a man not write to his wife who loves him soooo much? I'm waiting for a reasonable answer, Anthony Bravo!

In her voice, under the brittle school-teacher officiousness, Tony could hear only a mush of fear and confusion, not one note of the sparkling intelligence and confidence that had won her the Monuten Young Educator of the Year title two years in a row. He felt for her, but he felt self-satisfied at the same time, which surprised him but also didn't. For years they had treated him like a baby brother, an idiot cousin. As soon as Homer met Nancy, he had relegated Tony to the back seat of his car and talked only to her. And such stupid shit, because that's all he could manage in Spanish. How was your day? What did you eat for lunch? Do you have much homework tonight? Later on, Give me a kiss. Eventually, Tony came to like the rides in the back: a hopeful horniness replaced his humiliation and loneliness, as he watched them locked in kisses, separating only to promise, *siempre...para la vida...mi corazón.*

Last week, Nancy said, Anthony Bravo, answer my question right now! Does he still love me? Do you know for a fact that he's remained faithful to his wife?

Homer loved her still and only her—Tony knew that for sure. But he knew too that men did crazy things in war. He remembered the whores the lieutenant treated his company to towards the end, after they came back to camp for the last time. Eight girls in four tents behind the shitter. Thirty guys lined up at each, like cars at a filling station. But not Tony. For weeks before, unless he had to, unless his twisted bowels were killing him, Tony wouldn't go anywhere near the shitter. For two weeks straight he'd been on shitter detail, assigned, because he'd returned late from a desert run, to haul oil barrels of base feces to the "shit pier"—a platform at the edge of the sea. Each evening he was made to light the day's load, burning it into the air, then drag the barrels back for fresh dumps.

But it wasn't only location of the tents that had kept Tony away. Even if the whores were in a field of clover, Tony wouldn't have gone near them. When he was growing up, his house was like some Planned Parenthood clinic, strewn with pamphlets promoting "personal and sexual health," "knowing your partner," "respect for the human body—your own and others," etc. And, then too, though his father's body had been shattered in a Saigon alley, the image of his father and mother and their flawless love had been worshipped in their home. And so he willingly absented himself from the He-Man sex scene that surrounded him in the valley, in college, in basic training, and then in country. Until Lily, there'd been only Kim and one other girl, whom he didn't love the way he loved Lily, but cared about for the while he was with them. What would Homer have done had he been in his tent city back then? Besides his best buddy, Ernie Polanco, a science whiz whom he called Einstein, Tony was the only one that hadn't lined up for a free fuck.

In truth, he couldn't be sure of what Homer did or didn't do, but only that he *loved* only Nancy.

Homer loves you, Tony had said. He explained how exhausted he'd been when he first came back, how he'd slept all the time. How he hardly wrote home towards the end either. He's just sleeping a lot and dreaming of you, he laughed. Storing up all his strength for you.

Really? she'd squealed, sounding like one of her third-graders, then laughing her old bright laugh.


Tony hasn't been aware that he was worried, but today, learning that his best friend has arrived home in one piece, he is giddy with relief. Now life can totally take off. And the night of the day Homer returns, Tony takes Lily out for dinner. A special dinner, for a special occasion.

He drives them up Monuten Mountain to the restaurant in the ski lodge where his parents fell in love. They have never eaten here before—not only because the restaurant has gotten pricey but because it had always seemed a kind of holy shrine, not for mere mortals but for lucky lovers blessed with perfect love.

As if sensing that something's up, or will be soon, the waiter seats them apart from the other diners, at a table in a windowed alcove overlooking the mountains and valley.

How does the ceremony go here at love's shrine? Do the words come to lovers just like that? Will the perfect feeling inside him form perfect phrases that will pop from his lips? He studies her sad spaniel eyes and aches to have it settled between them. We should marry? Or, Can we marry? Or, Do you feel it too—that we should be together forever? As he waits for the right words to seize him, he leans against her and together they watch the sun descend, the hills darken from blue to violet.

I want to wake up beside you every day. To dream beside you every night. To live beside you for the rest of my life. When I'm old to die in your arms. Phrases shimmer in his mind.

"I feel like we're picking up where they left off," she whispers. "Mimi and Henry...."

There she goes, reading his mind. I want you to read my mind forever. And me yours. Could he start with that? He holds her hand and watches her watch the sun streak the sky before dark claims the valley, feeling he could sit here forever, just watching her in silent peace.


Homer sleeps nonstop in the studio apartment he and Nancy share, and then, after a week, he feels like his old self again and raring to go. First things first—he needs to see their best buds. It is the first of May and they arrange to meet in the long meadow on the west side of Monuten Mountain, just beyond Fort Monuten.

There is no fort at Fort Monuten, actually, just the natural fortress of the mountain itself—and the field below it. Here in the decisive Battle of Monuten, after the death of 7,000 Union and 2,000 Confederacy soldiers, the strategic mountain and the vast stretch of the Shenandoah Valley to the south were secured by the Confederacy.

In all but the coldest weather, Civil War buffs and vacationing families can be found walking the field. In recent years, the weekend before Labor Day, men and boys from all over invade the town to re-enact the Battle of Monuten. For the Fort Monuten Foundation and the Monuten township, this is the biggest money maker, generating more income in the single weekend than a whole year's battlefield's entry fee and gift shop sales combined. Lily knows the whole spiel. Not only from the two summers she worked here, at the little adopt-a-pet station that the county ASPCA used to run at the entrance. But from the happiest days of her earliest years, passed right around the corner, on the far side of the mountain.

Now it's a popular picnic area, but when Lily was little, it was a hidden meadow. Around the bend from the "fort," tucked behind the mountain, it had been untouched by battle, which to Lily had always seemed a miracle. And how fitting it seemed to her that in times of family peace, when the roaring ceased at home, her parents should bring her here for a day of munching and cuddling and cooing. For its river of blood—which, according to one of the fort's explanatory signs, rose two feet high and ran the width and depth of the field, washing an estimated thousand soldiers down the mountain—Lily had always called the field on the "fort" side of the mountain the "red" field; and her field—streaked with blue cornflowers and blue flax, bordered with the blue hills of the Blue Ridge and the blue sky above, the blue Shenandoah below—she'd dubbed "blue" field. Few people came to her meadow back then, and sitting beside her parents on the soft grass, it felt like the fighting at home and the battling at Fort Monuten were not just erased from her mind, but erased from the world, like she and Ronnie and Connie were not just another family on a picnic but angels of peace, vaporizing all the ghosts of war and hatred, sending beams of love and calm around the mountain bend, across the valley, over the Allegheny peaks and out across the world. Even after both of her parents were gone, the field remained a place of hope and possibility, and to her it has remained "Blue Field," even after the town claimed it as a park and named it Monuten West Recreational Facility.

Last year, it had been Lily's idea for them all to meet here on May 1st. Tony brought Kim, which didn't bother Lily at all because it was before the war and the birth of her true feelings. For the past few years the meadow has been host to special events, including the yearly May 1st celebration. The first of May, singers and dancers perform wherever they wish, and at tents set up along the park's edge, local artisans and farmers sell their crafts and flowers.

Because it was Lily's idea to go last year, and because she still had the tag-along kid status and felt she needed to bribe her way in with the "big kids," she brought the whole picnic. This year, with Tony's love racing through her, she feels confident enough to divide the tasks. Homer will bring the drinks, and Nancy a sack of biscuits and chicken. Tony will pick up the fudge cake that Lily has ordered from Stoehmer's, the same cake that Mimi surprised them with the month before, when they surprised her. And Lily will bring cookies and paper goods.

The day before Lily spent a half hour at Party Card at the Kmart shopping center deciding on the right tablecloth, napkins, cups and plates. She was itching to buy "happy engagement" plates, but of course that would have been presumptuous. Nothing's been decided. The engagement section was near the wedding section, which was lovely, all the paper goods patterned with silver bells and hearts, white roses and bursts of gold ribbons. But Homer and Nancy had been married half a year, tying the knot without any fanfare the month before he went to Saudi Arabia. So wedding stuff was out. The day after Homer returned, Lily and Nancy had one of their heart-to-heart sessions on the phone, and Nancy told her that she and Homer were going to start a family soon. At the card shop Lily amused herself imagining designs for "starting a family" party goods. Ovals for eggs, little paisleys for sperms, in pink and blue respectively? She knew it was ridiculous but when it was time for her and Tony to start their family she'd decorate some paper plates with these designs, for their private use. It would be funny but also serious, sending a serious message about her wishes and dreams.

They had nothing for returning soldiers, just one general "Welcome Home," which seemed too impersonal, white with thick blue lettering and stripes, looking like the Israeli flag. She found a patch of products called "General Congrats," and finally selected one that was covered with crimson hearts and stars and exclamation marks and the words "YAY US!" When she spent time on what Mimi would call nonsense and Tony would call silly shit, she wasn't ashamed, just secretive. Secretly she believes in such activities, which she thinks of as "creative explorations." They'd saved her life—all the name plays, Roco, Blue Field, all the searches for positive themes and motifs to vanquish her fear and sorrow.

Today Lily arrives first and sets the blanket down where they've arranged to meet at the south end of the field, just above the rose garden. When Nancy comes, they both sit silently watching a group of dancers emerge from where they've hidden behind a wall of white spirea to perform one of the many spring celebrations dotting the lawn. They form a circle and issue strange chants in a strange language — *gaia, waia, wanna, manna*. Then English chants to "mother god" for a "fecund, fruitful season," as a dozen dancers circle a maypole wrapped in red satin. Half of them are well into their forties, Mimi's age more or less; half of them are in their twenties and thirties; they all have rosy cheeks, though on two the skin is less pink and more lavender, making Lily wonder if some of them might actually be men, which Nancy doubts since there's a painted sheet on the grass that identifies the group as Women for Springtime. They all wear garlands made of red tulips and purple irises with trailing green ribbons, and green leotards and tights, giving the overall impression of dancing flowers.

Lily knows Homer and Tony will think the dancers are ridiculous and would much prefer to be at the front of the field where the bluegrass bands gather. She likes bluegrass as much as the next fellow but she hates the crowds surrounding the bands, and last year as well they came to the quiet part of the lawn, where a flock of women, who may well be the same group, skipped around the maypole singing, *moon, loom, womb...womb, loom, moon*, again and again. It was a bit much, Lily knew. But they did this great drumming too and then spun each other around the maypole, and Lily longed for a turn. After, whenever she got really excited about something, Tony would say, Where's your maypole! Today, again, there's something comical about grown women skipping around in Kelly green leotards. But Lily loves being near them. *To spring we sing...we sing to spring...*the women chant, a very different song from last year, and there's no skipping and spinning but instead a finale of cartwheels. The tiniest maypoler, a short, chubby East Asian woman with gray braids, accidentally lands on their blanket and sits to rest. She reminds Lily of Connie, after a sequence of strenuous flips, sitting and panting and Lily offers her a cup of juice, which she gulps down, holding the cup in two-hands baby style.

Lily is glad the guys are late. She knows they will laugh at the rituals or at least snicker and she wants to quietly enjoy them—and also tell Nancy, or better still to see if Nancy can tell on her own about Tony and her. Would Nancy think it was strange that only Lily was here with no Kim or one of the other girls Tony had dated before he was called up? Would she sense her new status—or just think she was still tagging along? They'd always included her—but more often as the kid. At Homer and Nancy's engagement party, Tony sat at Homer and Nancy's table, but Lily was put at a friends-of-the-family table—with parents and their little kids. She had expected more from Nancy; they'd always been close. But, of course, she had to realize, as she nursed her wounds, that it was a big-sister/little-sister kind of close, and at sixteen, she was stuck beside Mimi and various grown-ups, the table baby-sitter for a bunch of squirming brats. There was one other teenager, a fourteen-year-old boy who came up to her chin, which, since she is five feet, made him almost a dwarf. She was determined that at Homer and Nancy's wedding she'd be at an adult table if not the wedding party dais, and for months she kept asking Nancy about bridesmaids' colors like she was just curious but acting so concerned and kind that Nancy could not help but want her at her side to support her on the big day. Lavender, Nancy finally declared, but never a word more. Then Saddam annexed Kuwait. The day after he got the orders that his division would be shipping out, Homer and Nancy got married at the county offices. Then Desert Shield. Then Desert Storm. Then now.

Nancy laughs appreciatively about the paper goods and says, "Mad cute! I agree—Yay for us." But then she falls silent. The dancing flowers have started up again.

"Lovely words... *Glory be to fecundity*," Nancy says, smiling, without a glint of irony. Then she says she will tell Lily a secret if she can keep it to herself.

"You're starting a family...tonight?" Lily guesses.

"Warm," Nancy says.

"It started?" Lily says. "Last night?"

"Hot, little sister. First night back. I felt it take right away...in the morning my tits were tremendous and my belly was tingling like a spider was dancing inside. You're the only one I've told."

Lily studies Nancy. How had she missed it! Since last week, her breasts seem to have doubled in size causing gaps between the buttons of her blouse; her mouth and nose seem bigger too, spreading before her eyes like Mimi's cream cheese balls. Even if Nancy had not said a word, Lily thinks she would have noticed in time. Every part of her seems to be softening, readying itself for a baby's landing.

"You have a secret too?" Nancy says.

"Who told you?"

"You did," Nancy says. "Your eyes. Is it who I think it is...hope it is...have always hoped it would be?"

"Who?" Lily whispers, hoping she will get it right. A wrong guess would jinx it.

Nancy's breath tickles as she whispers his name in her ear.

The men arrive late but with good excuses. Tony had to work overtime at Southern Skies. Homer fell asleep after lunch.

Tony says, "Mark my words. In three weeks you'll be your old full-of-beans self." And he jumps up and down quickly to illustrate what Homer full of beans will look like.

"Full of shit," Homer laughs.

He has brought a case of Budweiser and is opening cans for all of them and whomever nearby showing an interest.

"Get your ice cold beer," he hawks.

Nancy closes her eyes. Is she really sleeping? Lily wonders, or just pretending to, like her mother used to when Ronnie would start up with his shouts and Stoly shots, chased with beer or dope or both. Lily closes her eyes too. Soon she is sleeping and dreaming about blue grass—a giant layer of it covered with a layer of blue sky, separated only by a thin band of horizon. And then the earth and sky, she sees, are the layers of a cake—and the horizon line is dark fudge. Mother Nature's Cake is written on top. Mother Nature, Lily calls in her dream. Mother Nature, you're so gorgeous and luscious!

"Shhh," someone is saying. Nancy is whispering in her ear: "Don't say mother. Don't give it away. Remember, no one knows but you."

Lily rubs her eyes awake and surveys the blanket. Tony's opened the cake box. She must have smelled it, vanilla and eggs and butter—and chocolate.

"I'm starving," Nancy says. "I'm craving that whole cake!" She smiles across at Homer, wondering if he will guess like Lily did.

"Look it—Yay, U.S.!" Homer says, pointing to the cake.

It's Yay *US*, the four of us—because we all have so much to be happy about, Lily wants to correct, but lets it go.

"Fuckin' Yay U.S.," Homer says. "Yay, we did it. Yay, it's over."

He's got a buzz on, so he says, "Over, no one buried in the clover, no bodies coming over… to Dover." He laughs.

The maypolers dance and sing: "Yay, yay, yay. To spring. To us. Human and beast. Fish and bird."

"Burd turd," Homer says.

"Guess why," Nancy says

"Why what? Why you got a little gut?"

Her belly, poking out of her shirt, looks bigger than he's ever seen it. He bends down to kiss it.

"Guess," she says. "Guess why I'm starving…and could eat a whole cake…a whole cow…."

She feels so warm, like an oven. Oven…lovin'.

Two beers on an empty stomach. He can't tell what he's thinking and what he's saying. Lovin' in the oven.

"You guessed, baby. A baby. We're having a baby."

Baby, maybe, he laughs.

"No maybe," she says. "I can tell. Your first night back—like magic. Can't you tell?" She means her spreading belly and breasts and ass and nose and lips and even, she thinks, eyelids and eyeballs. Everything feels about to burst.

"Oh, Jesus," he says. Then he can't talk.

"Devil dogs *feel*?" Tony laughs, patting Homer's back.

"I guess a baby devil on its way amounts to special circumstances."

"Guess what else!" Lily says, settling on Tony's lap.

"Oh, Jeez. A big bro cannot turn his back for a second. Little bro, Lil', what's going on?"

"I'm not Lil' any more," Lily laughs. "I'm a big girl. He's a big boy. We're all grown up." She beams.

"A grown-up Devil and his grown-up Devil girl! The corps grew you up, bro. And now you're a man...."

Devil man. Devil girl. Tony had always listened to Homer in rapt attention. It made him feel strong, or at least stronger, like when he was a child and he'd talk to his father. The truth is he never felt more like a child than when he was in country.

Perched in the LAV, riding into the desert, with no roads to guide them, he'd wait for Homer's or his father's words to come to his aid. He can still hear his father's whisper blowing through his mind: You're going to make it, son. Homer cheering, Go, buddy, go Devil. And he'd snap to for a while, only to have his nerve fizzle as they drove on.

A man? He looks at Lily. He was clueless about what that meant but it is with her, since he's been back, that he's felt the first flickers of clarity that he has associated with adulthood, if not manhood.

"Hey, man, remember, buddy, we're still *riders through peace and strife*," Homer says. "Hey, my main man."

Today all that feels so far away, and Tony can hardly remember the words. But poor Homer looks so ragged and he wants to give him a boost, so he closes his eyes and it comes to him: *"Death and life....* Who could forget that, buddy!"


The next week, while walking Roco, Lily stops to talk with Luisa Molto, the widow across the street. She is moving to Florida to be with her daughter and selling her house. On the chance she knows a friend who would want to buy it, she's telling Lily first. It's a nice house and it's nice to have nice neighbors.

Nice neighbors. Lily goes home to call Nancy, and at the end of the day, Nancy picks her up from Doc's to see it. Homer will come later when he wakes from his nap.

"Perfecto, right?" Lily says. "Sure dunk, right?" She's never used either of those phrases before but she blurts them out because they seem to perfectly express the certainty of their new lives. "Right, Nance?"

"Muy perfecto," Nancy laughs. "Muy sure dunk! Muy for sure I love it."

It's like the house she grew up in, like Mimi's house, like half the houses in Monuten, like half the houses in America, Nancy thinks, a 1940s bungalow, with a wide front porch, front and back yard, a first-floor of living room, eat-in kitchen, two bedrooms and one bath. When her father came back from World War Two, the GI bill got him a college degree, a job as a teacher, and the house on Sage Street, where she lived with her parents and grandparents, and then, when her grandparents died, just with her parents till they sold it to move to Arizona. Baby-boomer bungalows, her mother used to call them—because of all the babies born in these little houses after the War, when families were suddenly blessed with a bit of post-War money. She giggles with joy—the perfect symmetry. Back where she started, which is all she's wanted since Homer left for the Gulf. Another war over. Another beginning.

Later, when Homer and Mimi come by, they agree that the house is perfect, and Nancy writes a check for the deposit. Mrs. Molto takes out a bottle of marsala from the kitchen cabinet and pours everyone a drink.

"To my best neighbors," she says, looking at Lily and Tony but mostly at Mimi, who each year has helped her more and more, with shopping and errands and yard work, organizing Lily and Tony to mow and weed and shovel snow. "To my new neighbors," she says, lifting her glass to Nancy and Homer. "Alla salute!"

Then because she is not used to drinking or company or the idea of leaving, she tells her guests a hundred things about herself. Her parents came from the old country and died here, at home, in bed, like it should be. Her husband was a mason, and after a concrete block fell on his head, he still remembered everything about block and brick and mortar but not what happened each day, which made him a good worker and provider but a limited conversationalist at home, which she got used to sooner than she thought because she was so busy. Once upon a time, she worked as a milliner in New York City, but when hats went out of style big-time, she moved here and started working at home, beading sweaters and dresses for a fancy Baltimore manufacturer, until they moved the entire operation to various parts of Asia. By then her fingers were stiff and her eyesight strained, and her husband was dying from Parkinson's caused by the old injury. She had a special friend who was from Haiti, a beader too, who she met one day when she went to Baltimore to deliver her completed work. He was a beautiful man, who could ballroom dance and make love expertly—and sometimes, she swore, both at once. She liked the idea of "people of color" living in her house because she'd always wanted Jacques, who had gorgeous sepia skin, to live with her, but between his wife and kids and her husband, kids, and parents, there was no room. Then all the kids in both houses left, and all the others in her house died, but Jacques still had his responsibilities to his wife, who had developed early Alzheimer's, and so Luisa had to settle for occasional sex and lots of good feeling in between but also loneliness. Now they were both in their seventies, and her daughter was dragging her to her house in Tampa, mainly, she knew, because she wanted to work her to death cooking and cleaning while she played golf even though she said it was because she was worried about her. She didn't want to leave Jacques, but he was busy with his wife's care. The wife still recognized him, but soon she wouldn't and Jacques and Luisa had discussed his moving to Luisa's house, with his wife, the two of them caring for her together. But then the wife seemed to improve or at least stop deteriorating—some days she could recall all the presidents since FDR and count backwards by two and even three—so who knew when they could be together. So now it was *au revoir*, Jacques, who luckily had a cousin in Tampa who he says he will visit often, and they plan in the near future to take a secret cruise.

"All that!" Mimi says. "And I never knew."

"More than that…. Another time," Luisa says. "I'm not one to reveal so much. You've been my neighbor for how many years, Mimi, and did I once tell you personal details? But I'm leaving anyway so what the hell."

They pour more glasses of marsala and toast Jacques. "May his wife lose her mind entirely sooner rather than later," Mimi says, and giggles. "Oops. That's not very nice, I guess."

"Maybe. But I appreciate your saying it," Mrs. Molto says. "It's not like I made her sick, poor thing. Or that my thoughts could make her sicker. Or better."

"You're just frustrated, Mrs. Molto," Lily says. "Because you have a certain plan in your mind."

"And a lot of love in your heart," Nancy says.

Mrs. Molto hugs Nancy. "If I knew it could be so lively around here, maybe I wouldn't have sold. But a deal's a deal," she laughs. "Really, I'm done with this part of my life. And you're just starting. The house is yours."

For two thousand dollars, Mrs. Molto throws in her "sets"—dining room, kitchen, living room, bedroom—which she bought in 1945, when the war was over and Mr. Molto came home.

"That was some long war," Mrs. Molto says, turning to Homer, but he's fallen asleep.

For several days after, Nancy calls just to celebrate her good luck and thank Lily for the introduction. Lily is Lily, generous and jolly, but with each call she feels more and more jealousy sprout until there's a big ugly mass of it in the middle of her mind, like the nasty weeds they used to hack and heap in Mrs. Molto's yard. Mrs. Molto's yard. Mrs. Molto's house. She can't stop thinking about them. Her house is Mimi's and will always be. For Mimi will never leave Henry, who haunts the valley and who, until a few years ago, she talked to in the morning shower and sometimes in bed before she went to sleep, so that it sometimes seemed like four people inhabited the house, one dead and one nuts.

Sometimes when Nancy is gushing about her house, Lily thinks about Mimi's house without Mimi, if it were all hers and Tony's, with photographs of animals instead of Mimi's macramés and appliqués and pastels of nursing mothers on the walls, which could be painted fresh white instead of Mimi's old dusty rose and petal pink. Nancy talks about whose clothes will go into which closet, and Lily imagines Tony and herself without clothes, the two of them walking around like that, dressing only when company came. From her work with animals, who have neither clothes nor guile, she has become interested in nudity as a concept, and she finds herself wondering now if theirs might be a nudist house, even when they have kids. But her thinking about nudity now, she knows, is not conceptual but hormonal. Since Tony's been back, she's all sexed up and this is just one of the many fantasies that titillate when he's not there.


The second week in June, Roco dies in his sleep, at the foot of Tony's bed. They bury him in the yard and hold a little family service.

Lily says that Roco was her last connection to her parents, nothing to write home about as parents, but her parents nonetheless, for whom she named her dog. Looking down at

Roco in the sheet in the ground, she wonders if she would have done any better at life if she were in Ronnie and Connie's shoes. What if Tony hadn't been in and out of war in forty-three days! In and out of the ground war in one hundred hours! When Ronnie got high, he'd sometimes tell her what he'd seen in country. What if *Tony* had been in massacres, in villages torched to nothing, on roads lined with napalm-melted bodies and heads on sticks.

Her ma couldn't take the stories, or the way her pop went from nice to vicious on a dime, attacking when she least expected. If Connie took his darling girl, he'd follow her and kill her, he used to threaten. She remembers Connie carrying her to the car, locking the doors, the two of them just sitting there, as her father circled like a rabid dog and her mother cried, Calm down, calm down, Ronnie. Eventually, her mother left alone, convinced that he would never lay a hand on Lily. Which was true. In fact it was Lily who ended up hitting him a couple of times, when he was really impossible, and he'd already ignored all her *Calm down*s and *Or else*s. Sometimes, if he was too high to know who she was, her old threat shocked him and he shut up for a while, and sometimes, if he still recognized her, he stopped yelling to laugh, because she was "such a nervy little midget." But at least twice that she can remember, when nothing worked, she swatted his nose, which she knew hurt but did not harm him, and he took off to his room and stayed quiet.

She never misses those days, though she misses her father's hyena laugh and her mother's mama-bear hugs. And she'll miss Roco, whose name embodied her old dreams, and whose body—with its kisses, cuddles, compassionate cries—was always there to comfort. She whispers, "Goodbye, Roco....Goodbye, my old dog."

Tony feels too sad to speak. Maybe more scared than sad? He thinks he may have killed the dog. Maybe the dog caught some desert bug, licking him up and down when he started sweating. At the very least he was a bad influence on

Roco, keeping him penned up with him for almost a month. "Maybe it was…." My fault, he thinks.

"Are you thinking it's your fault?" Lily says. "If you are, don't. That's crazy. He lived a long life. He just got called to doggie heaven after a long life."

Mimi has never spent much time with dogs, and the children took care of Roco. But still she has gotten used to the old dog and she too would miss him.

"He was a good dog," she says, "and he had a good long life and lots of love and what more could you ask for?"

With the words "long life…and lots of love," the young people embrace. Mimi recognizes the stage of love when everything that happens seems to be about the two of you. She is happy for them, for their self-centered, shameless love. And she is happy for herself too. She's off the hook! Tony was twenty-one, Lily would soon be nineteen. She'd raised them well—and now they had each other, and she was finally done with the ceaseless fussing and fretting. She has many good years ahead of her, she thinks, before she follows Roco into the ground.


The next morning, Mimi inquires about a job that an ob-gyn friend had told her about at the Women's and Children's Institute outside of Washington, D.C. It was still available and it involved teaching in a new graduate program in women's and babies' health, which included advising some research projects in prenatal care. She'd birthed enough babies to populate a mid-sized town, and for a while now, since Tony went to the Gulf, for sure, her heart has not been in it. For years, she's lectured on midwifery at local colleges and medical centers; lately she's been liking this more and more, and has been wondering if it's not time for her to help birth young minds and leave birthing babies to the next generation. But there were no full-time teaching jobs around for midwives.

Leaving here had always seemed impossible. The area was relatively cheap, the schools were decent, the kids could play safely outside. And also Henry was here. She didn't mean his body, in the coffin in the ground at Mt. Hope, but the enduring Henry whom she'd meet in the secret spot on the mountain, and talk to in bed at night, less and less over the years, but enough to feel, at least for that moment, that she wasn't quite a single mother. Henry existed here in the Shenandoah Valley and nowhere else for her; and staying here meant moments—rare and fleeting but potent when they came—when she believed her son had a father and she the partner she needed to raise him well. She knew so much of what she thought about Henry verged on madness, but it was a madness that had kept her together. Imagining him looking down on them, looking out for them, she felt counseled in most decisions, and less alone. But now she didn't mind being alone. In fact, there was nothing she wanted more than a chance to walk off alone.

And she won't be *all* alone. Washington is her home town, and she still has some old contacts there. A few cousins. Some old friends. She still gets Christmas cards from Susie Montagna, the girl next-door, who became a firefighter; and from her friend Charles Schwartz, whose parents had a melons and citrus stall a row over from her parents'. Steven Amsterdam, who was by far the smartest person she knew in college, would sometimes send her reprints of articles from his lab at the NIH.

The next week she drives to Washington for the day and returns having accepted the job. She will leave at the end of the month, with some books and clothes. She wishes she had been able to afford decent furniture, to leave the kids something better than the battered thrift shop pieces.

When Mimi leaves, Lily doesn't spend the day strutting around naked but lying in bed in her pajamas, desolate. Be careful what you wish for, she thinks. She hadn't meant to chase her off, but that's what happened!

"We'll call her every day," Tony says, crawling in beside her. "Or write her. Or visit once a month. Don't cry." He wipes her tears with his hand. "We won't let her be lonely."

Later, Nancy calls and says, "There's a time for everything."

Usually, nothing comforts Lily like a wise saying, especially when spoken by her wise big-sis girlfriend. And she likes the sound of this one, but what does it mean? That there's a time when women should call it quits? Nancy's mom—who lives in Arizona caring for Nancy's emphysema-ridden father—often tells Nancy, Don't worry about me, I had my time, which made Nancy sad for days.

"I know you don't believe that," Lily says.

"I don't," Nancy says. "I'm distracted. I'm pregnant. I'm tired. I just said it."

"I owe Mimi my life. And I paid her back by pushing her out of her own house," Lily says, starting to cry all over again. "There's no right time for that!"

"You're right," Nancy says. "But I think she really wanted to go."

Mimi might be lonely for a while, but now she'd finally get some peace and quiet, Nancy says. And it would be nice for her and Tony to be alone.

"I love you," Lily says. "You make me feel so much better."

"And goodbye doesn't mean forever," Nancy says. "When people depart, they don't have to die. Like your pop and mom did." Like her mother won't, she hopes.

"We're not actually sure about my mom. But anyway you're right about the Mims—she has got a lot of life ahead of her. Right? You really think that, right?"

"Her own life! Which she deserves!" Nancy says.

# Summer

# 4. Fireworks

It's the morning of the Fourth of July, and Tony wakes with the sun. Walmart's is having a Star Spangled Sale on gas grills. He'd noticed it when he was reading the day before, and he'd put a check next to the ad, and one next to the ad from Jack's Lumber, which was selling picnic tables and outdoor furniture at wholesale prices. But when he showed the ads to Lily, she said, Later, after we take care of other things, which is what she said about most things he's shown her. But there was something about the way she looked at the pictures of the grills, some moist longing in her eyes as if the cooking surfaces were floors and the steel cover a roof, like the entire grilling unit was a little house, in which all their dreams and hopes could live. She wanted it. He could tell. And by the time she got up, it would be waiting.

When Lily wakes at nine, she smells coffee and eggs, and, following her nose, she makes her way to the backyard.

"Happy Independence Day," he says.

And she says the same, and wraps her arms around his neck. Happy *Dependence* Day, she thinks.

Could it be—for the rest of their lives, each could depend on the other? The two of them a unit? She looks at the grill. At the two levels, one with the coffee and bagels warming, one with the eggs and bacon. A warm little structure, which stood for what they were building together.

They bring their breakfasts back to bed. Homer and Nancy and Mrs. Molto will be coming for a 4th of July barbecue, but since Lily will not have to start coals on Mimi's baby hibachi, they can take their time, and till noon, they eat, and doze, make love, then eat and doze some more, and then more love.

Today will be the day. As Tony rakes the yard, Lily goes to the Kmart gift and flower shop. She had planned on roses but the only roses they have are not only expensive long-stemmed at twenty-two dollars a dozen but yellow, and she wants red and white and blue for the holiday, red and white flowers in her mother's blue bowl. But there are no red or white flowers left in Kmart's flower shop, so she goes to the Kmart garden shop and finds perfect impatiens on sale at fifty-nine cents a pot. Back home, she puts the diary in her mother's robin's egg blue mixing bowl and surrounds it with the pots of red and white flowers. She drags the green plastic tables from the shed and hammers the legs into place. There are three of them, big, medium, and small, costing together on a pre-season sale $14.99. Eventually, when they go on after-summer clearance, she will buy yellow Martha Stewart fabric tablecloths and cover the tables, using them throughout the house as accent tables; but for today the red-and-white picnic-check plastic cloths included as a bonus are perfect. She sets the centerpiece in the middle of the biggest table. Red, white, and blue. No one will know till she tells them— at the right time—that it's a double-whammy event.

Their guests arrive and Tony wonders if he could just do it, a little later, when they're alone getting stuff from the fridge, or if that doesn't work, after, when they're cleaning up. And should something accompany the words? Should he kneel down as he says it? Would he need a ring for that? Does anyone do it that way anymore? Maybe she will decide when to make it official, like she decided everything else. Or he'll look at her, she'll look at him, and then that will be it? Engaged? Fucking funny if it happened today on Independence Day because he feels so fucking dependent on her and it feels so fucking good.

Homer says, "It looks like a magazine."

Nancy says, "How do you do it, Lily?"

Mrs. Molto says, "What a perfect party."

The centerpiece is perfect; even Homer likes it. "Cool," he says and salutes it, like it's a flag and he's reporting for duty.

"The diary, what's the significance of the diary?" Mrs. Molto asks.

Lily had planned to take him to the kitchen, to show him the diary, ask him or tell him or whatever it took to get it done. But she can't wait another minute. She opens the book and reads, "I'm crazy about the guy!" Then she looks at Tony. It's his cue.

Now? he thinks, but isn't sure so he says only, "Oh, jeez, Lil', where'd you find that?"

"In the attic, in the box."

Which box? What was in the other boxes? My trains? Your books? She braces herself for his questions. He needs prodding. Another cue, clue.

"Right on top of your mother's wedding dress." It wasn't true but it was only a couple of boxes over. Close enough. She wants the words to tip him off. Wedding, marriage, engagement.

"The blue one?" he says. "Was it blue? Or purple?"

"In between," she says. "A perfect combination." Like us, she thinks.

Now, he thinks. It's the right time. "Will you...could you...maybe now...?" he says.

"Maybe now what?" She wants him to say it simply, clearly, in front of their whole community—that is minus Mimi, of course, for which she is so sorry. Especially since her periwinkle wedding dress has just played such an important role.

"Marry...be together forever...children...old age...the whole thing. Till death do us part."

"I, Lily Dawn Engels, before my community, accept…," Lily begins.

"Save something for the wedding, sweetie-pie!" Mrs. Molto laughs. "Not that it's not very touching and genuine, what you're saying."

"Happy engagement" Nancy says and Homer and Mrs. Molto join in. "Happy life together!"

"You'll have to save that centerpiece forever!" Mrs. Molto says. "What a creative idea. What a fresh beginning."

She says that if you put the flowers in a zip lock with those little packets that come in the box with your new shoes, they will never die. She has a drawer full of the silica bags waiting to be used.

"The happiest day of my life," Lily says. That's what they called it in the magazine article. Even happier than the wedding because there's less strain of preparation. Not since those days at Blue Field has she felt such joy. But this joy is better….this joy would last.

"The happiest day of my life," Tony says. Was any day better? The day when she came to live with them? The day when her letter came? The day when he came back to her for good?

Mrs. Molto says that now that she knows Lily is so creative, she will not throw out the closet-full of artsy-crafty stuff she thought she'd have to dump. "You name it, I got it. Pipe cleaners, lanyard, from when my daughter was little, not to mention sequins and beads and felt and feathers and ribbons and some beautiful fabric from my years of employment. It's a shame to waste. And now I won't."

Later, Lily thinks, even if she's tired, she will walk over to Luisa Molto's house and take some of the fabric. That way the wedding quilt will be started the way the article said it should be—on this wonderful day.

At eight, the sun has set enough, Lily thinks, to light the votive candles she has placed around the yard.

WSHV—the voice of the Shenandoah Valley—is playing oldies.

Nancy announces, "First dance...the happy couple."

Lily and Tony rise for their first dance together, ever. Debbie Boone. "You Light Up My Life."

Homer is sleeping on the grass. His face is pale but blessedly peaceful, Nancy thinks. Is he dreaming about the baby? Sometimes he wakes in the night, telling her things he will do with the baby. Places he will take her, things he will teach her, songs his mother sang to him, which he thinks she will like. Always he imagines his baby's a girl.

The next song is "God Bless the USA" and Mrs. Molto asks Nancy to dance. "I'll lead.... I think we could do this as a waltz...," she says. "I know your generation dances unisex and doesn't know from waltzes. So just follow me...." Mrs. Molto flies Nancy round the lawn. "Watch us, Lily and Anthony!" she calls. "You need to know how to waltz for your wedding!"

Then it's nine o'clock. On the field at the Monuten West Recreational Facility, the light show is beginning. "Are we ready to rock?" the announcer calls. "Right here, besides our very own fort, hundreds have gathered to celebrate our first American victory. Which gave us our great nation. Happy Fourth!" he says. "This is an amazing show, folks," he calls. "No doubt our best to date."

The sky to the west bursts with white flowers, blue stars, red showers, accompanied by the thunderous sounds of explosion.

Homer wakes. "What the fuck," he shouts. "Take cover." He slithers under the table.

Her engagement table wobbles. Her centerpiece slides. If the whole thing topples, Lily thinks, will that bring bad luck?

"Here, buddy," Tony says, kneeling. "Take it easy, buddy. You're home. We're back. Everything is cool."

Mimi has been in Washington for only a week and hasn't found time to call any old friends or to make any new ones.

But today, out of the blue, she gets a call at work.

"Is this the Mimi DiPalma who majored in biochemistry at Georgetown?"

"This is she," she says. She hates that formal phrasing, but the voice on the other end is formal and she feels she has no choice.

"This is Steven Amsterdam. I've been out of the country a good deal for work. I was working in London for two years and just got back. You may not remember me."

"Of course, I remember you, Steven."

"I sent you some articles over the years. I wonder if you received them."

His voice is low, which she used to think was an affectation and a maneuver, so you'd have to listen hard when he spoke. Today, he just sounds shy and she is ashamed that she's never acknowledged the articles or made a friendly gesture back.

"I'm so sorry," she says, "that I never thanked you."

"That's okay. I've wondered about you from time to time and your name came up when I was talking to some people over at the Women's Institute…. I told them I knew you, from years ago."

How long since she's thought of those days?

"You were a great T.A."

He was. He moved awkwardly and spoke hesitantly when he'd enter the classroom, she remembers, his eyeglass frames not quite centered on his nose. But as soon as he started lecturing about molecules and cells and proteins and the origins of life, he grew composed and certain, and she was spellbound. She has never thought of it this way before, but it would be fair to say that Steven Amsterdam had altered the course of her life. From his lectures, she learned about the wonders of DNA, which had won her over to biochemistry from a major in Latin. The double helix, the complete nucleotide, the four bases, adenine, cytosine, guanine, thymine—in a matter of weeks all that had conquered her heart and mind, overpowering the entire Imperium Romanum, the Twelve Tables, Augustus, Titus, Nero and even Catullus. She continued to love translating Latin poetry into English and Italian, but it didn't compare to studying the translation of DNA into protein and protein into life itself.

"Thank you," he says. "It was long ago."

"Twenty-five years ago," she says.

"Twenty-seven," he corrects her.

She smiles. For a whole semester, while most of the class giggled at the exacting lectures from a man whose shirt buttons and button holes were unaligned, whose tie, more often than not, was a clip-on, she was charmed. And when the term ended and they ran into each other in a deli on Wisconsin Avenue, with a boldness that was totally out of character, she asked if he had time for coffee. But one-on-one, that time and another time over coffee and one night over dinner, was disappointing. He continued to lecture her on science, which she enjoyed, but while in the classroom he'd look at her as she nodded in appreciation, alone, now he looked everywhere but across at her. Shyness, she suspects now. But back then she read it as aloofness. And then she met Henry, who looked in her eyes, carried her off to a secret grove, made love to her on a cashmere blanket in the snow. When she came back to Georgetown, they'd wave at each other in passing.

"1964. I remember details," he says, and she hears the diffidence she once took for indifference.

He proposes getting together. He was taking off Monday for the Fourth. If she was taking off Monday too, perhaps they could meet up at the restaurant they once went to. It was still there.

It was their one dinner date and her first Indian food ever, and she remembers the place well. She was on scholarship at Georgetown, and at that point in her life, eating out was still rare and memorable. It was on M Street somewhere between Wisconsin and Connecticut.

"It still exists?" she says. "After twenty-five years!"

"Twenty-seven," he corrects her again, but this time he laughs.

Red vinyl banquettes, dark floral carpets, a flurry of young worried waiters, the smell of cardamom and tumeric mixed with pine disinfectant—the place seems unchanged. It's still a student place, packed even in summer with kids from Georgetown and GW.

"Were we ever this young?" she says. Twenty-seven years ago she was younger than Tony and Lily, too.

"Well, I was a little older. I believe I'm five years older."

"But you were still a kid. I thought you were so mature."

"Mature as in boring," he says and smiles, then looks down.

He heard about her husband, he says after a while. He's so sorry. He asks about her son, and she tells him about Tony and Lily.

She asks him about his life. Wife, children, work?

He shakes his head. "Just work."

She isn't surprised. He'd been single-minded about science. You got your eyes on the prize, she teased him the few times they were together alone. She meant his eyes and mind were elsewhere and he should loosen up. He never answered her or even smiled. The last time she said it, they were here, and he snapped at her. I don't think about the Nobel Prize, just about advancing science. That's all I think about, he said. He was trembling, she thought, angry.

She feels his eyes trained on her now, and now she looks down.

No doubt he was surveying the damage of the past few decades, she thinks. The crow-lines around her lips and eyes. The pound a year. She looked like that Venus statue on the second floor landing of the National Gallery, he told her that once, after a beer in the one and only minute of expansiveness, outside of class, she can remember. And now, she thinks, I look like a middle-aged museum volunteer.

"Time," she laughs. "It takes its toll."

She studies him. His sandy blond hair has darkened and mixed with gray. Except for that, a furrow in his brow, and round horn-rimmed frames replacing oblong horn-rimmed frames, he looks much like the Steven of twenty-seven years ago

"Twenty-seven years," he says. "Twenty-seven years...ago... you stole my heart, Mimi DiPalma."

She laughs. Flattered that he is flirting with her, humoring the chubby lonely matron. "And now you want it back?" she jokes.

But he's not laughing. He's staring at her, stony-faced.

"Not at all," he says.


Outside the restaurant, legions of Washingtonians and tourists are advancing toward the mall for the fireworks. She's always loved fireworks, but this year, she knows, they will remind her of the exploding Iraqi skies, and she asks Steven if they can just walk back to her apartment in the second alphabet. It's a steamy night, but they sit on the sun porch high above Rock Creek Park and talk about everything—population control and AIDS, public health and the World Bank, the state of the quantum in relation to theories of time and consciousness, which is his latest source of excitement, he says.

"Till now." He smiles and takes her hand.

The one night they'd had anything to drink and he likened her to Venus, they kissed, but he was too awkward and she too uncomfortable with him to take it any further. Tonight, though, she feels totally at ease, which she's felt with no man before or after Henry. And she stands, pulling him up with her, and says, "Let's dance."

There's salsa wafting in from Columbia Road, and she says she will teach him. He follows her, inept but eager. She leads him in a rumba, a mambo, a meringue. Then when the music outside stops, she puts on some of her own tapes. They waltz, and then fox trot.

"You've changed," she says. He was fun, she means, and not bad at slow dances. He's clasped her hands around his neck and pulled her head down to his chest.

"Have I? You haven't. Why haven't you changed?"

He lifts her chin and pulls her hair back into the ponytail she used to wear. "You look eighteen."

"Fucking liar," she says.

"May I make love to you now?" he says.

She nods her head, but doesn't move, clinging to him in their dancing position,

"Teenage style?" he says.

She nods again, and then begins to shiver.

"No rush," he says.

He draws a bath and carries her to the tub. Together they bathe in the dark.

"Tell me," he says. "I want to know."


She can't remember the last time she's been with a man, she tells him.

After Henry died, when Tony was little, she brought a few men home, but when each man arrived, Tony would always ask, Are you my Daddy? And when the man left, he'd cry after him, Don't go, Daddy. Only once did she let a man into her bed, but Tony came to her room in the middle of the night with a bad dream. He crawled into her arms and said to the man dozing beside her, Wake up, daddy! She carried him back to his room and got him to sleep. When she returned to her bed, the man said, Your kid's got problems. You really need to set limits on where he can go and what he can say.

She had thought he was a nice man—he was a pediatrician from the hospital where she had trained.

"Nope," she said.

"What do you mean, Nope?"

"I mean I don't want to hear what you have to say. You should go."

It was the middle of the night and she took delight in watching his pointy, little ratty ass shimmy off the bed and into his clothes and out of her house.

Now lying between Steven's legs, her back on his chest, she says, "I can't remember the last time I even thought of that!"

"Tell me more," he whispers.

She tells Steven that for a good five years after that, the little sex she did have took place in cars. It was her preference, bringing less bother and more pleasure. She'd imagine she was young and carefree, with little history and certainly no catastrophe behind her. Sometimes, she'd make believe that Henry and she had just broken up over something silly and the man in the car was just someone she was fooling around with before they got back together. And sometimes she'd make believe that she and Henry were back together, and they were doing all sorts of magical things in the back seat to make up.

She even tells Steven how for years she felt responsible for Henry dying. At one point, in senior year, she had said that maybe they should cool it. She was scared of the way their individual lives were eclipsed. She had to study for her MCATs but when she was with him, nothing else existed. She had graduated Georgetown a semester early to be with him, and moved from D.C. to Miami, sharing his attic room a couple of miles down the old coast highway from Dade State. But for a month, with the exam looming, she'd been unable to study. What are you thinking? What are you studying? Is it interesting? Why or why not? He was driving her crazy, and so she suggested that she rent a room in the house across the street. He wouldn't hear of it and began weeping and shouting that she didn't love him anymore. She did, but when he went on like that she didn't know what she thought, and so she said, Maybe we should cool it. Anything was better than his hysteria. He stormed out of the room. He got drunk and joined up. When he came back two days later, there was no talk of a room across the street. They got married. Two months later, he was called up for basic training at Peabody, and two months after that, he went to Vietnam.

She tells Steven how she spoke to Henry often and visited him at their secret place on special occasions, and how leaving him and Monuten after so many years, she had expected to lose her will as soon as she hit the highway. But as soon as she got into the car, she felt sure and steady.

How could she have endured her life back there? Worrying about Henry, then his death, then worrying again, every day, that some similar fate could befall the children. Then Tony actually leaving for war, and his death transforming in her mind from a passing thought to a tormenting threat, which she managed to escape only by reviewing the ways she could kill herself if he actually died. She sped toward D.C., feeling like a soldier, admitting, only when he's traveling home, how terrible battle had been. Never again would she suffer such agony, she vowed as she drove, never again would she set foot in those deep, dark trenches.

"I'm so glad that you're here," Steven whispers. "Not there."

"I've told you everything," she says. "Now it's your turn."

The bath is cold, and they walk to her big new bed. All night they alternate between telling their stories and making love.

He'd had a 10-year relationship with a Czech anthropologist. She'd left him because he didn't want to "disclose."

"I wasn't a good informant, I guess," he laughs.

But when it happened, he was devastated. To dull the pain, he read two mysteries a day for a month. His favorite were Sara Paretsky's books, because her heroine, V.I. Warshawski, reminded him of Mimi.

"Working-class toughie with pearl earrings and heart of gold," he laughs. He blows in her ear and traces a heart on her chest with his tongue.

He says, "I thought maybe I'd meet you again, or someone just like you. But I'd fuck it up again. So then I read everything I could about the psychology and physiology of human communication. And guess what?"

"You learned how to disclose!" she says, nibbling his lips.

"How to diagnose!" he says. "A case of co-morbidity. A triple diagnosis of extreme shyness bordering on social phobia, mild autism or at least mild Asberger's, and a pinch of ADHD."

"A renaissance man," she laughs, holding him tight.

"It was a relief. I practiced looking people in the eye. One thing led to another. A glance to a smile." In stores, lobbies, on the metro, at work, he'd practice. "And then there you were...."

If he were a believer he'd call it a miracle, that she came into his life again. But he's a scientist, and will have to settle for "an improbable, statistical surprise."

And now, suddenly it's morning. They close the blinds and say, "Sweet dreams." Then they close their eyes and sleep.


Back in Monuten Tony and Lily are waking. In a couple of hours they will call Mimi to tell her the happy news. Last night, after everyone left, they tried her but her line was off the hook, which is what she does when she's super tired and wants to talk to no one and do nothing but sleep.

# 5. Bugs

Tony has never minded his summer stints down at Peabody. After the busy school year, juggling jobs and chores and school, managing field work and student teaching, papers and exams, for the four years of his reservist career, he has actually looked forward to his month at Camp Peabody, which Lily has always called Peabody Vacation Camp. Here Tony is on leave from all decisions and complications. He is active but not anxious, his busy schedule pre-decided by the corps: rise at 6, work out till noon, clean vehicle and gun till three, run ten miles, and then at 9 collapse. Like a boy who's been at summer camp, he comes home trim and energized and full of funny stories.

Since he's come home from the Gulf, though, the base has seemed different. The last two months, when he returned for his reservist weekend, the whole ride down his stomach churned, and his mind shook with explosions of light and sound, and it was hard to hold onto the fact that he was on the road to Peabody and not Kuwait City. But this summer will be his last time ever at Peabody, and he vows to make the best of it. As he packs, he manages to think only positive thoughts: the whole month he will get to hang with Einstein, his best devil camper bud; the tan, which Lily will find sexy; his mind, which will come home rested to face the blitz of civilian life. He still hasn't resolved the missing credits for student teaching, nor reimbursement for last year's tuition, which the corps has not processed yet, which has him worried, especially now with rumors of VA budget cuts. But he's finished up his courses in the first summer school session. And he and Einstein can brainstorm any problems together and talking about anything with Einstein is always a blast. And Homer is on base, too, so how bad could it be?


Einstein is standing in front of the barracks when Tony arrives, which is surprising. For Einstein is always late—not from laziness or indifference, but in fact from just the opposite. His fierce energy and passionate intelligence propel him from one thing to another, curiosity to curiosity, making him a successful student of theoretical biology and physics at the University of Virginia, but a disastrous marine. Tony and he had linked up the very first week of basic training. Ernie Polanco—he hadn't yet been dubbed Einstein—had staggered in from a ten-mile run, an hour after the last of them. Their sergeant—a super lean, mean Green named Morgan, who boasted that he never met a human he didn't hate or a dog he didn't love, earning him the base name of Hound Man—pulled Polanco by the collar to the center of the barracks, to announce his fate. Two weeks with no free time, three days with double push-ups. And you know why? Because you're a lame little cunt.

Say, I am a loser and a cunt, Morgan commanded.

I am sorry, sir, Polanco said. But I prefer not to use that word, sir.

The sergeant spun him around, kicked him in his ass so he fell forward to the floor. He said, I guess that means you prefer shit patrol, a month of toilet licking, you little shitty cunt? He offered him one more chance to repeat after him: I am a lame little cunt.

But Polanco said again, sir, I am sorry, I can't.

Tony's admiration was instant and immense. All those years of Mimi-training had established a similar aversion to this *full-metal* filth. But it was so dangerous to stand up to it, and his apprehension equaled his appreciation. What would become of Polanco? On the run, Tony had spotted him, stopping, then kneeling to touch something on the ground, but he didn't know what or why.

Are you Okay? he asked, slowing down.

Yes, but *it's* not, Polanco said. He pointed down to a rabbit. I squashed it a little. My foot went into the rabbit hole just when it was coming up. I need to fix it up.

You'll get in trouble, Tony warned.

He'd twisted his ankle in the hole and would never make it back on time so he might as well do the right thing, find a splint for the rabbit and so on, Polanco said. Then he went limping off towards the woods at the side of the path, saying, How large a splint, I wonder?

Come back, Tony called. I'll help you walk back.

No point in both of us getting in trouble. I'm gonna be in more trouble than this poor bunny, Polanco laughed.

For the rest of basic, Tony ran beside him to make sure he stayed with the group. He himself was an unlikely marine, he knew, indecisive and fearful. But Polanco made him look good! Ernie had joined the corps in high school for college tuition, he explained to Tony. Then, when he got a full scholarship to U of V, he felt it wasn't right to walk away. And besides his mother had lost her furniture factory job and their health insurance, and the corps provided medical care, which meant at least one item could be scratched off his mother's worry list.

For four years, weekends and summers on base, they were inseparable. Polanco was always dreaming and Tony was always pulling him back to earth, and coaching him in survival skills from time management to rifle cleaning, which was weird, considering how, at home, everyone was always advising him. Homer would be his best friend for life; but he had to admit it was a treat having an additional best buddy who made him feel—in comparison—focused, decisive, and self-sufficient.

"The early bird catches the worm," Tony laughs now.

Einstein smiles. "I don't know about worms. But I think I caught *something*."

Tony studies his face. His dark eyes always catch the light, glistening like black cherries. Today they look dull, like they're coated with dust or sand.

"Hey, man, I see. You got yourself a little bug. Maybe you should check it out in the infirmary."

He has already. That's why he came early. The doctor examined him and said he was fine. "I didn't sleep much last night—that's what you're seeing. I'm feeling a lot better today. I think I'm fine," Einstein says.

"If you say so. You're the genius," Tony says, squeezing his arm. "You're the amazing genius!"

When they spoke on the phone the week before, Einstein told him he'd gotten calls from Stanford and MIT, asking if they could interest him in applying to their Ph.D. program in biophysics when he graduated at the end of the year. They could promise free tuition and a reasonable stipend.

"I mean, look at you, on your way to being Dr. Einstein!"

"And you, almost a teacher, almost a husband!" On the phone, Tony had told him about his summer school courses, Lily. "How's all that going, Maybe?" Because of Tony's habit of saying Maybe this or Maybe that, that's what he calls Tony sometimes.

Tony tells him about the snafu with credits. "But, man, after the desert, it hardly counts as a serious problem, right?"

"A mere particle of a problem. Not enough to stop our forward momentum," Einstein says. "Lily. I never expected that!"

"Yeah, who ever *thunk*?" Tony laughs because that's the kind of thing that she would say.

"Not even sometimes, Maybe? A little thought or wish when you were young teens maybe, Maybe?"

"Hey," Tony says. Einstein sounded like just another green grunt. What would he say next: Not even a little hard-on? A little wet dream?

"Not even an inkling, a passing premonition that you'd be together forever? That you belonged together forever?" Einstein says.

Tony laughs, in relief. "I thought you were getting pervy on me.... Yeah, when we were little, we were sure of it...." He explains how they were "blood children." How terrible it sounded now. Kids in pools of blood—the image swims in his mind, but even before he can execute his captain's trick and blow it away, it mercifully dissolves.

"Blood children," Einstein laughs, uncomfortably.

"Or 'One kid...indivisible...under God....' I forgot that! That was another Lily creation. 'We pledge allegiance to ourself.' We'd face each other and place our arms across each other's chest and...." He blushes. "We were very young still...."

"It's possible, you know," Einstein says. "People linked with unseen connections. There are dimensions we don't have the apparatus to register yet. Physicists are positing a 10-dimensional universe. There are interesting scientific hypotheses being advanced to explain the experience of psychic fusion, telepathy. Maybe I'll do my diss on you and Lily," he laughs.

"When you get the Nobel Prize, bud, you still gonna talk to me?"

"Without words," Einstein says. "We'll just ride the whatever-we-discover-they-are dimensions, waves or strings or something else, back and forth," he smiles.

He's joking, Tony knows, but also serious? Ernie smiles bashfully, but also blissfully, imagining.

Tony remembers how he used to delight in the belief that his father traveled to him from the world of the dead on waves, light waves which he rode like a surfboard. In country, he found himself thinking the thought again. It saved him—imagining his father surfing on shimmering waves to his side. He feels his face flush again—with embarrassment. And that old pleasure?

"And you'll tell me all about this crazy world." Einstein says. "The one we can see. Governments and wars and all the stuff of history. Which you'll be such an expert on from teaching."

"If those credits ever come through. Which they probably will. Lily likes to say, Things have a way of working out. I don't think I believe it but I love to hear her say it. Her eyes get all shiny like she's seen God. I catch the feeling, at least for a while."

"How do you know it's not true?" Einstein says.

"What's not true?"

"That there's not a giant something managing the whole universe?"

"Hey, man. You okay?" Tony says.

Einstein has closed his eyes and is rubbing his brow. Like he's trying to determine the ways he could investigate the existence of that something? A scan that could image it? A formula that could prove it?

"Got it worked out?" Tony laughs, rubbing the top of Ernie's head.

"Do that again, would you?" Einstein says. "My head is killing me."

"From thinking too hard," Tony laughs.


In the barracks, they set up their racks, empty their rucks, clean their guns, then sit on their beds and wait for inspection. Latecomers straggle in today, like the last term of the last year in high school, Tony thinks. When all the grades were in, and you showed up whenever you woke up.

But in an hour, when Sergeant Morgan charges to the middle of the hall for the only late roll-call in four years, he announces, "We have record absenteeism, which will not go unpunished. Unless your pussy friends come up with better excuses than their periods. Anyone know the official term for these lying creatures? I'll give you a hint....We like to fuck them. And it rhymes with pearls."

Tony looks down. The only good thing about the desert was not having Morgan around shoving his garbage in their faces.

"Polanco? Look me in the eye and give me my answer!"

Einstein looks up. Tony knows what his answer will be. The usual: I don't know, sir.

But Einstein just shrugs. He's tired and not listening.

"Fags shrug, not marines," Morgan says. "One thousand push-ups for that fag shrug."

Tony knows the drill. First Polanco and then Bravo. He's used to it, but still his stomach flips, his heart skips.

"Let's try your twin sister. Bravo, what answer am I looking for?"

In the beginning, like all the others, he'd give the expected answer to shut Morgan up and escape extreme penalties. Pearl-girl. Runt-cunt. Lick-dick. But as time went on, he felt worse and worse complying. He tried mumbling his answer, but Morgan said fruits mumbled and mumbled answers didn't count, and lately, since they've been back from the desert, he's been giving the *wrong* answer, like Einstein, which he knows is *right*. For Einstein, it was a policy, based on principle: You did not degrade yourself or any other human, saying those debasing words, even if commanded. For Tony, it felt personal. Because he was tired of being a shitty friend, to Einstein—and to Lily somehow too, maybe? Not just because it was woman-hating filth that he was being forced to spout, but maybe because she believed he was, or would be with a little practice, a man—which meant, she said, "emerging from a boy's confusion into clarity," or something like that. He knows half the times she got these ideas from stupid magazines, but when she said them, every word glowed for him like it was painted in gold on some precious medieval manuscript.

"Bravo?"

"I don't know, sir. Sorry, sir," Tony says now.

"Oh, you don't, well you can fucking push up a thousand times next to your girlfriend Polanco and then fuck each other like the faggots you are....I'll give one more of you maggoty-faggoty losers a chance....Lard Ass," he calls. "Give me my answer loud and clear, Lard Ass."

Lard Ass's real name is Leo Ludhauser, but because he is as fat as a marine can be before being tossed from the corps, Morgan renamed him. But size and name aside, Morgan favors Ludhauser for his school-monitor, suck-up style, which everyone hates, but which Tony and Ernie have decided to just pity.

"Girls, sir."

"Girls, sir, what? Tell them, Lard Ass."

"Girls rhymes with pearls, sir."

"And you fuck them good. Or are you a faggot?"

"I fuck them good, sir."

"Excellent, Lard Ass."

"Thank you, sir."

"Men who come home from war, crying boo-hoo, and crawl into bed because they have a little headache or they're broken out or are very very tired are not men. They are girls with their periods...or faggots...or fucking liars!"

Then he orders everyone on their racks until supper. Everyone has to lie on his bed like a girl with her period. And not say a word. Except for Leo, who is to call out the name of anyone disobeying the order.

Usually, Leo looks happy when he gets these special jobs. Today, though, his face is especially droopy, and sorrowful. Because it's all ending soon? And soon he would be no one's favorite? And go unguarded into the world? Like all the rest of them?

Einstein has never been the most robust member of the company, but his stamina, once he stopped dreaming, was decent. The next morning, though, as they do their extra push-ups side by side, he is laboring, Tony sees, wheezing and sweating.

Tony thinks about all the men who hadn't shown up the day before. A few of them were bullshitters but most were straight arrows. But even the biggest bullshitters—Barr the Boozer and two party animals from Miami who'd run errands for Morgan—stood to gain little. Desert Storm was over. The time to play sick would have been before being sent over. This was to be their last time on base. Wouldn't everyone be eager to have the last of it behind them? Sooner or later, they'd have to make up the time, if Morgan got his way, maybe do double time. Maybe some of them were partying, too high to register consequences. But maybe the rest were sick with whatever Einstein had.

What did Einstein have? The doc at the infirmary said it was nothing. And Einstein said he felt fine, but then he said he had that headache, though Tony had thought he was joking. And then he didn't say, Sorry, sir, but just shrugged, not a dismissive shrug but a dazed shrug, like he was unsure where he was or why. And now the push-ups, which he would never finish today and would probably be ordered to double or triple tomorrow, which he'd never pull off.

Ronnie's face pops into his mind, not his actual face, which Tony barely remembers, but the face his child's imagination had grafted to it. Agent Orange, Agent Orange, Ronnie was always going on about Agent Orange, how you never knew when fucking Agent Orange would get you. How many mornings had he walked from his house to Lily's house, to play with her of course, but also to get a look at Ronnie. To see if the Agent Orange had arrived. *Asian* Orange—that's how Tony thought of it—a monster from the East that tracked down vets and made *them* into monsters in its own image. He imagined Ronnie's pale skin turned orange and no longer really skin but a thick and bumpy covering like an orange peel; and slashes of dark orange eyes narrowed in hatred;

and a nose and mouth all orange too but pale like those Halloween marshmallow candies, and soft like them, too, changing shape before his eyes into snouts and maws; and Ronnie's yellowish, nicotine-stained hands would be gone, replaced by claws, like those on the ducks in the window of the Washington D.C. restaurant that his mother once took him to, sizzling in bright red-orange flames. It was the claws shooting fire he most feared—and he'd ring the bell early in case the Asian Orange had transformed Ronnie during the night and he had to rescue Lily before the flames got her. But it was always just old Ronnie at the door, with his old translucent skin and bloodshot eyes and thin mean mouth jabbering crazy stories. Years later, when, out of the blue, he asked Mimi about *Asian* Orange, Mimi explained what it was and how it worked, and that Ronnie had been spared that at least, though several of his friends, and their kids, had not been.

Could the government have used Agent Orange again? It was a defoliant and there was little need for *that* in the desert. And, besides, they'd probably learned their lesson about using any dangerous chemicals. So if it was anything, it was probably something innocuous, passing, like the doc had told Einstein. Desert Flu? Tony tries out the name, but it sounds too serious. Maybe it was just psychological. How many Vietnam vets came home with psychiatric stuff? Not that this looked half as bad as Ronnie's crazies, but maybe it was a touch of that. Desert Depression—maybe that was all it was. Or maybe just exhaustion. Gulf Fatigue? He likes that best, because maybe then all you do is sleep it off? He'd probably had a touch of it, too, but after a few weeks of rest, he was fine. If he had the money, he'd take Ernie to the Caribbean or the Gulf of Mexico, carry him down to the beach, lay him on a raft, and say, Sleep, buddy. And he'd watch Ernie bob in the turquoise waves until the deep fatigue from the black water and black sky of the other Gulf seeped out of him, and then he'd take him back home to start his Ph.D. and win the Nobel Prize.

Einstein is shaking now. "Ernie, buddy," Tony whispers. "Maybe you should stop? Maybe take a nap and try the push-ups later, when you got your energy back?"


At chow only one grunt thinks it's bullshit. Some think it's nerves, stress; some buy the idea of a little bug. Most prefer exhaustion as an explanation for the hooky-playing. Gulf Fatigue. They like that concept and Tony's phrase.

Only Ernie objects. "We know nothing. You can't build theories based on nothing."

Tony says nothing. He is a little insulted by his friend's rebuff, but mostly worried. Ernie's shortness of breath, sweats, and shakes had scared him before, and now this—his voice was weak but there's no question he was shouting. He's never heard his buddy shout before. Maybe irritability went with the fatigue?

"You have to look at the evidence. Who has what. Who was where. I don't know what kind of cohort you'd work with, or which approach you'd do first. Longitudinal studies would eventually need to be set up. But first a registry and protocol for tracking …."

He stops talking mid-sentence and lays his head on the table, rubbing his cheek against the cold metal.

"You're right, bro," Tony says, laying his hand on Ernie's brow.

Ernie's head feels hot; maybe he had a fever. His thoughts were always pretty wild. But this was stratospheric—a dissertation out of nowhere. What was going on? Right now, Tony wants a simple answer. He wants down-to-earth thinking. He wants Homer now, he thinks, to talk this through with, step by step. Homer hardly knew Ernie, but he knew just about everything connected with war, which this might or might not be. And overall, he was so smart, a practical smart, which could probably help him see something that he and Einstein hadn't seen, though it was there all the time, just lying there.


After chow, Tony drives over to Regina's, a bar near the highway, where he and Homer have met up over the past few years, not as the camper and lifer they were on base, but as the old best buds they've been most of their lives. He tells Homer about Ernie and the other camper absentees. He tells him his theory—that it's some sort of fatigue or maybe a flu from the Gulf.

"It's nothing, bro," Homer says.

"We have twenty-five percent no-show and they all have called in with the same story. Exhaustion. Aches and pains." He tries to remember all the ailments. "How can that be?"

"Ever heard of telephones? A good idea—like playing fucking hooky—travels fast. And answer me this. How come none of my lifers are sick? How come it's just your fucking campers? Sure people get tired after war. But look at us. We both rested up and here we are. Good as new."

"You know Einstein. He is as straight as they come."

"War brings out character. Don't take this personally, buddy, but your friend may not have the real stuff you thought he had."

He and Homer have never disagreed about anything substantial. They were both Democrats. Both Senators fans. They both rooted for the underdog. Homer walked the corps walk, talked the corps talk. But face to face, he always talked to him as a friend. None of this, Me Jarhead, You Pinhead shit.

"How can you be so certain?" Tony says.

"We were all in the same places, Ton. How could it be that only the kiddies get sick? Answer is—they're kiddies. Not men…marines."

"Next you'll be calling them pussies," Tony says.

Suddenly it felt like his best buddy was gone. Like he had ridden off without him. Stranding him. And Ernie, and all the other losers with their loser problems, on some path where no one would ever find them.

"That's not what I'm saying. Maybe my vocabulary is a little rough. But my point is we have a group of men who have had zero experience or training in enduring real stress. And, yes, maybe, their bodies are having little nervous breakdowns and maybe need some R and R. I'll go that far."

"You will...oh good." Tony can hear how childish he sounds but he feels so relieved. *Go that far.* Like Homer's still with him, and he's with Homer, riding life together. He can see Homer's point about bodies having "nervous breakdowns."

"You mean like when I have finals," Tony says "and I'm not sleeping and I get these sores on my face, and after my last test, I usually get a vicious headache and sleep for a week?"

"There you go, bro," Homer says. "Your college friends just need a post-war intersession. I'm just kidding. Yeah, it's like that but more because it's post-combat and these guys aren't used to that or probably to much stress at all. You tell Einstein to take it easy and he'll be as good as new."

You promise? Tony thinks. That's what he was always asking Homer when they were kids, when the older boy would listen to his problems and assure him they would vanish. That he'd save up enough from his paper route for a new bike, pass trigonometry, stop sweating like a pig when he talked to a pretty girl.

"You tell him that Big Brother Homer says so and that I've never let you down."


The infirmary distributes mega doses of vitamins to Ernie and other fatigued men. Each day Ernie wakes with energy and, though he's tired by the afternoon, he feels reassured.

They've run tests on them all, which have all come out normal.

"Tests, unlike people, do not lie," Ernie says.

Ernie isn't exactly Einstein again— bouncing from here to there and back, like sound or light. But he manages to do everything he needs to—eat, walk, talk—and Morgan is off his case. There are absolutely no data suggesting that he and the others are anything but fatigued, tired from the stress of the desert war, and maybe a little desert bug, undetectable and fleeting. That's what the docs posit, and barring any new empirical evidence, it's as decent a working hypothesis as any, Ernie says.

By the second week of August half of the absentees are back. Some say they had rashes or coughs or sweats and dry heaves. Some all of these. Some all of these and more. Most of them feel better. Not just from taking the vitamins but from having people who understand.

The base doctor, for one. He calls a meeting of the entire battalion and tells them all, "You've been through a lot. Feeling the pressure is nothing to be ashamed of."

He reviews the signs of stress. Headaches, fatigue, irritability, stomach cramps, rashes. They have excellent medication for anyone who needs a little extra help in putting the desert behind him.

Ernie goes to the infirmary and is given Prozac.

"Goodbye, stress," he says, showing Tony the little blue pills. He found his time with one of the doctors very interesting. "The doc said that trauma can actually change the brain's appearance. New imaging techniques demonstrate changes in the brain with severe post traumatic stress disorder, which is not what he believes I have. He suspects what I have is milder than PTSD and just a little fiddling with my neurotransmitters should do the trick. For everything. Energy, mood, concentration. Soon you can call me Einstein again," he laughs. "Lately, I've noticed, you don't call me that much."

By the third week, the reservist area is ninety-five percent full. The brass has decided to cut them all some slack. The truth is they were all tired. The rest would do them all good. The base commander has brought in a specialist to explore modes of communication in their organizational culture.

Sergeant Morgan is put on desk duty and is replaced by an avuncular older sergeant. Sergeant McCormack tells the men stories about Vietnam. How much worse that was. How many of his unit had died, or lost limbs, or lost their minds to drugs or PTSD or both. They are lucky. It's their last season and soon all this would be behind them.

"You did so well, men," Sergeant McCormack tells them. "You won the war. Why wouldn't you be a little ragged. It's only human."

"It's sexy," someone calls. "Ragged is sexy."

"That's the fighting spirit," the sergeant says. "Give yourself time to get back in sync."

Homer comes to say goodbye to Tony.

He probably won't see him till Christmas and wants him to know that he's aware that he'd been a bit of a prick about Einstein and the others that night at Regina's. The base was running groups to sensitize lifers to stress issues, so they can deal respectfully with colleagues less experienced in battle and trauma. Camper colleagues. He's genuinely sorry.

"I'm here, little bro," he says. "If you need me, call. For anything at all."

The next time they're together, Tony will be a civvy. A devil no more. But still his best buddy, Homer says, hugging him and calling, "*Semper Fi....Through peace and strife.*"

His Homey could be an arrogant prick sometimes but he was his Homey still, Tony thinks. Always there, in the end, always faithful. "*Through death and life*, bro," Tony says.

And then August is over, and Tony prepares to head home with the other grunts.

"You have your whole life shining before you," the captain says. "And the corps behind you, supporting you in all your future ventures."

"*Semper* behind you....The corps nevermore," someone cheers when the captain's gone. "The corps' behind...Take it up the ass, corps. Take it up the ass, Morgan."

Then there's lots of ass-slapping and hugging. Promises to connect sooner rather than later. In a couple of months, at the most, Ernie will organize a reunion since he's the one with a computer and everyone's address on a floppy.

# 6. Surprise

The end of summer has always been Lily's favorite time of year. As a kid, before fall really came with its cold mornings and rigid routines, Lily loved end-of-summer musing about what was coming next. She loved imagining new teachers, new friends, new math skills, new topics and projects in social studies and art that awaited her. She loved late-summer preparation for fall, trips to the mall with Mimi for new sneakers and socks, sweatshirts and sweatpants, a rainbow of cotton turtlenecks and barrettes. And now that she's grown, she loves the clinic most at the end of August, when dogs and cats return from wholesome country vacations, blowing her away with their lean beauty. She loves the valley most at the end of summer, too, when the trees are still mostly green and full, then suddenly surprising you with splashes of color that take your breath away. If she had to summarize what she loves best about the end of summer, it would be that sense of surprise. And she can think of nothing better to welcome Tony back from his last summer ever at Peabody Camp than the almost-fall shocker she has planned.

She wakes extra early to get there before the office fills up. A secretary is just unlocking her desk and files, and Lily knows she's the one. She is a hoot and exactly as Tony has described her—with an old beehive, baby blue cat's eye glasses, face powder dusting a hearty moustache, dandruff on a navy polyester blazer.

"Good morning," Lily says. The woman looks up. Her face is a worn battleground of mean and scared, Lily thinks: Slashes of no-frills lips keeping all at bay; slits for eyes, just big enough to scan for sudden advances and end-runs. She is Josephine Hayes, Secretary to the Principal, a plastic sign sitting on her desk says.

"Good morning, Ms. Hayes. Is Dr. Moser here?" Lily says.

"He's a very busy gentleman," Ms. Hayes sighs.

"I can imagine," Lily says. "Is he here this morning?"

Ms. Hayes sighs again, this time more peevishly, as if Lily has been harassing her for hours. When she sits and starts fussing with her computer, Lily estimates the time it would take to dart through the wooden gate, cross the main school office, make it to the far door, marked *Private. Principal. Dr. Arnold Moser*, and push it open. No more than five seconds, Lily estimates. But Ms. Hayes's desk is too close to the gate to try, Lily thinks. She'd cut her off at the pass.

Ms. Hayes looks up. Her eyes blink a certain message: Don't give me trouble, don't even think of it!

"Please give him my card," Lily says. "Please tell him I'll be expecting his call."

"Oh, he's expecting you?" The secretary's whole face softens, the mouth relaxing into a wobbly smile.

Lily nods. Lucky she had taken time this morning getting ready. She had given her clothes a scotch-tape go-over, removing most of the dog and cat hair. And with the coat of fur gone, who was to say she wasn't just another young professional in black slacks and a black blazer?

"He's had dealings with my...associate," Lily says. "He's probably been expecting him."

She presses her lips together to contain the laughter bubbling in her as she imagines how Tony will crack up when she tells him what she said, pulling "associate" out of the hat, just like that.

"Shenandoah Animals, Inc...I see. Here to talk to the chief about our internships and intro-to-the-professions programming? Why didn't you just say you were one of our community corporation partners?"

Lily smiles, silly me. And then the next thing she knows she is standing in the open doorway of Dr. Moser's office, and he is saying, "Our corporate community partners...where would we be without you!"

And again she has to swallow giggles, because that was probably the kind of bullshit he'd given Tony and she can't wait to act out the scene for him. She knows exactly the voice she'll use for the old bullshitter!

"We'd love to come to talk to your students," Lily says.

"Yes, yes, I think your associate mentioned something along those lines."

Dr. Arnold Bluffer. That's what she'd call him from now on.

"Perhaps," she smiles. "Before he went to the desert."

"Desert....You work with exotic animals? Yes, I think I recall that. How exciting."

And then she can't bear another minute of the crazy charade. She tells him she means the war in the desert. Desert Storm. And then she says Tony's name and feels tears fill her throat. "How could you, Dr. Moser?" she cries. "He trusted you...."

"I trusted *you*," Ms. Beehive says, listening by the door. "You'll have to leave."

"I've got this, Josephine," Dr. Moser says, and closes the door. "My young lady, please sit down...so we can talk. And do the best for...your...."

She watches him search for the right word. If not associate, boyfriend...husband...brother?

"We're officially engaged to be married," Lily says.

Sorrow rarely brought her to tears, but anger rarely failed to. Anger and frustration. And she can't stop crying as she says, "We've got everything planned....But if he can't graduate...after everything ...." She means after working and studying, after student teaching and basic training. After the desert. And before any of that—when she first knew him, marching around with a soup pot on his head, saying it was his helmet and his name was Henry; and then for years, alone in his room, asking his father for tips on growing strong and unafraid.

"He's such a nice person. He's worked so hard and is so close to reaching his goals," she says. She sounds like she's gargling and she wishes she could stop crying, but she can't. "It's just not fair," she says. "Do you think it's fair, Dr. Moser?"

Dr. Moser shakes his head. "I meant no harm....I am just very busy. Between developing and meeting my performance objectives and strategic goals...I can't breathe...."

Please don't, she thinks. For she knows the signs. His face was collapsing. In a second, *he'd* be blubbering too.

"Okay, what's next?" she says, trying to seize them both from the pit of humiliation.

She watches him struggle for composure, snorting to recall the tears and related gunk welled up in his nose. Then blowing into a tissue, which does the trick.

"Getting this matter settled of course is next....It's in the works, of course, but we can surely facilitate... expedite...." He will take care of everything. Chop chop. "That's the least we can do...for our young men and women....The very least...."

His eyes moisten again and search out her eyes. He grabs her hand. From all her time with beasts perhaps, she is skilled at reading looks and touches, animal and human alike—and can tell he is sincere. They were having a *molten moment,* which is her name for times when the edges of people soften and they flow towards one another. But she knows these pass, and half the time people congeal right back into the turds they'd been.

"Please, Dr. Moser, don't forget." She almost says, You promised. But it sounds too young so she just says, "Thank you so much, Dr. Moser," and waves goodbye, telling herself not to skip but to walk down the hall.

The whole half-hour ride to the clinic, she giggles. Where had she found the nerve to do what she did! She was a planner, but not a schemer, and if it were for herself alone, she never would have dared. But it had broken her heart watching him, each day before he'd taken off for Peabody, checking the note pad by the kitchen phone, as if staring at it hard enough would make a message appear: *Dr. Moser called, all is well.* She couldn't bear the thought of him coming back from base to wait and watch all over again.

By the time she reaches the clinic, the letter from Dr. Moser has arrived on the fax machine. *Anthony Bravo has been declared AAC: All assignments completed.* Five minutes later a fax from the college comes through certifying *Anthony Bravo CFG: Cleared for graduation.*

Tomorrow he'll be home, and she tries to imagine what he'll say when she surprises him with the certificates and then all her impersonations!


"You rascal…you charming weaselette," he says. "You did it…you…*associate*…you." He lifts her up and spins her in the air.

Associate. She had thought that he would love that, and call her that for a while. He had been coming up with new names for her forever. A few weeks back she had read an article, "Tender Terms," about the names spouses use for each other. It was kind of stupid about how Baby and Babe have replaced Sweetheart and Darling as the most common terms of endearment in the last three decades. But it said nothing about coming up with your own name or names for that matter, and seemed to assume one fixed "tender term" for your "private life and private moments," and so on. But she liked the variety, the playfulness, and never ever wanted that to stop. Associate was fine. So was Pony, Midge, Short Stuff, Teeny, Tooter, Hooter, Spinach-mouth, Beasty, Bean, Fur,

Pup and Pits and a hundred others he had thought up over the years. She has no names for him but Tony and Ton, but she laughs now, thinking, Mr. CFG, cleared for graduation, Mr. CFM, cleared for marriage. Mr. AMF, all mine forever.

The second week in September, Homer calls and says he's arranged to come home in two weeks for a two-week vacation. Nancy has sent him a sonogram photo, which he has taped to his rack. But he needs more than pictures.

He says, "I need to be home. I need to be with the baby." He says he wants to pat it, feel it kick, lay his head on it and listen to its heart. He knows he can never be as close to the baby as Nancy is, but he wants every intimacy he can manage.

Before he went back to Peabody, when they had sex, after he'd climax he would stay inside her, satisfied and still. It was "family time," just him and her "and the baby," he'd say, and it was the happiest time he'd ever known or imagined. As he told her this, Nancy would climax. Before, they had always tried to come together; but now she waited for him to settle down. It was practice for parenthood, she said, when at all times at least one of them had to be clear-headed, responsible and ready. But it was more than that, she knew: she loved him more than ever when he just lay there, quiet and still.

It was the baby that had changed things, of course, she thinks. The baby and the war. In the early days, it's true, she had tried to slow him down, but just long enough to look at him and hold him. All in all, back then, his natural might and spirit had thrilled her. "The most talented marine I've come across," his captain had told the whole company, at the end of basic training; he called Homer a "natural warrior." Back then, with no wars in sight, she was proud, admiring his physical and mental agility, his discipline and fairness. She never tired of hearing Lily and Tony tell the story of how he taught the local kids that he was no one's slave. And in those early years, when he'd rock in her arms, hard inside her, howling that he'd die for her, she had no doubt that he would, and she'd radiate with joy, and sometimes, after, they'd joke they had really both just died and gone to heaven.

*Die for you. Go to heaven.* All that heroic talk only terrifies her now. When he was in the desert, the nights she slept, she slept lightly, listening for the doorbell to ring and officers to announce they were sorry to have to report....From night to night, the scenarios changed: her husband had been gassed...lost in the dunes...exploded with a Scud.

For what? she'd think. He'd talked about fighting "to keep the peace." She wasn't sure what that actually meant, and his explanations never really helped. He sounded a little goofy, like some of her old high school classmates, when they'd try to explain why and how they'd been born again. It had something to do with justice. And honor. It was his moral responsibility to use his natural might to do right, to right wrong. She had never seen him start a physical fight, but twice she had stood by helpless as he jumped into raging brawls. Both times, he'd stopped the car and, after a quick briefing from someone on the sidelines, charged into the middle. He was lucky. Both times his massive presence stopped the fight. But what if it hadn't? And what if he had the wrong information about who was right and who was wrong? Or no one was—it was a pointless fight?

If you drive quickly, which Homer does, you can get from Peabody to Monuten in two hours. And for the past three years, Homer has lived on base, and she has stayed in Monuten, and they've hooked up on weekends one place or the other. But it was only temporary until they started their family. Nancy's school district was the best in western Virginia, and they'd agreed she couldn't leave her job. They'd talked about Homer requesting a transfer to the Marine Outreach Office over in Downsville, which was only forty-five minutes away. But now, she wants him out of the corps entirely.

His might and soldier talents scare her. She knows Homer couldn't change his being but couldn't he temper it—become a slightly less eager, slightly more reluctant warrior? A few marine wives had called to say their husbands were getting out—the desert had killed their taste for battle. Most were retraining for security work. She couldn't quite see Homer doing that—it wasn't active enough. But she could see him doing something with kids, in self-defense perhaps. Or in conflict resolution. Imagine the impact of a powerful marine telling you to solve your problems with words! She knew first-hand how much the schools needed those kinds of programs. And she needed him home. And in one piece. The week before he returned to the base, she practically ignored him, fretting about ways to keep him with her. The two weeks at home would give them time to really be together and then, when they're feeling close and trusting, she could make the case for a new course of action.

Every day, after work, the women get together. Tony is working long shifts and overtime at Southern Skies and he helps when he can, but most evenings it's just the two women who get together to make Luisa's house Nancy's and Homer's and the baby's house. Now Homer's upcoming visit provides an incentive for the transformation to be complete.

Bare windows are dressed in flounces of pastel gauze. Mayonnaise or in extreme cases turpentine is applied to remove all mars and scars from wooden pieces. Ancient wall-to-wall is attacked. The walls of the baby's room, which Mrs. Molto had papered with a butterfly and daisy pattern in the sixties, are stripped and scrubbed and treated to two coats of "Meadow Dreams"—a serene pale green from the Laura Ashley Mother and Child Collection, which has been discontinued and put on sale at Valley Paints. At the end of the week, Lily rents a machine and scrapes the grim wood floors back to their original bright white oak.

Lily knows a lot about toxins and fumes and for even the smallest job—washing or polishing—she supplies masks and gloves. The nastier jobs involving turpentine, ammonia, epoxy, and lacquer she has claimed for herself. A new mother must be extra careful, she has told Nancy. She must be safe for two. Much of her health awareness has come from her training in animal care, but many ideas have come from the mothering magazines she has been buying to find ideas for Nancy's new life.

There is much more attention to health and safety in *American Mother* than in *American Bride,* but many of the articles stress similar social concerns. The importance of support. A network both inside and outside the home. Calm and security for the mother as much as for the baby. Communication. Information. These all seem so valid to Lily and she is committed to providing Nancy with as many of these essentials as possible so that her entry to Motherland is not only physically but emotionally satisfying and safe.

It's the least she can do for Nancy, who for so many years has given her so much. Not only barely-worn sweaters and sneakers, free movies and popcorn, dancing and driving lessons. But something way more important. If she were authoring an article, she'd write, "Nancy Jackson taught me to be a woman. From her I learned womanhood's essential principles and practices...."

Some of it Nancy imparted without knowing through what one article referred to as "women's naturalistic modeling." Small stuff it might seem, but detail upon detail added up to a whole womanly style, the article said and Lily agreed. Nancy's sway when walking, her head-toss when starting to laugh, her sincere gaze when hearing your point of view even if she disagreed—all these Lily would watch spellbound. Then later, at home, she would try them out. She'd never be a swayer, but studying then practicing Nancy's amazing taffy walk brought such significant change. One of

Nancy's nicknames for her had been "Jumping Bean," but soon her own improvised slo-mo walks and turns glimpsed in the mirror seemed so beautiful that she swore her Jumping-Bean days were over. She must have caught that spastic stuff from Mimi, from Mimi's naturalistic modeling. From watching Mimi running, running everywhere—to and from the car, to get to or from a birth, and in between careening to the supermarket, the bank, down the hallway to the phone, the stove, the bathroom. It could be thrilling, racing around the valley at her side, to sex ed and prenatal classes, even, in an emergency, to births. Lily knew that in other homes, women would walk from room to room, and sometimes sit down, to do nothing in particular. Till Nancy entered her life, though, she'd rarely seen it up close.

In long leisurely afternoons, Nancy demonstrated this other way. They'd wander through Kmart, sometimes for no reason at all, looking and touching item after item, aisle after aisle. But with no rush or anxiety, important things still got accomplished. First bra, first lipstick, first heels, first tight jeans—all these Nancy oversaw. From Nancy she learned to detect and stop certain "beast moves," as Nancy jokingly called her habit of circling like a dog when nervous, or whinnying when embarrassed. And Nancy gave her the greatest tool of all, an actual tool, the duct tape mitten, and taught her to make them herself to remove the "beast fur" which clung to her, especially on winter wools. Without Mimi, she doubts she would have survived; without Nancy, though, she would have remained a puppy-girl. Nancy guided her to the gates of womanhood, and assured her that when she was ready she could enter and no one would laugh. And now here she was. Holding Nancy's hand as she wobbled towards Motherland—that was the least she could do.

Eventually, she'd journey there herself, following in Nancy's footsteps. And Nancy would hold her hand again. Like the bridal network, the motherhood network wove back and forth, inside and outside the home and family, growing stronger through the years.

Homer will come home the next Friday. And by then, Lily is determined, the house will be "baby-set." A mother magazine article used the phrase, by which the writer meant not only having the baby's crib etc. ready, but a whole house calm, organized and welcoming—or COW. Babies can perceive more than we think, and "only a home that has achieved a COW state is truly baby-set."

Nancy works beside Lily but achieves very little. She is useless, she says. But she is content. A cow, she laughs; a cow in COW. She used to find Lily's little systems silly but now every last idea and arrangement about how and what to eat, breathe, touch, and think seems charming. She remembers when Homer first brought her over to Mimi's. Lil' was eleven or so, and Nancy would brush her hair into high pigtails, and Lily would beam and insist she was part cocker spaniel like Roco. Once she even put Roco's collar and leash on and made Nancy walk her, but Miss Jumping Bean didn't walk but flew down the street, breaking the leash. She was her pet, her little sister, her little fairy. Today, she looks like Tinkerbell, flying around the house, spreading magic dust.

If she could only toss some magic dust on Mrs. Molto's furniture, Nancy thinks. She totally hates it, which only now, as their work on the house draws to an end, has she come to realize. Despite the wondrous transformation of floors and walls and windows so everything is lighter and brighter, she feels some heavy sorrow as she looks around the rooms. Her grandparents on both sides were children of tenant farmers from the outskirts of New Orleans, Panama City, Port au Prince, and Norfolk, respectively, all of them equally eager to escape the dirt floors, the tables and chairs hewn of discarded legs and salvaged boards, the muslin curtains dangling from strings and prayers, and other signs she'd glimpsed in family photos and stories of precarious pasts on the edges of vulnerable tropical ports. She never knew her father's parents, who both died young, but her mother's parents both migrated as children to the Chesapeake region, becoming the first in their families to finish high school, then college, and in their small town just outside of Newport News, the first blacks to become civil servants. When her parents married and settled in the Shenandoah Valley, her grandparents came to live with them in their new house in East Monuten. Nancy always felt so safe in the bungalow, "built with five hundred tons of bricks," her mother used to boast, and filled inside with sturdy 1950s variations on American colonial—plaid skirted sofas and chunky maple side tables, thick captain's chairs, a walnut table that would transform from square to octagon to round at her mother's bidding, a raised-panel credenza big enough to double as a daybed, she discovered, climbing up there many days, when her homework and household chores were done, to watch the news and wait for her parents and grandparents to walk in the door from work.

Growing up, she was so proud to say to friends, as her mother had said proudly to her, Our home is Early American. To Nancy, it had sounded substantial, dignified, like her forebears had come to these shores not as brutalized African slaves but as fortunate ship's captains and merchants and traders, acquiring their homes, furniture, and futures with relative ease. Her family's beefed-up stuff, she realized later, was the kind of factory-made Early American found in coffee shops owned by Greek immigrants, and the homes of other recent escapees from drudgery and poverty. But still she has always felt so proud of what her family had assembled.

Seeing Mrs. Molto's furniture for the first time, she felt so comforted, like her childhood had never ended, her grandparents had never died, her parents hadn't moved far away, her mother buried under the weight of her father's illness. Today, though, the Molto marriage sets seem monstrous. She feels especially hormonal this week and knows her fear that the giant pieces will squash the baby, or displace the air the baby needs to breathe, is neurotic. But when these particular terrors subside, she finds she still has an aversion to the massive hardwood pieces. She craves furnishings that suggest a light, carefree existence, not the one awaiting her. One day, she hopes to have enough money to go up to New York City and buy a whole house of whimsical grunge in the East Village, where, according to a *People* article she's read at the dentist, Madonna buys her furniture. Wrought iron butterfly chairs and slim Scandinavian couches and flat pile-free rugs woven with playful triangles and dots. With furnishings like that she could be happy and her baby safe.

Two days before Homer is to come home, as they wait for the last coat of polyurethane to dry on Mrs. Molto's floors, Nancy and Lily eat a supper of sandwiches together in front of Mimi's T.V. It seems to Nancy that she is seeing Mimi's house for the first time. How could she not have noticed the way cool stuff all around?

"Funky funky, grungy grunge...and def cool. I never noticed before...."

"You like it?" Lily laughs. She has grown up with this junk–each room an array of unmatched modern pieces, the wood ranging in color from black to blonde with a fake-teak mud-brown dominant. The upholstery is all sixties synthetic, in screaming oranges and mustards, hopeless olives and umbers. "I can't believe you like it.... I mean what's there to like?"

Mimi had said they could toss whatever they wanted to, which is what Lily has planned to do as soon as they have some money for some real furniture.

"Surprise," she says, "it's all yours."

"And you'd just take Mrs. Molto's monsters for now?"

"You mean that? I don't think they're monsters. I'd cherish them forever. If you'd let me have them....Oh my

God, they're classic," Lily says. By which she means furniture all the same color and in a style that was securely established well before her mixed-up life began. "You sure you don't like them?"

"I like them for *you*," Nancy lies.

The next day two buddies from Southern Skies help Tony move the furniture from one house to the other. And then it's all done. Nancy's house is totally COW. Totally baby-set.

Was anyone ever so blessed? Nancy thinks. A baby. A loving husband who may very well decide on a new career and stay safe by her side forever. Friends, one of whom might very well be an angel. The rest of the week as she checks children's homework, she finds herself dozing, uncertain when she wakes if her perfect life is just a dream.

Then, with Nancy's house done, Lily starts in on theirs. Like Nancy's, it must be totally COW, and Tony helps every chance he gets. He doesn't remember what COW means exactly— an environment that's healthy and natural, like milk maybe? But he is sure he remembers Lily saying that they could achieve it with less bother since they didn't have to be baby-set, only baby-friendly.

He loves transforming Mimi's house into their house. He loves that for all her clipboards and task charts, the actual work Lily has organized feels often like a game. He calls it, Lily's Mystery Tour because he never knows what's coming next. The only thing he can be sure of is that she understands him perfectly. When she'd announced they would swap Mimi's furniture for Mrs. Molto's, she knew what he was thinking before he did. He can visit the old furniture any time he wants, she told him. Or if he finds he's missing a particular piece, like Mimi's bureau on which his father's picture used to sit, he can borrow it back temporarily or even for good.

Other things, though, are banished forever. Each

morning, like a midget queen, she stands in her nightgown at the foot of the bed issuing her latest edicts. What is fated for the garbage, what to the thrift shop, what to a neighbor to use or dump as they wish. She laughs as she declares, "Out," or "Be gone," one day banishing ancient clothing, the next day tattered mismatched sheets and pillow cases or half-colored coloring books and heaps of broken crayons.

And each morning, though he knows what her answer will be, he asks, "Are you sure? Absolutely sure?"

And she laughs. For better or for worse, she says, she is always sure.

She is sure that she loves him, now more than ever. She is sure that he is the kindest, most loyal person in the world. She is sure that when she is old he will not dump her. When she is battered, like her Popeye lunchbox or ragged like her Spiderwoman nightgown, he will call her cute and want to keep her. She is sure they will be together forever.

It is only when he proclaims loyalty to the color of the walls—the loud oranges and sad pinks and brutal blood reds that Mimi thought exciting and that Lily finds depressing as hell—that they clash.

"You always hated those colors," she tells him.

And it's true. As a kid, he complained all the time about the *girl* colors. And recently in their new talk that combines the old bluntness of kids with the new openness of lovers, he has told her how he was embarrassed when boys first came to visit. It was bad enough that everyone knew his mother spent all day with her hands in ladies' vaginas. Why did she have to publicize it? Why did she have to plaster the walls with those pastels and watercolors of nursing ladies? The colors alone were embarrassing—the pinks and reds shouted vagina, breast, womb. Why couldn't she leave her work at work!

Now, the day the spackling is done and the painting is to begin, he pulls his "Are you sure?" routine, and they fight.

"Kind of cute?" she says. "Nipple mauve is not kind of

cute on a living room wall! Give me a break!"

He shakes his head. "Not cute but...." What does he mean?

"You mean that it feels disloyal, banishing them forever." And then she declares a compromise: whites and beiges everywhere; but in special spots, like the inside of closets and the stairwell to the basement, an array of those special reds, there for him always.

For three frenzied days, they paint their walls, and then their house is set too, just in time for Homer's visit home.

They will celebrate Homer's arrival with a special dinner, a "back-and-forth supper." It's Lily's idea, a variation on something called the "move-along supper" featured in a recent *Modern Mother*. The idea of the move-along is to reduce the burdens of mealtime by having each of a group of neighboring families assume responsibility for just one course, with all the families going from course to course, house to house. There are course rotations each week as well as rotating meal captains, and Lily wonders who in the world would find the time or energy to do it. Just reading the plan was exhausting—even to her. But to celebrate Homer's special leave, a meal made together, then shared in both homes—the four of them, between courses, walking back and forth in the autumn night—seems perfect.

Lily has insisted on doing all the shopping over at Oleans Organic Produce and Meats a few miles down the road from Blue Field. Lily is a vegetarian but when she thinks of the vegetables not to mention the poultry, fish, and meats down at IGA, she shudders. She knows the mammalian digestive and circulatory cycles by heart and knows it would not happen the way she imagines—bacteria, hormones, antibiotics, chemicals, fungi marching down Nancy's esophagus to Nancy's belly, then quickly blasting through the stomach walls to Nancy's uterus—but she knows her basic idea is right. The avocado, mushrooms, chicken, grapes, and pumpkin in the supermarket are not what they seem. They might well be time bombs, and it is worth the half of a paycheck she's spent at Oleans to safeguard both mother and child.

Then the week of shopping and preparation is over and Homer is expected. And, just as Lily finishes pouring the pumpkin custard into her pie crust, Homer is back. They hadn't heard his car, but then there he is, at Mimi's kitchen door.

He looks tired still but so handsome and happy as he stands there in his uniform, calling, "Anyone home?"

"Now *everyone's* home," Lily says, running into his arms.

The men embrace, and then Homer tiptoes to the living room, where Nancy is resting, and wakes her with a kiss. And Lily declares it's time for the celebrations to begin.

Nancy can't drink, Lily doesn't, and the men are on a health regime, to lose the weight they gained and gain the energy they lost in country. But they must celebrate tonight. Tony prepares the drinks that Lily has planned. "Champagne-free mimosas"—organic orange juice, which he squeezes in the ancient red juicer that had belonged to Mimi's mom.

"To friends," he says. "…old friends…best friends."

"To my husband," Nancy says. "Who's come home to our new home. To Lil' and Tony and our what-you-call-it special meal."

"Back-and-forth supper," Lily laughs, with not a speck of embarrassment, as she explains to Homer how it will work, back and forth, back and forth, between their two homes, which tonight might as well be one.

The two couples, the two houses, the two futures shining before them—it all seems so right, Tony thinks, looking out the kitchen window as the light leaves the sky and the houses light up like jack-o-lanterns. The twin ranch houses where he and Lily used to live, he with Mimi, she with Ronnie or Connie have always come to mind when he thought of home and more than once he's said, "Barberry Lane" not "Maple Lane" when asked for his address. Halloween is weeks away, but scarecrows, witches, goblins, and blinking jack-o-lanterns are already adorning the street, just like they used to on their old street.

He remembers Halloweens trick-or-treating on Barberry in an olive drab t-shirt with a stock pot on his head. I'm Henry, he'd say, which meant a soldier in camouflage and helmet. How long since he thought of that. When he was little, he couldn't wait for Halloween to come so he could turn into his father.

He used to think of his father all the time, never imagining him in heaven but right there beside him. What name to give a stuffed animal, what color to paint his bike—always even the littlest decision tortured him and for years, day after day, he'd turn to Henry to help him choose. But it was the big things that his father helped with most. What to do when bullies attacked, when teachers railed, when his heart raced and his mind stalled? He'd say to Henry, I shouldn't be scared, right? And his father would tell him, Right, you're strong and brave like me, not a scaredy-cat. Or if he was in a gentler frame of mind, Henry might say, Everyone gets afraid. It's okay, son. Tony's favorite part of the private catechism was when he'd say, Everything's going to be all right, right? And his father would say, Right…everything's going to be fine. Why? Tony would say. His father would say, Because it wasn't for me. You mean that's the way it works? Tony would say. You mean it's a special system? Exactly, his father would say. I died so you can live.

When his company landed back in the States, his colonel said, American pride got broke in Nam, but you men fixed it. Tony doesn't know about pride: he can't remember much about the desert but what he remembers, like the kids on the wharf or the whores by the shitter or the ceaseless sirens, fills him with despair, not pride. But tonight the colonel's words replay in his mind.

"Earth to Tony," he hears her say.

Their *old* families got broke in Nam....But they'd come back to their *new* families alive, alive and healthy. Since he got called up, since he joined the reserves, since he can't remember when, he hasn't felt the peace he feels tonight. Like the world got put together and now he could live in it less afraid? Not the whole world for sure, but their little corner of it here on Maple Lane?


Over Nancy's chicken at Nancy's table, they light candles and talk. House talk first—gutters and rakes, furnaces and oil. Then work talk—the clinic, teaching, the base. Then gossip. Mrs. Molto has called and told Nancy that Jacques is planning to move to a senior complex not far from Tampa, where his wife will be in a dementia unit and he will be in a regular apartment, where he wants Luisa to visit as often as she can, and Luisa is thinking that her daughter is a bigger pain in the ass than she remembers and has already put her name on a list for her own apartment in Jacques' complex. Einstein has called and told Tony that he has more good days than bad days.

"He sounded upbeat," Tony says. "Which was great to hear. He really had a rough time...starting classes and feeling so lousy. We were lucky...."

"Maybe not just lucky," Homer says. "Maybe we're just stronger."

Tony had thought Homer was done with his super-hero routine. So much for sensitivity training for the lifers! he thinks.

"I forgot all those guys who feel sick are just fags and cowards."

He doesn't remember ever snapping at Homer in all his life, and he hates doing it. But it was Ernie he was talking about! His mind replays that morning with Ernie down on the floor, unable to do his push-ups, unable to move at all, leaning on him as he hobbled back to the barracks.

"I never said that," Homer says. "I did say it's funny that the reservists have all these stress symptoms. And my guys don't. But what's it got to do with you? You're a camper, but a brave camper, and my best bro."

"Maybe the lifers are afraid to say they're stressed too. I mean if you are a lifer and you're having crazy dreams or psychosomatic rashes or your belly is in knots maybe you'd be too afraid to admit it? Maybe you'd be afraid they'd think you weren't corps material and you'd be out on your ass?"

Homer shrugs, then laughs. "Afraid? It doesn't ring a bell."

"Homer, honey," Nancy says. "Everyone gets afraid. It's only human."

Homer laughs. "We Devils are different. They sear fear from us in basic. Greens are fucking fearless—that's the whole idea. If you're shitting in your pants, you're fucking *brown* not green."

"Enough," Nancy says. "Enough green crap! Grow up. We're having a baby. What's gotten into you?"

She smiles to temper her words and reaches for his hand. But he is reaching for Tony's for a quick high-five.

"*Semper fi,*" he calls. "Right? You and me, we sear all fear with fucking cheer!"

Tony shrugs. He often shrugs in confusion. Then sighs. But now he feels a pain in his chest, like his heart is being torn in two. Ernie tugging on one side, Homer on the other. "I don't know!" he hears himself cry.

"Bullshit, bro!" Homer shouts. "That's just fucking bullshit!"


Outside the window, the street lights flicker. The jack-o-lanterns and goblin lights blink quickly—one, two, three. Then all the lights dim.

Lily feels her stomach tighten. What was going on? The street darkening. Tony yelping. Homer ranting. And Nancy all upset. Her goal for the back-and-forth dinner was just the opposite—making them individually and as a group content and peaceful.

Lily stands and walks down the hall to the bathroom. She turns on the sink and sits on the floor. When she was little and Ronnie would scream, Who the fuck left the Cheerios out, or the screen door open, or the wet towel on the fucking carpet? she'd slip into the bathroom and run the faucet, to wash away his "Fuck Talk" and the grenades of hatred she could hear hissing in every word, getting ready to explode. Scaredy-cat, Ronnie would call. Can't take the fire get out of the kitchen, he'd shout to her as she hid in the bathroom. And then the talk would stop and the breakage would begin.

What if Homer was becoming a Ronnie? Would Nancy become a Connie? Would Tony change into someone else too? Was that weird cry the beginning? What would become of *her*? Would she have to become a Mimi, stepping in to save the baby? Lily and Ethel, Ricky and Fred, that's us, Tony had joked before when they first sat down to eat. They'd watched the Lucy reruns together and she knew what he meant—that it was fun again, they were all together again, even closer than before, sharing their meals and lives. But now it was all going down the drain.

One step at a time, Miss Lil, Doc used to tell her when she first started working at the clinic and had thought that every scratch on every dog or cat meant certain death. One step at a time, she tells herself. She was taking all the steps at once and falling down the stairs. It was all the stress of getting engaged, then baby-set, and then and then and then, and feeling like she was doing it all at once and not just for herself—but for them, Ronnie and Connie, and time was running out. Time was *not* running out, she tells herself. There was lots of time to take it slow.

"Hey, Lil'," Homer calls. "Come on back, Lil' honey so we can eat….I don't want my Lil' upset. I'm just talking shit. Your big bro's a little tired tonight and is just talking shit. Come back, Lil'!"

She shuts off the water to hear better.

"Pup," she hears. Tony's voice now. His old voice, boyish and tentative but so sweet—not that horrible yelp she heard before.

She looks out the window—there is light in the street again. She waits for her stomach to finish un-knotting. Then she walks back to the kitchen, one step at a time. Then it's time to move-along back home for her chemical-free pumpkin pie.

Over pie, they talk about names. Nancy takes out the pocket-sized baby name book that Lily treated her to the week before when they were at Party Card browsing through baby announcements.

"Here, Lil', read the ones we like…the ones we checked," Nancy says.

It's a trick, an old teacher's trick, Lily thinks. It's been pulled on her many times before. A special job to boost the esteem of an orphan in need. When she was a kid, she used to run from the room when a teacher would pull one of these, but she's just run from the room, and besides best friends surround her, not classroom goons. She should feel proud about helping with the names. She'd bought the book, after careful comparison. She'd selected the one with the fullest explanations of the roots of the name, and space to write your thoughts so you didn't have to bother carrying a notebook too or organizing a million pieces of paper.

"And remind us of what they mean, Lil', and what we thought of them. Lil' found us the best book."

"That's my *associate* for you," Tony says, kissing her cheek.

Lily clears her throat and begins. "Abigail—father's joy. Ann—favored by God. Elizabeth—consecrated for God. Matthew—gift of God. Jacob—held by the heel. Daniel— God is my judge. Michael—like the Lord. Joshuah—God is salvation. Ashley—from the ash tree. Nicholas—victory of the people. Mark—the god of war. Vera—Latin true or Russian faith. Gregory—vigilant."

"Those are the ones we liked best. The names themselves. Not necessarily all the meanings. Like we liked Ashley as a sound but not as an idea...like what's the big idea in an ash tree?" Lily says.

"Still it's better than calling a kid, Oak or Maple or Birch or Pine...," Nancy laughs. "And it works for a girl or boy."

Homer doesn't like Ashley for a girl and definitely not for a boy. But he likes Abigail for a girl—a father's joy. And for a boy, Gregory the Vigilant. Or Mark the Warrior.

"We liked those boy names too. But, Lil', what did we think about the meanings?"

"We thought, 'Mark sounds strong and would be nice if we could think of strength but not violence and war.' And 'Gregory has an interesting sound. Like a spice.' We also thought that 'the meaning of Gregory—vigilance or watchful—is good. A good trait in a child...protecting himself from accidents...and looking out for others.'"

"So Abigail for a girl? Gregory for a boy?" Tony says.

"I like that," Homer says. "I mean I still like Mark, but either's okay. I'm not going to fight," he laughs.

Then it's time to call it a night. Tomorrow is a work day. They stand to say goodnight and take turns patting Nancy's belly.

"Nancy means favored by God," Lily says. "Did anyone know that? Nancy's belly, Nancy's baby, everything having to do with Nancy is blessed."

"Nancy's husband," Homer says. "He's blessed...to have Nancy. The most blessedest guy in the world."

Did he ever really believe she was anything but perfect?

Had he really pinned her picture to the Wall of Shame? How far away that all seems. Her gone, with all his hopes, and the will to go on.

"Father's joy," he whispers, placing his hand on the mound of baby. Then he shouts, "Hey, I think she kicked! Hey, Abigail just kicked. She's a kick-ass kid." And he bends to kiss what he's sure are her perfect, powerful, kick-ass toes.

All week Homer takes long morning runs along the Blue Ridge Trail, and then comes home to putter. When his mother moved to Alabama shortly after his father died, she left him boxes of childhood books, *Mother Goose, Brothers Grimm, Monkey King, Anansi the Spider.* He takes the pictures he loved best as a child to the print shop to color copy, then frames them for his child. In darkening afternoons, trimming, mitre-ing, gluing, staining, he thinks about his parents and all the things they made him, all the books they read him, all the songs they sang him, the endless animal sounds his father would produce on his banjo just for him, all the times they said they were proud of whatever he did, even when what he did was laugh in their faces. Their embarrassing slave shows, their hideous African pajamas, their revolting meals of legumes and roots from recipes passed on by the obese cook at the history center—he wanted nothing to do with any of that weirdness. And everything he did—becoming student government treasurer, captain of the wrestling team, be-ribboned jarhead—was intended to make that perfectly clear. But they'd just beam with pride at everything he did. And then when he was nineteen his father died suddenly from a stroke, and his mother left.

She moved to a small town near Mobile, where his Aunt Malvena had lived forever, in an old decrepit schoolhouse, whose bottom floor housed her community children's theater, which was always on the verge of condemnation for some crumbling wall or broken floor. His mother sent him photos of the renovations she and Aunt Malvena had done together. She squiggled notations all over, identifying "Anderson windows," "Ikea cabinets," "our new stage," "our mini green room," "your room." She sent him announcements of productions, schedules of upcoming events, xeroxes of two cultural council awards; but he never visited, hardly responded. When the baby came he'd try to make it up to her. He'd invite her to visit them in Monuten; and they'd visit her in Mobile. He'd listen more, pounce less, allow her to show him off, show the baby off—when Abigail was older maybe even send her down a week or two during summer vacations and she could star in one of the productions!

At night, he and Nancy loll in bed, wonderfully tired from all the preparations. He is so much gentler, in every way. He is rested now. Before he leaves, she will talk to him about the corps, careers, etc. and she knows he will listen.

His last day, he feels tired and has a little cold, and they go to bed early. She settles his head on her shoulder.

"Want to know what I'm thinking?" she says.

He says he does.

"Seven years your way....now seven years my way?" She's not sure why she's put it that way. They'd been together seven years, of course. But does she want him to feel a sense of danger, like there could be seven years of bad luck...like from a broken mirror...if he doesn't listen? Or has she said it to suggest the good luck of the number seven? Her way and good fortune would follow? She doesn't mind that she doesn't know exactly, and she thinks Homer won't mind either.

This last week, he seemed to be accepting her lyrical mode. Not just tolerating it but actually welcoming it as a kind of tonic, it had seemed. How do you come up with those ideas of yours? he'd asked her a couple of nights before, when he watched her make a worksheet to help the children decide who they'd be for Halloween and why. They had to draw their Halloween selves, write their character's history and futures and secret dreams. He wanted to live in her, in her brain, he said, filled with *her* secret dreams.

But now he looks at her like she's a madwoman. "What are you fucking talking about?" he says. "I didn't know you had such bullshit in you."

She tries again, straightforward this time. "I'm just asking you to consider making a change. Now that the baby is coming. Something that didn't put you in such danger. I'm not saying right away. But eventually. Maybe you could have another life. Eventually."

"Another life! The corps is my life. As much as you are. It's like another wife. *Semper fi. Till death do us part.* There's no difference. Jesus Christ, I thought you knew that."

He looks like a maniac. His eyes are popping, and his arms are punching the air, Rocky-like. What a brute he could be. And what a bore. *Semper fi, semper fi*—he should tattoo that on his ass and go away! But she says nothing, silently burrowing under the covers and turning away.

But Homer hardly notices. The corps has been so good to him. The corps was probably going to let him transfer to Downsville. He wouldn't be a staff sergeant forever. Eventually the corps would be offering a special new officer training program, which he would probably get into, which would mean more pay, more home allowance, more educational benefits. He is so grateful to the corps and she is so ungrateful.

"I thought I knew you. I thought you understood everything," he says. "You understand nothing."

She says nothing. She is ignoring him, he sees.

"What's wrong?" he says. "What now?"

She turns her head and begins to tell him. But when he snorts, she stops. Whatever she says will be fodder for another attack.

"What's the point?" she says.

"Look at me," he says.

He doesn't look like himself. His chocolate complexion

has drained to mauve going on gray. His bright eyes are filmy and droopy, like he's been drugged.

"Come here," he whispers.

"Why?" Was he going to give her his, I want to visit you…and the baby routine? He was a bully, a creep. How could she ever have found the smallest speck of that creepy routine attractive!

"Not now," she says.

"Now!" he says. "I said now, goddammit!" He is ashen and trembling. He has never laid a hand on her, but now he grabs her wrists and pins her down. Sweat pours from his face onto hers. "That's a goddamn order!"

"Stop!" she cries, as his fist descends.

# Fall

# 7. Help

Nancy escapes to Mimi's couch, not sleeping a wink, just surveying the room, studying the miserable stains and scars on all the horrible furniture, which only weeks before, she'd thought so fine.

By the next morning her horror and hurt have transformed to worry. That monster last night was not her husband. Her husband doesn't do what that man did. True, he passed out on top of her, before he could punch her. But her husband would never even threaten her. He fell off like a junkie and snored like a drunk. In the night, she heard howls, growls, like a wolf was in her bed.

The next night Tony calls, and she tells him that Homer is still sleeping from the night before, which is true. Almost 24 hours. She tells Tony he acted strange the night before. She spares both of them the violent details.

"Stress?" Tony says. "He thought he was immune to it. But he's as human as the next guy. He may be in for a shock. Realizing that might do him some good."

The next day Homer wakes up and says he had the worst dream. Enemy forces with her face grafted over their faces to trick him had entered the room. And he had no weapon. Just his fists.

"I know."

"You know?"

"You weren't sleeping," she says.

"I wasn't sleeping?"

"No. I was there. I saw…."

"Oh, Christ, oh, Jesus, am I all fucked up? Did I fuck up bad? Did I…hurt anyone…you…?"

"I'm okay," she says. "And that wasn't you...."

"I feel like shit. My joints ache. I feel hot."

She feels his head. It's burning.

She takes his temperature; it's 102.

"Last night it was probably higher," she says. "And probably you were delirious."

Nancy calls the VA triage desk. It sounds like a common flu, the nurse says. Tylenol and sleep.

Nancy gives Homer two Tylenol and he sleeps for three hours. That afternoon he vomits six times.

"Maybe it's food poisoning," he says. "Can food poisoning make you crazy? Can it go to your brain?"

Gastrointestinal problems are a common stress symptom, the VA nurse says when Nancy calls again. It's not uncommon for a fever to accompany them. Responses to fever vary from individual to individual. But delusions are not uncommon and no cause for alarm. Keep the fluids going and let him rest.

The next day Homer is too nauseated to eat and his dry heaves leave him limp on the bathroom floor. So he'll be nearer the toilet, he drags a blanket and pillow into the bathroom, and sleeps in the tub.

The next day, Homer takes down some food, but just when they begin to feel hopeful, his torso turns purple, then breaks into a crimson rash.

"Classic post-trauma response," the VA nurse tells Nancy. "When he's rested, bring him in for some assistance."

"Assistance?"

"A good serotonin re-uptake inhibitor like Prozac. And some good talk with peers. Both are valuable adjuncts in the healing process of the war-stressed soldier."

Tony says Homer seems just like the guys at camp. Ashen and weak. Itchy and achy and nauseous. The docs at camp said stress too. And gave them Prozac too. And encouraged them to talk about it, and it seemed to be working. The last time they spoke, his buddy Ernie told him that he was still tired, but that many of the other symptoms were lifting along with his spirits. He was beginning to catch up on his course work and was filling out graduate school applications.

Nancy tries to see the bright side of Homer living in the bathtub to get over his stress. She rests her head on Tony's shoulder and gestures to her rooms. "Our very own spa—a few weeks of fasting and purging at our facility and all the toxins leave you....Devil toxins, testosterone toxins," she says, laughing a quiet, tired laugh. "Maybe for good. Maybe when he's feeling all better, he'll listen to me. And stay here for good? With us," she says, rubbing her belly.


There have been forecasts of hurricanes that haven't materialized, but many days in mid October the rains are still too heavy to work at Southern Skies, and Tony stays with Homer. He's not quite sure what Nancy means when she talks about a new Homer, but like her he is hopeful that a little rest will do the trick. That with rest his friend will return and the creature living in the bathtub will vanish.

But Homer likes his new haunt. The boils and sores on his skin and the exploding fires in his gut and the raw sore of his anus and the memory of Nancy's tear-slicked face telling him what he'd done, and the image of what he *could* have done, her beautiful lips and nose and cheeks shattered or splattered—only the hot water gives him relief from the pain of all that, if just for a moment.

After a few days, though, the bath loses its charm

"Should I just die?" Homer calls from the bathroom.

Stretched out in the water, staring at the ceiling, he looks dead already, Tony thinks when he enters the room.

"Come on," he says. "Come on, bro."

"She'd be better off without me.... You all would."

"Not true, bro. We need you, man. You just need some

help!" Tony says.

"Help? Where's help? It's coming...?" He looks around bewildered.

Quickly, like *he's* the big bro, Tony lifts Homer from the bath and pats him dry, dresses him in sweats and walks him to the van.

"Where now?" Homer says.

Sprain, just twenty miles due south, was the nearest military hospital. But was it any good? A three-hour drive would get them to Bethesda Naval or Walter Reed, but Homer looks too weak for that.

"Sprain," Tony says.

It's a rotten day—the rain is ceaseless and dark, and it's hard to see the road. It reminds Tony of the oil raining down in the desert, blackening the sky, half blinding him. He feels his belly flutter with dread. He wishes he could turn to Homer and say, Everything will be all right, right? But he's the one in charge now. So he just drives and whistles and Homer snores.


Urgent Care is standing-room only, packed with troops of all colors and stripes—Air Force, Army, Navy, Marine Corps, National Guard. Their desert tans are long gone, even the "dark greens" a medium gray. And pencil thin. Most everyone is with someone. Because they're all too beat to drive, like his Homey?

Nurses circulate through the room, jotting information, reviewing symptoms, taking temperature and blood pressure, drawing blood, when spaces become available, leading soldiers, one by one, into treatment rooms. Body on body, not an inch of privacy. The soldiers whisper, but everyone can hear. Tony feels like he's back in the desert, in Tent City, where you heard every word, laugh, cry, belch, and fart down the bay of racks, and smelled them too. Sweat and blood, piss and shit—their scents fill the waiting room today, pungent from today's barfs, bleeds, spills and dumps; subtle from ancient deposits impervious to Lysol and Airwick.

Tony has to breathe through his mouth not to gag. But no one else seems to notice. Tired, tired, tired. Sleep, sleep, sleep. They declare and compare maladies. Anxious, forgetful, confused. Confused, forgetful, anxious. Joint aches. Rashes. Bellyaches, nausea. Dry heaves. Night sweats.

It breaks his heart. Why them? Why not me? Tony thinks. He had been majorly scared and stressed. But except for the three weeks in April, when he was worn out and worn down from the desert, he's himself again. Better than himself! He feels guilty feeling happy, happier than he can ever remember. With Lily beside him for life.

Homer has fallen asleep again, his head on Tony's shoulder. It had always been the other way around. Homer's strong shoulders beneath *him*, him holding on tight as Homer rode them down the Blue Ridge trail on his bike, or on his back across the Shenandoah, once in a hellish fog, once at night.

They've arrived at noon. At three, an orderly calls out Homer's name, and Tony taps him awake.

"I dreamt I was in a hospital," Homer says, opening his eyes.

"You are, buddy," Tony says. "They're going to help you."

"Oh, yeah," Homer says. "What did they say? I'm going to be okay?"

"We're going in now," Tony says.

"Oh, right," Homer says. "Now I remember."


The doctor is kind. He reviews Homer's vitals. Everything is normal, except for a slight elevation in white blood count, which is nothing to be alarmed about. "We're seeing it in lots of our returning soldiers. A few months of struggle and then a resolution."

Homer tells the doctor that something is definitely

wrong. He isn't himself.

"Stress....I know it's hard to believe. You have been through a lot. The heat, the oil, the death, which is not easy even for a marine."

Homer shakes his head. "I am a marine. I'm trained for disaster. Easy or hard, we're prepared. This is something else."

"Stress is very quirky. You never know what will trigger it. Why one person and not the other."

"I'm a marine," Homer says again.

"Lots of marines coming in here with the stress symptoms. Lifers like you. You got to fight it like a marine. Face it. Battle it. Beat it. It's an enemy. An internal enemy. And you need to be armed for the battle."

He gives Homer a prescription for Prozac. He signs him up for de-stress training. A group of servicemen and women will meet with a doctor and talk about what they're facing and how to defeat it. He gives him breathing exercises and a flier on PTSD—Post Traumatic Stress Disorder—and other stress conditions.

"I don't *feel* stressed," Homer says.

"I know," the doctor says. "I know."

Homer says, "Stress. It sounds fruity. Like Seth...."

The doctor laughs.

"I'm serious, sir," Homer says. "I'm a marine."


Homer insists on driving home. If it's just stress, he'll kick its ass. But a couple of miles up the highway, he starts to shake and sweat.

"Maybe I should drive?" Tony says.

"Maybe. For a little while." Homer pulls to the side of the road, opens the door, vomits, then crawls over the seat to the back. "I'll take over half way, bro," he says. "You'll see. Mind over matter."

The next day Tony calls National Navy Hospital and describes the symptoms.

The same story as Sprain: stress and maybe on top of that a little bug, a cold or stomach flu. Prozac can't hurt. If his blood tests remain more or less normal, there's nothing to worry about. If he has a fever, give him Tylenol. Keep fluids going and let him rest.

Homer says he can do it—face it and beat it. He moves from the tub to the bed. He rests and takes his pills. He repeats the word stress again and again till it sounds normal to him. On Friday he wakes up and says he's ready.

"Ready for what?" Tony asks. The days are beginning to blur as he sits by Homer's side.

"My group," Homer says. "Don't tell me your mind is going too, bro! You drive there and this time I'll drive home....Watch out, stress—your days are numbered!"


"I'm a doctor," the trainer says to the dozen people in the room. "But you're not sick. You're stressed and stress does strange things."

His name is Doug Meloni, M.D., his specialization is pain and stress syndromes, and he believes that he can heal them. They should call him Doug and feel free to ask questions and say anything they want in his session.

There is something sweet about Doug, Homer thinks. Red-headed, full-cheeked and freckled, with sincere dark eyes flashing through little round glasses, he looked from the neck up like a child. The result of his own anti-stress training? he wonders.

"You take a rat and shock it again and again, and the rat doesn't move. It doesn't eat, digest, or sleep," Dr. Meloni says. "We humans are luckier than animals. We can use our minds to locate the stressors and neutralize them. We don't have to hide in the corner of a cage and tremble."

"First thing you need to do is understand what stressed you out." They will do an exercise called "Find the Stressor."

"Tell the group what scared you most in the desert," the doctor says. "Think hard, it might be hiding in the back of your mind."

But no one has to look hard. No one has to look at all. It's there, ready to pop.

"Saddam Insane's gas warfare...every day I was expecting it."

"The sirens. For the Scuds."

"The Scuds...though they never came near me."

"The biological bombs. We knew he had 'em."

"Seeing the napalm melt a whole company of Iraqis...."

"Seeing them trying to crawl without their arms or legs."

When it's Homer's turn, he says, "I saw a lot...but I don't think that stressed me. What stressed me was my wife. When she fucked another. I mean when she was an angel but I thought she was a whore and I hung her picture on the Wall of Shame with all the other harlots. Problem is I'm still getting crazy and fucking everything up. I was ready to kill her with my fists. She says I had a fever and was delirious and thought she was the enemy. But now you got me thinking maybe it was stress that caused my fever and my confusion....And Nancy as well as Abigail or Mark—they're gonna stress me for sure. But I can't lose it again."

"Who are they?" Doug asks.

"Nancy's my wife. Abigail or Mark or maybe Gregory are my unborn babies."

"Triplets?" Doug says. "You're expecting triplets? That can increase your stress."

"Just one," Homer says. "Do you know that Abigail means father's joy, and she's due to arrive in seventy-two days and I am a fucked-up, miserable mess!"

Tony sits at the side of the room as a "guest of the group." But Homer's remarks alarm him. Not just the things he's said but how he's said them? The sharp staccato. The odd precision in the midst of confusion. Like war, he thinks.

"You, okay, Homes?" he calls.

Homer nods vacantly.

"He's okay," Doug says. "He's opening up and draining the psychic toxins. He's really okay. But thanks for caring....You're free to share any time you want and move from group friend to group member," he laughs, and smiles a sweet boyish smile.

Caring, sharing—was there anything in any of this? Tony wonders. Were he to join the group, what would he say? How he's stressed about Homer for sure? And before that...in country? Something about that night on the wharf with Homer and those kids? How that had gotten to him, making him wonder what they were doing there? Or something about the highway? Though it remains a blur, the image of a highway sometimes crashes into his mind. Just fire and smoke, and then smoke letters spelling a phrase: "Highway at the end of the war," or other times, "Highway at the end of the world."

What was on that highway? He remembers someone saying, It was a fucking buffet, and laughing. Someone else saying, One from column A, One from column B. Which suggests lots of different kinds of something. Bombs? DU? Napalm? Phosphorous? He rubs his head. Every time he tries to remember this shit, his head hurts. Which maybe means he should just try to forget? Blow it away?

Booom, booom, Tony thinks.

"I'm okay, Doug," Tony says. "But thanks."


"Let's review," Doug says. "I think we're ready to review what's come up in terms of your stressors....The fear of illness and death. From multiple sources. Biological agents. Nerve agents. Fire. Traumatic suffering. Withdrawal of love. For some people it's one thing. For most of us, these stressors come in clusters."

"Clusters....Cluster bombs," someone says. "They stressed me bad. When I thought of them dropping all those bomblets and then every bomblet breaking into a gazillion fragments, then seeing it...."

"I saw a kid in a field," someone says, "bending down to pick one up. It looked like a can of soda pop. I called to him to stop. But I guess he couldn't understand English...."

"You were afraid," the doctor says. "Which is human."

"I'm afraid of what I did," a young man says. "We went in so close, man. We flew those fucking A8s so low you could touch their turbans before you let them have it....It was a turkey shoot, man."

"You did your job," someone says. "To keep your country and its friends safe. That's our job."

"I got a charge," someone says, "a goddamn fucking rush...like I was coming or snorting. Swooping down, dropping every kind of shit we had...with Metallica and that Lone Ranger song blasting. I don't sleep for more than an hour. I can't walk a straight line or think a straight thought. I'm still in that warthog going down and up and up and down...so low...man...."

The doctor looks tired, like their stressors along with their fatigue have rubbed off on him, Homer thinks. His face looks middle-aged now, with creases on a brow that only an hour before had been as smooth as a baby's butt.

"What we've learned from our work today is that you all faced multiple stressors. Now I think we're ready to examine symptoms. Your homework," Dr. Meloni says, "is to talk about the symptoms. Talk about them in any way you wish. Expose them to the light of day. They're like sores. They need to be open to the air to dry out and heal."

Homer feels under his shirt and rubs his scabby rash. "Not *like* sores. They *are* sores. I see them and think I'm dying. So now I'm wondering is the sore a stressor or a symptom?"

"An interesting question....Hold it till next time," the

doctor says.

Turkey shoot. Tony remembers that. Someone on a highway saying, Turkey shoot.

All week, to anyone who will listen, Homer talks about his rash and his memory, his balance and his bowels. He smiles as he recounts his miseries. He is a hopeful man, a disciplined marine. If he works hard, he will achieve his goal to be stress-free and well.

In the evenings, Nancy and Tony and Lily listen, but they're all busy.

"Your job is only to heal," Nancy says. "Think about nothing else." And she scurries off to lay a rug or hang a shelf, which he knows he should be doing. She pats his head as she goes in and out of the living room, where he's stretched out on the couch, where he spends both days and nights. But she is clearly tired herself—tired of hearing him recount when the rash first itched him, the tremors first shook him, the heaves and diarrhea first left him empty and immobile.

When she drops by, Lily says, "I'm here to listen." But then the next thing he knows she's gone, helping Nancy with the breathing exercises or something. Why would she want to spend a minute with him? He's a baby, a monster baby, pissing and shitting round the clock.

Tony spends the most time with him. But the truth is he feels queasy when Homer goes on and on about explosions or bodies. One morning on his way to work, Tony brings him a notebook.

"Write," he says. "Your symptoms, man, what you're suffering. Get them down so you can feel better."

It feels so strange to be giving Homer orders when it had always been the other way around. Doubly strange maybe because he's not sure he believes a thing he's saying. Is it really good to dwell on the details of the war? The stress, the symptoms. Maybe he had no symptoms because he didn't remember anything!

"Doc said to *talk* about your symptoms…," Homer says.

"And you've been doing that real good and we've been listening. Writing is like talking. But you can keep doing it when no one's around."

"You're going to be around later? To check it over?" Homer asks.

Tony remembers how he'd trail Homer after school so he could check his writing. Take a stand and defend it, Anthony, teachers would write on his book reports and compositions. Problem was he saw things from lots of sides and could never decide what his stand was. So Homer would decide for him! The *Iliad* was better than the *Odyssey*; the most original American presidents came from the South not the North, and so on. And the teachers ate it up. The truth was Tony liked the *Iliad* and the *Odyssey* equally; his favorite presidents— Washington and Jefferson and Lincoln and the two Roosevelts—came from the North *and* the South. Things were complicated. It was scary to take stands and not budge. You could be wrong. You could offend. You could start fights.

"Write it all down," Tony says. "It's as good for you as talking."

"You're sure? And later you'll read it over and we'll talk?"

"We'll talk, bro. Later, for sure."

# 8. Teach

Soon Tony is not around much either—to read or talk.

A letter comes from Dr. Moser: "If you are still of a mind to teach, we would be pleased to consider you for a position at John Adams High." Could he come in for an interview?

Tony can't believe the words when he opens the letter. *Of a mind* to teach. He was *out of his mind* to teach. Southern Skies was only temporary, till his application for a teaching license was approved by the state. The daily drill at Southern Skies had left his arms and back permanently bruised, he's convinced. And the new shit raining down feels as shitty as being in country some days. That morning, he woke up sure that his whole life would be spent wiping up Homer's puke and hearing about stress symptoms and dosages of Prozac.

He had always had a respectful appreciation for teaching, but never anything approaching the passion that has suddenly gripped him. Life goes on, the war in the desert didn't destroy everything, Lily lectures to Homer every day. But suddenly only the prospect of teaching makes Tony think this may be true. He was, for sure, no Einstein—neither an Albert nor an Ernie—but lately he has had daydreams of standing in front of a class, pointing at places on a map of the world, talking about what they'd been like once upon a time. Ancient Greece. Byzantium. The Mayan kingdom. The desert doesn't exist in those daydreams, only those other worlds, shiny with treasure.

His interview goes well. Dr. Moser starts off talking about Lily. Tony was lucky to have such an "associate," he says laughing. Mostly he talks about Tony's student teaching reports, which were outstanding and highly recommended him for the social studies position. He reads from one class observation: *This able young man never settles for easy answers. He asks students to dig and dig some more, approaching history and government with an outlook refreshingly clean of dogma and certitude. In this lesson on George Washington, he showed students an outline of Washington's face and asked them to supply details. They worked from facial features to his whole body. To his uniform. To his childhood. To his character. To his style as a general and president. The teacher encouraged every point of view and never dominated with his own. With this talented teacher at the helm, the classroom is a forum for inquiry not simply assertion.*

Tony blushes. He is shy and embarrassed by the praise of his *ability*. But also flushed with pleasure. The essential Tony came out in that lesson, for better or worse. Inquiry, not assertion. Every point of view and not just his own. After a decade of being told he was deficient in the point-of-view department, he was being applauded for his openness!

He remembers the lesson. They spent almost half an hour on Washington's face and it was the students who decided to move on to his body. They'd saved the observation. Just like Homer and Lily had saved him every day of his life! If it weren't for Lily marching in here, demanding the principal respond—wouldn't he still be at home waiting for the phone to ring so he could ask for the credits so he could get the certification so he could look for a job? He feels his momentary pleasure topple. He didn't assert his own position because he couldn't. He didn't have one.

Dr. Moser says he likes the fact that Tony has served his country in a time of war. The boys and girls today don't have a sense of service. He wants those values imparted to them, and Tony would teach those values by example. His rich experiences as a marine would enhance his classroom and perhaps re-shape the larger curriculum. They're revamping the 10th grade curriculum. What does Tony think about a semester for 10th graders focusing on modern war?

Tony feels his heart quicken. He wants to teach old history, not recent history, old wars not his war, or even his father's. He probably couldn't anyway. His mind hits a roadblock when he tries to approach them. Which is probably just as well.

"Modern war…," he says. What should he say?

Then he imagines again that Lily is there coaching him, saying, Just nod your head and express interest. He nods and says, "Modern war…interesting." Then, "How would you want to define modern war? Are you thinking of modern versus ancient? Post Renaissance? Post Enlightenment? You're not thinking late twentieth century, right?"

"It's yours to define," Dr. Moser says. "I have total confidence in you."

That's dumb, Tony thinks and smiles.

He feels Lily's presence again. Say, Thank you. Say, When would you like me to begin? I can be available before the semester to get oriented.

He smiles and speaks her words.

"Well, we start up the new term on January 5. But I'd like you to come aboard for a few weeks before the holidays to see how we do things, fill in for prep periods, and absences, which there are always too many of in December. Come, I'll show you the social studies office if you have time."

He follows Dr. Moser down the crowded, bustling hall. The memory of the hall at Sprain crowded with bodies comes to him. He hears a cry behind him and he startles, but when he turns he sees it's two kids plugged into the same Walkman shrieking over the same song. He smiles. They smile back.

"You'll do well," Dr. Moser says, as he leads him into the office. "You've got an easy way."

Each social studies teacher has a little cubicle, but each cubicle has a window, a desk, a file cabinet, and a bookcase.

From the window, looking north, he can make out the Monuten peaks in the distance, and looking south, the old road toward Richmond.

"Lots of history outside the window," Dr. Moser says. "Lots of opportunity for field trips. To local battlefields! Exciting opportunities!"

Tony smiles. "Modern War. Starting with the War of Independence...the French and Indian Wars...."

"Yes," Dr. Moser says. "We could have a whole new curriculum to present to the state board. We could put John Adams's Social Studies program on the map along with our award-winning Language Arts program! I can actually see it now in the local papers as well as our professional magazines: Marine Leads the Charge for War Curriculum. I'm being playful, but I'm also quite serious about making real change. Our young people know very little about wars and you, young man, could play quite a role here in helping John Adams lead a generation from darkness to light."

"I like what you represent, young man. I'll run all this by my honcho. And we'll talk soon, young man."

When Tony gets home, the phone is ringing and it's Dr. Moser.

"The district superintendent is thrilled about the possibility of a new curriculum. We've been talking about it for years but the recent war and then you appearing made it a must-do! We just had a quick conversation about a few approaches. One possibility is something 'methods-driven'—The Field of War, structured around field trips to battlefields culminating in individual field reports. And a more 'content-specific' idea is Patriotism and War in Modern America. Exploring the values that provide the backbone of our great democracy and the how, when, and why that we, as a nation of patriots, have defended them in battle to make us the greatest nation on earth."

The old fart liked to hear himself yak. The how, when, and why. Our great democracy. A nation of patriots. The greatest nation on earth. He sounds like he's running for office! Tony thinks. Lily will crack up when he does an imitation later.

Hilarious, she will say, and imagining her, he feels a laugh coming on and he searches his mind for something serious and sober to say.. "Experiential *and* analytical," he says. "Physical artifacts and abstract values combining…to construct history."

"Exactly, young man. I couldn't have formulated it better. And our suggestions are just that—suggestions. Curriculum development is an interactive process, a didactic dialectic," Dr. Moser says.

He is about to tell Dr. Moser that he concurs. Followed by phrases he knows the old fart would love. Dialogical, intertextual, exploratory heuristic. But he can't trust himself to say them without cracking up. So he settles for, "I'm so happy, Dr. Moser. I can't wait to begin teaching."

It was the simple truth. And he laughs. Because he *is* very happy.

"Well then we're in accord. And I look forward to our collegial collaboration…."

"Thank you, Dr. Moser," he says, only slightly embarrassed by the joy and gratitude quivering in his voice.

Most afternoons Homer spends at Tony's, lying on the couch in the living room. So Tony has entered the house through the kitchen door. Soon he will go in to check on him. But now he has to concentrate on what he and Dr. Moser talked about, not Homer's bleeding nose, his crusty eyes, the rash on his neck, the boils on his chest. He tiptoes through the kitchen to the hallway and down the hallway to his bedroom.

"Tony," Homer calls, "Wanna check out my journal?"

"Later, buddy," Tony says.

In his room, he jots down snippets of his conversations with Dr. Moser. George Washington. The republic. The beginnings. That's where he'd start. And when he got his feet wet, he'd trek on, one foot in front of the other. Till he figured out where to go from there.

"Amazing shit," Homer calls from the living room. "I'm on a fucking roll."

*Writing is like talking*, Homer writes in the speckled notebook that Tony gave him.

He writes, *I can't remember what I'm supposed to talk about exactly. Symptoms? Because if you look at them, they dry up or something like that?*

*Could any of this be true? It feels kind of dumb, but what's the harm in giving it a shot? Besides I promised Tony. It feels like he's my big bud now and I'm the kid. They called him yesterday and he's going to be a teacher soon. I could tell he was tired of my shit, which is why he came up with the notebook so he wouldn't have to listen to it any more. Who could blame him?*

*Here goes:*

*Hey, listen up, I'm talking. I'm telling you a story. The Story of My Symptoms.*

*Once upon a time, I went to Saudi Arabia. My first day in that faraway land, I felt shitty. Now I remember that, but back then all I knew was that I was ready to rock 'n' roll. It was war. You're supposed to feel like shit. Fuck it! If I thought anything it was that.*

*Now I'm wondering what was the shitty-feeling stressor? Being far away from home and lonely for Nance? All the fucking sand? I remember thinking I could get lost in it easy. All the fucking flies and fleas? We had to wear a collar around our necks like a dog. It was DEET and it stunk and made me dizzy like I was breathing in a can of Raid. I forgot about that too. Someone said, Is this approved at this strength for humans, and someone said, Step outside, wise-guy. Then they had a meeting about gas agents. They gave us pills, ten of them, against the gas agents if Saddam Insane used them. Pyridostigmine bromide or bromide pyridostigmine, I think was the name. BP for short. No, PB. Someone said, Maybe this PB shit will help against the Raid, but no one laughed. Now that I'm trying hard to think*

back, I swear I felt the pills doing something. The next day after
we took the ten pills, they told us we were actually supposed to
take one a day for ten days. Tony says they gave him two a day
for two days. Ten in one day! Shit!

So maybe it was not one thing, but a lot of things? A cluster
of stressors, as Doc Doug said, that gave me my stress and then
my symptoms?

Other stressors:

Could it also be

1) the oil rain? Isn't that toxic?

2) maybe some bad stuff that got us when we entered their
bunkers after we hit them with bunker busters?

a) it felt like a flu for a while and still does lots of days.
Could it be some bacteria they had in there?

b) or chemicals? Right after we left the bunker, I had
trouble not shaking. Not an afraid kind of shaking but like my
nerves had been blasted. I paid it no mind then but now I'm
wondering. Someone told me they felt like that when they went
into a weapon storage facility to clean up after we bombed. The
same exact shaking, on the spot. Who was that? Where was
that?

c) depleted uranium. We hit lots of places with DU,
including the bunkers so maybe when we took the bunkers apart,
the DU got us. And later on the highway, the DU blasted through
everything and we were right there. Walking through the dust,
breathing it in. They say it's harmless. But isn't it nuclear waste?

d) vaccinations. They kept giving us vaccinations. Before
we went and when we were there. Vaccinations for anthrax and
other shit all the time!

e) the sand? There was sand flying all around all the
time. I swear it got inside me! It was the weirdest sand ever—
the tiniest grains coated with something really sticky.

So I'm thinking now there were lots of different stressors
causing lots of different symptoms. My symptoms took a while
to develop. I mean there was that headache my first day there. I
guess there was a stomach ache sometimes. I didn't think about
it though and I laughed at guys who said they felt sick. When I

got home, I felt so fucking tired. And I'd forget little things, sometimes where I was. I'd say some strange stuff sometimes, rhymes for example. Then there was the time, later, which was the big sign, when I thought Nancy was the enemy....I couldn't bear if I ever hurt Nancy (or the baby) in any way. Come to think of it now, when I put Nancy's picture up on the Wall of Shame, if she'd have shown up, I might have shot her on the spot. Luckily she didn't, and luckily Tony wrote me and I trusted what he said cause he's my best bud, and I calmed down.

Question for the doc. Why does he call them stress symptoms? I think he explained this but I can't remember. Does he mean that there is no physical basis? Or that the physical stuff develops because your nervous system goes wild because you have so many different things coming down on you. A kind of nervous breakdown, I mean as in the actual nerves, a neurological breakdown?

I kind of hope the doc is right that if we understand it, we can begin to control it. Minds can play a role. Because I have always been disciplined and if I have to direct my mind in a certain way to train it to control my body and my symptoms, I will. All I know is that by January, I have to be symptom-free for my fam! That gives me two months to get my shit together.

Maybe the group can be like basic training, when the corps stripped us naked of every response but rage. Now they could take away everything but staying calm. And if Dr. Doug is right, that would alter the nervous system, which mediates everything in the body? I could take a little rash hanging on and a little stomach stuff. But not the nausea and runs and not walking like I'm drunk and feeling confused and forgetting and getting ballistic over nothing.

Homer photocopies his journal for Tony, so he can read it on the go in his busy new life as an almost teacher.

He staples the pages together and prints on top, in red marker, FOR YOU, TEACHER. DON'T GRADE ME HARD!

# 9. Listen

Dr. Meloni asks who wants to share, and Homer raises his hand first. He clears his throat to begin, then suddenly loses heart. He feels like an old man, phlegmy and weak. But around him in the circle, all are smiling, nodding encouragingly; and then just as suddenly he feels like a boy. Like when he was a cub scout, sitting around the campfire, telling the other boys everything he knew about knives and hatchets, which was more than anyone else in the whole cub troop. So he begins to read.

"You got it," someone says.

"That says it all," someone says.

"Multiple stressors…I can see that."

Most of the men—and both of the two women—say that they'd been exposed to the same things, and had the same concerns. PB pills, DEET collars, vaccines, oil rain, crazy sand, and maybe chemicals and germs.

"And depleted uranium?" someone says.

"It's depleted," Dr. Meloni says. "So it's not a problem. But, yes, you've faced many stressors. Let's consider your response. When you think about these stressors," Dr. Meloni asks the group, "what do you feel?"

"You gotta be kidding," one of the women says. She looks in her teens but says she's thirty-two. She's been in the Army three years, has two kids, and her name is Lisa. "You want to kill someone—for exposing you to all that. Risking your health, your life, your family!"

"My very point," the doctor says. "You get angry. And anger itself is another dangerous stressor. I mean it helps in battle, but you're home now…."

"So are you saying if we can get calm, like Homer said in his journal, our symptoms will subside?"

The doctor nods. "The mind and body. They can't be divided. The more we understand and foster a connection between the two, the better off we are."

Meloni, baloney, Homer thinks. There he goes again, doing his rhyming shit, like when he first got home. Nancy would look scared, like she was afraid he was crazy drunk and so he stopped rhyming out loud. But when he felt his mind wandering, he'd do it, like, Let me just grab onto a couple of words, anything, man, not to float away. But, till now, he can't remember thinking even one rhyme all week. So maybe it wasn't baloney at all. Maybe there was something to what the doctor was saying. Reduce stress, reduce confusion, reduce dumb rhymes...and all the other symptoms.

He's been calmer this past week, just resting at home, talking about his stress experiences, writing in his journal. He thinks his rash is actually less itchy. When Lily and Tony were touching up the trim in the baby's room the week before, the rash was awful, and so was his stomach, and his thinking and walking. The thought crossed his mind that it was from the chemicals, that the paint fumes had activated something that had started in the desert—a reaction to the oil fumes, or air in one of the bunkers. But now Doug has him wondering if it wasn't that he felt guilty not helping, and the guilt stressed him, which made him suddenly susceptible to paint fumes? Then the painting stopped, and his guilt stopped, and his symptoms seemed to lift a little. He's never been very psychologically inclined, but could it be?

"I don't buy it," Lisa says. "I think we were poisoned, and this is bullshit."

"Do you have any evidence that you were poisoned?" Dr. Meloni asks.

She shakes her head. "I just feel it. I felt sick as soon as

I swallowed those damn PB pills. Five pills for four days. Every day I felt worse."

"Consider this," Dr. Meloni says. "There was talk of gas warfare, and so you were given pills to counteract the nerve agents. You felt endangered. Your mind sent a message to your body—we're in trouble, do something. The body did something—its skin, its intestines, its balancing mechanism. The body is a good listener."

"I don't know," Lisa says. She is finishing an AA degree to be a physical therapist assistant. "We studied the psychological components of illness in several courses in my program. This just doesn't seem psychological to me."

"What I am proposing is something more complex than a psychological explanation," Dr. Meloni says. "The body and mind whisper to each other day and night."

"And we gotta listen?" a man named Frank calls. Like a hunting dog listening, he juts out his head. "We gotta learn to listen…to ourselves?" he barks nervously.

"Just listen," a few people call.

"Yes, just relax and listen," the doctor chants. Then quietly, "Listen…listen…listen…."

Homer closes his eyes to listen with the group. To open up the channels between body and mind to allow messages to flow freely.

"I hear you," someone calls.

"I hear," someone whispers.

"I hear," Homer tries. He feels like he's in church, like he's a boy again, escaping the boredom of his parents' at-home Sundays in the local Baptist church. Here, here, here I am, Jesus, he'd call out with all the other boys, loving the loud camaraderie. But after a few visits, it started to seem ridiculous. And when the pastor shouted, See him, find him, love him, and the other boys called, Jesus, Jesus, I believe in you, come to me, I'm over here, here…sometimes even giving Jesus directions and tips… next to the door…or at the back of the room…wearing a red tie…or black glasses…or whatever, he would just lose it, falling on the floor and writhing in laughter. The first time, the pastor thought Homer was experiencing religious ecstasy, and he knelt beside him and praised him for finding Jesus and the joy of salvation so quickly. But the next time Homer fell to the floor, his irreverence became obvious, and his hilarity contagious. And soon the pastor asked him to leave and not return unless his attitude changed, which it never did.

Today, though, he wants to believe so badly that his whole body aches. But his mind feels empty. He looks around the room. Everyone's eyes are closed, to hear better and heal better, he imagines. They look so vulnerable that he can hardly look at them—their faces bare, exposed, like peeled cantaloupes. He feels exposed too suddenly, like he did the first days with Nancy. Opening up and feeling scared like his skin had been sliced and pulled back and maybe she wouldn't love him that way and he'd never be put together again. That same dread now. But a similar excitement too. If he just opened up and listened, all his suffering might lift!

"I hear," he says, louder now. "I hear...."

"Good work," Dr. Meloni says. "Mind and body, body and mind. Hear them, listen...."

He apologizes that they haven't had time to talk about their symptoms more. Next time, that will be their focus.

He distributes a group roster, in case they want to reach out to someone during the week, and he assigns written homework. He has read about writing-to-heal techniques but has never used them. But Homer's writing did them all so much good that he wants them all to keep journals from now on. This week they should write in their journal about new stressors. And symptoms. And the relationship between the two.

"Think of it as a story," Dr. Meloni says. "Tell your story. What your mind thinks, what it says to your body, how your body feels, what it says back to your mind....Next week we'll share our mind-body narratives."

The doctor ends the sessions with a tip. "There are two kinds of LISTEN. The LISTEN we've just talked about. And another one we haven't. LIS-TEN. It stands for Let It Slide, count to Ten. The second LIS-TEN frees you up for the work of the first LISTEN....Write that down, ladies and gentlemen. Put it on the fridge. Practice it every day."

Listen....Listen....Listen. Wasn't that what Nancy said to him way back when they first met? You don't listen. You have to listen. He listened—and learned to speak a language that had escaped him, and then she loved him back. It was a miracle! If it happened once, couldn't it happen again?

All week, Homer walks around the house counting to ten. He feels too hyper for the first Listen—hearing his body talking to his mind and his mind talking back, except to say, Shape up, sick bastard. But the second Listen—LIS-TEN. Let it slide, let it slide, count to ten—he practices over and over. A glass breaking. A car alarm screeching. Chills or sweats or a touch of confusion. Don't react. Just LIS-TEN. LIS-TEN. LIS-TEN. And by the end of the week, he feels calm enough to sit quietly. And then he can hear his mind tell his body, heal, heal, and his body tell his mind that it is hearing and cooperating....He doesn't think that he is only imagining that his stomach, joints, and skin are responding! His barfing is down for sure.

Nancy agrees that he's in better shape. Most nights now, he is calm enough to lie on the bed and let her rub his joints with Ben-gay and his scabs with vitamin E oil and cocoa butter. And a couple of nights, he feels clear enough to rub her belly back so that her silky skin is not marred as the baby grows. Those nights, they feel certain that bliss and perfection are right around the corner, and more than once they have talked, half seriously, about calling the baby Perfect, at least at the beginning.

The captain in charge of the stress program has issued a memo that one meeting a week is sufficient for stress training, but the group and Doug feel otherwise. And since in a month, the old wing that holds the offices will close for two months to deal with a rat infestation, they decide to hold all meetings in a home. Doug will go to these meetings and help them along. More meeting and more talking means less stress means fewer symptoms means health, he tells them.

Because it is centrally located, Homer's house will be the meeting place. Those days that Nancy comes home from school early, the group will go across the street to Tony's. Homer asked Tony, and of course he said yes. He has a heap of work, but he is determined to make the stress group feel at home. His life is moving right along while they are all so stressed and stuck. His living room and a few six-packs of Coke seem the least he can offer. He's quit Southern Skies and is holed up in his bedroom preparing for teaching. He can hardly hear the soldiers and marines in his living room when he's reading about Valley Forge or Stonewall Jackson's final march.

Toward the end of each meeting Tony returns to his living room to drink coffee with the soldiers and marines and say hello and goodbye. It takes forever for them to stop talking and start leaving, and as he sits with them, he can't help but hear about the subject of the day—chills and sweats, breath and coughs, joints and tremors and dreams. Lily calls the troop sessions the "organ recital," and the day there are meetings she calls before she heads home to ask if the "organ recital" is over and the coast clear.

Secretly, when they are alone, Tony and Lily wonder if the talking does any good. Tony hadn't talked, and his fatigue and sweats just vanished. Those crazy shakes on the highway—it's been ages since he had to pull to the side of the road to wait for them to pass. His memories were shadowy at most, but even the shadows have lifted now, without either of them doing or saying a thing.

At the end of each meeting, Doug asks them to stand in a circle and hold hands and say, "Mind over matter. That's the deal. Remember that and heal."

Tony joins the "goodbye circle" but he doesn't chant, nor does Lisa. She has her doubts, she's explained, not about Doug whom she loves for his genuine concern, but about the validity of his theory.

One night at the end, as the circle begins to form, Lisa says she can't join them.

"Can't or won't," Doug asks.

"Both actually. We're sick and that's that. Our bodies are sick."

"Your mind feels your body is sick," Doug says.

Lisa's face turns an angry red, then gray, and she runs from the room.

The sound of her retching floats down the hallway from the bathroom.

When she returns to the room, she tells them she can't stay. "This isn't working," she says. "I won't be coming back, but I'll keep in touch from time to time. I wish I didn't stink from puke so I could kiss you each goodbye."

She blows a kiss, then salutes, then marches down the hall and out the door.

# 10. Breathe

By mid-November the plans for Modern War: A 10th Grade Curriculum are coming along. Tony hasn't decided on his organization. Chronology? Generals? (Washington? Lee? Grant? MacArthur? Patton?) Themes? (Leadership of War? Media and War? The Public and War? The Psychology of War?)—but he's reading enough and taking enough notes to feel confident that some unifying idea will emerge. Field trips would play a big part too, but it needed another engine. Dr. Moser has called a couple of times and seemed positive about Tony's ideas. He doesn't want Tony to feel under pressure. Exploring patriotic values through war and vice versa was just one heuristic. He believes in him and wants him to feel free to experiment. This year's war course will be a pilot. He went on about the curriculum development process he had created, which several districts had adopted: Classroom trial, Evaluation and Revision, Dissemination, Adaptations and final Review. CEDAR, they were calling it. An acronym that carried the sense of something strong and lasting.

He wants Tony to relax. Rome wasn't built in a day. It took him three years to get his CEDAR method into shape. Again, Tony must will himself not to laugh when Dr. Moser goes on and on with his nonsense systems and theories. But it's getting easier to focus on the important stuff. Dr. Moser's basic decency and warmth. He kept talking, didn't really listen, but somehow, somewhere understood? Like a father?

Lily has designed an invitation for the baby shower and printed it out on Doc's color printer. She has arranged the menu and bought the paper goods. Which is good. Because when the shower is over, she will have more time to plan their wedding. Of course, she will help Nancy with the baby. Even now she is her partner in the pre-natal classes, filling in for Homer, who, despite improvement, is still too tired for the two-hour sessions.

By the time the baby comes, Homer will be strong enough to be Nancy's birthing partner. He has extended his home-leave till the end of December to work with Doug and attend additional groups over at the VA, especially designed for memory, concentration, relaxation, and anger-control, which in turn will diminish the experience of stress, which in turn will diminish the physical symptoms. She is glad they're nearby to help. Tony is glad that his teaching will end at three so he can continue to keep Homer company. Tony has never stopped being a best bud to Homer, but now as Homer starts to improve, Tony actually looks forward to their time together. It will be like old times, like all their afternoons doing homework side by side—Homer's homework now visualizing or journal writing, and Tony's preparing lessons and marking papers. And he will still drive him when possible to the hospital and after drive for pizza or ice-cream, like they used to over at Valley Mall. Lily's down with all of this.

The only problem for her is that Homer's at their house more than he's at his own. Some days, even when there's no stress-group meeting, his stress-group buddies are there too, chilling on Mrs. Molto's upholstered pieces. In so much of life she has strived to emulate Mimi's openness and generosity, and when Mimi's house became her house, she was totally comfortable keeping Mimi's do-what-you-want policy regarding food and drink in the living room. It was Mimi's big-hearted, big-picture nature, Lily knows, that accounted for her *laissez faire* attitude in so many areas of life, but Lily can't help but think that Mimi's furniture being so crappy to begin with played a role. If Mrs. Molto's furniture had graced the living room when it was still Mimi's, wouldn't even Mimi have noticed the pale peach color and peachy-fuzzy texture, how what made the pieces beautiful also made them vulnerable and in need of protection—and wouldn't even Mimi have reacted to soda and chips and chocolate dropping all over? Both houses have No-Smoking rules, but some of the men light up in the yard. In the morning, the lawn is strewn with butts. How long till beer and vodka? Pot and heroine? How long till she could put up a sign: Welcome to Ronnie-land!

When Ronnie was high, he used to trim his beard with a hunting knife, and leave his hair everywhere. Homer doesn't drop hair but a confetti of dried skin from his rashes. From living with Roco and working with dogs, though, Lily knows there's a way to set limits that is both kind and firm. Why not lay out parameters and reward good behavior! She could live with him bringing his buddies to their house but they had to do their eating and drinking in the kitchen, and clean up before they left. Because she is used to talking about bodily functions with animal owners, she is even willing to discuss the skin flakes with Homer, and teach him how to make Nancy's tape mitt to remove them from surfaces. She has already picked out the notebooks and pens and vitamin E products she will buy him to reward him if he honors the rules. They'd be hosting the baby shower very soon, and the house needed to be ready.

She knows it's a no-win situation and she tries the LIS-TEN trick several times a day. When the LIS-TEN trick doesn't work, she feels like Ronnie—reckless and mean. Once she collected Homer's droppings in a mug, which they nearly filled. Her plan was to mix them with the sugar in the sugar bowl and when he barged into her house and fixed himself a cup of coffee with three teaspoons of sugar and settled on her couch to watch TV, she'd watch him. And when he was done with his coffee, she'd tell him what he'd just downed and he'd experience the disgust he inflicted on her every day!

A couple of times when Lily could see Nancy across the way, floating around, oblivious to the fact that Homer was not home, but in her home making a major mess, Lily had flown out the door, wanting to go to Nancy's and push open the door and yell, You fat cow. You fat shmoo. And punch her in the belly! But she never did. She'd stop and do the LIS-TEN trick and the temptation to punch would lift and positive thoughts and feelings would descend.

She would see things in the best light. The anti-stress group, she'd tell herself, was probably a positive for Tony too. He's never had the stress rash nor the stress cramps nor the dizziness. But he'd had the fatigue early on and some sweats. And she knows he's had his stressors—the grenade, the blindness, the terrible sights and fears, and then shitting and pissing his pants. And sometimes, when they're driving on the turnpike, he seems far far away, like he's back in the desert. But since that first night he's told her nothing. And she's asked him nothing. Because it's no use dwelling on these things—that's her philosophy. But maybe what works for one individual doesn't necessarily work for another. *Dwelling* wasn't the way to go—she still feels that. But maybe *visiting* the experience was of value. The group talking down the hall was a safe little trip, to war and back. So when she isn't stressed, she sees the meetings in her house as a win-win situation. The last grains of the desert were washing off Tony. And the group was making Homer stronger and clearer. He'd be back on base in no time. And the times he came home on leave, he wouldn't want to hang at her house, but be snug as a bug in a rug with Nancy and the baby.

On Wednesday nights, Lily goes with Nancy to the natural childbirth class and for two hours they can feel the baby play and kick, stronger and stronger each week! It's her favorite night of the week. Driving with Nancy to the hospital, just the two of them yakking about everything or not, just sitting quietly and watching the night outside the window. Then walking through the doors of Mercy Women's Clinic, hearing people she doesn't even know calling, Hello, Lily, whispering as she passes, That's Mimi's girl. Then, in the class, helping the teacher. She's no expert in midwifery but years with Mimi have taught her enough to demonstrate the basics of pelvic stretches or diaphragmatic breathing or whatever it is Liz Blum, the instructor, asks of her.

And, of course, then there's the highlight of the evening—kneeling beside Nancy, timing pretend contractions, helping her through waves of pretend anguish, wiping her brow of pretend sweat. Those nights, life seems perfect, perfectly on course. Nancy is always beautiful and strong as she pants and pushes, her baby healthy inside her. Lily feels strong, too, helping and teaching. And also happy that she can learn, for she knows that eventually she will be following Nancy down Motherhood Lane.

Liz Blum used to be Mimi's assistant and now she directs the prenatal program. She is a lively redhead and her class keeps everyone busy with alternating stretching and concentration activities. Tonight is no exception. The mothers and their coaches, all fathers except for Lily, work hard on breathing their way through the much-feared Titanic contractions, and Liz rewards them with a special and extended relaxation activity. Lily demonstrates first. And then the whole group joins in. Liz guides them as they lie on their backs: Close your eyes, count the stars, claim each star, breathe each one in and then out, in and out, claim and release in healthful, natural relation…to the light…the source of all power…and peace…."

At the end of the session, as they still lie on the floor relaxing, Liz always lowers the lights and delivers a brief talk, speaking softly on a new topic.

Tonight she says, "Please, dear parents, consider spending time alone. Away from the stress of the everyday. A serene, pre-baby respite. Just the two of you. To replenish the fountain of feelings at the heart of your lives together."

There's rustling in the room—and Lily turns to watch the mothers and fathers smiling, locking eyes, and holding hands. One couple kisses, a kiss that is entirely too long for even a gooscy-loosey birthing class. And Lily looks over at Nancy to laugh together. But Nancy's eyes are closed.

"Don't be sad, Nancy. You'll have a respite soon. Maybe just a little later," Lily whispers.

Nancy nods, but Lily can see her mind is elsewhere.

In the car, Lily says, "Sad?"

"No, just thinking. Happy thoughts actually. How the stress management is making Homer so much calmer and how the rash, the joint pain, and everything is calming down too. At this rate, he'll be back on base in a couple of weeks. That will be his respite, and mine. Our reprieve. I was just thinking that."

"Good," Lily says. She is so glad. For him. For her. That he'll be gone. For herself. That she didn't turn into a total bitch and start training Homer like a dog, or trick him with the sugar bowl. Or turn on Nancy, which she almost did a couple of times, resenting her like she'd sometimes resent Connie, for not protecting her from her father, because she used her as a babysitter for a madman, never so much as saying, Thank you, Lily, for lightening my burden.

"But, Lil', I was thinking also how you and Tony should get away. This illness or whatever it is has exhausted all of us. You should get away now. Before Tony starts teaching."

A pre-wedding respite? Built on the same idea that Liz talked about? To rekindle love for the long haul ahead? One of the bride magazines recommended it, and it had appealed to her then and even more now. Moving into *Living Your Life* was not an easy transition for anyone but when that life was more complex than you ever dreamed, with friends sick, and you helping in their care. Time away would strengthen them for each other, their friends, all that faced them in this central phase of life, being godparents, then parents….She stops herself. It was out of the question. Every cent they had saved had gone into the house or the baby's crib and layette or their little fund for wedding expenses.

"It's kind of corny," Lily says. She hates not telling Nancy the truth. But Nancy had worse problems than a low checking balance.

"Corny. Then you should love it," Nancy laughs.

"There's so much to take care of here."

"It will all be waiting for you when you get back. I know you're worried about money. Let it be a pre-wedding present from me to you, sweetie. How does that sound? I've put money aside for something special for you. Why not this, Lil'?"

"I couldn't," Lily says.

"You must."

How lucky was she that the LIS-TEN trick had worked for her in the end and she had kept bad thoughts from becoming bad deeds—and her becoming a bad friend.

"You sure?" Lily says.

"Positive, baby. And I'll be a mama soon so you have to do as I say. Like that corny shirt says."

*Because I'm The Mommy And I Said So*. Nancy and Lily had seen the shirt in the mall and laughed together.

"Oops," Lily says. "I was going to buy that for you."

On the trip, she'll come across other cute things that Nancy *will* like, she's sure. Little things to say, Thank you BIG time, BIG sis. Which is probably what she'd write at the bottom of some fun card she's sure to find in their travels.

She pats Nancy's belly goodnight. What a bitch she had been thinking even for a second of punching her there!


Tony has saved enough from his job at Southern Skies to stop working until his teaching job begins. And Lily makes all the arrangements at Doc's for a week off. She picks up brochures of motels and historic houses at the Virginia

Hospitality Center near Fort Monuten, and Tony makes a list of battle sites and battle museums to visit for his course development. Tony doesn't know what "pre-wedding respite" means and Lily isn't quite sure either, but they both know they're tired and eager for time together, alone, riding from the Blue Ridge Mountains across the state.

The morning they are to leave, though, Homer wakes with a fever of 103. He hasn't had a fever since the first week he was sick, and Tony wants to wait till he's checked out before they leave. So it's off to the hospital again. Tony drives and Nancy sits in the back with Homer's head on her lap.

"Something's wrong," Nancy tells the Sprain triage nurse. "Now I'm thinking that something's really wrong."

Then to the nurse practitioner, who takes his vitals, she says, "You see that something's wrong. Right?"

Finally, when a doctor comes to examine Homer on a stretcher in the crowded hallway, Nancy says, "Everyone's making believe that nothing's wrong. And they convinced us that it was just, you know, nerves. But now his fever's back! Another marine we know has had all the same symptoms and suddenly a high fever too."

Tony nods and explains how Einstein's rash and vertigo had subsided, but then the fever came out of nowhere. "Maybe something's really wrong," he whispers so Homer won't hear. "With all of them...maybe. Besides just stress?"

The doctor is a plump Indian woman with a wide, white smile. "Let us focus on this one patient. 102 is not a high fever."

"Before it was 103. I gave him Tylenol. That's why it's only 102 now," Nancy says.

Homer looks up. "I tho I wa get better," he says, and closes his eyes.

"He thought he was getting better," Tony says.

"Does he always have trouble speaking?" the doctor says.

Tony shakes his head. "I think he's just too tired to talk."

"Are you tired today, sir?"

Homer opens one eye, then closes it again. He shivers and moans.

"How do you feel, sir?"

"He feels like he looks," Nancy says. "Lousy! I thought he was getting better. But mainly because he kept saying he was getting better. His rash was better but that's about all. All they've done here is give him Prozac. And get him together with other sick people, telling them they're not really sick just stressed. That's their explanation for the fact that these people can't walk, pee, eat, swallow, think, breathe...Look at him. And we're having a baby."

"How nice," the doctor says. "Your first?"

But Nancy does not answer. She meant only to communicate that her husband needed to be healthy, now more than ever! She will not be sidetracked with chit-chat. She is determined to have him admitted and worked up.

She says, "I am requesting he be admitted and worked up. He needs to be totally worked up and for that he needs to be admitted."

She knows the lingo. Let the doctor think she's a madwoman, she doesn't care. She'll say it again and again, till she's heard. "He needs a total work up and needs to be admitted today."

She feels like Mimi, who always pushed for all of them. A few years back, when her father turned blue from emphysema, and the ER just let him sit there, she got hysterical and called Mimi, and Mimi called the desk and said something like, Either you bring him a tank of oxygen now or I will come over with one...and you don't want me there in your ER...believe me.

"We shall keep him overnight," the doctor says. "And then we shall see. Fevers can come and go and mean nothing. Try to relax. Nothing is adding up here. It does not meet the criteria for any diseases with which I am familiar."

"How bow one tha new," Homer says, his eyes still

closed.

He said, "How about one that's new?" Nancy says. "Please listen to my husband, doctor!"

"Fro the deser."

"From the desert?"

"The symptoms are all over the place, dispersed in every system. That's almost unheard in a single disorder," the doctor says.

"So maybe it's lots of disorders!" Tony says. His mother would have said something like that. Once when he fell from a tree he was climbing with Homer, the ER kept them waiting half the night and then said the pain and weakness in his leg and foot were probably from a sprain. Probably or certainly, Mimi had said. Which got him an X-ray, which showed a fractured femur. I was almost a cripple, he used to tell kids.

"We have many people reporting diffuse symptoms much like Sergeant Joyce's and so far the stress theory seems the most plausible. He must learn to relax and so must all of you."

"Not... stress," Homer whispers. "Not...stress."

"He doesn't think it's stress anymore," Tony says. "He feels too bad."

"That's a very subjective measure...how one feels. I can't go around admitting or spending a fortune on tests on the basis of how someone says he feels."

"Look at him," Tony says. "Look at him, doctor!"

His own voice shocks him. And the fact that he has strode across the room to the other side of the bed, where the doctor is standing.

"Look at his face, doctor. It's gray!"

"There are guidelines for these cases."

"How can you get around the guidelines in the case of my friend here?"

"Perhaps I can justify a night or two...because of the fever," the doctor says.

"And you'll work him up?" Tony says. "In that time?"

"I will do my very best," the doctor says.

"Do let him dow," Homer says.

"Don't let *him* down," Tony says. "Listen to my buddy. He's in trouble," he whispers.

Homer begins to doze and Nancy and Tony walk to the lobby. In an hour or two a porter should arrive to take Homer up to the ward.

"You did what we needed. You kicked ass," Nancy says. "Now go. Go on your trip. I'll be fine."

"I'm not going," he says.

They're both tired and worried, but they both begin to laugh.

"Getting ready to kick ass in the class?" Nancy says. "The new you. Way cool."

He blushes. "It's bullshit. He needs a real diagnosis. Not that voo-doo stress shit. And be treated with more than Prozac!"

"He will be," Nancy says. "You can bet on that! In the meantime, there's no need for two of us to be here. He's staying and I'm staying with him. Not a problem. "

A Lilyism. And they both laugh again.

"Take Lil' and go," Nancy says.

She looks school-teachery, resolute. Not to be messed with.

"We'll call you every night," Tony says. "We'll come right back if you need us. We'll never be more than a few hours away."


When Tony gets home, it's Lily who isn't sure they should go. His description of Homer scares her, and she holds herself responsible. "I was mean-spirited and he sensed it."

"And what if that were true?" Tony says.

She shrugs. "I don't understand this whole stress thing. But isn't that the way Dr. Ron says it works? I was mean-spirited and he sensed it, which stressed him and caused a downward turn? If I'm extra nice to him, he could take a turn for the better. If we stay and I send him only loving thoughts....Something like that?"

"It's not stress, Lily," Tony says. "I wanted to believe it was just that. You had to see him today! Stress can't do that."

"Maybe not my thoughts, but my actions?" she says. "You don't know how I was to him the other night. I asked him to take the bottles and cans to the curb when he was leaving. It's true he'd drunk them all, but I didn't say please and my voice came out bitchy and what I really wanted to say was go away and don't come back and he knew."

"That's it? Your vicious act?" he laughs sadly. "Lily, listen, this has nothing to do with anything you did or thought. And nothing you can do or think can fix it."

"Nothing I can do? Nothing? Are you sure?"

"I'm sure," he says, with a certainty that surprises them both. "I'm convinced it's from the Gulf, Lily. The war did this. Not you."

"That stupid war is over!" she cries. "You're wrong."

Both houses were set. The baby shower invitations out. Half the food made and stacked in the freezer. The pre-natal classes almost finished. Homer improved and returning to Peabody in a month, they'd thought. Now just the heavenly parts—the birth and the wedding—beckoning them down the long happy road of life.

"I wish I were, Pup."

"Everything was supposed to be better!"

She means this wasn't Vietnam. That was the whole idea, if a war could have an idea. In and out, fast. Five weeks, not fifteen years. Forward not back. She wants to lie here till she dies. What was the point of getting up?

Did he ever see her look so desperate and doomed? Tony thinks. When Connie disappeared the first time, or was it the last time—maybe then? Tony remembers Ronnie running in with her, hopped on what he realizes now was speed, saying, Here, take the brat, I gotta go. And Lily just lying on the floor, like a rag doll. He thinks Mimi rubbed her back, like she rubbed her ladies' backs when the contractions began. She sang a song. And then another and another. He remembers because he had a junior guitar and he went to his room and got it, and Mimi whispered, Play very softly, sweetheart. Then Lily slept. She slept for a long time, right there on the shag rug, and he sat beside her. Her mother had taken her away on a trip and Ronnie had just brought her back, and Tony hadn't seen her for so long. He couldn't take his eyes off her—her upturned nose, her rosy skin, her long blonde braids, her thick dark lashes still glistening with tears. She was perfect! Can I keep her? he'd blurted out. He was only five but he knew as soon as he said it that there was something wrong with it, and he braced himself for his mother's laugh—and lecture: She's a person not a pet or doll. But Mimi said only, We'll see, sweetheart.

All he has ever wanted is to guard her from misfortune and make her happy.

He rubs her back and quietly croons her name. Lily. Then all the other names he loves to say and she loves to hear, whispering them into her hair.

After a few minutes, she begins to giggle. "That tickles," she says and jumps to her feet. "It feels like that day when my dad dumped me on the rug. Look how things worked out then for the good. It's so stupid to cry."

She walks outside, and climbs in the car, which they've packed the night before. "I bought two phone cards. So we can call them all the time," she says. "People get sick and then get better. You don't have to be a rocket scientist to know that happens all the time!"

He can't reach Ernie, but he'll try again on the road. He wants to know if *his* fever's down. Maybe if there was time, they could loop around and see him on the way back home. He misses Einstein a lot.

# 11. Crimson Woods

There is much made of Virginia in the spring, the dazzling bloom of cherry and magnolia and dogwood. But Virginia in the fall, in the foothills of the Alleghenies down to the Roanoke River Valley and across from Charlotte to the coast, is the state's true glory, with yellow gingko, crimson sumac, and screaming orange oak claiming the earth and sky. When Lily and Tony were little, one Columbus Day weekend, Mimi drove them to see the sites in Washington, DC, circling the whole state, it had seemed, to get there. They shouted out at every blazing tree they passed, now and then convincing Mimi to pull to the side of the road so they could gather special specimens. They must have been very young, because they declared the back of the car, which they'd piled thick with leaves, their "forest." Don't ever throw out our forest, they begged Mimi, who said, Of course not....Who would do a thing like that!

It's already mid-November, but Indian summer has delayed the fall, and the leaves are still bold and beautiful. They can think of no better vacation than a retrace of that old one, ending with a surprise visit to Mimi. Tony is excited. The trip will allow them to visit war sites he's never seen: Appomattox maybe, or Lynchburg, Winchester, or Mannassas. He's feeling all wound up about teaching in general and the war course in particular. He wants to take notes, buy historical facsimiles and dioramas to use with the kids.

Their plan is to divide the trip in two: his and hers, and ours. Lily's plan, of course. And he's game. They will drive south-east, toward the coast. They want to enjoy the leaves, pick apples, and visit a few war sites. Tony's picked out a few sites to visit, one Revolutionary fort, two Civil War battlefields, and an historical replica. Dr. Moser said there might be money for travel. Even if there was no money for that right away, they'd have the materials he'd bring back.

But as soon as they hit the highway, at every exit, another sign for another war site beckons. Fort this and Fort that; The Museum of the Confederacy, of the Confederate Sons, of the Southern Soldier; Infantry Village, Cavalry Village, Guardsmen's Grange. Which one mattered most? He can't decide.


Lily decides that nearby Front Royal should be their first stop. They start down in the valley town, then trek up the hills to the mountains, which like Monuten are sprinkled with snow. The first tier of mountains has markers and descriptions, but Lily's heard about a giant waterfall on the tier above, and when they reach the first plateau, she sees it gushing down the east side of the mountain, flashing bolts of morning sun.

"Look," she cries.

But Tony doesn't seem to hear her, which she refuses to take personally. It's his time, not her time. And she executes a quick about-face and follows him to the interpretative material posted on a vast outcropping.

She tells him to sit and relax and she will read to him:

In March 1862, Union forces under Maj. Gen.
Nathaniel Banks started to advance up the valley.
General Jackson retreated to Mount Jackson in order to
defend the Valley Turnpike. Then Jackson led his
forces down the Turnpike and engaged Union forces in
battle. Jackson was defeated, but his aggressive move
convinced Washington that Confederate forces in the
valley posed a threat to Washington, and Maj. Gen.
George B. McClellan was denied reinforcements at a

critical moment in the Peninsular Campaign.
She stops. "Enough?" she says.
"Go on," he says.

At the end of April, Jackson left Maj. Gen. Richard S.
Ewell in charge of troops to confront Banks, marching
with about 9,000 men under Maj. Gen. John C.
Fremont, approaching ... from western Virginia. Banks
believed that Jackson was leaving the valley to join the
Confederate army at Richmond. But, Jackson appeared
again...at McDowell. He then led forces back to join
with Ewell to confront the Union forces.

"Enough?"
"Go on, Lil," he says. "Try not to condense as much
though. How much are you leaving out?"
"Just a little."

Banks resisted....Jackson attacked and routed the
Union forces....They fled to the Potomac ....
Banks...started up again .... Linked up with Brig. Gen.
James Shields's Union division.... Jackson
withdrew...almost lost line of retreat because of
converging columns....Union offensive against
Jackson starts. Fremont's troops....Shields's column
marched up.... 25,000 men challenged Jackson's
17,000. Confederate cavalry commander Brig. Gen.
Turner Ashby was killed while fighting a rear guard
action....Confederate forces marched 650
miles...inflicted 7,000 casualties, at a cost of only
2,500.

She stops reading. "Brig. Gen. Turner Ashby," she says.
"Sad when any human being dies. But they don't give the
name of anyone else who died. That doesn't seem fair. I mean
I don't see how they have the nerve to say *only* 2,500! That's
a lot of people. Maybe not Brig. Gen. Turner Ashby kind of

people, but human beings just the same! Let's go to the waterfall," she says.

"You scout it out," he says, distractedly. "I want all the details."

She finds a narrow path up the mountain, but a short way up, fallen rocks thwart her advance, and she retreats to the car waiting for him to be done. Out the window, she makes out two robins settled on the branch of a cherry tree, and on a branch above a sparrow. Generally by November the birds of the northern Shenandoah Valley have retreated south for the advancing winter. But lately warm autumns have allowed them to stay longer, only to encounter starvation and death with the sudden onset of winter. She recalls an article she read at Doc's on recent climate changes altering migration patterns. A truck backfires on the road below and the birds lift off. She exits the car to watch where they go, searching for spots of blue and gray, but she's lost them.

When Tony returns to the car, he asks her to drive.

"Get ready for a big one," he says. "The Second Battle of Manassas. It's also called the Second Battle of Bull Run. It was a much larger battle in terms of scale and numbers than the First Battle of Bull Run, also known at the First Manassas, which was fought in 1861 on the same site."

His voice sounds unfamiliar, like he's giving a speech. He doesn't seem like her best friend let alone the man she's pledged to marry, but like that annoying boy brat who used to jump up on Homer's handlebars and pretend she wasn't running beside them. But those times were long gone. Now was a new time, and right now it was his time, not her time.

When they reach Manassas and he wanders around the rocky plains and hills, she sits in the car again. The image of the robins and the sparrow flying off, perhaps in the wrong direction, gnaws at her. She takes out her pad and writes herself a note to send a $10.00 money order to help the birds. But why stop with birds. Each month, she can send a $10.00 money order to help a different concern in nature: birds, reptiles, amphibians, mammals, humans, air, ground, mountains, sea, lakes, rivers, the Arctic. And once she has that planned, she reminds herself it's his time still, and it's only fair that she apply her skills to *his* project. She will make a template on a notecard to record the essential facts. She's learned the value of templates at Doc's, where the consistent formats she developed would organize facts needed in the service of saving animals' lives, not in the service of recording its opposite—war and killing. But if it will help Tony and speed things along, she'll lend her skills—and add her perspective when she can. Name of Battle, date, commanders, how many injured and killed. She knows she should add a last item, who won, but she's not sure she understands what that means anymore.

When he returns to the car, he insists on reading aloud from a "really amazing account" in a pamphlet he's bought.

In order to draw Pope's army into battle, Jackson ordered an attack on a Federal column that was passing across his front on the Warrenton Turnpike on August 28. The fighting at Brawner Farm lasted several hours and resulted in a stalemate. Pope became convinced that he had trapped Jackson and concentrated the bulk of his army against him. On August 29, Pope launched a series of heavy assaults against Jackson's position along an unfinished railroad grade. The attacks were repulsed with heavy casualties on both sides. At noon, Longstreet arrived on the field from Thoroughfare Gap and took position on Jackson's right flank. On August 30, Pope renewed his attacks, seemingly unaware that Longstreet was on the field. When massed Confederate artillery devastated a Union assault by Fitz John Porter's command. Longstreet's wing of 28,000 men counter attacked in the largest, simultaneous mass assault and devastation of the war. The Union left flank was crushed and the army driven back to Bull Run.

"Interesting, right?"

Assault. Mass Assault. Attack. Counter Attack. Crush. Disaster. Devastation. It sounded like one of those stupid comic books her father used to read out loud when he was high. *Crash. Crack. Agh. You'll regret that, you heinous lout. Zoom. Boom.*

"How many casualties?" she says.

"Let's see....22,180 total. Union 13,830 and Confederacy 8,350." She hands him a notecard with a template. "Use this to write down the important facts." He studies the card. "I like the idea of a repeated format or protocol....That's good. I can give the students my notes and articles, and your summary. I'm trying to figure out learning activities from all this. Divide them into groups. Each group could be responsible for bringing a different battle to life for the rest of the class. It might take up the whole semester, but they'd learn a lot. About military decision making, tactics. They could use a lot of role-playing, which the kids always like."

"They could play the 22,180 dead and injured," she says.

If he hears her, he doesn't show it. He's studying a map to figure out what battleground to advance to next.

"I don't see how you can win with over 8,000 dead in two days!" she says.

He smiles vaguely.

Hey, remember me? she wants to say.

It begins to rain and she's glad. Maybe they can go to a motel and take baths and fool around and read. But he says they're lucky. A few places have drive-through tours.

"War Tour Radio," he says.

The rest of the day and the next day and the next, the rain continues and War Tour Radio comes to the rescue. Tony records the narration on a mini tape-recorder and stops at each gift shop to buy maps and battle chronicles. Lily fills out her cards of essential facts.

They drive through the Chancellorsville Battlefields. *May 1-4, 1863. Commanders: Gen. Robert E. Lee (CS) Maj. Gen. Joseph (US). Estimated Casualties: 24,000 total (US 14,000; CS 10,000).*

They drive to the site of Five Forks Battle. *April 1, 1865. Commanders: Maj. Gen. Philip Sheridan (US) Maj. Gen. George Pickett (CS). Estimated Casualties: 3,780 total (US 830; CS 2,950).*

The third car tour is at the site of the Battle of the Wilderness. *May 5-7, 1864 Commanders: Robert E. Lee (CS) Ulysses S. Grant (US). Estimated Casualties: 25,416 total (US 17,666; CS 7,750).*

Their fourth car tour is at the site of the Battle of Spotsylvania. *May 8-19, 1864. Commanders: Gen. Robert E. Lee (CS) Gen. Ulysses S. Grant (US). Estimated Casualties: 27,399 total. (US 18,399; CS 9,000).*

He packs the growing stock of books and pamphlets and maps into his backpack and when there's no more space there, he fills up the rucksack he's tossed into the trunk.

She keeps the note cards in the glove compartment. She reads a book Doc has given her on the treatment of worms in household pets. There are lots of cases showing up, especially in the smaller pooches. But she can't think of worms today without thinking of the dead soldiers. Winner or loser, it doesn't matter, the worms got you.

The next day it's sunny and in the fifties. They've never been to the Historical Triangle—Williamsburg Historic Village or the Yorktown Victory Center or Jamestown Settlement Festival Park. They don't have time for all three, and when they reach the Colonial Highway, they agree on Jamestown. Yorktown and Williamsburg were the sites of big battles, and even Tony is ready for some R and R. Lily knows that Pocahontas lived at Jamestown, and she loves the story of the princess. Tony knows that the first Europeans landed in Jamestown, and called the local Indians Powhata. There's old-fashioned dancing and music and costumes and food,

Lily's heard.

"Food!" Tony says. He's starving.

Last night, to save money, she insisted they sleep in a Walmart's parking lot, where you're never bothered because it's open 24 hours and they never check. It was actually fun, because every few hours they'd go inside and pee and buy something. A notebook and pens. Pretzels. A clearance baby onesie in yellow for Nancy, good for either boy or girl, and pearl post earrings for Mimi because she was always losing hers and they were real gold and real pearls and with 80% off came to the grand total of $9.88! And now they have enough money to eat lunch at the Jamestown Settlers Inn, which a large billboard on the highway says is the best in the entire historical triangle.

Their table overlooks the James River and replicas of the first settlers' ships.

"The Susan Constant, Godspeed and Discovery," Tony says.

"Good for you," Lily says, taking his hand.

The two of them together, settling into their own new lives, like the settlers in a new land—this is what she had in mind, and it was worth trekking and waiting and sleeping in a car to have this now.

The waitress, a woman in her thirties in a muslin dress, gingham apron, and her dark hair in a long braid, brings menus.

"Let's get something old-fashioned," Lily says. "Check what they ate," she says, gesturing to his backpack.

He takes out a book and reads. "Deer and squirrel."

"No thank you," she says. "That's all?"

"Corn."

"We like corn." She opens the menu, "Corn fritters. Turkey and creamed corn. How does that sound?"

He says nothing. "Actually, most of the settlers starved the first year, it says. That's the ones that didn't die of disease."

"Go on," she says. "This is tragic but interesting!"

"Corn fritters," he says. "That's what I want."

"Tell me," she says. "It's just history."

"This guy says they ate rats and may have died of the plague. Some of them...." He shakes his head, closes his menu.

"Some of them what? I can take it. It was almost 400 years ago! You learn from history. What to repeat and what not to."

She grabs the book. "Starving and desperate, they dug up graves and ate corpses. By the end of the first winter, only 38 settlers were left at Jamestown."

The waitress appears again. Her caramel skin reminds Lily of Nancy, and Lily blurts out, "We just read something terrible and won't be able to eat. Are you aware of the history of this place? What people ate?"

The waitress shrugs. "My people are Upper Mattaponi. They ate corn and deer for the most part. Some still do. On the reservation. I was born on the rez, but there's work here so I'm here now."

"I mean the settlers," Lily says.

"The invaders," the waitress smiles. "That's what we call them."

"Whatever you call them. They ate corpses, which I call cannibalism."

"I've heard that. The grandmothers tell that story. Men eating the darkness of excrement and putrid flesh. One white man slew his sleeping wife and ate her every part. But I didn't know it was written down. A white man wrote that?"

Lily looks at the photo on the book jacket. "Looks white. His eyebrows are very dark. Harold Tinn. Is Tinn a white name? I don't pay attention to these things. I think everyone's a bit of a mutt. You look like my best friend, Nancy. She's African American. But now that I see you I think she's probably a little bit Mattapori too. Some of her people are from this area. So are Homer's, her husband's."

"Matta*poni*," the woman laughs. "The first Africans landed here too. That's another grandma story: Twenty from across the sea…cargo in a pirate ship. I don't know why they call it the Jamestown Festival."

"I wouldn't choose that word either," Lily says. "But you're not going to get many people to come if you call it the Jamestown *Funeral*!"

The waitress's names is Darlene. She has three kids and she shows Lily and Tony photos of Dierdre the Devil, Desiree the Darling, and Baby-boy David. Although they haven't eaten, they leave Darlene a five dollar tip. For taking up her table and her time, and telling them about a better, cheaper diner about ten miles north of Yorktown, right next door to a super clean and super cheap motel.


Revolted as she was by the tales, Lily is invigorated by the conversation with Darlene, and at the Freedom Diner, she talks about Darlene's three kids. "How cute is Baby-boy David!" she says. She bets Nancy and Homer's baby will look like him. "Baby chick hair, but dark, and chirpy eyes!"

Tony doesn't respond. He lays his head on a paper placemat on the table and closes his eyes.

"Ton, are you okay?"

"What am I doing?" he says. "What's the point?"

"The point is living life. Starting our lives together and individually. Think of how much you have to teach….How much you have to choose from now." She points to his backpack. She feels bad that she criticized his articles and accounts. "You've gathered so many fine resources."

"Have I? Five hundred miles and a thousand facts later, why do I feel like I know less than when we started out. Like I'm less sure about what I'm teaching and why."

She rubs his head. "You have to process what you've learned."

"What have I learned?" he says.

He lifts his head and reads the placemat. *Virginia is for Lovers.* The usual late 20th century *I LOVE* graphic, a red heart and black letters. But there's the outline of the state on one of the heart's lumps, filled with the words: *Did you know the six interesting facts at the bottom of this placemat?*

He looks at the bottom of the paper and reads out loud:

*1. The American Revolution ended in Virginia with the surrender of Cornwallis in Yorktown.*
*2. Over half of the 4,000 battles fought in the Civil War were fought in Virginia. Half of the 700,000 soldiers who died in the war died in Virginia.*
*3. The tomb of the Unknown Soldier is in Virginia's Arlington National Cemetery.*
*4. The Pentagon building in Arlington is the largest office building in the world.*
*5. The system of slavery in the colonies began in Virginia.*
*6. The lands of Virginia once belonged to the Confederacy of the Powhatan People, which was destroyed in 1646, though today offspring can be found on Virginia's many reservations.*

"Interesting. Very interesting," he says.

"What, in particular, do you find interesting, Ton?"

"It sounds like me. My little lessons. Class, fill in the map with the facts. So what? Who cares? George Washington's nose...."

"What?"

He'd been too embarrassed to tell even her about the half hour he spent on Washington's face. From wooden teeth on. He pats his knapsack. "Just a heap of information. All these maps, replicas, notes, lists, dates. They're about as interesting as the placemat. Four thousand battles, 700,000 dead, the system of slavery, the native nations destroyed. People eating human shit and flesh. Actually, that is all amazing. Problem is that you read it one minute, then spill your coke on it the next."

"What do you want to do with it?" she asks.

He shakes his head. "I don't know. Walking through battlefields. Role-playing generals. It's no better than memorizing facts or the crap they taught us in junior high. Remember?"

She knows he means the rote formulas of history. The revolution was a combination of this and that. The basic causes of the Civil War were that and this. The immediate causes were a, b, c.

"It *was* pretty dull," she says.

"What I've got is worse. At least that was orderly crap. Mine is a jumble of junk. I'll open my backpack and my rucksack, and say, Class, look at the junk heaps. Take your pick."

He traces the Virginia is for Lovers heart on the placemat. "Virginia is for war. Virginia is for death...killing. What more is there to say? End of lesson."

He rips up the placemat. "That's all I know. I have no course. I give up," he says.

"You do have a course. Think. With your gut."

In his gut. That's where he knew it was hopeless. His gut was churning and he felt queasy and dizzy.

"Really, Ton. Just close your eyes and what do you see?"

He's afraid if he closes his eyes, he'll puke, but he's too tired to fight her. When he closes his eyes, he sees it. It's bigger than Jamestown or any of the battlefields they've seen. It's blind like a bat, with the black hair of a rat, and countless suckers. He opens his eyes to clear his mind. But the giant bat-rat monster remains. Homer is hanging upside down from one of the suckers. Don't eat him! Tony thinks. Please.

"Please what?" Lily says.

"I'm losing it," he says.

It was war, she knows. Assaults. Attacks. Invasions. Starvation. Disease. His sick friends. Thinking about all this was making him crazy. You couldn't dwell on it for long.

"Please, someone help," he calls, looking past her.

When Ronnie was off his rocker big-time, conversing with the dead piled inside the wall behind the couch, she learned to stay calm so she could calm him. Sit still, breathe deeply, she'd tell him. She'd shut off the TV and bring him a Coke and sing him a song he liked. Sometimes that would relax him and he'd lie down and fall sleep.

Now she whispers, "Ton, it's okay. I'm going to sing you a song. What's your favorite song, Ton? Funny I don't know, right?" She rubs his head and hums.

Then he's back. "I don't have one....Remember...I couldn't decide...."

They both giggle and she takes his hand. "I like 'You Light Up My Life.'" She hardly knows it, but they'd danced their "first dance" on the Fourth of July to it. "You like 'You Light Up My Life' too?"

"I do."

He lays his head on the table and she strokes his hair and sings the song softly. *"You light up my life, you give me hope to carry on.... Rollin' at sea, adrift on the water, could it be finally I'm turning for home....Never again to be all alone...."*

"Nice," he says.

"Maybe just teach the other classes? Do you have to teach this war course?" she says.

He nods.

"Can't someone else?"

He shakes his head. "*I* should. I know things...," he says. "But I need to rest. I'm too tired now to figure out what they are."

"It's normal to be tired. And scared," she says. "Rest a while and then we'll see how you feel...."

There's a cup of crayons by the sugar bowl for bored kids. While he dozes, she takes a red crayon and writes on her placemat. She wishes he would just give up the course, but if he won't, she'd have to help.

She tries not to think about war, but about learning. The learning she's been doing and how much she's loved it. All the stuff about animals. All the stuff about safety and nutrition. About marriage and relationships and weddings. She loved the subjects, of course, animals, health, love. But why was this so extra exciting?

She watches him sleep, listens to his breathing.

Because there was a reason to learn? Wasn't that the difference? It felt like she was learning for the people and beasties she cared about.

"What are you doing?" he whispers, feeling her eyes on him.

"Thinking about…your curriculum."

"So nice…sweet," he says, sitting up. "What are you thinking?"

"Shh…wait…I'm thinking."

She was so corny! Her gestures as canned as her speech! How he loved watching each one. One hand under her chin, to show *pensive*. The other rubbing the top of her head…to show she had on her *thinking cap*….While he was resting he'd been thinking he should never have dragged her with him through the battlefields. *Red fields*—he thinks, remembering how she'd avert that side of Monuten Mountain. But here she was, trudging though what she feared most, for *him*.

"Okay. If the students got to learn for a reason…. Like before with Darlene, I was interested in her and her stories. If we hadn't gotten nauseated, I could have sat with her for hours and just listened. If your students got to care about a person or persons who'd been affected by war, then wouldn't they want to know what happened and why to the person or persons?"

He wants to laugh. Where did she get this stuff! Person or persons. But he doesn't want to hurt her feelings, and besides it makes perfect sense.

"So you create the personal connection?" he says. "Is that what you're saying? And then the desire to understand the person's experience or background comes naturally? From that desire...that need?"

"Just a thought," she says. Persons and *animals*, she is tempted to say. She doesn't like to dwell on it but she knows how pets and livestock are left behind in war to starve or burn. But she's not in the mood to be laughed at. This was all very serious.

"It actually makes a lot of sense.....I like it," he says.

He thinks about the old man who cashiered nights at the 7-11. He told Tony he remembered his great-grandfather, who was a freed slave who fought in the Union Army. He had his uniform and some photos, he'd told him. The night shift was slow and he liked to tell his stories and Tony liked to hear them. He could introduce some of the kids to Clarence. They could drop by and talk. A kind of friend-informant?"

"What do you call your method, professor?" he says.

What could they call it? She rubs her chin. "Connect and Detect? Connect and Reflect?" she says. "First one and then the other?"

"Sounds cute, like you, professor." He leans across the table and kisses her nose.

"First the kids become friends with someone. *Connect.* Then they learn stuff with and about the person. *Detect,* okay? Then they put it together, try to understand what's important there...they *reflect*, okay? *Connect, detect, reflect,* it sounds silly when you say it, but it could be...lots of fun and more...."

He sees students working side by side with the person who experienced the war...directly or indirectly. A soldier...his child...mother...whatever. To find out all this stuff and try to understand it together.

"I just remembered something little. About my father's

VA disability check...." Her father would sign it "under protest." How did it go? "'Under protest...because you bought my life with a lie...and $300 a month won't buy me a new life....' Funny how things come back. I couldn't read but he'd tell me every month what he was writing....Now why do you suppose I remembered that now?"

"Because we *connected, detected*, and *reflected* together," he forces a laugh. He is still imagining her hearing Ronnie's explanation about his check each month. Her skinny legs running around the house, her chubby hands foraging for coins to help pay for her father's new life?

"Don't laugh at me...or I won't tell you what I think should come next."

"I know already."

Was it just that she gave him the confidence to think or did she beam her thoughts to him? He thinks of Ernie in front of the barracks saying, Beams and waves, why not? He smiles remembering Ernie's shy, hopeful smile.

"Oh, yeah. Tell me if you know it!" she says.

"And then...after they connect with people and learn their stories and understand with them how war shaped them, made them...or unmade them...then they do something with that discovery?" he says. "Is that what you're thinking? They tell people about it?" He likes it. With this last part, all the hard work of the kids and their persons, their informants, their friends...wouldn't just sit there...."

"You read my mind!" she says. "They *project* it into the world."

He teased her, he called her Professor and Pup and Associate and a lot of silly things. But she was amazing to him. A little goofy girl, and then a goddamn genius, and sometimes both in the same second...in the same sentence. She'd just put everything important about teaching into words. The muddled inklings and tangled musings and longings he'd tossed somewhere, and she'd found.

He imagines out loud how the last part could work. The

kids could teach the rest of the class everything they've learned about a particular war from their person. Or maybe they could go on local TV or radio shows. Or publish a little monthly newspaper. *The War Reporter, The War Gazette?* With stories of wars...wars near and far. In the words of local people. Hand them out at the movies, the supermarket, on street corners?

"I like that," she says. "Like Jehovah's Witnesses," she laughs. "And it feels kind of holy, don't you think. Saving history. Saving the truth. Move over, *Watchtower*...we're coming through. *War Watch* coming through!"

*"War and Peace Watch?"* he says.

"People would learn about war...and want peace forever?" she cries, clapping her hands.

He remembers a letter she sent him in the desert. How she had a feeling this would be the last war ever.

"We could publish your letters," he says.

"Some of them," she squeals. "Not all of them!"


They stay in the motel that Darlene suggested. While Lily reads one of Doc's books in bed, he paces between the bathroom and the window. Like Homer, he thinks, on the pier at Jubayl, back and forth, back and forth, mobilizing himself before battle. But he was mobilizing for *after* battle. For peace maybe! Teaching history, knowing history was a matter of life and death! Finding the road to the past, mapping it, leading the kids down it and back, was not just a job...but his duty...in a new corps he was joining. Marching back and forth in the room, he feels pumped with hope, not just for himself and his life, but for the whole world—messed-up, confused, battered, but maybe...maybe fixable! It had happened again. She'd marched in and his fears had flown away, like they were scared of the midget.

Operation Connect!—maybe they could call it that. He sees the stages clearly: *connect, detect, reflect, project.* And another one, he thinks. *Protect.* They all linked together. People work together (connect) to locate experiences and artifacts of war (detect), then figure out what they mean (reflect), then tell other people the truths they've found (project), so that history doesn't repeat itself (protect)? Dr. Moser—creator of the CEDAR method—would probably go for the schematic, rhyme and all. And the basic process... evolving "from personal connection...to public engagement!" Isn't that how Moser would put it?

How would a sequence work? Juniors or seniors would work with public documents and other official material? Congressional testimonies, executive orders? Maybe even some Freedom of Information Act material from the Department of State, Department of Defense? What the government knew before Desert Storm about various medicines and munitions they used, like pyridostigmine bromide and depleted uranium? Why and when certain strategies got decided, like to strafe the Basra Highway? And again, engage the public with their discoveries? Town meetings? Policy proposals? Eventually, satisfied that it's getting clearer, he settles down beside her on the bed and writes a letter to Dr. Moser. "An update on the course as promised."

He includes just the basics of Operation Connect. A local, experiential approach with emphasis on people's stories and original material. Local community involved as both informants and audience. The many opportunities for public forums, purposeful learning, civic engagement around war as a personal and community experience. And next year possibly a junior or senior curriculum focusing on less personal, more official materials, with maybe an investigative reporting element? (He doesn't mention Freedom of Information Act because he doesn't want to scare the old codger.) They could explore various media for transmission of findings, from student publications, to educational journals, to community and public media, where possible forging partnerships. That's his thinking so far. He is very eager to get Dr. Moser's feedback and input. He feels so honored to join the school in this challenging time in our history. At the end he writes about peace. Learning about wars so there are no more….Imagine if we could do that?

At midnight they reach Nancy. She's convinced Sprain to keep Homer for a few more days, though they still say nothing is showing up. There's a new young doctor who is testing for everything. Homer's white count is up, and the doctor is thinking it may be a bacterial infection, in which case antibiotics should do the trick! His fever is down to 100. She's back in the house. She's feeling hopeful again. They're both catching up on sleep. Though the baby is kicking like crazy.

They were back on the right road, Lily thinks. Sometimes you think you're lost, but you're just on a detour, seeing new things, and then tired but wiser, voilá, you're back on course. In the dark, as they fall asleep she tells him what she's never told anyone, About her phases, her phrases for her phases. How all she wanted for them and their friends were the phases of a normal life. The other day, when she was crying so hard, it was because she was sure Homer would miss out on a *Future to Face*, a *Life to Live*. But now it felt like all that would be his. She felt hopeful now, like the kind of misery their pops and moms had endured was over for good. She didn't just hope but believed that a new era was actually beginning, an era of tranquility, that planets like people have phases, and that in the phase that had just begun the earth and its people got to live their natural lives all the way through. She feels so embarrassed telling Tony these things, but also so satisfied. Because she can tell him anything. How safe she feels being with him because of all the humans she knows, he is the one whose honesty and loyalty most resemble a dog's, which she means as the highest praise.

He says he never wants her to be ashamed of anything she thinks. That he loves everything she thinks. That he'd be lost without her phrases and phases.

In the morning, she wakes before him. The room-darkening drapes are drawn and she tiptoes to the bathroom, where, without waking him, she can turn on a light and read. She draws a bath and opens up her tote. *Knowing Your Bird* is on top, which seems so right. She feels as free as a bird this morning. Seeing him so happy and confident. Remembering how she told him everything last night and he heard her. Feeling so excited about every aspect of their future, including her professional development, which he respects as much as she does his! She's borrowed the book from Doc because more and more birds and reptiles are showing up at the clinic and in order to provide them with proper care and herself with a foundation for the pre-vet program she is eager to start, she must expand her knowledge base, which is totally mammal-centered. She is a quick reader and in an hour she's finished the book. There's a gray parrot that comes to Doc for vitamin treatments for lethargy, and the book has her thinking about the role of light in the life of the transplanted tropical bird. She has a gigantic reptile and amphibians book in her suitcase, but she doesn't want to go back and risk waking him, so she dips into her tote and brings up a magazine.

It's last month's *Bride Today*, and she finds an article that she hasn't read but that seems particularly apt for now. "Driving Your Marriage," it's titled. Think of life as a ride, it says. Think of your marriage as a car that you will be sitting in for a long ride. To minimize trade-ins and crashes, you need to ask yourself many things *before* you get in. Is my marriage/car beautiful inside and out? Is it comfortable to be in? Is it safe? Then when you're starting out, think about your fuel—is there enough love and understanding to take you on a long trip? Think about your glove compartment; do you have the road maps and directions for where you're heading—which is to say are you sufficiently oriented as individuals and as a couple, big-picture and small-picture, long-term and short-term. Are all your signals (directionals, brake lights, etc.) working—so that there is sufficient information/communication? Okay, then in the car, under the hood, you need to think about maintenance—regular check-ups and tune-ups and even overhauls. Marriage is complex with many mechanisms that need regular attention. Properly attended to, though, your marriage/car should last for the extensive trip that is marriage. She laughs. It is so ridiculous, she knows. But she gets a kick thinking that the last few days have given them a superior vehicle all around, along with improved preparedness and skills for a mighty long ride!

He calls her name, and she goes to him, spooning and giggling in his ear all the things she just read.

He calls her, Navigator.

"You'd be lost without me," she squeals.

"Lost without you," he says, lifting her nightshirt and asking where he should go.


At noon the phone rings and he grabs it. It's Nancy, he knows.

"Just calling to check in. His temperature is down. Probably from the antibiotic they put him on yesterday."

She's trying for cheerful chirps, but everything sounds like a scared yelp.

"Tell me," Tony says.

"There's not that much to tell. He's just a little moody, I guess. He says people are trying to kill him. He called me a dozen times yesterday to tell me that. It's probably just fatigue talking. I spoke to the nurse. She said that antibiotics can be very depleting."

"We'll come back," Tony says.

"Give it another day," she says. "Let's talk again later. I asked this smart young doctor if she thought there was something wrong with his brain and she said, 'Let's not jump to conclusions.' So let's not, Ton."

But the whole day he feels a conclusion gather in his mind and while Lily reads, he stays trying to sleep and not think.

In bed that night, Tony shakes and shivers in his sleep.

"You okay?" Lily says. Is he sick too? She feels his brow, but it's cool.

"A dream," he whispers.

"Just a dream?" she says. "That's it?"

"Just a dream," he mumbles. "Don't worry."

And she doesn't. Tomorrow *her* time begins. She falls off quickly, eager to sleep so she can wake refreshed. She has a million plans and only a couple of days.

It's not even six and the phone is ringing.

"It's what we want to do," Lily hears him say. "Just hang in there. It's probably just that he's not used to being home. Probably he's gotten used to having nurses wait on him. And when he feels bad, you know, he knows he can take it out on the person he's closest to."

"Bad?" Lily says when he hangs up. "He's bad? They sent him home? And he's acting crazy?"

She looks tragic, hopeless; her eyes droop like Roco's.

She imagines Homer lying on the couch, barking out terrible things. Like Ronnie used to. First you hack the arms, then the legs, then the head…then when you got all the parts in a nice neat pile, you light the fire….You got that? These things happen…for real….Arms, legs, head, fire! Even when she'd cover her head with a ski cap and hide under the bed, she'd hear her father's every word.

He can see the fear on her face even as she tries to cut it with a smile.

"There's so much to be done," she says. A pre-honeymoon vacation is often not a real vacation. You're in a relaxed setting, away from everyday stress, but you're still

185

tying up all the loose pieces. "So much to be tied up," she says. Her stomach feels tied up in knots.

Big Lily. Little Lily. That's how he thought of her sometimes. She was small but so brave and bustling sometimes that he saw her as a giant...like a float in the Macy's Thanksgiving Day parade on TV. This morning, she looks tiny and scared, just like she used to when she'd hide in his house before it was her house too. He kisses her hard, puts his tongue deep inside her. He wishes he didn't have to go, but could just stay inside her. Guard her from the inside from all the hurt and disappointment waiting to pounce.

"No need for both of us to go," he says. "I saw a Rent-a-Wreck down the road. I know you have things to do."

"I do," she says. Her part was to include shopping. A surprise pre-wedding gift for him. The wedding clothes for both of them.

His chest is still golden from the summer. Ever since they were little, it has been her favorite part of him, and now she nuzzles it, and kisses it with gratitude.

They agree that she will call him every night. And every morning. It shouldn't take more than a couple of days to settle Homer down. If the physical symptoms are really fading and it's really only psychological now, they'll have it under control in no time. Then he'll meet her and they can get back to their trip.

"Test drive?" he says, trying to remember. Suddenly yesterday seems months away.

"Test is when you're not sure if the car is for you!" she says. "You mean practice drive not test drive, silly."

# 12. The Dress

If Tony couldn't go, Lily would have sniffed her way back to Monuten, sat at Nancy's feet, guarded her as long as she needed her, and then some. She is a loyal mutt, and if no one else could go to be with Nancy, she would have gone for sure. But Tony did go, and she will take his word that her presence isn't necessary.

What she's doing now *is* necessary, and she packs quickly. She is compelled by love and loyalty, not only to Tony, whom she wants to marry in a way that reflects all the feeling inside her now, but going back, back, back, to *her*, to Connie, who never got to marry or to have a lasting love.

She makes it to Washington in just over two hours, and in just a few more minutes, it seems, she's on the outskirts of Baltimore and exiting the highway. She remembers the exit, which sort of surprises her and sort of doesn't. She has tried to forget everything about her time with Aunt Sally, but seeing the sign—Hemlock Avenue—she knows that's it. Because she used to think, Hemlock Avenue, Poison Avenue, how she wished to poison them all, or herself, if they wouldn't let her go.

She was eight when she was *kidnapped*. That's how she thought of it. It wasn't right for a "stranger" to keep her when there was family, her aunt had said, packing her up and hauling her away from Mimi. To Lily, though, Aunt Sally was the stranger, hiding her in her poison house. Each day seemed the terrible part of a different fairy tale. She was Gretel, locked in the witch's house, all alone, pining for Hansel and home. She was an orphaned changeling waiting for her rightful guardian to appear. She was Rapunzel locked in a tower, Cinderella enslaved in misery. Each day a different story, but always always she was there and captive.

She remembers the number, 77 Hemlock—because she always thought how seven was a lucky number and maybe her luck would change—and she finds the house easily. But nothing about the house—an unremarkable two-family attached to a row of identical houses—rings a bell. Over the years, when thoughts of this time invaded, she remembered a vast gloomy house of giant stones, never this hum-drum Depression-era gray-tan brick row house. She climbs out of the car, looks up at the top floor where they'd lived, then slowly climbs the steps to the second-floor porch.

An iron gate blocks her entry, and now she remembers the bars, her standing on the other side of them, dreaming of escape. The smell of the place—there it is again—a smell not easily forgotten. Mold and... something else. She sniffs the air to get it right. Vinegar, yes, that was it. She used to call it "witch liquor," and it was the basic ingredient of all her aunt's brews—witch soup, witch shampoo, witch mouthwash, the latter used on her often when she would yell that she belonged with Mimi, not here with a mean old witch who just made believe she was her aunt. The smell is repulsive, but it tells her that her aunt is still alive. She will breathe through her mouth to minimize the effect like she used to, she remembers now, then quickly do what she's come to do, and then fly away.

She had right on her side. It belonged to her and taking it would balance the scales, set the record straight. Her mom had shown her pictures of her grandma and then Sal in a long spill of ivory satin, with seed pearls and lace. When she and Ronnie tied the knot, her mom was going to wear it, and then Lily, when her time came. Aunt Sally used to have the gown on a tailor's dummy in the little room off the front hall; and when she lived here, the rare times she was home alone, Lily would pat it and think of her mother, her satiny skin. Once Lily crawled under the skirt, imagining her mother was all around her, an angel of white light enveloping her. Then Sally walked in the room, saw her legs peeking out, and yanked her out, telling her she was never ever to go near her gown again.

A head appears in the front window.

"Who's there?" it says.

"It's me, Aunt Sally."

Then Aunt Sally walks onto the little porch and opens the gate. She extends her hand, then thinks better and offers her cheek. Vinegar cheek, Lily laughs to herself, holding her breath and pecking quickly.

"Well, look what the cat brought in," Aunt Sally says. "Well, what do you know. What brings you here?"

"I'm getting married," she says, smiling. Her aunt would see that she had been wrong about her, and her mother. She remembers her poison words. A tramp. A bastard. Worthless. She'll regret that and give her what is coming to her.

Aunt Sally nods. "When?"

"In June. Nothing formal, but it will be a real wedding."

"Good for you. Who's the lucky fellow?"

"Tony. You remember?"

"Your kinda brother?"

"Kinda. But now kinda not," Lily laughs.

"Whatever turns you on," Aunt Sally says. "Funny…they were little ones together too—Constance and Ronald. But it didn't work out for them. They didn't have the strength. They were weak in so many departments, poor things."

On the ride, Lily has coached herself in restraint. She will not fight. Fighting would only sabotage her plan. But the unfairness and cruelty of Sally's words rile her and she can't help but say, "It's easy to judge others. What's hard is to judge fairly." Which you never did and for which I will never forgive you, she wants to say but doesn't.

"Where'd you learn that?" Aunt Sally laughs.

"I'm a grown-up, Aunt Sally. I know things."

Like the difference between fact and opinion, she thinks. Which you don't know, which your daughters, Lois and

Bernadette, the *witchettes*, never knew. How mad she still was! But why not! Day after day, they had plagued her with their cruel judgments—and punishments. Every Friday, they inflicted their weekly report card, evaluating her Personality, Social Skills, Sense of Humor, Intelligence, Dress and Appearance. Each week it was the same determination: she was Unsatisfactory in all. And each week an "Overall Summary" would report: "Lily is weak in all departments and shows no signs of ever improving." There was space on the card for a parent's signature, but since she was an orphan, *she* had to sign that she had read the report and agreed with its contents, or else be detained—locked on the front porch till they said it was okay to come back in. She'd sign, but always write below, "Signed Under Protest." She laughs because she knows now where that came from. And because she's pleased: her father had given her something of use. Which is more than she can say of Aunt Sally!

"Well, I have a very positive opinion of you. A bona fide bride with a June wedding no less. A far cry from your ma. Going steady, then shacked up."

"It's not fair to say, 'shacked up,' Aunt Sal," she says. "We were a real family. We just had bad luck. With the war and all."

"Your opinion," Aunt Sally says. "Which you have a right to just as I have a right to mine."

Lily has a woolen mitten in her pocket and she thinks how satisfying it would be to stuff it in her aunt's mouth, to silence her and maybe make her gag and choke, then knock her head against the brick wall. But she remembers her coaching.... Stay on purpose. Gown...gown...gown, she thinks. "Okay," she says.

"Okay, what?"

"Okey-dokey," Lily says and laughs. Okey-dokey is what she used to say to everything Aunt Sally or one of the witchettes said to her. At first she said it to be cheerful so they'd like her, and then when she saw they never would she said it to provoke. Food's waiting. Okey-dokey. You're ungrateful. Okey-dokey. You're Stupid. Okey-dokey. We hate you. Okey-dokey. Okey-dokey, okey-dokey, okey-dokey, she'd cry—until they'd lock her on the porch.

The first few times they put her there, she just stood there studying the distance from the *tower* to the ground, trying to assess if she could survive leaping to the pavement to escape, or at least fall in a way to assure a quick and certain death. In time, though, she used her time in detention to carefully plot her escape. And as the cousins cackled inside, she'd practice crawling unseen to the side of the porch, where she'd review her final exit—one quick jump onto the hemlock bushes, then a dash on tip-toe to the back alley. Okey-dokey—she said it every chance she got so that they would throw her out here again and again, until she could muster up her courage to execute the plan.

"Marriage is underestimated in our self-indulgent society. My marriage to your Uncle Bob is my proudest accomplishment."

As far as Lily can remember, marriage was her aunt's only accomplishment, and judging from the state of her apartment and her kids, Aunt Sally failed miserably in it. Uncle Bob was a refrigeration salesman who Lily saw only fleetingly, when he'd come back from his Maine to Miami route, sleeping for days, then taking off again. Aunt Sally was a poor housekeeper, her vinegary foods mostly inedible, her cleaning—whose prime technique was application of the vinegar-soaked rag—would never hit the mark, streaking but never removing vast stretches of grime.

"Your uncle and I were very happy. He traveled and I missed him and him me. But there were wonderful reunions and much mutual respect. He never drank. And of course never used drugs, not even those no-doze pills which lots of long-distance salesmen with less character used and abused. I miss him now that he's passed but I have very rich marital memories."

"I'm sorry he's gone," Lily says.

"My girls have left me too."

"Dead?" Lily whispers. She used to wish them dead but now she feels nothing.

"Lois ran off with a drunk drummer. Bernadette is a lesbian. I guess it could be said that you're what's left...and here you are. I guess it could be said that you're following in *my* footsteps," Aunt Sally says. She produces a big yellow smile.

Lily smiles back, glad she hasn't risen to too many baits. Maybe her aunt was actually softening. Maybe soon she'd ask her inside, they'd peek inside the little room with the gown....Lily could say, Oh, that's still there?

"Got your gown yet?"

"Gown?" Lily says. Had the witch read her mind? Next, would she cackle and say, I have a beautiful gown, which you can't even touch. Or was the old witch melting, and forming into something new, something aunt-like?

Lily shakes her head, tentatively. "I don't have a gown...."

"I wore a lovely gown which was my mother's."

"I sort of remember," Lily says.

"Satin to the floor. V-neck. Very classic. I keep it in my sewing room to give me solace. I could see you in something like that."

"You could?"

"I could let you try in on."

"You would?"

"Well, come on," Sally says. "You may as well come on in. For a *fitting*," she laughs.

The house had always been messy with piles of things on every surface. But it's worse than ever, with mountains of clothing and towels and mesas of newspapers and magazines.

Lily walks behind Aunt Sally. The hair on the back of her head is a mess. Short here, long there, the botched handiwork of someone with no one in the world to turn to zip you up or trim you or check how you look from behind. She feels a stab of pain on her aunt's behalf, which she's never felt before. She will try on the dress and if it fits, wrap it up carefully, just like her aunt would want. Then she would clean Aunt Sally's house for her and then take her to the beauty parlor. They wouldn't have molten moments exactly, but improved relations because the old witch was changing.

It's been so long since she's talked to Nancy, her main confidante, about the wedding specifics and she feels the urge to tell her aunt what she has planned. The boldly colored wildflowers from Blue Field. The presence of children named Abigail or Gregory, and others too. The simple hearty food such as Mrs. Molto's lasagna and Mimi's chili and Nancy's tropical fruit salad; she'd already gathered the recipes and Marie Edwards, who catered parties from home, had agreed to prepare it all and run the show at a friends and family rate. And then, of course, the wedding cake—a gigantic version of their favorite Stoehmer's fudge layer cake, rising as high as it could go, and topped with daisies to match her simple daisy bride's bouquet.

She taps her aunt's bony back.

"What?" Sal says. "What do you want?"

"Want me to describe the wedding I have in mind? Or you want to wait and see for yourself?"

Months ago, not in relation to Aunt Sally, but thinking about co-workers at Docs and neighbors on their block, she had decided on a policy of "inclusion." Nothing bugged her more than the stingy mentality in the magazine articles on guest selection. If people wanted to be at her wedding, they belonged there. That was how *she'd* select.

"You mean I'm invited?" Sal says.

"If you'd like," Lily says and laughs because she almost said, If you're nice.

The sewing room is cluttered but no more than it used to be with the same exact contents: a gray corduroy recliner that looks like a small rhinoceros, a rusty ironing board with a cover of scorched violets, a sewing machine that never worked. And the gown.

"Here, try it on," Sal says, taking it off the dummy.

Lily slips it over her head. Even with her jeans and flannel shirt, it billows out. Room enough for two of her, she thinks. She is the smallest one ever in her family and she stands on her toes not to drag the hem on the floor, and tiptoes to the closet-door mirror and smiles. She is a size one or two, with her period sometimes a size three, and this must be a size ten or twelve, but it could be altered. She loves the way the ivory satin blends with her ivory skin, the way the seed pearls shine like the palest strands of her hair.

"You look like Constance."

Lily nods. "I feel like she's here. Looking at me," Lily says. She points to the mirror. "I feel like she's there, you know, admiring…the dress."

"You know she's dead, right?"

She nods weakly. She'd never heard the words before.

When she graduated from elementary school, Mimi bought her a white organza dress with a triple tiered skirt and had a party for her afterward in the yard. Mimi had spent a fortune on Lily's favorite foods and invited the whole block, and Lily held herself together until the last guest left. Then she lost it. She knew Ronnie had died the year before. But she had expected Connie to show up for her big day. Especially now that Ronnie was dead and there was no danger.

Mimi knew from the silent shaking what Lily was thinking. She said: She would have come if….

Lily said: She always has an excuse.

Mimi said: There's no easy way to say this, sweetheart. It happened so fast on the heels of your dad's accident.

Lily covered her ears and ran to her room, locking the door.

In the morning, Mimi said, You want to talk? But Mimi

and Tony had given her riding lessons for graduation, and she told Mimi she wanted to concentrate on horses for a while if she didn't mind.

"Lung cancer, from secondary smoke," her aunt says. "She begged me to come to the hospital. It was really tough, though, being with her the way she looked."

Lily looks everywhere but at her aunt's face, the skinny lips producing the terrible words—*Yellow, weak, bald.... You can't imagine...what it was like to sit across from that.*

"I would have gone to her if she had called me," Lily says.

Her mother wouldn't have had to beg. I would have begged to be with her, she wants to say. I would have given anything to kiss her cheek, stroke her head. She tries to imagine her mother's head, yellow here, bald there. I would have said, Poor darling, can I get anything for you?

"I would have been happy to be with her. I would have slept by her bed and been glad for every minute I had with her."

"Sure, sure," Aunt Sally says. "You say that now but you didn't see her. Or hear her moaning and babbling about how crazy she was about you and about that Mimi. And there I was the one visiting but every other sentence she had to rub in that she was so glad you had *that* woman. How an intelligent and creative child like you needed someone who appreciated her. I'm not a dummy. I knew she meant that I couldn't or hadn't when I took you in. She looked so pitiful that I didn't get into the fact that she wasn't any great shakes in the care-giving department. But she knew that in her heart of hearts. She kept rationalizing what she had done. You know, how she was sure he'd kill her if she took you but he'd never harm you. How when you went to stay with that woman, he told that woman never to let her near you, or there'd be trouble. She thought he'd overdose soon enough, at which point it would be safe to come and get you. When that happened, she was already sick."

Lily touches the mirror, the forehead in the mirror.

"Poor Mommy," she says and watches the mouth in the mirror widen to a smile.

Her mother was dead, but she seems there, too, smiling. She presses her lips against the mirror and kisses, little tender pecks, like the ones they used to give each other for good morning and good night with always a few extras thrown in for good luck. And then a longer kiss, a goodbye kiss. But not a goodbye forever, she thinks. I have your gown. You'll be with me, marching down the aisle, and after...in my happy life.

"It's okay, Mommy, it's okay," she whispers.

"Hey, what the hell are you doing? Get away from that mirror. You'll soil my gown!"

How perfect—the queen of grime screaming about a little dust. "Sorry. I'll have it cleaned," Lily says. "Before and after."

"Before and after?" Sally says.

Lily smiles. "My wedding," she says. "June 18 or 19. Write it down."

"You got the wrong idea. I said you could try it on. I can't let you take it. If your mother had married and worn it, you'd be entitled to wear it. But otherwise it's not proper."

Lily says, "That's totally wrong. Those are stupid rules. The only rules that matter are those that rule the heart." She just thought that up, but she likes it, believes it. "The rules of the heart are the rules I follow," she adds.

"Very nice. That's your approach and I have mine. Now give me back my gown."

"*My* gown," Lily laughs. "That's what my heart tells me."

Out the front door, onto the porch, she runs. The gate to the stairs is locked so she races to the side of the house, climbs on the ledge, then flies down to the bushes.

"My mom's and mine," she calls up to the porch, lifting the skirt as she takes the corner fast.

She knows the entire mall is watching her, a girl in a wedding dress and parka and sneakers, but she's had no time or place to change, and she doesn't really want to anyway. The satin weighs a ton and her back is aching, as well as her arms from holding up the skirt, but after all the years of lacking and longing, she is not about to take it off so fast. She feels like one of those heroes in that book of world myths Mimi used to read to them, who endure heinous conditions and battles to get something remarkable—a special sword, a ring, a shawl. So what if all she did was enter a stinky house, fight a major bitch, and take off with a dress. It was a pretty dress, but that wasn't the point. Fighting for what was hers was the point, and winning.

She races past strolling shoppers feeling super powerful and brave, like now everything she wished for could happen. Homer would be well. All their plans would proceed as scheduled: baby shower, baby birth, wedding. Then her own children and their special celebrations! And it would start with the dress she'd wear, which her mother should have worn at the wedding she should have had to start the life she'd deserved!

The Harbor Mall has it all. A TJ Maxx, a Saks, cute kiosks, a mile of shops with everything she needs. Party goods, baby furniture, clothing of every type and price. Usually when she's upset she window shops at the Monuten Mountain Galleria, walking up and down each level till all the colors and textures, the poses and displays, sweep away the heap of misery that brought her in. Today, though, she will shop for real. Compare items, make large purchases, maybe even impulse shop, at the end, if there is any money left over. A funny book, a few crazy key chains, some outrageous sunglasses, and not at Valley Dollar, her usual haunt, but at Hallmark or Kooky Gifts or both. She imagines she is one of those rich girls from the Freemont Estates on the other side of Monuten with their wads of credit cards and flamboyant show-and-tell sessions on the school steps, flashing their boots and vests, digital cameras and cellular phones. *Shop till you drop,* they'd giggle to each other. *Shop till you drop,* she chants to herself, not sure if she is saying it aloud, and, if so, people think she's nuts or just a richie—with one of those new cell phone ear attachments that keeps your hands free to get at your wallets and the keys for your SUV. I'm on my way to Saks, she says into the air, aware that this is the first—and probably last—time in her life she can utter the words. But she has saved up all year and wants to buy the very best.

First, there's her pre-wedding gift for Tony. Several articles, using pretty much the same logic as proponents of the pre-honeymoon, suggested it as a way for the couple to express their affection, which too often gets buried in the wedding blitz. She knows exactly what she wants—a blazer he can wear to school, something light in weight but dark in color that can take him from fall through spring. If the price is right, she can buy him two so that when one is in the cleaners, he'll still be set. He can wear it at the wedding, too, and any other special event that arises. She wants it to be a quality blazer, which is why she starts at Saks.

The first one is the one, she knows. A navy cashmere with brown bone-like buttons. She strokes the soft wool and imagines Tony in it, striding to the chalkboard, looking as composed and confident as a senator. Then coming home, feeling tired but accomplished, throwing himself on Mrs. Molto's velvet loveseat and pulling her down on him, tucking her inside the jacket. But it costs two thousand dollars.

"Scottish cashmere lasts a lifetime," the salesman says, seeing her disappointment.

She takes out her solar calculator: even if it lasts only ten years, that's 200 workdays a year x 10=2000. 2000 into $2000 is a dollar a day.

"A dollar a day," she smiles and the salesman smiles back.

"I never heard it put that way...but that's probably right."

"Well, I'll certainly put that in the blender," she says, turning red because wasn't the expression really "put it in the hopper"? Embarrassed, she makes for the elevator, surrounded by a group of Fremont Estate types. Blender was right, actually, as in smash up that plan. It was out of her team. League, she means. Totally out of the question.

Sir Sport on the second level has one that has 20% cashmere and costs only $500, but that's most of what's in her account and so she walks over to TJ Maxx. Even there, though, the blazers start at $200. Had she not imagined him in the Saks blazer looking so hot, she might not have noticed that the fabric on even the ones for $299 was almost as shiny and flimsy as her fourteen dollar cheapo high school graduation gown. Besides, he also needs slacks and shirts and ties and shoes. Two blazers and two slacks and a pair of shoes will cost more than she has. There is a Modern Male store that has jackets for $99. But they smell like burnt plastic and make her sneeze.

Totally unacceptable, she thinks. And she takes herself to the food court, to a little table at the side of the court, where she takes out her check book to look at her balance, as if staring at it long enough will make it grow. Seven hundred eighty dollars. It had seemed like a fortune till now.

Her eyes well up. What a total loser she was. Her hokey magazines were making her into the biggest jerk in the world. A pre-wedding gift. A surprise of a new wardrobe. Running up a debt of a couple of thousand dollars, when she was already in debt for the baby's crib, the layette, the paint and rugs, etc. for her house. She was so level-headed and sensible, and then suddenly she'd go on some lunatic loser campaign.

In a gesture of dismay and disbelief, she shakes her head and little drops of water fly around. She feels like one of

Doc's dogs, when she bathed them and they shook water all over her like they were bathing her back. She laughs, which makes her feel spunky, and she ventures to the nearest counter and buys a slice of pizza, then goes back to her table. How would she ever find a way to buy him the gift that told him how much she thought of him and his future as a teacher? Especially now with his new curriculum.

Where there's a will there's a way. That was her motto, a gift from Mimi, which she carries with her most days. She hears Mimi's voice, cheerful and steady, like a kindergarten teacher, saying it. She remembers the feel of her hands on her face, arms, legs as she lay on the shag rug as limp as her Raggedy-Ann, wondering if she had died, Mimi pawing her till she knew she was a living girl again, then lifting her and carrying her into her bed, where she said she would always help her, if she promised to help herself too. She told her a secret—that not too long ago she'd thrown herself on the rug and cried for three days and three nights till there were inches of water all around and the rug was almost ruined. They laughed. So then I had two problems. Did that make sense? They agreed it did not. So I changed my attitude. Want me to help you change attitudes? When Lily said, Please, she rocked her in her arms and said, Repeat after me, Where there's a will, there's a way.

It had always worked for Lily. When Mimi turned forty, Lily decided to buy her a new van, a newish van to replace the junk-heap she was driving. But scouring lots and classifieds, the best she could find was a three-year-old Ram for $10,000. Still she kept her positive attitude and then someone bringing his cats to Doc's for a check up said he was moving west. Driving out in your old van? she said. She had spotted it in front, an old orange VW, dent-free and dazzling. Nope, selling. It had only 50,000 miles and he wanted only $1200. She drove to the bank, withdrew her life savings, got a money order, then drove him and the cats home, where he transferred the title.

Mimi, Mimi—how beautiful she looked as she said, I will always help you, always be there. When she was growing up in Mimi's house, Mimi was often not around. She was busy with her births, afraid to turn away any patients, not only because she loved catching her babies, but because they needed the money. Babies came at all hours, and so dinners were often late or makeshift, holidays often celebrated the day after, parents days, school plays, and soccer games often missed. But she and Tony hardly cared. Not only because they had each other but because when Mimi wasn't with them, she still seemed there. He'd say, What do you think she would want us to make for supper? And Lily would come up with something that seemed right. Probably because he thought about his father so much, she more than Tony seemed to have direct access to Mimi's mind and ways.

She closes her eyes to imagine her. In a soft, furry turtleneck sweater that matches her eyes. She imagines reaching for her arm, saying, Please help me. She imagines the feel of her sleeve when she touches it. Cashmere, or angora. Then she whispers, That's it. Thank you. Not with words, but with the softness of her sweater, Mimi had told her what she needed to know.

She finds an old phone book at the phone booth on the wall and studies the listing of Baltimore thrift shops. Every house of worship, medical center, and disease seems to have one, but which is near, which is best? St. Joseph's? Judea? Mercy Medical? Sufferers of Joint Diseases? Where should she go? And again, it's Mimi who guides her. Her miserable year stuck in Aunt Sally's house taught Lily little about Baltimore. But she always remembers Johns Hopkins, not the place, but the name, because Aunt Sally used to say that her daughters were sure to go to Johns Hopkins because they studied so hard but she, being unruly, would never ever be admitted to such an outstanding institution. I don't want to go to snotty, disgusting John Hopkins, Lily would cry. Johns, not John, Sally would correct her. But now she did want to go. You go to the thrift shops near where the rich live or work, Mimi used to say. She finds the listing she wants. Hopkins Exchange, Inc.—the Charity Shop of Johns Hopkins University.

Hopkins Exchange, she learns when she calls and asks if they have any men's blazers, has the largest selection of used traditional attire, including blazers for men, women, and children, in the Washington-Baltimore area. She gets directions—the highway to North Charles to Centre—and she drives there in a state of joyous anticipation. Thrift shops—they had enriched their lives forever. Mimi rarely took them with her to her shops—the few times she had, Tony held his nose and Lily gagged, and on the ride home they both declared it the stinkiest place in the world. But Mimi haunted the thrift shops, swooping down to seize the best, which she immediately washed or dry-cleaned, presenting Tony and her with thrilling trophies of the rich world. Ski sweaters with reindeer. Jeans and leather jackets. Bright yellow raingear and once matching seersucker suits. Mimi's favorite thrift store was one near the medical center, where she said lots of stuff came from doctors' families and was top quality. 100% wool, full-fashioned, hand-knit, made in Italy, made in France, or England, or Scotland or the Shetland Islands. Tony never listened but Lily couldn't get enough of Mimi's lessons in quality. Ooh, woven in Ireland. Oh, thank you, thank you, she'd say.

Hold your nose, she coaches herself now, laughing, as she pushes open the mahogany doors. But the smell of lavender greets her, and though it is dark inside, it is not a grim, dank dark like those smelly places of her childhood, but a cheerful dark of burnished hardwood and forest green mohair, like the shop in Georgetown, where Mimi took them once to escape a blizzard, buying each of them a handkerchief with their initial embroidered in gold.

The sections have names, like that store. Regency and Country Lane, and Tailor Row, which looms just beyond the entry with ten racks of men's jackets and blazers, arranged by color. The first blue blazer is his size, and so is the second, and the third. They are only ten dollars apiece, one a light wool, one a gabardine, one cashmere and wool; in all of them, she knows, he will look radiant, his tawny skin and bright green eyes set against the navy. There are unworn or hardly worn Oxford shirts at $3 a piece and she buys ten, which was the price of two at most, even on sale at TJ Maxx's, which is at least 40% off to begin with. Chinos and slacks are four dollars and she buys five. And ties are one dollar and she buys a half a dozen. Half of the stuff is from Brooks Brothers, which she's heard of and another big chunk from Bailey's of Baltimore, which doesn't ring a bell, but which she can tell, from the touch, is just as good.

He's set. School-set. Grown-up-set. Gorgeous-guy-set.

She leaves her selections at the counter and moves on to Regency.

Tuxedos and ball gowns, a row of each.

There's a tux, from Brooks Brothers too, with a shirt and bowtie included for ten dollars. Maybe, for fun, even though it will be in the house, he'll want to dress up for the wedding. There's one a size up, which is Homer's current size, and she decides to buy it for Homer, and one a size up from that too, which she takes as well, in case Homer puts on some weight. He could wear it at the wedding or maybe just some special fun occasions they think up when things settle down.

Three blazers, five pairs of slacks, ten shirts, twelve ties, three tuxes and she hasn't yet reached a hundred dollars. She can see why Mimi went crazy in these places.

And now what?

"Do you have bridal party dresses?" she asks a young clerk. He is tall and thin, milk-chocolate colored and confidently gay, and he looks down at her and laughs.

"Come, little one," he says, taking her hand and leading her to the petite section. "This is you," he says.

He has pulled out an ivory silk gown with a sweetheart

bodice. Its big sash makes it look like a child's party dress or Halloween costume. It is a size 1, her size, and she holds it up and spins around, laughing, like she's playing dress up.

"Sixty, including the veil," he says. "Wish it was my size," he laughs.

"Wish I needed one," she says, handing it back to him. "I meant bridesmaids' dresses in case we go fancy. I mean I'm getting married but I have my gown." She opens her parka to show him.

"That is not you. You are a little person and need a little gown and the one in my arms is little and precious."

"This one," she touches her skirt, "was my grandmother's."

"They should have buried her in it," he laughs.

"That's not nice," she says.

"Fair enough, but neither is that dress."

"It was going to be my mother's…but they wouldn't let her wear it. My aunt that is because my mother was… different."

"So forget it. Look, I was joking before. It is a lovely, heavy Italian silk with classic lines. But you're lost in it. You shouldn't be lost in your wedding dress. Consider another option?"

He has a very certain eye, very definite opinions, but she likes the way his voice goes up at the end of sentences, like he's not sure and wants your input too.

"Maybe you're right," she says. The important thing was not necessarily wearing it, but the right to wear it if she wanted to.

"Start fresh?" he says. "Slip this one on?"

She shakes her head. "Don't worry, I know value when I see it and I'm definitely going to buy it. Someone will definitely wear it," she says.

That's what Mim always used to say about her thrift shop purchases: I couldn't pass it up. Someone will use it. Lily suspects she will use it. In which case the family gown would still get used, by her daughter and/or Nancy's daughter, both of whom are bound to be bigger than she is. But she can't pull herself from the old gown just yet. Lost in it, he said. She doesn't feel lost, but found in it. Like Connie and she have found each other again. That old feeling, like Connie is surrounding her with softness.

"Make sure that someone is you?" he says, turning to a long stretch of pastel flounce. "Bridesmaids' Lane," he laughs.

She laughs, too, giddy at the sight of organza and taffeta, satin and voile on either side of the aisle. She finds Nancy's size and selects a short chocolate brown satin strapless gown tucked amid pinks and yellows, and a matching gown for Mimi but with three-quarter sleeves, which Mimi claims, along with the A line skirt, is a lost classic. There's a brown strapless the next size up and she grabs that one too in case Nancy doesn't take off the baby weight right away.

"It's silly," she says, "since it's in our house. But it will be so fun dressing up."

Maybe she'd write an article when she was done—about a new solution to the nagging old problem of dressing the wedding party. Countless articles and letters in her magazines spoke to the challenge—the burden to your favorite people of expensive dresses and tuxedos, how to show your appreciation in the wedding party gifts. She would explain about thrift shops in areas frequented by the wealthy. Suggest the bride buy all the clothing there. Dry clean, then give as gifts to members of wedding party. Talk about double-whammies. She tells him about her idea for an article one day.

"I like the way you think...like me. But, hey, girlfriend, what if everyone followed your advice? There'd be no inventory left for us poor gals?"

"Maybe you do a means test," she says. "No one with income over a certain level can buy from the fancy section of thrifts...."

"Perfect, girlfriend," he says. "Perfect solution. Let's co-author?"

He says his name is Sean and although he is now an associate at Hopkins Exchange, his goal is to be a wedding and gala specialist. Articles would be great for his PR package.

"And testimonials," she says, "from people who like your work. That's what you should really look for. And I'm sure you'll get tons as soon as you start." She knows the importance of recommendations from her bride magazines, and from work, where most of the new clients say that they've been referred by some pet owner.

"I've started," he says. "With you, girlfriend. My first and favorite client?" For nine dollars an hour, he'll do her makeup, flowers, music, whatever she needs.

"It's going to be amazing. Unless Aunt Sally comes and spoils it," she says. "Like that fairy tale where that bitch-witch intrudes 'cause she wasn't invited to a christening I think it was...."

"You must take charge?" he says. "Say, Off with you, horrible thoughts. Like pantyhose falling down, heels catching on trains, tripping and ripping your dress and/or breaking your leg. Be gone, all horrible situations and people?"

"And witches?" she says. "That woman is a witch. If she shows up...oh, my God."

"And there are no witches," he says. "Not around me. Only good fairies?" he laughs. In the morning he is going to Wilmington to visit his brother or else he'd suggest meeting again tomorrow to explore her preferences in colors, flowers, and music. He looks so excited, that she doesn't remind him that it's just a house wedding, a house and yard wedding, a two house and two yard wedding at most.

However small, with him helping it would be small-substantial not small-pitiful. How lucky to meet him now, when all her peeps had too much on their plate to help or even think about wedding planning.

As she is paying, he taps her shoulder. "A little something…from our Heirloom section. Imagine it with a champagne punch and lemons and daisies aloft…?"

"That's the biggest bowl I've ever seen," she squeals. "And I bet it's Irish crystal." She has no idea what Irish crystal looks like but she means it's beautiful and best best quality, she can tell from its shimmer, and he is an angel to think of her!

"I like to find a way to express it when I like people?"

"I like you!" she says, noticing his eyes are huge and more than a little sad. Like maybe he doesn't really have a brother or anyone. "I'll call you soon," she says.

"I'll call you too?"


She finds a motel near the harbor. Because the clothing can't fit in the trunk and she is afraid that the gorgeous glamorous satin and fairy-land voile will attract robbers, she carries it all inside, heaping it on the side of the bed where Tony would have slept were he with her.

She is glad, actually, that Tony wasn't with her when she shopped. Not only because she can now surprise him, but because he is not a good shopper, and chances are, were he there, she would have rushed and never met Sean and never gotten all the goodies and the promise of near-professional advice and support.

At night, when she can't reach Tony, she imagines they are together in the room. Dressing each other in their wedding clothes, declaring their love in the dark, then stripping and making love till morning. She will always treasure those long confessions and collaborations about life and work that have brought them closer than ever on this incredible trip. But except for that one amazing morning when he called her Navigator, their pre-honeymoon, cut short as it was, has been limited in that other department. Tonight, she is heady with longing. They have never had a youthful romance together. Best friends, then pledged for life. Now she wants to have it all. And knows she will.

All night she wakes in starts to check that the clothing is still there, that her life is really on its course. And to check on the time; she wants to call him at the crack of dawn. At seven, she reaches him at home.

She'd beaten the bitch-witch, gotten gorgeous clothes, made an adorable and talented new friend. Everything in her life seems charmed, and she hears herself say, "Everything okay there?" Could it be anything else!

"Homer's holding his own."

"Excellent," she says.

"He's not worse."

"He's looking better you think?"

"Maybe. It's hard to tell. He's sleeping most of the time."

"Good. He needs his rest."

"Right...right," he says. She should give him a day or two. He'd meet her at his mom's in a day.

But hearing him say, Right, right, that special way he says it, low and slow, like he agrees but is also bewildered in that adorable way of his, she feels she can't wait a minute to have him with her. She tells him about the wedding clothes she's bought them. Her idea to dress and undress together. She takes off her T-shirt, and puts her breast in her hand, and tells him what she's done.

"Oh, baby," he says.

It sounds like the "oh baby" he says when he's inside her.

"Baby," he says. "Baby, there's so much I want to tell you." Then stops. "In person."

The starts and stops of his speech excite her. Like when he teased her nipples with his tongue, starting and stopping, starting and stopping.

"I can wait," she whispers, then hangs up.

She can think of him, then stop, think, then stop. Till he was with her in person. In only a day or two. With Homer feeling better, he'd be all hers; the only disruption to their passion would be sleep!

Before they go to Mama Mimi, she wants a fabulous night alone with him. She isn't sure they can afford another night in a motel—so maybe they could meet up at Mimi's and then drive somewhere. It wouldn't have to be night even. Washington was surrounded by deep, dark woods.

# 13. Fruit

She will surprise Mimi on her own, which is probably for the best. Though he did get all excited on July 4th when he surprised her with the grill, Tony's constitutional uncertainty and indecision clash with sure, swift surprise. What should we say, when should we call—he'd go on and on second-guessing the plan—and as for the surprise itself, it too would be executed with changes of heart. Let's call to make believe we're home...but then who should dial and what should they say? Maybe don't call but send flowers to make believe they're far away...but then which kind? So she alone will ring Mimi's bell, cry, Surprise, and then, Ta-da. Look at this wedding stash. Were he with her, she would sense his boredom as she showed Mimi all the loot, and she'd rush rather than taking her time so Mimi could really enjoy it.

She wants the surprise to be perfect, which means not just showing up but bearing gifts, perfect gifts. She drives to Silver Springs and finds the old market, where Mimi's parents had their stall. She never met Mimi's parents, because they died when Tony was little. But Mimi used to bring her and Tony here. They'd run around from stall to stall, gathering armfuls of fruit from Mimi's parents' old friends, and Mimi would sit with a couple of the old merchants and talk about old-times, the fruit and vegetable business, the future of American orchards, her parents short lives. Mimi said she preferred coming to the market than to going to the cemetery, that she came here when she was sad, but always left happy. The fruits were like her babies. There were always more coming and, to her mind, one was more beautiful than the next.

It is still a produce market, though the owners are all Chinese and Indian, not Italians and Jews. She buys things

Mimi loves like black grapes and persimmons, pomegranates and dark bosc pears. And fruits that are unfamiliar—lychees, guava, papayas—because she knows Mim would ooh and ah over them just as she ooh-ed and ah-ed about new mothers and babies from places that were new to her—Belize, or Cameroon, or Uzbekistan. She finds a cheese store, the last Italian store left in the area, and buys Mimi's favorites— Italian fontina and bufola mozzarella.

And then she's on her way. She giggles with expectation as she looks for Mimi's building, and then with joy when she finds it—a giant limestone with decorative flowers and bows going round and round, like a wedding cake! How perfect was that! Giddy, she drives up Connecticut Avenue to the nearest phone booth. She will say that she's calling from Monuten to tell her she misses her and wishes she were with her. Then the next minute she'll be at her door and ringing her bell.

"How wonderful to hear your voice," Mimi says. "I miss you so much. I wish I could be with you. I want to visit soon."

"It's very busy here in Monuten," Lily says. "But we'll try to visit you soon. How fun would that be!"

"So fun," Mimi says, using the youth phrase that she finally succumbed to when her children had almost outgrown it. "I'll believe it when I see it."

"One of these days," Lily sighs sadly.

One of these days, Mimi thinks, she will have room for the kids. She doesn't mean a room for them to stay: eventually when they come, she will happily sleep on the new convertible sofa and give them her bedroom. She means room in her life. Right now it feels filled to capacity with work, Steven, and what she has come to think of as her rehabilitation.

She sees the past two decades in dire terms—that sometimes seem shamelessly self-dramatizing but often apt.

She has suffered, she often thinks, from a chronic palsy of the soul, an intermittent trembling at the core, advancing under stress to psychic convulsions that have left her wondering if she, and not only Henry, had died. Regular exposure to babies and births had treated the condition, every baby she caught jolting her being like an electroconvulsive shock, changing her brainwaves from desperate to blissful. Then just when expectations of joy and birth had replaced the certainty of misery and death, war came again. She doubled her workload when Tony went to the Gulf, but nothing could stop a full relapse.

With her own baby gone, even catching babies brought no relief. Why usher them to life if they could die in just a few years? she'd think. And until he was back in the States, her calls of courage to crazed mothers were rote cant. When he returned to her, she felt she had to leave him—she couldn't endure worrying like that ever again. And when she knew Lily and he had each other, she quickly fled. Her survival seemed to depend on caring less, about her children and all the children.

You care, Steven has said, when she's explained her condition to him.

He means to reassure her that she remains a nice person, and she laughs because for the first time in her life she really doesn't give a damn. In the beginning, when she first realized the change, she was alarmed. But quickly she grew comfortable with it. She came to think of her new mode as "cool" care, as opposed to the "hot" care of mothering and midwifery. And if she could sign up for a lifetime of this, she would die a happy woman. She misses her old life like a reformed drunk misses boozy highs, but she wouldn't return to it for anything.

Her husband died young and her parents in early middle age, but now she has come to believe that if she has no new shocks and threats to endure she can live a long life and die a natural death. Indeed she feels like she has just begun to live her life. The week before, walking in the park, she felt like a young child seeing the riotous colors of fall for the first time. And when Steven took her hand, she felt like a teenage girl with her first boyfriend and her whole life before her.

But she knows she is a middle-aged woman who, after a hectic week of work, needs her weekend rest. They'd gotten in late from a jazz performance at George Washington University, and then an NPR show on the Savings and Loan debacle caught their attention, and then it was two in the morning before Steven stopped his tirade about what the trillion dollar buyout would mean for public health and research, and how Neil Bush belonged in jail and maybe his brother too, who had one of those preppy names she'd never heard before, Bib or Jib or Jeb, who'd done his own shit with some thrift association. Then he was off about thrift associations and *their* hanky-panky. And then he started on another Bush son named George who...she can't remember what he'd done, for by then she was falling asleep. It seemed only a little later that Lily called but it was in fact 11 o'clock. She sounded so lonesome and far away, and when she had asked to talk to Tony, Lily stalled, like something was wrong. He's...out, she said. She should call her back, she knows, but she doesn't want to. Steven has been up for hours, working at his laptop, but now he's come back to bed and has opened his arms to receive her. She is a middle-aged woman who is catching up on love, and Lily is a young girl with her life ahead of her. So she will stay here with him and call back later, saying, You must come visit!

And now the downstairs bell.

"A delivery," the doorman says.

"Of what?"

"Fruit," he says.

Then the doorbell, and then a small mountain of half the fruits of the world is in her face, held up by some midget delivery guy, calling...Surprise.

"I fooled you," Lily says. "I fooled you good." She sets

the bowl down on the hallway floor and gets on tip-toe for a
hello hug. "There's no way you expected me, right?"

"Right…right," Mimi says.

"Right, right," Lily says. "Woof woof."

Woof. It's an old intimacy, the origins of which Mimi
can't remember right now but she remembers the tinkle of
her voice, the lemony scent of her hair, the feel of her frail
frame in her arms. She remembers five minutes ago, how
glad she was the girl was far away and, now, the thrill of her
really here.

"Woof yourself," Mimi whispers, remembering now that
it had something to do with pure feelings, exchanges immune
from human language and lies…a theory of Lily's involving
dogs….Then to make sure she doesn't cry, Mimi barks,
"Where the hell is all of this from?"

"North Street Market!"

North Street Market. And now there is no possibility of
escaping tears. The words are a password to her heart,
signifying knowledge, indeed shared ownership, of its
contents.

Then Steven pads to the door. "Lily?" he says. "Is this
your Lily?"

"My Lily," she says.

"What a treat!" he says. "Why are you crying?"

"She cries when she's happy," Lily says. "Nine times out
of ten when she's really happy, she starts to bawl. We always
laugh—me and Tony."

"And Tony? Where's Tony?" he says.

"He'll be here tomorrow."

"Well, we've got some planning to do," Steven says. "For
some real celebrating….By the way, I'm Steven," he says.

"This is Steven," Mimi laughs. "I was going to tell
you…guys…when you visited."

"Well, here we are," Lily laughs. "Hello, Steven."

"I'm the boyfriend," he laughs. "I mean I used to be her
boyfriend. I mean I wanted to be her boyfriend. In college.

Now, I guess, I've become her man-friend...."

"That sounds so old-person," Mimi says. "Isn't that what you have in the retirement home—a man-friend or a lady-friend?"

"The serious scientist?" Lily says, blushing, remembering the rest—how he was a cold fish, how glad she was to find Henry!

"I've changed," he laughs. "But, yes, I used to be a dud."

"What's this?" Mimi says.

Beyond the bowl of fruit are bags of more fruit, and huddled behind them, like shy refugees wondering if they will be welcomed, her plastic bags of wedding clothes.

"Wedding clothes...I didn't know about Steven or I would have gotten him a tux. I mean maybe you have one already, Steven. Not that you have to wear one. It's just that they were such good quality...and cheap. Hey, I actually got an extra one in case our friend Homer goes up a size. If that happens, I can get him another. So one of these is yours!"

"How wonderful," he laughs. ""No one's bought me a suit since my bar mitzvah."

"That's cute," Lily says.

"You're cute," he says. "She's the cutest," he tells Mimi. "You raised the cutest kid."

"Wait till you see Tony," Lily says.

While Mimi makes lunch—of fruit and cheese and bread—they carry in all the bags from the hall.

After lunch comes the fashion show. The label show. Brooks. Saks. Made in England. Made in Paris. Merino wool. Italian silk. The quiz show—how much each item is worth, how much she actually paid.

Lily explains that she used the basic Mimi rule.

Mimi smiles, trying to hide the fact that she doesn't remember the basic rule that bears her name.

"Thrift shops in wealthy areas," Lily says.

How far away that all seems. The wearisome searches, the depleting struggles for survival. Everything in the room came from catalogues.

"You taught me good. See?"

"I see," Mimi says. She regrets that her voice sounds weak. But suddenly she feels so tired, as if the heaps of clothing, the strewn plastic, the sudden clutter of family life have displaced all the air in the room. She pads over to the couch and lies down.

"I should say so," Steven says, in a strange, loud voice intended, she thinks, to make up for hers. "What amazing quality," he says, "and all in perfect condition."

When Mimi wakes, she finds the note by her side.

"The tux fit Steven to a tee. Here is your dress. Wait till I'm back to try it on. We've gone to the marina. Steven thinks we should have the wedding there. I don't know if Homer will be up to it or Nancy with the baby and all. Or what Tony will say (he'll be deciding till a year after the wedding, yes or no, ha ha). We had planned on something at home. But I figured, What's the harm in looking. I've never been down on the Potomac so it will be a fun afternoon even if we decide to have the wedding back home. Don't worry, I won't decide on anything without talking to you. I know you'll say you want it here, but I know then you'll want to make all the arrangements, and I don't want to bother you even though I know you'll say, Nothing would give me more pleasure….And I know you mean it. But still."

The wedding. The baby. The arrangements. Just reading the note exhausts her. Nothing would give her more pleasure than to stay lying here till everyone goes home again. She staggers to her bed, and falls back to sleep. Then the next thing she knows she's hearing the key in the lock, footsteps. They're home again.

"Time to wake up," he says, rousing her with a kiss on the cheek.

"Steven, I feel so ashamed," she whispers.

"Steven!" he laughs. "Wake up, Ma," he says.


The kids want to go to the "famous" Indian restaurant, which evidently Steven has told them about. But Mimi still believes that her old life and her new life should not be mushed together. Right now family life feels like a giant monstrous meatloaf pulling in everything that comes near. Family loaf, she thinks, trying for humor, which she doesn't feel.

"How about something light," she suggests.

"Tony is famished," Steven says. "If not Indian, how about Italian?"

Tony suggests the place Mimi used to talk about, near grandma's market in Silver Springs.

"It's closed down," Mimi says, frowning. But she is glad there's no excuse for trekking to Silver Springs and back.

They settle on a café overlooking the river in Georgetown, a favorite spot of Mimi's.

By day it is another bustling, hustling joint, where politicos and movers make and break deals; but at night, like the city, it is more hushed and still, with a view of the capital so beautiful and majestic that it is easy to forgive its daily callousness and coldness. Mimi orders a salad and a martini, and stares out at the water, the monuments, the light of the monuments gleaming on the water.

Lily is telling Tony about the marina, but Mimi hears it as background, a little light music. "You wouldn't believe how stunning....Steven says it's available....We have to decide...home or here. Don't take it wrong, Mimi. You know what I mean."

Take what wrong? Mimi thinks. "Of course, sweetheart," she says.

When they were little, and she'd space out, no matter how much she nodded her head and said, I see, or, Wow, to fake concentration, they could always tell. You weren't listening, don't try to pretend you were, they'd say, annoyed that her attention had wandered from them. But now they seem not to notice.

Tony says, "Wherever you are we consider home too, Ma. But we do have to decide…which home?" He looks across at Lily. Is that what she wanted him to say? He's not really paying attention.

"Of course," Mimi says, trying to focus, and braces herself for her son's Talmudic inquiry. Which place is better for their purposes? And what exactly are their purposes? And will they change…?

But he says only, "At least that's one problem we could solve…fast."

He looks so sad when he says the word, problem. In one second all her ideas about spending the rest of her life in peace and privacy vanish and she can see only her son's sad face saying the word. Problem.

"What's wrong, darling," Mimi says. "What's the problem?"

He shrugs. "Just tired. From helping with Homer. He'll be all right, I guess…."

"Tell me," she says. "Why does he need help? What's wrong?"

"Homer's his best friend. The one who'll wear the other tuxedo," Lily explains to Steven. "And his wife is Nancy, who is going to wear the other brown satin dress. They're having a baby. That's who I bought the embroidered Irish linen suit for because it's going to be in the wedding party. So come to think of it maybe it would be easier if we did it in Virginia…for Nancy and the baby."

Tony takes her hand. She always speaks quickly, but when words fly from her mouth, crashing full-speed into everything and anything, it means she's scared.

"I see," Steven says. "And what's the matter with Homer?"

Tony shrugs.

"First they said stress," Lily says. "They gave him Prozac. Like they gave Einstein, another friend who wasn't feeling well. And now they've added an antibiotic, which brought down his fever. He's still not himself 100%...but doing better? Right, Ton? A lot better?"

Tony shrugs. "Einstein's because he's so good at science," he tells Steven. "He's going to be a physicist. He is already, I guess. He's got a million scholarships waiting."

"Shrink theory," Lily says. "He's an expert."

"String theory," Tony whispers.

"Great stuff....But how are he and your other friend not feeling well?" Steven asks. "What are their symptoms?"

After three days with Homer, Tony knows the symptoms by heart: "Vertigo, insomnia, fatigue, joint pain, rashes, stomach aches, fever, confusion, mood swings. And they said stress for all of that."

Mimi says, "You know, when humans are stressed, their immune systems can weaken. I know it sounds like a grandma's view of human illness, but...." His eyes look so worried, and she wants to reassure him, and she *has* seen that happen! "Right, Steven?"

"Could be," Steven says.

But he seems suddenly far away, like he used to, distracted, uninterested. "What's wrong?" she says.

He shakes his head. "Nothing. An article at work. I forgot it on my desk."

"Can't it wait till morning?"

"I need it for a morning talk.... And the talk's at eight. And I want to make copies to distribute."

"We'll drive you up after dinner."

"I forgot about the talk entirely somehow. I'd really better go. I'll catch up with you later."

And then he's standing up, walking toward the door, and gone.

"This is how he used to be....All work." Mimi manages

a laugh, but she feels confused and scared.

"Don't worry," Lily says. "He just got worried about work. You do that too. So do I. Or maybe since he works in medicine, he doesn't like to hear about it after work. We'll have to check if he feels that way and be careful if he does. Anyway, he's really nice. We like him…Tony…right…we like him a lot…?"

"Right, right," Tony says. Then, "Something's wrong? Right? We mentioned Homer and Einstein. He asked a few questions. And then he was gone?"

"Steven is very honest," Mimi says, not knowing what else to say. "Totally trustworthy. He said he had to get a paper. I believe him. Please, honey, we don't know at all that something's wrong."

# 14. Butterfly

Mimi tells the kids she will sleep on Steven's boat to give them time alone. They should take a taxi home, and she'll take her car. And then she leaves.

The truth was she had to get away from them. Steven's disappearing act had unnerved her too, and if she stayed a minute longer they would see that. She made excuses for him, but she hasn't a clue about what was going on. He wasn't used to kids, the mess of family. He likes intellectual talk about politics and science, but all he heard today was family *squawk*: Lily's wedding guests and how many could squeeze onto his deck, or whatever she was going on about, Grandma's favorite restaurant and when it closed, Nancy's cervix and when it would open. Homer's headache and rash.

Had they tired him out? And had it suddenly fizzled for him just like that? Had he just decided it wouldn't work? And so what was the point of staying with her another second? Reason tells her it could be something else, but her heart feels like it's breaking as she gets into her car and speeds away.

For the pure melody, the perfect harmony, the heart-piercing story—she had been raised to love Puccini above all other composers. And the fact that her parents named her after a dying consumptive has never bothered her. She loved *Bohème*. But *Butterfly* had always been her favorite. Until Henry left and didn't return, when she stopped listening. Men leaving forever, women bereft of love and hope, orphaned children—she couldn't bear it. But now, when she turns on the radio, she hears *Butterfly*, for the first time in ages. Her heart heaves, but she can't bring herself to turn it off.

*Ma or quel sincero. pressago è già....il triste vero apprenderà.* Sharpless sings as Mimi drives down to the harbor. *She must learn the miserable truth. Once again. The miserable truth.*


He is lying on the hammock with his eyes closed when she climbs onto the deck.

"There is no talk tomorrow at eight? Right? Something's wrong?" She feels like a banshee, appearing suddenly, towering over him, howling. But she has to know.

"Right."

"What's going on?"

He shakes his head. "I'm not sure yet."

"But you're having second thoughts?" she says.

"Oh, Jesus," he says. "I have to tell you something."

"I don't think so. If it's what I think it is. Oh, Christ...I don't think so."

"You look so scared. Come here," he says, pulling her onto his lap.

She studies his long lean thighs, his wide shoulders, his pensive eyes looking up at her. She longs for him to comfort her, but can the man who's destroying you by leaving you comfort you before he goes? Marrying young, she had escaped all this. Men didn't leave her, they simply died.

"If you're going to leave me, what's the point?" she moans.

"You can't be serious....Come here, Mimi, this is serious...."


He really had gone back for a paper. Just not a paper for a talk. He'd made up that part. An unpublished paper that someone from the Institute of Infectious Diseases had shown him the other day.

"Some findings on a group of patients with symptoms

like Tony's friends," he says.

She nods but she isn't sure what he's getting at. The symptoms were hardly unique. "Vertigo, joint aches, stomach complaints, skin eruptions, fatigue...what's reportable about that? What's the punch line?"

"They all were just back from the Gulf. Every last case. All just kids, just back from the Gulf."

She knows she has begun to shake, there in his lap. And that her intestines have gone wild and that there is a small chance she will shit her pants, her tights, her skirt, her fastidious boyfriend's freshly laundered chinos. But it's not this that shames her, but the survivor's glee that quickly follows, dispersing the terrible dread. Soldiers may be coming back riddled with disease, but Tony was fine! His eyes their sparkling sea green, his skin and hair glowing like amber, his cheeks a dark rose. How handsome and healthy he'd looked tonight across the table—and tomorrow night would be the same, and on and on, for years to come. He was hers and he was fine and that's all that mattered. Then she remembers Homer, of course, and the boy they called Einstein, her healthy son's best friends.

"Oh, shit," she says. "Oh, Christ, what do they think it is? Viral? Bacterial? Chemical? Shit, don't tell me they're using Agent Orange again. I mean something like that. They wouldn't do that again."

"The paper calls it Persian Gulf Illness and proposes that it may not be one condition but several. Someone at Southern Maryland Hospital has started a registry to track the cases and the symptoms. A community hospital! But it has some connection to the NIH. It's a remarkable place."

"Good...good....And what are the treatments? Tell me there *are* treatments at this remarkable place!"

"Some seem to have elevated white blood counts but not all. They're doing IV antibiotics for that group. And for everyone, aggressive chelation. To cover several bases. Gas. Germs. Radiation. Until they know more."

Gas. Germs. Radiation? "You're not serious," she says. "They don't really think it's that." She tries to do some lady-in-labor breathing to stop the shaking, which has started again.

"Something is definitely wrong. But some seem to improve quickly if they get treatment early."

"How early?" she whispers.

"I've arranged an admission at Southern Maryland for tomorrow morning."


For years, to tell Tony where she was or when she expected him to be home, Mimi has dialed Homer's number automatically, and she picks up the phone and dials it now. She gets the machine, Homer's voice saying they're not home but to leave a message.

"It's Mimi," she says. "Don't worry. I'm just calling with some information...."

"He sounded sweet," she tells Steven, when she hangs up. "Like a friendly little boy. 'Leave your number and we'll call you back...right away.' Like he wanted to make new friends. I remember when he first moved into the neighborhood and they became friends...."

"He's not dead, Mimi. You don't have to write his eulogy yet. He's probably going to be fine."

She laughs sadly. "That's what he said to me."

When Tony joined the reserves, she'd blamed Homer and when he'd come back from the base to visit, she couldn't look at him.

He's going to be fine, Mimi, he said one day while he was waiting for Tony in the kitchen and she was doing her best to ignore him. He said, Mimi, there aren't any wars on the horizon. And if one pops up, I'll kick ass. Don't you worry, Mims. He had on fatigues and boots and he extended his leg to show his killer kick, and said, Man, I'm ready. Look out.

In his letters from basic training, Henry wrote how each day made him steadier, readier. Soon he'd be ready for Charlie, he said. They'd been novice hippies and peaceniks but as soon as he got to boot camp, he started talking the talk. To rev up his courage engine, she'd thought. Ready! His first trip to Saigon, he got killed by a sniper. You play war, she told Homer. Dress up and play war. But I've lived it, Goddammit. Then she walked out of the kitchen.

Now she tells Steven, "I should have talked to him more. I took the high ground. I should have taken more time."

"You were afraid for your son, sweetheart. You were being honest."

"But if I hadn't been so busy shaming him, maybe I could have reached him. I could feel that war was coming. Not just in my war-widow, disaster-is-around-the-corner way. But because the PR campaign had started. You know, Saddam's our friend when he's killing communists and Iranian fundamentalists. Then suddenly he's not just another killer thug tyrant we've supported but the devil out to destroy our lives and all that we hold sacred. And this idiot bought it. Saddam is worse than Hitler and if we don't get him, he'll come and get us! You should have heard him—and my idiot son. And I said nothing!"

"You said plenty, I'm sure. But changing people's minds about these things is almost impossible, in wartime or close-to-wartime maybe totally impossible. But you think you should have succeeded and I should add your failure to your list of unpardonable sins?"

"Yes. Please."

"For a lapsed Catholic you still run a great guilt trip on yourself."

"It's the one concept of the church I truly value."

He says, "But the good people are racked with guilt. And the bad ones rationalize all guilt away. The Kuwaitis and Saudis are world champions in torture, amputations, beheadings, and enslavement of women. But somehow

Thatcher and Bush convince themselves and us that it's a better world with them as our best friends. And little Neil Bush bleeds Silverado dry and then gets his daddy to get the government to bail him out and that's for the greater good too! Christ, by the time they're done, that bailout's going to cost us a trillion dollars, which could have paid for half a century of healthcare for the entire fucking country. Not to mention food. And shelter. And science. And art. But they're good people…waving at the cameras outside church, every Sunday."

He is only warming up, he knows. Soon he'll be all revved up and then blasting off. He is thinking about an article he read about James Baker, which claimed that before he invaded Kuwait, Saddam checked with the U.S. ambassador and the ambassador said that the Secretary of State said that Iraq's relations with its neighbors was not a U.S. matter, and then Baker said he never said that but the author said there were transcripts of cables and maybe Saddam thought he was being given a green light even though that may not have been the U.S. intention, though maybe it was, to trick Saddam into invading so they could go after him. The author thinks it likely. Impossible, Steven had thought when he read it last week. But tonight—seeing her son's scared eyes, reading the miserable article, feeling her tremble in his arms—he's not so sure. More and more he feels he knows little for sure. More and more the demarcation between possible and impossible has begun to blur for him. Global war, global domination, global economy, global poverty and disease, global rains and floods from global warming—especially when he's tired, the stuff of science and futuristic fiction spins around his mind like a meteor shower, sometimes crashing into what, despite his atheist inclinations, he can only think of as his soul. Then personal and global extinction seem imminent….

"One day soon…" he hears himself say.

"What?" she says.

He can hear the fatigue and dread in her voice. What a fool he was. He had meant only to comfort her, not demoralize her more with his doomsday explosions.

"One day soon what, darling?" she yawns.

"One day soon everything will be fine again," he says, taking her hand.

She calls them her peasant paws, the natural selection from centuries of clawing roots and vines, garlic and tomatoes. Big and rough, an adorable contradiction with her frail wrist, he thinks, which he holds now, working his way up her arm. How he loves to touch her, to feel her heart beat with his hand, or with his chest when she lies on him in the morning, or with his dick when they've made love and come but he's still inside her and she's pulsing softly all around. The other week, after a site visit to an Ohio environmental disease center—whose pre- and post-clean-up data were supplying many missing pieces of the dioxin-exposure puzzle and whose director he had to inform before he left that funding would end at the end of the year, for no good reason except that fucking Neil Bush was a fucking pig gobbling up the federal budget with his bail-out—he stayed up half the night sipping bourbon to dull his despair. And only the thought of her, her big eyes and heart, kept him from getting totally trashed, and to muse instead on the technology that might keep her with him always. Not digital phone with photo, transmitting her voice and face, but something that would attach to the back of her head, perhaps, and register her moods and eventually even her thoughts, transmitting them wirelessly to a receptor/monitor no larger than a quarter, which could sit on a band on his wrist, like a watch, and when he looked down to check on her, people would think he was checking the time. She was the most decent person he had ever known. In every way, the opposite of Neil Bush and his whole scheming, thieving family and their pirate pals!

"I'm here for anything," he whispers in her ear.

That's what she should have said to Homer, she thinks.

One day, shortly before he shipped out, he'd asked her, Are you still going to deliver Nance's and my kids? Or are you still mad at me, Mims?

Not mad. Just disappointed. I expected more....She'd actually said that!

"Poor Homer....Poor Nancy....Poor Tony," she says. "You don't know my son. He is a very tender boy."

Steven nods. "I know....I know his mother."

"Poor Lily," she says. "You can't imagine how dogged she becomes once she's launched a plan. The shower. The wedding. All bombed to bits."

Bombed to bits, my ass, he thinks. The Bush family's plans aren't bombed to bits. The Bush family isn't canceling daughter Dodo's Camp David wedding! Bullshit...Bush-shit, he thinks. But he must swear off these rant-a-thons—after the initial thrill, they depleted him and depressed her. So he says only, "It won't be as lavish as Dodo Bush's wedding but it will happen!"

"Doro," she laughs. "You really think everything could keep going?" she says.

Usually when he thinks of meteors and their penetration of the atmosphere, the shocking collision with earth, the vast chasms, and dark dust everywhere, he imagines himself alone and asleep. But now he imagines something—an asteroid or missile, he can't tell—shooting towards Lily and Tony and the other kids. Him calling to them to follow him to a secret safe place. There was still time, if they moved fast.

"They're all such close friends. And if Homer's really sick.... I don't know, Steven, I just know I hope you're right. I don't mean just Lily's sweet, silly plans. I mean everything, you know...."

"I know," he says. "It will. We need to move fast, though."

She tries Monuten again a few minutes later, but still gets the machine. She dials her own apartment to tell Tony and Lily what's going on, but the line is busy.

The apartment is all theirs—the terrace above the creek. The bathtub with a view of the Capitol. The new queen-size bed.

Lily shows Tony her Hopkins wedding dress and his tux. "Want to...you know?" she asks.

He know she means dress and undress the way she has planned.

He nods. "Soon....After I rest...."

Last night and the night before he hardly slept. The stress had finally gotten to Nancy. She was pacing and crying, and he'd insisted she go to their house to rest. He remembered the staple of advice his mother fed to all her "new mommies": sleep when baby sleeps, or you'll be done for. And every time Homer fell off, Tony would too. But then horrific noises—Homer gasping or moaning or farting or calling, sometimes to him, sometimes to someone in a dream—would reach him, and he'd walk down the hall to check on him, never really getting back to sleep.

"You mean a little rest now? Or like after a night's rest...like in the morning?"

"Big rest...," he says.

He can hardly talk...let alone dress and undress and hold and kiss and stroke....Which he wants, of course, but later....He needs to sleep. Dinner was a strain. He liked meeting Steven, seeing his mother happy and Lily so Lily-ish, so excited about her plans and her people. But just holding his head up, not to mention listening, answering, smiling, or nodding as the moment required, took everything he had. Homer had sucked him dry. Not nice to say about a best friend, but for two days Homer was at him non-stop. Do this, do that. Get me water, a towel, not that towel, not a towel now but a blanket, I'm cold, I'm hot, get me ice....Then at night, the noises.

Last night, Homer's calls came without a break. Clipped, dream speech, a generic jarhead dream, it had seemed. *Yessir.*

*You bet, sir. Got it under control, sir.* Over and over and over. Then just before dawn, Tony heard a long moan, a long groan, some quick, awful gasps. He ran to him. He was still asleep, sweating like crazy, and Tony sat down and wiped his face and neck with the baby wipes Nancy had begun to keep by the bed.

You okay, Homes? he said.

He looked okay. But then the noises started again.

There was an inhaler by the bed for when he got short of breath. But before Tony could pick it up, the noises stopped.

Those hadn't been real noises, but dream noises, he realized then. The sick Homer lying in bed wasn't groaning and gasping; the sounds were coming from the dream.

Homer cried, *Oh no, oh no, oh no, sir.* Then: *Why, sir? Oh why, oh why, oh why, sir?*

The sun was rising but watching Homer, Tony felt like they were back at that time when the sun was setting down on the Gulf and they were sitting on the wharf in Al Jubayl watching the hungry kids and he'd asked Homer, Why are we here? What are we doing here? And Homer had answered, Devil dogs don't ask.

But yesterday, from his dream, Homer said, *Is this right, sir?*

*Should we be doing this, sir?*

He said, *Why are we closing the highway, sir? I'm just trying to understand why the road's being closed, sir. Why, at this point in time, sir?*

Until it was time to make Homer his breakfast and give him his morning meds, Tony just lay beside him, trying to think. He drove a light armored vehicle; Homer drove an Abrams tank. Roads and highways, highways and roads. That's where they spent the war. He remembers so little, but the memories that flash in his mind from time to time are of roads, some paved, some just a furrow in the sand, him and Ernie in the LAV, covering their dread with jabs and jokes. But the road in Homer's dream…where was that? Was it the same road as in *his* dream? That road he can't remember except as a smoky message in the sky: "highway at the end of the war," "highway at the end of the world." And maybe a smell, like a cook-out?

Lily tiptoes into the bedroom to check on him "What are you thinking?" she asks him. "Tell me."

She pats his head and says she wants to know *anything* he's thinking like he had said that night when she explained to him her ideas about life's phases. But what if he was thinking terrible stuff? Even more terrible than Ronnie's piles of arms and legs and heads on sticks?

"You're just tired, Ton?"

She looks so scared. He couldn't bear to scare her anymore. Or himself, by speaking it out loud. "Just tired," he says, closing his eyes.

Lily has a special term she's used over the years for Ronnie. He wasn't MIA, missing in action, but MAA, missing *after* action. When she was in grade school and the Vietnam Memorial Wall was going up and the families of the MIAs won the fight to have the names of MIAs up there too with the DFS (her phrase—dead for sure), she wrote a letter to President Reagan suggesting the category and asking that names of MAAs be put up too. When she didn't hear back, she thought of involving others in her campaign, other kids with MAA pops. She thought of starting an organization; she had the perfect name: Children of MAA PAs (Missing After Action Pas). There were also the mother-casualties like Connie, the women waiting back home who got fucked up and destroyed afterwards. MAA MAs—that could be an adjunct designation and organization. Like AA and AlAnon, which she knew all about from her MAA PA and MAA MA.

Homer was MAA. She hadn't thought about it before in those terms, and she can see why. Little Greg or Abby part of a whole new generation of MAA kids! It was too horrible to think about! True, Nancy had resources that her mom hadn't—a teaching certificate, a master's degree, professional awards at a young age—but if she had to stay home with Homer, she could end up a MAA MA too.

She and Tony would do everything they could to help. She loves Tony for being such a loyal, helpful human being. But lying there before, weak and drained, he hardly seemed himself. What if he got lost in the process—and ended up MAA himself!

After her mother was long gone, she used to leaf through her old AlAnon and family of addicts pamphlets and books for tips on dealing with her father. She always disliked the way they put things: words like "boundaries" and "limits" sounded stingy and mean to her. She could see the value in the concepts, but then and now she liked more kindly words, like "edges." You flow towards those you love and vice versa and your *edges* touch and overlap, like she used to overlap doilies in her favorite collages—so that you could see each doily fully as well as new beautiful lacy spaces that the doilies created together. She doesn't think any card she's ever bought or made matches those old collages for expressing how she feels about people and their warm feelings for each other. Or people and their pets, for that matter. You look into your dog's eyes and touch his spirit and he yours. You are cozy and overlapping but you have remained an individual human who can say, See you later, Puppy, and Puppy as an individual dog can go off, maybe sniffing those scents that he loves as a dog and that you as a person cannot even detect. You *touch* each other but you do not *tear*? She likes the way that sounds.

Though she knows she would miss the dogs and cats at the clinic too much for her to take it from concept to plan, she sometimes thinks the smart thing would be to drag Tony to New York for a while and make a million dollars in advertising! There are so many ideas flying around in her mind that want to and should get out. The *About to Be Married* sign for the pre-honeymoon, for example. She'd brought the paper and the markers, her idea to execute the sign in bold print and tape it to the front bumper the night before her part of the trip was to begin, as opposed to just taping *Just Married* to the back after the wedding. But then they spoke to Nancy, and Tony left, so there went acknowledging not only accomplishment but aspiration. To her, it was not just about a particular couple honoring all stages, but the public at large, who would see the sign and be reminded to place more emphasis on planning for the future.

Tony was so tired, but maybe with a night's rest he would be as good as new. They had so much to do. When's the last time she thought about the shower, which was only three weeks away! As for the wedding, Mimi had not tried on her gown, and, of course, she and Tony have not even tried on their wedding clothes, never mind...taking them off together. Worry and sleep, worry and sleep had replaced dreaming and doing. She's being a bitch, she knows, but she wants her special time to be special. Only Steven, who she is beginning to think she will ask to give her away, has given a damn about her upcoming wedding, trying on the tux, showing her the party room and deck at the marina. But he is a busy, grown-up scientist, so she can't just pick up the phone and run plans by him. Not that there's really anything to run by. No one picks up on the hint, when she says things like, Marina or Virginia? Any thoughts?

She woke up this morning, not sure what phase they were in anymore—*Facing the Future*? *Living Your Life*? Then in the bath, watching the mall in the morning, the glass and stone glistening with light, she looked at her body, which Nancy had coached her to like, and Tony to totally love, and thought, This is a skinny, pathetic body of a skinny, pathetic female human. She has always felt so accomplished just surviving her childhood; and caring for animals and being with people she loved are all she's ever wanted to do, making her not a very special person, perhaps, but a very contented one. Now the bathwater had shriveled her skin, and she felt like she was shrinking before her eyes, a feeling she used to have a lot the year she lived with her aunt and the witchettes, when there was nobody to love her or to love back. But when she's with Tony—or any of her people—she feels the exact opposite of that—like she will be strong forever and ever. But not lately. Not at all lately.

Usually at this time of night, she and Nancy talk on the phone. Girlfriend, whassup, they say, discussing everything in their lives from start to finish, from big to small. She misses Nancy so much, though she understands totally why their daily heart-to-hearts had to be on the back burner for now. She wishes Sean were around. He hardly knew her but he understood her. She'd called his cell once and left a message; he owed her a call. But when you like and trust a person, you don't keep count. And she dials him.

Sean is happy to hear her voice. He is still in Wilmington. To get experience for events planning, he took a restaurant job which they call assistant manager but which is really busboy? Cutting butter and bread? It would be cool to take a few days off and come up and get things going?

He understands her ambivalence about the venue, marina versus home, grand versus homey. Which is the struggle in most weddings. Frankly he sees her near the river in the early evening, with a 8-ish sunset ceremony, then dancing under the stars. Was there room for dancing at the marina? He could DJ as he has said or provide simple background music if space was an issue? Accordian music, which he finds charming, is coming back, he says. And tends to be inexpensive because of all the hard-up émigrés from the former Soviet bloc nations.

He asks her how the viewing went, and she lies and says, great, and that everyone preferred her in the Hopkins gown and agreed the other one should be saved for someone else's event.

"They thought you were drowning in the satin, right?"

"Drowning," she says.

"And the brown satins. Everyone's down with the brown satin program?"

"Totally down with the program. Everyone loved everything and can't wait to meet you."

"Let's see," he says. "Maybe I could come down in a day or two and we could tour the marina?"

"Come as soon as you can!" she says. The wedding was only six months away. And once the baby came, she'd probably be too busy helping to get back to D.C.

Then Mimi calls. "I've been trying you forever. Who were you talking to?"

Expecting a birth? Lily wants to ask? Mimi was always rushing them off the phone to leave the line free for the call from some mother with quickening contractions or broken water. It might as well be a delivery again, for Mimi is calling orders into the phone like she used to call to her poor assistant during a difficult labor. Now it's Chelation. IV. North Maryland. ASAP.

They're still AWOL, Lily wants to say. As soon as they report in, you'll be the first to know, Sarge.

"No answer still," Lily says. "But I keep trying, believe me."

Then, not only because she feels Mimi bearing down on her to help, but because, of course, she wants genuinely to help, even though she doesn't know what the problem is exactly, she suggests one of them call Liz. Nancy's class with Liz was Tuesday night and her weekly exam with Liz was Wednesday morning and now it was Wednesday evening so Liz would probably know how they were doing and where they were.

"Honey, you're the best," Mimi says. She'll call Liz as soon as she hangs up.

"What's going on?" Lily asks. "Why ASAP?"

"I'll explain it all later, honey," she says. "Okay? Can we put it off till a little later? Don't worry, honey." And hangs up the phone.

Chelation. Doc did that for the fire and police dogs—when they'd been exposed to toxic fumes after the huge tire plant fire or when there was a bomb scare at the county office and they sent the dogs in and then worried about chemical exposure.

But Mimi said not to worry so she won't. She goes to snuggle beside him.

"Brrr," she whispers. "It's almost December."

# 15. The Parameters of Responsiblity

Liz isn't sure of the exact address but she will try again when they get closer. It was never her intention to lay this at Mimi's feet, but the girl would not comply with any of her instructions lately. She would not stay off her feet, stop driving, or really rest. She called in her partner as well as her covering ob-gyn, to provide a fresh voice. They advised what she advised but their words, like hers, went in one ear and out the other.

Nancy had changed, and in the past week her usual concern for her husband had swelled into obsession. The VA had discharged Homer, no other VAs would admit Homer, if she found another hospital that might, the military insurance, which was their only insurance, would not cover Homer's stay. The corps had sent Homer a certified letter to "clarify the parameters of responsibility." Then just yesterday another letter: If Homer didn't report to base by Jan 1, "dishonorable discharge might be pursued." Nancy repeated the exact phrasing a couple of times, clearly traumatized. And Liz said that she could imagine how much distress all this caused, and she sympathized. But *she* was her responsibility and Nancy needed to follow her orders.

She had an unremarkable medical history but in the past week or so her blood pressure had spiked, which was not uncommon. But it had to come down! Liz said she had to insist on no working, no walking, no 24/7 solo care of Homer.

"I'll think about it," Nancy said, and left.

Liz felt she had no choice but to write Nancy her own letter to convey the seriousness of her condition, and yesterday afternoon she faxed Nancy at her school so she would get the message fast: "If you do not follow my medical advice, I cannot oversee your care and the birth of your child."

Nancy's response was less formal. This morning, she stormed into the office and said, What's this shit! What am I supposed to do with Homer?

Liz said, It would be irresponsible of me to let you believe you are not putting your pregnancy in jeopardy.

She didn't mention Mimi on her own but only after Nancy brought up Mimi for the hundredth time. It seemed the only way to influence Nancy these days. When she wasn't talking about Homer, every other sentence out of Nancy's mouth was about Mimi. Did Mimi recommend the same vitamins? Did Mimi use the same blood pressure monitor? Finally, Liz said, You know I'm sure that Mimi would agree that this is a dangerous situation. No responsible certified midwife in the world would keep the case without complete patient compliance.

Nancy said, Mimi would. She's different.

That's when Liz lost it. She said, So goddamn go to Mimi! She didn't mean it. A spark of fleeting fury ignited her mounting frustration—and the words just exploded from her.

I'm on my way, Nancy said.

Liz watched her from the window. Opening the passenger door. Rousing a sleeping man, who must have been Homer. Opening the back door and arranging some pillows. Before she knew it, Liz had flown down the stairs, and was at the car asking Nancy what she was doing.

Going to Mimi's. As soon as I get Homer settled in the back seat. He'll sleep the whole way.

She asked her where Lily and Tony were. Maybe they'd talk some sense into her. Take Homer. Let her rest for at least a few days.

With Mimi, Nancy said.

Liz told her she'd drive. It was wild, she knew, but what were her choices? She had no more patients scheduled, and if she let Nancy drive who knew what could happen. She helped Nancy settle Homer in the back seat, then helped her squeeze in beside him. She was not unaware of the irony that she was doing what Mimi would have done, not just for Nancy, but for her, or most anyone, to avoid catastrophe, and another time she would have smiled. But now she just fixed her eyes on the dark road, and before they even hit the highway, she heard them snoring, thick synchronized snores like you hear in old age homes.

It had been five o'clock when Nancy appeared in her office, and it was just six when Liz commandeered the car. Because Homer had to stop to pee three times and vomit twice, they didn't reach D.C. till nine. Then they overshot their beltway exit and had to circle back up to the NW. Then Mimi's number was busy for hours though Lily's directions, once she picked up, were perfect, and at eleven they are ringing Mimi's bell.


They are young children playing grown-up, and have discovered a closet-ful of clothes to help them look their parts. They are teenagers back from someone's prom with a posse, tuxedos and gowns tossed between sleeping bodies in boxers and tees. At eight in the morning Mimi opens the door of her apartment and the scene rockets her back to such moments, and now like then she feels a mix of excitement and annoyance. Nothing new for a woman with children to come upon but shocking here, where she has lived alone in orderly peace.

A quick count puts the number at six, her two and four others. When she puts on coffee, she peeks from the kitchen. One stirs.

"Liz?" Mimi calls. For the red bun looks so like Liz's.

"It's me. Mimi, I have so much to tell you." Liz patters into the kitchen to embrace her old friend.

Then a boy joins them, extending his hand. "I'm Lily's

new friend? Sean? I'm a wedding planner? Sorry for the mess. I had everyone try on their wedding clothes last night and when we were done we were all too pooped to tidy up?"

He is a genius at reading situations. He poses everything as a question, but is certain of everything. The women have to talk. He needs to give them time alone. He knows a patisserie over on Connecticut with *pain et chocolat* to die for. He'll go and get some for everyone.

"There was nothing else to do," Mimi says, when Sean tiptoes out. "I would have done the same. You have nothing to apologize for, Lizzie. I owe you a debt of gratitude...."

Liz tousles her hair. "You sound like you're giving a speech at a memorial or something. Poor baby. You're still in shock. This is a lot. Believe me, Mimi, I would drive them right back if I thought they'd stay there...and listen to me. But she's hell-bent on being with you. Sweetie, if I can help in any way, let me know. She's a handful."

Liz looks out to the living room, to the sleeping bodies, Nancy and Homer.

"They're two handfuls. I'm leaving you with a lot to care for....A ward," she laughs. "Your living room looks like a damn ward."

"A ward," Mimi says, trying to smile, for, of course, Liz meant no harm.

"I'm sorry," Liz says. "I'm so sorry. I'm just tired. Please don't cry."

Her Neapolitan grandma used to call it a *mezzo. Half a laugh, half a cry. You wanna a mezzo to enda with a mora haha thana boohoo*, she used to say. *Or you loosa you amici.* Mimi knows that, more than ever, she needs all the friends she has, and when her mezzo lasts only a second, dissolving in sobs, she retreats to the bathroom.

*"Ma or quel sincero. pressago è già....il triste vero apprenderà...,"* she cries in the hot shower. Misery... again.

By the time she's all cried out and dressed, Sean is back,

and has set the table, cut up fruit, and laid out his pastries. Liz has put away the clothes and is folding up blankets. The kids are seated around the table, looking worn but happy to be together. Mimi takes her seat and surveys her table. It's like old times. Her son, Lily, their friends, old and new. A teacher. A marine. A party planner. A compulsive planner. The chief of midwifery. Except for her son, they were all confident people, like herself until today. Now she sits there looking as dazed as Tony. There's so much to do, but where would she start? She was out of practice with this family business.

"What's everyone doing today?" she says. She needs time to gather her skills and courage.

"I'm checking in fast," Homer says. He is so relieved to be with Mimi and her guy and finally get some serious care. While Mimi was showering, Steven called and explained everything to Homer. He was driving over from Bethesda to Southern Maryland and Homer would meet him there. How cool to have a doc say that the stress diagnosis is bullshit but not to worry because he is taking you to a great place that does a great job washing out all the toxins. Nancy has to rest so Homer will take a car service up. He recites his plan, then lays his head on the table.

Liz says the hospital is on her way back to Monuten. She will drop Homer off. "Southern Maryland is great, I'm sure, Homer. But you need to be patient…a patient patient," she says. "Not like Nancy," she smiles.

"Of course," he whispers. "Way to go."

Nancy says she is sorry she caused Liz so much trouble. "It's not like me to be such a pest," she says.

"I know," Liz says. "She's a doll," she announces to the table.

"Best Young Educator of the Year for two years," Lily says.

"They should take it back…. I'm so stupid," Nancy says. But from today on she will do whatever she must to push out a healthy baby.

Lily says she will do everything she can to help Nancy do that.

"Everything short of delivering the baby, that is," she laughs.

She'll call Doc and take the next few weeks off and keep her eyes glued on Nancy, making sure she gets proper rest and nutrition. She says, "Nancy, you're the best friend anyone has ever had and I want to be the best friend I can be right back."

Last night, she wasn't so generous. Last night, when everyone descended all at once, she smiled and said the right things, but inside she was freaking out, thinking this is our special time...the last moments of our pre-honeymoon, so, please, scram. Then Sean appeared too, and she knows she actually looked at him like, Do I even know you? Sean, who had agreed to assume the enormous responsibility of her wedding for less than she'd have to pay a bartender! Sean, who was so perceptive, who, more than anyone she'd ever met, grasped every nuance of beauty and ritual, was sure to have registered the ugly meaning of the expression on her face. Everyone went to sleep but she couldn't. Hadn't she learned her lesson when Nancy came up with the idea of sending them on a beautiful trip while she was planning how to mix human skin with sugar and feed it to a friend! Homer and Nancy were their oldest friends and Sean was her newest friend, and it was shameful to even think the thoughts she had about friends. And only after she promised herself that from now on she would be more sensitive and flexible and make it up to them did she fall asleep too.

"Thanks, Lil' Sis," Nancy says, blowing a kiss across the table.

Sean says, "I came here to get the wedding plans rolling. But I see that this is not the time? I will go back to Wilmington but I could come back for a bit if needed to help in a variety of different ways? I'm a serious multi-tasker?"

"Multi-tasker and multi-talented," Lily says. "Come back soon, Sean!"

"I have a cousin in the District with whom I could probably stay?"

"Stay here," Mimi hears herself say, surprising herself. She thought she'd broken the habit of leaping before she looked. But she'd actually looked. His voice might be cheerful, multi-tasking, but his eyes were dark sad pools. No cousin, no family, they said. "The more the merrier," she says.

"Tony?" Lily says.

Mimi's heart flutters. Her heart always flutters, with both worry and hope, when she waits for her son to make a decision. She studies his face to see if she can guess what he will say. How horrible he looks! Ragged, tired—like he'd aged five years in one night!

What will I do? Tony wonders. Today and the next day and the day after that?

Just before they sat down, Nancy had handed him the mail. Bills, magazines, advertising circulars, a postcard from Mrs. Molto—and a letter from Dr. Moser. *Some feedback was in order. He had shared his comments about the course with the superintendent and....*

"Ton, what are you thinking?" Lily says. "You trying to figure out how long you can stay? Until you have to go back to teach?"

He says nothing, so she calls, "Hello...hello....Earth to Tony," laughing a thin, tinny laugh.

"Oh... I'm just thinking I'll go with Homer and get him settled in....After...you know...I'll see...."

"When's your first day of classes?" Lily says. "I forgot!"

Tony raises his shoulders in a tentative shrug.

"He forgot too," Lily laughs again.

"What's wrong, darling?" Mimi says. "Are you worried about the teaching, darling. Don't worry about the teaching."

"He's just tired," Lily says.

Everything is falling into place, Mimi thinks, surveying

her table one more time. Liz would take care of getting Homer to the hospital and Tony would take over once they got there. Tony was just tired, and probably more worried about the teaching than he knew. Lily would perk him up. She'd perk everyone up. She'd cut up buckets of fruit, and buy organic vegetables and make soup and hover over Nancy. And Sean would go to Wilmington or Baltimore, wherever it was he'd come from, at least for a while though he'd probably be back soon. He was an orphan, she suspects, or something along those lines.

She used to call those times she was up for days, birthing baby after baby, her Fire and Ice days, because only a combination of the hottest coffee and the coldest ice got her through, the former drunk by the liter, the latter applied to the back of her head and brow, to revive her energy and nerve. She walks to the kitchen to put on a fresh pot of coffee and check on her ice supply. Only one person to take care of. So why does it still feel like it's the whole world?

"So everyone has a plan," she calls. "And the sooner you all take off, the sooner I can get started…with my plan."

"What's that?" Lily says.

"To take care of my patient."

"Him or me?" Nancy says.

"You, baby," Homer says. "I'm set. Ready to go!"


When they're alone, Mimi studies her patient. Nancy looks drawn, her lovely caramel skin is now a yellow-gray, her cheeks hollow, her golden eyes engulfed in purple puffs. So though Mimi hadn't intended to examine her here but to take her, after she rested, to her office at the Women's and Children's Institute, she pulls her stethoscope from her bag to check her heartbeat.

"I feel better already," Nancy says when Mimi is done. "With you in charge."

"Liz did everything right, honey," Mimi says, laying the

stethoscope on the chair and her hand on Nancy's shoulder.

"But I feel better with you delivering the baby. Here with everyone close by."

At the WCI, Mimi has been doing no clinical work, but even if she were, she would not deliver Nancy's baby.

She shakes her head. "Your heartbeat is fast and if I took your blood pressure I know it would be high. I don't think you're a candidate for a midwife delivery."

"What if I take care of myself? Now that Homer's okay, I'll take care."

"I can't make any promises," Mimi says. "We'll have to see."

"We'll wait and see?" Nancy says. "But maybe yes?"

"We'll see. Right now a doctor should see you. We could get you seen at WCI quickly. Get your blood pressure under control."

"Tomorrow," Nancy says. "Or the next day….Today I want to see Homer. Know that he's settled in. That will be a load off my mind. Probably my blood pressure will drop then on its own."

She sounds like the kids when they'd make deals against bad odds—snow days in October, Santa Claus in July. It always amazes and amuses her—how some women dart back into childhood just before they take the irreversible leap into motherhood. Today, she feels alarmed, annoyed.

"Today," Mimi says. "I'll drive you to check on Homer. But you have to see a doctor today. A short visit with Homer. And then off you go."

"Okay. Homer. Then off I go."

# 16. Treat

"Steven arranged everything," Homer explains. He is already lying in his hospital bed, on a medical ward, with an IV and catheter. "We walked into Urgent Care and everyone's racing towards us like the docs on *St. Elsewhere*. Right, Ton?"

"Right," Tony says.

"And then ten minutes later, I was here, all set up."

"Great," Nancy says. "That's a sign—that this is the right place!"

Mimi can't take her eyes off Nancy. She doesn't like the way she looks, her breath seems short, her slender ankles look as wide as her calves, her back is swayed, its muscles clearly weak. Which makes sense. Even now, she is doing everything she shouldn't be doing. Standing, pacing, bending down to raise Homer's bed and give him water.

"Sit down, Nancy," Mimi barks. Another time, she'd temper her harshness with humor. A Lily-ish, Down, Nancy. Down, girl. She's not sure what's going on with Nancy, but she knows it's not a joke. "If you want half a chance to push out your baby, sit down, right this second."

"You're scaring me," Nancy says.

"Good," Mimi says. "Someone's got to scare some sense into you. You just sit there while I go call Dr. Foster and see if she can fit you in."

Lynn Foster, her favorite ob-gyn, specializes in complicated pregnancies and deliveries. She'd worked with her for years at Mercy, and it was Lynn who'd told her about the opening at WCI. When she explains the situation, she knows Lynn will tell her to bring Nancy right over. *If she can fit you in*—she said that because she wants Nancy to worry enough to do the right thing for a change. She's acting like a mindless child. Even her teen mothers had more sense!


What was that all about? Tony wonders. What was his mother barking about before she zoomed out the door and down the hall? He was nodding off, but he heard most of what she said. *Half a chance to push the baby out.* Did she mean that the baby might never come out or just that Nancy could have trouble pushing it, or just that she couldn't deliver it, but would get her friend Lynn to? *If* the doctor agreed. She made it sound so bad, so scary. But wasn't that one of her routines? Next time you climb up a tree at night, you'll probably break your neck not just your thumb when you fall. Next time you make prank phone calls, the cops will come and take you off to jail. Wasn't that the routine when she got scared herself, and a little mad too at the person who'd put her through it?

"She gets carried away," Tony tells Nancy. "Tough love or something along those lines."

Nancy has begun to cry. He feels like crying himself. Nothing was turning out right. But he forces a smile, and pats her hand.

In the last few months, his affection for Abby/Greg has grown slowly but surely like the baby itself and now he feels a big ball of love inside him. So if he's afraid now, what's Nancy feeling? This couldn't be good for her situation and if he gets the chance he will tell his mother to tone it down. He feels his mind wandering, but he tells himself, Stay calm, stay here, stay present, one of those Dr. Meloni baloney routines.

"It's okay," he tells Nancy, "just stay calm," and he pats her belly.

He loves when he and Lily do that together, sit side by side and pat the baby together. Sometimes, Lily whispers, Imagine…. Imagine that it's our baby, he knows she means—

that they've reached a mature enough stage in their own lives for that. Her eyes shine like Roco's then, and he strokes her head and whispers back, One day, Pup, you'll see.

Right now, though, he's glad she's not here. Why have her worrying too? Or staring at him? Since he arrived in DC, she's been staring at him, like, Hello, hello—are you there? Anyone home? And he honestly doesn't know where he is any more. Where his life is. In the letter in his back pocket, he thinks. Crushed under his ass!

"You sure?" Nancy says.

He can't remember what he said to her last, but he nods and says, "I'm sure."

"I just get these silly ideas," she says. "But if you say everything's going to be okay, I know it will be. Because you're a worrier...."

Then his mother's racing in just like she raced out, like she's trying to get appointed chief resident, waving a vial and a syringe that she's nabbed from her bag in the car. If she draws bloods right away and runs them over, Lynn Foster will have the results by five, when she has agreed to see Nancy. She whips out her blood pressure kit and slaps it on Nancy's arm.

"Take it easy, Mom, you're scaring her," he says.

She's scaring me! Mimi thinks. Her blood pressure was 180/100—and who knew what else was wrong! But she registers Tony's words, and says only, "Let's just get you strong, Nancy baby. There's nothing scary about you getting good and strong."

"In a hospital? How am I going to look out for Homey here if you put me in a hospital?"

"I said nothing about *putting* you in a hospital. Just doing the delivery there."

"You promise," Nancy says. "You really promise?"

She rolls up Nancy's sleeve and finds a vein for the needle.

"This is it for needles today, right?" Nancy says. "No

more needles?"

Grow up, Mimi wants to say. But she says what she used to say to the kids when they pushed her for reassurances she could not give. No shots, no yukky vitamins—you promise! "Let's just take it one step at a time....How does that sound?" she says. Then she runs out with her vials.

"Little steps," Nancy says. "Baby steps....Then everything will be fine. Right?"

She's looking at Tony, waiting for an answer.

"Right," he says. "She's making a fuss over nothing." He studies the dark rings under her eyes. "Lily used to have rings under her eyes...from allergies...." He is impressed that he's come up with this, because suddenly his head his killing him and he wants to get the hell out of this scary, hopeless place. When he went to the john, he'd read the letter again. Dr. Bullshit with his bullshit words. *We have serious concerns....*

"I heard my name," Lily says, opening the door.

"Tony was saying how you used to have allergies and that's probably what I have."

"Yeah, and Tony used to tease me. Remember you used to call me Racoon because of the big dark rings around my eyes? When I first came to live with you?"

Lily is looking at Tony, but he is somewhere else.

"Mine went away," Lily says. "Yours will too, Nance."

Homer is falling asleep, his head on the "baby."

"Mine too...if I take baby steps...tiny baby steps...." Nancy says. Then she's sleeping too.


Out in the hall Lily tells Tony that she called Doc who said it was okay to take time off. The clinic was slow. He gave her the numbers of some DC vets for part-time temp work and they were very nice and said they'd call if anything came up. Then she got brave and called the National Zoo, and she was lucky because she hit it off with the person in personnel and they need extra help in the monkey house! She makes a few chimpanzee shrieks, which always make him laugh. But he doesn't seem to notice.

"Are we really staying?" he says. "I told the doctor everything I know about Homer. He seems set. Do you think there's really anything else for us to do?"

Lily says, "I want to make sure Nancy takes care of herself. Help her get around too. She doesn't ask but she needs help."

"Maybe we'll be getting in their way. I don't want to bother them...."

The truth was everything was bothering him! Nancy crying like a baby and Homer snoring and snorting like a hog and his mother flying around like a ghoul. He wants to pack Lily in the car and drive off and never come back. He wants to be anywhere but here. Nothing nothing nothing was working out

"What's wrong with you?" Lily asks.

He doesn't want to upset her but he doesn't want to lie. And besides he knows he can't keep up this act much longer. She was already seeing though it. "A letter came...," he says.

She thinks she may have seen a postcard with a photo of a dolphin on Mimi's coffee table. "From Luisa, right? Don't tell me she can't come up for the shower!" Before he can answer she's turned away.

"Do you hear that, Ton? What was that, Ton?" she says.

"Nance, is that you? Nance, what's wrong?" she calls down the hall. "We're coming, Nance! Hold on, Nance! Hurry, Tony! Find a nurse!"

Nancy is on the floor near Homer's bed, flopping around like a seal in a pool of red and brown.

"Lily, what's this? Shit or blood or what?"

"Meconium...I think," Lily says, and she rings the bell for a nurse.

"Uh-oh, that's no good," Nancy says. "That's very bad."

"A nurse is on the way," Lily says. "Tony's finding one."

Then Nancy starts pushing, and Lily calls to her, as she'd

called to her over and over in Liz's class, "Hold on. Breathe."
She rubs her back, her front. "Don't push. Wait for the nurse.
Keep it in...."

Kneeling before her, Lily sees more dark stuff coming.
More meconium? Or the baby's head? Or both?

"Help us," Lily calls. She was only a stand-in coach in a
pretend-birth class practicing pretend-labor. "Help us!"

"Oh, Christ," Nancy shouts. "It hurts...so bad. So
bad...so bad...."

What was it that Mim used to say when her mothers
wouldn't stop screeching and pushing, and it wasn't time?

"Sweetheart...just a little while longer," Lily whispers.
She remembers that, but then what?

"Look in my eyes...stay with me....Soon...soon,
Sweetheart," she hears herself say.

"Now," Nancy shouts. "Fucking now...not soon...now,
you fucking hear me!" Nancy shouts.

Then she's silent.

Like a baseball, it pops into the air then descends, and
Lily squats. The Yogi Berra squat Mimi always called it. She
cups her hands, like she'd seen Mimi do all those times, then
scoops it up.

"What happened?" Nancy whispers. "Lily, what
happened? Did my baby come out?"

Lily nods. Is it alive or dead—the silent, slippery thing
she is holding in the air?

"No nurse," Tony says, running back into the room.
"What should we do?"

No nurse...no hope....The baby just lies in her hands.
No movement...or sound...or breath. What have I done? Lily
thinks. She just mimicked what she saw Mimi do and Liz
and all those midwives in all those films she used to watch
when Mimi took them with her to work. But it turned out all
wrong. The baby lies in her hands, bloody and still, looking
like a roast beef fresh from the butcher.

"Did my baby die, Lily? Yes or no?" Nancy calls.

Her voice is light, care-free, like she just wants to know, so she can plan the rest of her day. It's hormones, Lily knows, that secrete a barrier between mothers and terror, so they can face all that birthing entails. But how long until the terrible truth breaks through? She hadn't birthed Nancy's baby but maybe...*deathed* it?

Lily cuts the cord and turns the baby upside down, then holding it by its feet, slaps its back.

But nothing happens.

She turns the baby right-side-up and covers its lips with her own. She sucks as hard as she can. She remembers Mimi doing that once and the baby squealing suddenly, thrilled, as if from an amazing kiss.... But now, though Lily sucks and sucks, her mouth a frantic pump, nothing happens. The baby's color's changing, blanching from brown-red to gray-pink. On its way to blue?

With the baby in her arms, Lily advances to the door, to fly down the hall, to grab someone to help—when one last giant inhale pumps out a dark stream. And then the cries. The first one sounds like a puppy yelping. The second like a beeper. And then it's one long screech, like a siren.

"A girl," Lily calls, lifting her in the air.

"Hello, Abigail. Hello, my darling," Nancy calls from the floor. "How's my darling, how's mama's pretty darling?"

And then a pair of doctors and a nurse rush the room.

One takes the baby. Two lift Nancy onto a gurney.

Nancy calls, "Hey, Homer, wake up. Your girl is here. Wake up and meet your darling!"

Homer opens his eyes, just in time to call, "Hello, hello, father's joy." Then wave goodbye.

# Winter

# 17. Mother's Milk

So that the family can be together in what Lily calls "their first home," Homer's doctor, Dr. Chavez, has arranged for Nancy to visit Homer's room many times a day, bringing Abby with her whenever she can. Born six weeks early, Abby spends half a day in the incubator. But she is doing so well, that she can spend almost half the day "at home" in her mother's arms.

For a few days, everyone gathers around studying the "angel." They all see signs of her strong character and her happy future.

Her hands are big for her tiny body, which tells Homer she is a born fighter who no one will mess with.

Lily says that her coos, which seem exceptionally varied and expressive, tell her that Abs will be gifted with language, and people will want to listen to her and follow her advice.

Even Tony comes up with something. Wise eyes, he says. They are golden like Nancy's and he wants to say she will be a natural teacher like her mother, but he finds himself unable to say the word, teacher, and just says, She will be …something else! Everyone laughs, and for the rest of that day *Something Else* is their pet name for Abby.

Nancy says her constant smile shows she will know much joy and give much joy and enjoy many friendships. One day she sees her future in politics, another day in entertainment.

Mimi knows the bowed mouth is a sign of gas not joy, but she doesn't say so. She knows also that you can never know how they will turn out and can only do your best and hope. She's glad she's too busy helping with the nursing and burping to take part in the game.

It's the actual birth, which she's missed, that Mimi will stop work to talk about those first few weeks. She loves to hear about the Yogi Berra catch, clapping joyously when Lily squats to demonstrate. She loves to hear the part when Nancy calls, Is my baby dead or alive? and Abby wails the answer.

"The first exchange between mother and child," Mimi tells Nancy one day. "You'll never forget it, Nancy."

"Remember *our* first exchange, Lily?" Mimi asks.

Lily can't remember Mimi not being in her life, but she knows she means that morning on Mimi's front lawn on Barberry Lane. A crying Connie rushing into Mimi's arms, and Mimi whispering, Don't worry, sometimes mommies get sad too, Lily. But then, *poof,* they feel better. Poof, Lily said, to get Connie to stop crying. It worked, that time, and sometimes later on. Poof, Ma. Poof, poof, she'd say, and her mother would sometimes laugh, and say it back. Poof, poof, yourself, my angel.

"On the lawn," Lily says.

The bright miracle of meeting Mimi more and more eclipses the pain of losing Connie. And Lily can't get enough of Mimi stories, Mimi and her, Mimi and Tony.

"What was your first *exchange* with Ton?" Lily asks. She remembers but she wants Mimi to tell it again.

"I was scared, too, like Nancy," Mimi says. "I was alone on a crowded ward with no nurse or doctor in sight, no clue of what to do when the contractions seized me, how to ride them through. The woman in the next bed, a mother of three with hours to go till her fourth, heard me crying and jumped out of bed. She wiped my forehead and gave me ice, and told me how and when to push and stop, push and stop, then push all the way…."

"She put him on my stomach and the next minute he was on my breast and sucking. I asked her her name. It was Antonia and I said to the baby, I'm going to name you after this nice lady. I said, Antonia, this is Anthony. Anthony, say hello and thank you to Antonia. That was our first exchange, introducing him to the stranger who had delivered him. Then I thought, *I* want to catch babies…for scared strangers. I said, Hey, Tony, how would you feel if I did this, too?"

"And he said, Enough, Ma. One exchange is all I can take. I need to sleep. No more exchanges, please Ma." Lily laughs, looking across at Tony snoring in the chair.

Homer is in his bed, dozing too, but listening. "I like the story," Homer says. "Go on." He is so grateful that Mimi is here. There was a time when he thought she'd never talk to him again.

"I said, 'It means I'll be very busy. You might be lonely.'"

"But then you got me, to keep him company. Right, Mims?"

"Exactly. Lucky Tony."

"We are very lucky," Nancy says, beginning to cry. "That we have each other…for company….How many people are so blessed?"

Lily whispers in Tony's ear that when they have a baby, she wants it to be just like this. Everyone sitting together. She bets he can get some time off…teacher's parenting leave or something like that?

Tony startles. "Something like what?"

"You know, new-baby leave. As a teacher," Lily says.

"Oh, Jesus," he says. Was that him? he thinks. What do you call that weird sound that just came out of him? A wail, a yowl, a howl?

"What happened?" Nancy screams. She'd been daydreaming about Abby's first senatorial swearing-in, a cold but dazzling day…."Why's everyone shouting?" She looks around the room. "Where's my baby? Who hurt my baby? Where'd they take my baby!"

"Wa wa wa," Abbie cries from her breast.

"Oh, there you are!" Nancy says, rocking with laughter. "Mama's joy."

Dr. Lawrence, Abigail's pediatrician, is a gentle man but there is no way to buffer the blow. He had thought her slight prematurity explained it and that the time in the incubator would resolve it. But they haven't. Abby's heartbeat often sounds normal, but sometimes it's quite slow. They've done a cathaterization and something's shown up. Incubation alone would not suffice. Abby would have to be moved to the ICU.

He assures Nancy and Homer and Lily that there's nothing they could have done to prevent it. If it was any consolation, they weren't alone. They were seeing this in a number of babies born to Gulf vets.

"It?" Nancy whispers. "What's it?"

"In this case, a small…hole."

"Small hole?" Nancy says. "Where?"

"In the heart…but it's really small. You're lucky. We're seeing some Gulf babies with bigger holes, bigger problems…."

Mimi is glad he has stopped there. The other night, Steven showed her some photos of Gulf vet babies—with noses sprouting from their necks, hands poking from their thigh. With hearts with holes the size of a quarter that might never close up.

"And the treatment?" Mimi says. "Tell us the treatment for this *tiny* hole."

"We are just monitoring it carefully for now. We want to see if it will correct without any treatment. Besides oxygen and electrolytes and an anti-inflammatory."

"And the cause?" Lily asks.

"We're not sure. We think depleted uranium may be involved. DU weapons destroy everything they touch, and then burst into flame….That means lots of uranium dust floating in the air."

"But they said DU was harmless to breathe," Tony says.

"They said Agent Orange was harmless," Dr. Lawrence says. "Until recently, the military held fast to that."

"So it's just going to heal on its own?" Nancy says.

"Let's give it some time," the doctor says. "I don't think there's any reason to get alarmed. And rush into surgery."

"That's good," Homer says. "I mean that there's no need for surgery. That we just got to give it time....And with all the research that's going on here, I'll be better in no time. And we can all be home again. We're lucky, Nancy," Homer says.

Nancy says nothing. She feels her milk letting down and she hooks Abby onto her breast.

"There there, there there, little baby. Don't you worry. Mama's gonna make you strong... and fine...."

She needed to focus on healing her baby and nothing else. Only the natural, wholesome soups and salads Lily has been preparing would pass her lips; she wouldn't add a grain of salt to anything and she'd stop all sugars, even the Mounds bars from the vending machine she's been turning to when she's particularly tired and scared. Her milk would be the healthiest in the world, and it would give her baby the nutrients necessary to close up the tiny hole. She needed to block out things that could make her anxious and interfere with her milk production and the healing process.

"We'd like her in the sterile chamber for a while," Dr. Lawrence says. "She'll be cared for well there. They'll feed her well there."

He says it twice. Nancy says nothing. "Did you hear what I said, Ms. Jackson?"

"She needs to be fed well....I heard that. I'll pump," Nancy says.

"Pump, sweetheart," Mimi says. "And freeze it. Then when she's out of the unit, you'll still have a good supply to give her...."

"I mean now," Nancy says. "She needs my milk now. Now more than ever!"

Dr. Lawrence shakes his head. "Not now. I'm so sorry. Mother's milk is not advised now. We need to control what she's getting, know exactly which nutrients and how much."

"Please" Nancy says.

"Soon," Mimi says. "Soon she'll have you…and you'll have her. And everyone will be back home. You'll see."

"It really has to be this way, Mimi, to make my baby strong?"

"It has to be this way. For now," Mimi says. "But soon…you'll see…."

"Soon…little baby," Nancy croons. "Don't you worry, little baby. Don't worry, little baby. Don't you worry," she whispers.

Then the baby's asleep.

"She'll be in good hands," Mimi whispers.

And Dr. Lawrence wheels Abbie away.


Every night Lily cooks and every morning she brings containers of brown rice and steamed vegetables, sprouts, pureed fruit and organic yogurt to the hospital. One day a week, at Mimi's insistence, she gets away, temping in the small apes area of the National Zoo. Most days, though, she's with Nancy and Homer. Homer sleeps and Nancy ferries back and forth between the ICU and her room, upbeat on her way to see Abby, morose when she has to leave. Lily stays at her side, coach and mascot, telling Nancy over and over, Looking good. Doing great. You go, girl.

Tony stays with Homer. It was Lily's understanding that he had signed on to do for Homer what she does for Nance. But half the time, he's asleep on the job. And then Lily has Homer to look after too—feeding him her food, checking on his spirits, wheeling him twice a day to the ICU to peek at his girl! If Tony were truly sleeping when he was asleep on the job, Lily would understand better. But often he isn't dozing...but *dazing*, she thinks. She'd imagined he'd used the time when Homer was resting to prepare specific lessons and materials, but if he's not sleeping, he's staring across at Homer or down at some papers. Sometimes he looks up when she enters the room, but he doesn't seem to see her.

A couple of times, she's shoved her face up close, and kissed him, nose to nose Eskimo-style, which he's always loved. And once he rubbed her nose back, but the last time he just jerked away, like he couldn't breathe with her so close. That hurt so bad, and she raced from the room, and he called after her, What? What? What's wrong? Did he really not know? Cooing doves one day and the next...he's looking at her like, Are you even my species!

Now, it's a couple of days later, and, leaving Nancy at the ICU, she hears thin, high sounds nearby —like a newborn kitten's purrs. She stops moving to make them out. They are sighs and they are coming from her! How could that be! Her mother sighed all day long the months before she left, and when she realized she was never coming back, Lily vowed never to sigh. If only her mother had not sighed! In her child's mind, she'd see Connie sighing and sighing till she became one big sigh, rising into the sky and floating away. Only promising herself to make a grown-up life, where safety and stability would not vaporize daily, taking your hope, your breath, and you with it, eased her agony. But look at her now!

And who could she turn to with her strange, sudden sorrow? Not Nancy. Not Homer. Not Mimi, who was doing too much as is these days. Not Steven. He was way too busy, and even if he wasn't, too dignified a person to expose to the ugly vibes and sounds she's emitting of late.

# 18. Toast

"Wilmington is a downer," Sean says, when she reaches him on his cell. "My job...my brother."

"So come here again," Lily says. "You said you would."

"I know but it got complicated with my brother for a while. Now it's not."

His cousin in D.C. has been pushing him to stay with him indefinitely. Maybe he will.

"I'm actually packed. I've known for a while that I should not be here in Wilmington? It's a very sad city? All the plastic and poison production...with plastic, poisonous people to match!"

"That's not for you," she says. "You're a nourishing person. You give nourishment and you deserve it in return. You should come here soon."

"There's a train at one," he says. "If I rush I'll make it?"

She is so glad she followed her feeling and did not go to the zoo this afternoon as she had scheduled. She felt too sad to do much of anything and besides, monkeys, way more than people, in her experience, sense human sorrow and become depressed themselves; and life was hard enough for her spider monkeys, stuck in *habitats* that were actually smaller than Doc's large-dog cages.

She is so glad that she did not just wallow; but reached out to Sean. One little action can lead to a whole bunch of positive outcomes. They spoke, he was on the train, he'd stay here, at least for a while, which would cheer her and everyone up. They all liked him. He was kind and trustworthy, Tony said the first time he met him, and reminded him of Ernie.

She meets Sean at Union Station, and after they find a locker for his bags, they walk over to the mall, stopping at the reflection pool to drop pennies and make wishes.

"What's with the sighs?" he says. "Tell me, Little One. A penny for your thoughts?"

"I think Tony doesn't love me any more. And doesn't want to share his life with me...." Before she spoke, it had been only an uneasy feeling, but now there it was a whole, horrible thought!

"Tell me the signs, hon."

"Ignoring me, for one....Ignoring me, for two....I don't exist. He doesn't love me...."

"Oh, that space-cadet look? I saw that when I was last here? It has nothing to do with you, girl? And all to do with the fact that his head, at present, is up his ass way high."

"You mean he's *distracted from* me...not *disgusted...by* me?"

"Totally totally distracted. But so might you be if you came back from a silly, murderous war...which is still attacking your friends...? The stare I detected on your man is so totally an I'm-so-worried stare. So not a leave-me-alone, I-don't-love-you-any-more stare?"

"Oh my God, it's not just not looking at me. At night he paces out on the sun porch and when I call him in, he pretends not to hear! I try to offer comfort. It's just a rough patch, I say. Everyone's on the mend. And soon we'll be back and your glorious teaching career will be launched! But it's like he's deaf...at least to me."

"Listen, child, I had a true love once, a not-so-true love, I should say, and, honey-bunch, when he was done with me he looked at me with positive hatred...and mocked my every word and tear. When I entered a room, he left. And if my personal belongings were in the wrong place, on his chair, in his side of the closet, etc, etc, he'd cut them up with horrible, giant scissors."

"How mean can a person get!"

"Very. My ex was very very very mean. Your man is not.

My ex was my brother….I mean the one I said was my brother. He wasn't anything though but a cruel human being whom I had mistaken for my true love for life."

"You should have told me," she says. "You shouldn't have held all that sorrow inside you. Poor you…."

"Stop….I cannot think about…that any more? Or accept pity however well-intentioned."

"You sure you don't want to talk…?"

"Not now, best girlfriend. I *cannot* go there. I *can* talk about *you* now though. And, honey, I cannot reiterate enough that your Anthony situation is so totally unlike the destructive relationship I was just ejected from."

"It doesn't mean anything that he ignores me?" she says. "Imminent ejection…rejection?"

"It means he's wrecked and dazed, but hardly devoid of feelings of love…."

"Thank you, thank you," she says.

She's so glad they talked. She feels so much better. Tony still loved her and she loved him. But he was worried and preoccupied, and how could he not be? He'd been back from the war for less than a year, and it was like war all over again! All the anxiety about Homer and Ernie, and now the baby, and all the guilt because *he* was fine. And the stress of preparing for teaching like nothing was wrong—and as if all that wasn't enough, on top of that, teaching about *war*!

"I have a future, but so do you, Sean," she says. "Tony and I have a life to live together but so will you…with someone who deserves you…."

"Thank you for your kind wishes. My here in D.C. cousin…my not-cousin, that is, is fun but not deep like us. So we shouldn't expect more from Milton. Milton's lots of fun. But probably nothing more?"

When the time is right, he will tell her about Milton and the other *cousins* and *brothers* and his dear dead mother and his cruel and might-as-well-be-dead police-officer father, who ripped up his dress-up items, and smashed his dolls and him every chance he got until he, Sean, could take no more....But dwelling on negatives did him no good. He needed to pursue only the positive aspects of life. He and Lily were experiencing mere pauses in their pursuits?

"Now is not the time to plan your wedding, but one day soon...I will and it will be well worth waiting for. We're not stuck but just still, you and I, poised like dancers readying ourselves for a gorgeous, gigantic leap? In the meantime, we have to stay affirmative in our outlook?"

"Right," she says sadly. "I guess you're right." She'd been feeling happy again until he mentioned the wedding. "The baby was going to be...a flower girl or something. *Bud baby*...that's what I called it." She laughs a low, sad laugh.

"Think of the good stuff....You're a wonderful godmother to her—catching her and all. A wonderful friend and birth coach to her mother?"

"That was an accident....I just caught her. I didn't plan it. What about all my plans? I had their whole shower set. I have most of the food in the freezer."

"Can't you still give them their shower? Something small but lovely for Ab and Nance. In an intimate quiet space...?"

"Like the pediatric ICU?" she cries. "Give me a break!"

"Never heard of a solarium?" he says. "For use by patients and their families? Why not a lovely solarium gathering?"

Why not! Dr. Lawrence was permitting Abby to leave the ICU in her bubble-cart for brief family visits, but they haven't happened yet. "Seanie, that's brilliant! A lovely solarium gathering," she laughs, unable to stop.

And he joins in. On the edge of the pool, where they've stopped for their talk, they rock back and forth, like they haven't a care in the world besides not falling in the water.

She says she will drive back to Monuten to retrieve the quiches and meatballs from the freezer, the fudge cake from Stoehmer's.

She will do nothing, Sean says. She will stay with Nancy,

try to take it easy. He will do what needs doing: assorted wraps, chocolate covered strawberries, a carrot cake to die for.


Dr. Chavez books the solarium and Dr. Lawrence gives the OK for Abigail to attend the shower. Her two weeks in the ICU have helped them sort out the situation. No infections have emerged, no allergic reactions, just an intermittently lowered heart rate, though less remarkable than before. They can transport her to the party in her sterile incubator. A half hour seems a good length of time for her first party.

They do it on a Saturday so that Mimi and Steven can attend without taking off any more time from work than they already have. They have both been troopers—Steven translating when the doctors' words are incomprehensible, Mimi coming by the hospital every day to check on Nancy and the baby. They will keep the party short and sweet, Lily says.

She and Sean arrive early to decorate. It is a pleasant room, even in early December beaming with late afternoon sun. The furniture is standard seventies institutional—*L*s of stainless steel chairs and couches with orange vinyl cushions that show mars and scars that vinyl was made to resist but always suffers in the end. Lily finds them depressing, like Mimi's furniture. But the walls are cheerful enough—a pale green-gray on which landscape and still-life posters from unknown museums hang, generic, unobtrusive hospital art. It is the trees, though, that make the room—potted ficus that have become popular in lobbies and banks and yuppie homes. But these are gigantic with glossy leaves, sending a clear message to patients and their families—You are in a place where living creatures thrive and so shall you.

"Nice," Lily says, taking in the room. "The light...the plants."

"Perfect," Sean declares. "As the sun sets, our light will

rise…?"

He has brought strings of clear bulbs and gets to work tossing them on trees and along the border of the room. At five, when the party is to start, the white lights begin to twinkle, and Lily and Sean agree that anyone coming into the room would not think hospital at all but a private place, peaceful and pretty, fitting for baby's first event.

Nancy arrives first, and she loves it all—the lights, the tablecloths, the flowers.

Sean knows Lily is about to say, The tablecloths are plastic sheets and the flowers cleaned-up patient discards, both donated by Homer's nurses. But if she does, illness will enter the room, and tonight it is to be banished. So he whispers in her ear, "Keep your trap shut."

Before, through the ICU window, where she spends her days, Nancy watched the attendant dress Abbie in the white linen suit from Hopkins, which Lily has washed and ironed. Sean had implored Lily to tell Nancy and Homer it is an old family treasure. But Lily explained that Nancy and Homer know she has no family, that they are more or less her family, and besides it's too late. Proudly she has bragged to Nancy that it cost only two dollars but when new probably went for over a hundred. And together they had read the label—Irish linen, embroidered in Firenze by hand!

"Wait till you see her," Nancy says. "In the little suit."

In a way, Lily thinks, it's good that the baby is coming later. It feels, for the moment, like the real shower she had planned when the baby was still inside. Sean had wanted it to be a surprise, but Lily thought that Nancy had had enough surprises in her life of late and anticipating it would counter the gloom enveloping her since Homer came in for treatment and she learned that Abigail came out with the hole in her heart.

Homer is the second to arrive. Then Mimi and Steven. Then Tony. Then nurses Arlette Adams and Jeffrey Chin, and the two other Gulf vets Homer and Tony met at SM Urgent

Care, who occupy the room across from Homer's. They're all there, except Abby.

Lily distributes party hats, which tie under the chin. They are paper plates, which she has decorated with a drawing of a hand crafted from the letters that spell the word *hand*. H-A-N-D—the best word for the best baby and family, Lily explains. H for Homer, A for Abigail, N for Nancy, and then D for Determined, which describes them to a tee.

"I thought of Delightful too and ...." Dazzling she is about to say. And Dears. But she stops. In another second, she knows, they'd all start coming up with D words, and then how long before someone said something that would ruin everything. Diseased, Depleted Uranium, Dishonorable Discharge, Done for, maybe even Dead?

"Determined is excellent," Homer says from his wheelchair. "That's what we are. We'll beat this for sure." The hospitalization and the baby have energized him.

"Determined...," Nancy says wearily.

"And *hand* to express the idea of giving a hand, as in applauding and also helping." Lily says.

"And you made the hand small but chubby like a baby's? Perhaps so we think above all of baby Abigail?" Sean says.

"Abigail isn't chubby," Nancy whispers.

"But she will be," Homer says.

"She will be," everyone says.

"She's a *determined* one," Homer shouts.

And then, as if on cue, the nurse opens the door and in wheels Abigail.

"She is chubbier today," Lily cries. And it's not just the thick linen suit, she's sure.

"She is!" Mimi says. "I read the chart and it said she gained eight ounces but I thought maybe it was an error. Look at her. She's a fatso. Look at her belly."

Through the incubator's plastic dome, Nancy studies the dome of Abigail's belly. It does look bigger today, and she wants to believe it's because her baby is becoming a fatso.

But could it be that her abdominal muscles are straining to help her breathe? Up up up, the belly goes, like a beach ball filling with air. But then she watches it go down, and become a skinny belly again, not as skinny as it's been maybe but hardly fat or even chubby. She studies Abby's skin, translucent and yellow like the plastic wrap she gives her kids to wrap their Easter baskets.

For the first time since they pulled the baby from her breast, Nancy is glad not to be nursing. Steven has supplied several bottles of champagne, and she feels like drinking a bottle all by herself. Maybe then hatred for her husband, which floats like a monster in the middle of her mind, would drown and sink out of sight. When Abby first came out, she had cried, Is the baby dead? But it was, odd as it sounds, a mere request for information. For weeks she's been on a free-fall from the hormonal high that could produce such a question with no trace of alarm, to a dark vicious depth she's never known before. When she's not sleeping, she's been staring at Homer as he slept. What have you done to my baby? Why are you alive after doing what you did? Again and again, she thinks this. The handsomest guy, the coolest boyfriend, the tenderest husband—she knows that she has thought him each of these over the course of time, and even a week ago would have said that she loved him. But now he is her tormenter, giving her a child only to take it away.

She knows he was already sick when he raised his arm to beat her, and he didn't think it was her but the enemy attacking; but still the miserable beast in the middle of her mind gnaws on the memory day after day, hunting and devouring other memories to fuel its hatred. She remembers one night before he went to the Gulf, telling him she had her doubts about this war. She said she was sure the problem could be worked out peacefully. Saddam was a bully, he said, and bullies only understand might. She is generally regarded as altruistic and generous, but she couldn't stop herself from saying, Who are the Kuwaitis to us? What has Kuwait done for you and me lately? That was mean and irrational, he said, and he didn't want to talk anymore unless she was going to be decent and rational. She began to say, In what way is war decent and rational? But he left the room, saying he didn't listen to lunatics.

He never listened. He couldn't hear anything but the words in his head: get them, show them, *semper fi*.

Today she studies him as he lifts his cup to make the first toast. What bullshit would he come up with now? she thinks as she watches him try to gather his thoughts.

"People," he says, but he is clearly exhausted today, and his voice is so weak that it comes out, "Pee." "Friends," he says, which comes out "Fred."

Once more with feeling, she thinks. Courage and all that shit. She's dying for the drink. She could use a little courage now, to get through everything. And discipline, so she doesn't go crazy despising him. But the hatred satisfies her so, like sex, or nursing, or breaking everything in sight.

And then, somehow, his voice gets firmer, and he says that these have been the happiest days of his life. He says he owes it all to his Nancy, giving him his Abigail, his "father's joy," brightening the darkest days they've ever known. He says he knows how hard it's been for her, but she hung in there with him. He will get healthy again to be there for them both. He can't believe he brought all these problems home and wishes he could draw them all back, into his own body. He hopes he never has to go to war again.

Still no toast, so she empties her glass and pours herself another. She's not impressed. He couldn't go to war again, even if he weren't half dead. Unless he got back to base soon, which was highly unlikely considering his condition, the corps would probably boot him out. What else did he think the letters meant! "Dishonorable discharge might be pursued." What a bunch of bastards they were, and what a dope he was, deaf to everything she ever tried to tell him, blind to everything but their green shit.

"To my fam," Homer says. "And my buds." Then he's too choked up to speak.

Steven says, "Homer, Nancy, I know this is such a hard time for you and it should be only a joyous time. But things can look up...truly...."

He meant it as a gift, and considering his scientist's exactness, it was a generous gift for him, but it sounds like a death knell, Mimi thinks. She puts her finger to her lips, to signal across the room to him to say nothing more.

Things *were* looking up! He hadn't read the chart today, and she had.

"Sweetheart," Mimi whispers to Nancy, "the baby will leave the ICU in a couple of weeks. You'll both go home soon."

If she lives, if that bastard didn't kill her, Nancy thinks. "How do you know that about the baby?" she says.

"I read her chart today. The hole is smaller. They think it's closing up and anticipate normal functioning."

"Really? She'll be okay? Can I give her my milk again? I've been pumping so much...." As she speaks, the front of her shell pink blouse turns crimson from the sudden flow of milk.

"We'll see. But she'll be fine and home soon. She's very lucky."

"And *him*?" Nancy says.

If the baby is okay, she will not hate Homer any more. She will love him again. Just like she did all these months, and all the years before. Her soaring boy, who slowed down just to be with her.

"What about Homer? I don't want to leave my Homey all alone."

Mimi wants to smile and say, He's lucky too. He'll come home, he'll be okay soon. But they knew too little about the disease to say. His lab numbers looked better when she peeked at his chart this morning, but they weren't yet normal. They'd just have to do their best for him and see.

"I could rent a hotel room nearby till my Homey's ready to leave."

"No hotel. You'll stay with me," Mimi hears herself say. "You and the baby....Till...."

"Just till Homey has a discharge date. Then me and Abs will go home to get the house ready. Hear that, Homes," Nancy says, finding Homer by the window, and wheeling him in circles. "Things are looking up, Homes. We're going home with Mimi and soon you'll go home with us!"

"Thanks, Mimi, for taking care of my girls," Homer says. "Thanks, Mama Mimi."

Mama Mimi. Was it only a few months ago that she kicked up her heels and escaped? Mimi thinks. Just a few months ago when she left the aches of mothering children and babies and babies' mothers, for a new carefree life? A few months off, and now look where they were!

"We'll help, too, Mims," Lily says. She's checked her calendar this morning. Tony had staff meetings this Tuesday and Wednesday. Classes Thursday. So they had to go back to Monuten in a day or two. "Every weekend. You'll see. Like old times," she says, patting Mimi's back. "So stop mezzo-ing, my sweet Whatever. 'Cause no one's gonna leave my darling Whatever alone."

Then Sean announces that it's time for presents...then cake.

If the government makes good on its threat to discharge Homer, they will be totally hard up, not just new-baby hard up, Lily knows, and so she's told everyone that money and not presents was in order.

No time to shop, Didn't know your taste—everyone says a version of this, then hands Nancy an envelope.

"Here comes the cake," someone sings.

And Sean marches in with a cart. It could be a wedding cake! Seven layers, and then a tower of three more topped with a doll—a candy baby doll, which looks like Abby— milk chocolate with gold wrapped chocolate coins for eyes.

"I made it," Sean says. "But Lily designed it? Everything's edible. Even baby's rattle. It's a pretzel I dipped in chocolate?"

"It's big enough to feed an army!" Homer laughs.

He wheels himself to the door and waves down the hall for other vets to join them. He has made friends here on the ward, and a couple of hospital buddies along with a couple of new arrivals wave back, and then join the gathering.

He looks so frail! Nancy thinks, watching him as he wheels around the table distributing carrot cake with cream cheese-coconut icing. But the champagne helps her shoo the thought away. Friends. Lights. Cash. A good hospital. New treatments. The party has pumped her with energy—the party and the small hand resting trustfully on her chest, and the small mouth sucking hopefully on her finger and soon maybe on her breast. Soon, when they're with Mimi, waiting for Homer to come home.

Tony hears them singing—"Happy Birthday Dear Abigail"— and in a minute he intends to open his eyes. He doesn't want to be rude, but he feels so fucking zapped. Driving back and forth to the hospital several times a day has worn him out. And more and more, especially at dusk, when the sky darkens to charcoal gray, he could swear he's not on the Beltway but on that other highway. He smells its burning smell sometimes and starts to gasp, and then he pulls onto the shoulder till he can breathe normally again. Several times this week, with no luck, he has called Ernie, to see how he is, to tell him to come here to Southern Maryland. And ask him what he remembers. It's not like Ernie not to answer his calls. He thinks he left messages, but maybe he didn't.

The truth is, since Homer and Nancy arrived, the only thing that's clear in his mind is the letter. The letter from Dr. Bullshit. By now he has memorized every word. *I'm not sure we see eye to eye on what young people need to know.* There was *a difference in values. A clash of core beliefs.* He and the superintendent liked peace as much as the next fellow, but young people needed the nourishment of *core American principles.* They had counted on him to impart these, not to concentrate on the *inevitable difficulties of war.* Moreover *not all institutions within a democracy could be or should be democratic: students are students, there to learn from authorities....*that was a key John Adams's tenet and tradition. They had no choice but to *rescind the job offer at this time,* and wished him every success in the world.

A face is in his face. Its eyes are wide and wild with something. Fear? Fury? A mixture? The eyes and the mouth join forces in a crazy grimace, or grin. The face of a maniac? A marine? One of these or maybe both? His own face? His soul splattered on the site of his old face? A face with no future. No future to face. Lily, Lily, he thinks, searching for her across the dim room. *Facing the Future* on the cusp of *Living Their Life* together. Where was she? He needed to see her!

He sees her eyes first, lighting here and there; then her mouth, chewing and talking; then her nose, crinkled to smile and dotted with white frosting; and finally her hand in the air, waving to him. He feels those terrible loony thoughts seep out of him, and something else trickle in. He's here, near her, his soul, his life, which, with her, he feels he can maybe face....

That strange face is before him again, but now he's sure it's not his.

"Tony?" it calls. "Tony is that you? Private Maybe is that you?"

The face looks familiar, like Leo Ludhauser's, that fat, suck-up who Morgan called Lard-ass. The same nervous smile and stare, he thinks, as if Lard Ass had been boiled in a cauldron and shrunken down to only mouth and eyes.

"You don't recognize me....It's me, buddy. Lard Ass."

"Hey," Tony says. "Hey...Leo?" It's inconceivable that

only a few months ago this wreck was Lard Ass, the barracks snitch. "You okay, Leo," he says. He pats his skinny arm.

"I'm what you see, bro. But this place is good. Finally, people are listening to us. So great that we're both here at the same time. This place is our best shot."

"I'm not in here, bro," Tony says. "I mean I'm a visitor. Homer...the proud pop inside, he's been my best buddy forever. He's here...."

"So you escaped Desert Rot....Good for you, good for you, man. I'm saying that with all my heart....Listen, we gotta talk, bro....I gotta tell you things."

Leo propels his wheelchair across the room and Tony follows him out the door to a hall bench, where Leo parks and Tony sits.

Tony says how his body feels back to itself. But not his mind. He tells him about driving on highways, convinced he's on another highway...in country, the burning smell, his pounding heart. "I know we drove to a highway...I think the highway from Kuwait City to Basra. But I don't know what we did there...what happened there. I tried not to think about it but it won't leave me alone. I remember the smell, but not much more."

"Lucky man," Leo says.


"There'd been a ceasefire. The Russians and U.N. had brokered it, and the Iraqi soldiers began their retreat north from Kuwait along the highway to Basra. Then the brass gave the order to shut down the highway at either end. The Abdali Road... A80, we called it....Any of this sound familiar?" Leo says.

"A80," I remember that. "The name A80. But I don't remember shutting it down. We did that?"

"Not us but *us*. U.S. And then when the highway was totally clogged with soldiers thinking they were going home, we got them. It was night. The night of February 27th and all night we pounded them with everything we had. Napalm. Depleted uranium. White phosphorus? Tens of thousands ...incinerated."

"I don't remember that...."

"We got there after. After our A10s strafed the A80 all night."

"I remember we drove north...."

"Right. We'd driven north. The air war was won and it looked like it was all over but we were deployed north in case the Iraqis had a surprise waiting. But in the meantime...they had surrendered. Or so they thought. And the U.N. thought and the Russians thought...and other allies. But we hadn't brokered it so it did not exist...and so...bombs away. By the time we arrived, it was all over. Remember? We waited on the side of the road till we got the order to move in for...clean up," Leo says.

"Clean up?" Tony says.

Leo nods.

"Plowing? I remember being on the LAV. Then on a plow?"

"You remember well, my man. A tank with plow blades...."

"What did we plow, Leo?" Tony says.

"What didn't we plow, man! Thousands of vehicles with thousands of retreating soldiers. Civilians too...Palestinian and Iraqi families living in Kuwait. When they heard there'd been a ceasefire, they high-tailed it to the highway, scared the Kuwaitis would slaughter them. But mostly there were military convoys on the road. Fried soldiers still sitting in their fried vehicles. Or pieces of soldiers blown all the fuck over the place ...charred soldier parts...."

"You know what I can't get out of my mind?" Leo says. "Maybe some of them were alive when we plowed....The order was to clear it...yesterday. A couple of photos had found their way into a couple of newspapers. And I guess they wanted no more nasty images getting out."

"The Highway at the End of the War...The Highway at the End of the World," Tony says. "That's what I keep dreaming, those words written in smoke in the sky. It looked like the end of the world...didn't it?"

Leo nods. "The Highway of Death—that's what people in the rest of the world are calling it. Crazy, right? We'd already bombed them to shit in their bunkers...in the berms. We'd hit Baghdad hard...all the big cities. Basra was...like finished, man. Half the country was like bombed back to the eighteenth century, man. Factories, homes, gas lines, electric lines, hospitals...gone. They were done for and then some, man. I mean we dropped more bombs in five weeks than were ever dropped before in the all the wars combined in all of history....But that wasn't enough!"

"Why, Leo? Why would we do that? Just last licks. Like a game?"

Leo shrugs. "Your guess is as good as mine. You seen that interview with Bush in the rose garden the next day? We will not accept any cease fire we have not signed...but we will not attack retreating soldiers. Like he knew what had happened and by saying it wouldn't, it hadn't. Insane, right? Fucked, right?"

"Sometimes Homer talks scary stuff about a highway. Do you think it's the same one?" Why, sir. Why? He remembers his words.

"There were a couple of Highways of Death, bro. The A80. Then a few days later the highway up the coast. Your bud could have been at either one. Army-AF op but some jarhead units helped out. Same deal...close down all exits on the road....Create a fifteen mile traffic jam. Then bombs away. Jesus. Their cannons were in travel-lock, facing backwards. They were flying fucking white flags...."

"But we got ours....We thought we got off Scot free. But, man, we were punished good. Highway of Poison. That's what I call it. I mean the highway wasn't the only place we got fucked. Just the last place. Operation Desert Poison, that's what we should call the whole fucking war. Shit, look around this fucking joint...and we're the lucky ones."

"So everyone here was *poisoned*?" Tony says. "Is that what you think? With what, Leo? Chemicals? Germs? The DEET? The vaccines? The DU?"

"All of the above probably," Leo laughs. "Different strokes for different folks probably."

"They told us we weren't exposed to Saddam's gas."

"How would they know that? I know we had troops cleaning out their bunkers after we'd bombed them....So if he had any shit, it could have gotten our guys then. And those fucking broken masks and suits were for shit from the start. And there was fucking DU everywhere. Penetrates anything, cheaper than anything. Munition of choice. I don't care if they say it's safe. They said the PB pills were safe. And they're not even fucking FDA approved. Remember someone said that and the Sarge said, Take it or be court marshaled. I was the first in line cause I was a pathetic little ass kisser. I felt sick right away."

"So it may have been our own shit...not their gas? Oh, shit, you think it was our own shit that got us?" Tony says.

"Either way it was our shit. You know who Saddam got the gas from?"

Tony shrugs. He'd never given it a thought.

Leo pokes his index finger into his chest, then Tony's. "*Us.* U.S."

"Tony, come get cake," Lily calls into the hall. "It's going fast!"

"You know, I got ideas brewing that I've told no one. They keep me sane. I was going to tell Einstein because I wanted him to work with me on a special project, which I thought would be right up his alley...."

"Up his alley?" Tony says.

"Something that made use of his knowledge of physics. $E=mc^2$....Get it?"

Tony shrugs. "Tell me straight, Leo. I'm really wiped...."

"Something that would teach certain high-up mother-fuckers a lesson. Think of shit…bullshit…manure…fertilizers. Think along those lines and think of things combined with things and blowing up in certain lying faces. It's so fucking perfect. I seek revenge for what those bastards did to us. And to all those people over there…."

"You gotta take it easy, man. That's not the way."

"What is?" Leo says.

"Talking…telling people the truth?" Teaching people, he thinks to say. But stops. "We just gotta find a way…to tell people what happened over there…."

"Who the hell's gonna listen? People don't listen. That's the problem, man. But, you don't have to worry about me and my crazy ideas. I'll be here for a while."

"Maybe you'll be better and home sooner than you think," Tony says. "This place looks great. You know, Einstein's got it too….We got to tell him about this place so he can come….I haven't been able to reach him in weeks."

"He was planning to come here."

"When? He shouldn't wait. When's he planning to come?"

Leo shakes his head. "He can't, man. Not anymore," he says. "Ernie's gone…man….Man, Einstein…he's dead…."

Vertigo and nausea. Rashes and cramps and joint pain and fever. Down the road a patch of cancer even. But not death, just like that. He hadn't seen it coming. He'd talked to him a couple of weeks ago, a month at most. He had a full scholarship, free tuition and a stipend. He had a 160 IQ.

He doesn't remember how he got to the floor, just sitting there between the bench and a wheel of Leo's chair, and Leo stroking his head.

"I had written to him to contact me about a 'science project.' One of his housemates found my address and wrote me. She said Ernie had a bad headache and she told him to lie down and when she came back with some Tylenol…he was gone. Shit, man."

"If I had just found out about this place sooner. And brought him here," Tony whispers. "Maybe then...."

"Imagine what I'm thinking," Leo says. "Listen, Maybe, you were a bud to your bud. I was a Lard-Ass, Morgan's fat-assed, ass-kiss enforcer! I snitched on Ernie when he couldn't finish his push-ups....When he just lay on the ground trying to catch his breath, I ran and told Morgan.... But I got mine....You know I called that Morgan prick to see if he had any insider info on Gulf Rot and he never even called me back. Don't cry, buddy. Wipe your tears...and get revenge....I'm on a fucking mission, man. As soon as I can fucking walk...which may be fucking never...."

"Tony, Tony, you do not want to miss this cake," Lily calls down the hall. Or maybe it's his mother? Or Nancy? His brain isn't working.

"Mary...that was the girl who wrote to me. She said one of the cats that lived in the house died a few days after. The cat had spent a lot of time with Ernie...."

Tony remembers Roco at the foot of his bed, day after day. Then dead in Lily's arms.

"Oh, shit, Leo....Oh, shit....You really think that's why...?"

"You hang around with us sickies, you could get sick," he says. "Look, man, there was oil everywhere, right? All the poisons in the air could have mixed in with the oil...and then settled on clothes, blankets, sand, skin....And then we brought them home! Student Health told her her problems come from stress...her reaction to Ernie passing...."

"What ...?" Leo had been talking about the animals and poisons and then...he kept talking. Student Health. Problems. "What... problems?"

"Mary's."

"Mary?"

"The girl who wrote to me. First she got a rash. And then she was feeling kind of weak. Trouble waking up for classes, she wrote me. She must have gone home. I can't reach her. Who knows, maybe she's a goner too," he laughs. "Me. I'm like no dog, no girl, no nothing. It's better. Right? You're like me. Alone. You feel a little lonely at least you know you're not hurting anyone you love. Not spreading any rot. Right?"

"Leo, you don't really think....Oh, Jesus."

"I don't think. I plot."

Tony stands up and looks down the hall. He had to get out of there. He had to think. "I got to go, Leo....I got to go...."

"What's your rush, man? You can't take everything I say seriously. I'm pretty fucking crazy."

But Tony's lifting his backpack, getting ready to go.

He finds a piece of paper in his wallet and quickly, before he can change his mind, writes her a note.

"Could you do me a favor, man?" he says. "Stay out here for five minutes? Then go back in and give the girl with the blonde braid this note?"

"The cute dwarf running the show? What's she to you?"

# 19. Closure

He has wanted to do this for the longest time, but never had the courage. It's not that he feels brave or ready tonight, just too fed-up and tired to worry.

Tony knows he's speeding, but now that he's set the plan, he's impatient. He takes the Foggy Bottom exit off the Parkway and turns a corner and the fucking Saudi Embassy is in his face. Saudis, the shitty war, and all the shitty oil and sand, are in your face, no matter where you turn. And he floors the gas pedal to speed away, and there he is on the wrong road and then in some fucking circle going round and round. He is so tired of this fucking city. The circles snaring you, the giant buildings shouting, You puny little shit. What made you think you could have a life! You and your dead friend....

He manages to escape the circle only to find himself at the Tidal Basin and trapped in another screwed-up circle that he spins around twice—from the Korean War Memorial to the Holocaust Memorial Museum—and back again and then again. Wars and memorials, memorials and wars. Would it ever end! A bunch of bullies playing games. Traps, tricks, gang-ups, last licks! Our side beats your side!

Ernie was *out*. Now who would be next? Homer? Him? Then...her?

By the time he finds a place to turn around, then finds his bearings, the street he's been looking for and a space for the van, he is drenched with sweat and too tired to move. He rests for a few minutes, with the window wide open and the radio full blast, so that he won't fall asleep and miss his chance.

Even on a clear night, the air down here is thick, and he

remembers his mother explaining that the area—Foggy Bottom—was named for the fog rising from the Potomac here at the bottom of the city. The bottom of the world, he thinks, that's where he was heading. He feels chilled from the wet dark all around, and feels like he's in one of the myths Mimi used to read to them, crossing a river from the living world to the underworld, because there's someone he needs to see.

When the party is winding down and that weird guy gives her Tony's message, Lily whispers to Mimi that she'll meet her later, then grabs Sean and runs.

What drama! Mimi thinks. Her son disappears and then Lily. No one says why or where they're going. It was infuriating how childish they could be, her drama prince and princess!

"Don't get mad," Steven says. "Maybe something's wrong."

It hasn't crossed her mind, but at the suggestion she quickly shifts from annoyance to dread. Steven's car is parked right in front of the hospital. They could probably get to it before Lily got to hers in the lot, and then meet up with her before she left the hospital grounds. Mimi knows she's been busy with Nancy lately and hasn't been very attentive to Lily. They will catch up with her and she'll ask her what's wrong and if she can help. At the very least, she wants to give her directions. Washington is so easy to get lost in. Especially at night.

But the elevator takes forever and even though Steven speeds, they arrive at the parking lot only to glimpse Lily's Corolla zipping out of the driveway and onto the service road leading to the Parkway.

"Follow her," she says. "Please, Steven, fast."

He laughs. "Talk about dramatic! I didn't mean we had to follow them. I was only suggesting an attitude shift."

"Well, you got one!" she says. "I'm so scared. Everyone

getting sick around them. God knows what's going through
their minds!"

"The odds are against it happening." he says. "Them
getting sick too. If that's what you're thinking. He would
probably have sprouted symptoms by now. And the theory
that it's catching…that whole approach…is highly
speculative still. So the chances are slim that either one of
them will be ill…."

"Please, Steven. Don't ever say that again! I can't
hear…anything like that! Nothing like that had crossed my
mind!"

What had crossed her mind? That Homer was very sick?
That they were thinking that too, and distraught? That other
thing, the thing that Steven said, was unthinkable.

"I'm so sorry," Steven says, taking her hand. What could
he say to ease her mind?

I will swallow a bottle of aspirin, she thinks, if anything
happened to them. Or drown myself. From her childhood,
she knows just the spot, between Foggy Bottom and the
bridge to Arlington, where swift currents and monstrous
rocks hide under the Potomac's calm surface.


When he was younger, Tony doubted he'd ever come here, or
if he did, he imagined it would be with his mother and Lily.
All three of them entering the dark realm together. The incline
into the earth, the dark rock, the miserable flowers, the crying
faces. Every image he ever saw or imagined scared the hell
out of him, and he swore he would never do this, certainly
not alone.

It is almost seven o'clock but there are still some families
going down and coming up. He is the only one walking by
himself, but he coaches himself to ignore the empty spaces
beside him, the hollow sensation inside him. Very soon he'll
be with *him*!

He had always thought this was bullshit. He remembers

a news show when it first opened. A kid about his age was coming out and the reporter asked him how he felt.

Funny...because I never knew my father.

The reporter said, But funny-*good* because you got to know him a little today? Right?

The kid shrugged. His mother nudged him.

I talked to him, the boy said.

What did you say?

Another shrug.

He told his father he knew he was happy in heaven...and that he was proud of him, the mother said.

He hated those shows. He'd yell to the reporters on the screen, Mind your own business. And to the families, You don't have to answer if you don't want to. Don't answer. But they always did and it was the same crap, recycled show after show: I told him I loved him....He told me he loved me....I got closure.

He remembers they asked Mimi what closure was. It sounded like the dead closed you out, or you got to close them out, like in a game when someone calls out, "gates are closed."

It means it's behind you, his mother said.

Good behind you like you don't have to worry, or behind you like it's following you close behind and could pounce? he had asked.

It means you have peace, Lily said. They're close but in a nice gentle way, not that old scary way when you feel like you're squeezed beside them in a coffin and you could hardly breathe....

Lily loved those news shows. She liked magical mush with happy endings, not hopeless dreams of being buried alive with her father. She started saving up so they could come here for closure. She also had this crazy idea about a special section for men like Ronnie. MAA men....Missing After Action...or something like that. The MIAs got to be included, so why not the MAAs! She started writing letters;

then, when no one answered, she lobbied to come here to sign up other families. But that was years ago. Now she'd probably forgotten, and here *he* was.

"I'm at peace," a middle-aged man says and the woman walking beside him, back up towards the street, says, "Because I felt he was at peace...."

Tony feels old revulsion churn in his gut. But he feels his heart flip too—just like it used to when he thought about making the journey. *Peace* and *heaven* and *happy*—he had no use for that. Because he had his own conjuring tricks to bring his father back?

With Lily and Homer in his life, he had pretty much given up the habit of talking to his father. But then in the desert, he found himself turning to him again. With death all around, panic would seize him, and he'd say, How do I know I'm not next? Day after day, he'd imagine his father's voice saying, Remember, I died so you won't. Remember the drill? And Tony would trek through the fields of bodies, his father's voice comforting him.

Then he's there.

It is solemn, like a church, with flickering candle light. Someone is singing a lullaby, and someone is calling, Love you, love you, love you. Does he really want to do this? He looks back at the street, the thick, dark fog, then marches toward the Wall.


"Foggy Bottom." Sean reads the sign.

"I know," Lily says, taking the exit.

She wishes Sean would just shut up. She knows she's not being fair—he was an angel. But he was really getting on her nerves. He felt like a parody of her. Can-do cheerful 24/7. The perfect cake, flowers, lights. Had she spent less time the last few days with him and all their perfect plans, and more time with Tony, she might have observed critical signs and signals!

"Why Foggy Bottom?" Sean says. "That's a strange name. What's there?"

Were Tony with her and not Sean and everything was still okay, she wouldn't have to explain a thing. She'd say, *Farty* Bottom. Ha ha. Remember we used to call it that? Remember Mimi would say, There's so much to see at Foggy Bottom. She'd rattle off every memorial and museum up and down the mall, and they'd say, No way we're going to that scary Wall or anywhere near that stinky old Farty Bottom.

After a while she did want to go but he didn't and then life got too busy. Now life had turned too terrible. He told the weird guy to tell her he was going to see his father. Which she hopes means the Wall. And nothing more.

"You're speeding," Sean says.

"Tell me something I don't know," she snaps.

There is another place, a spot in the river just south of the Wall and the Mall and the Tidal basin, where Mimi had said she'd lost a friend when she was young. Showing off, he had climbed on another boy's shoulders, dived in, and hit his head on a rock. They were never to dive into waters whose depth they were uncertain of. It haunted them, the idea of quick annihilation. And growing up, when things looked bleak, they'd say it was "dive-time." Dive-time. See his father. A quick dive and he'd see him forever?

The promontory is just ahead and she guides the car to it. A couple of guys in high-heeled pumps are leaning against a parapet, smooching.

"Can I ask you how long you've been here?" she says.

They laugh. "About an hour....Though time flies when you're having fun....Maybe longer."

"Seen anything strange?"

"We're strange...but that's about it. Why, Sweetheart?"

"Too long to explain," she laughs, relieved.

Tony walks along the early years slowly as if to slow down time itself, for now that he's at the actual Wall, everything is racing. His father's year—1970—is right ahead, but he stops and leans against 1969. To pass the time until he feels steadier, he inventories all he knows about 1969.

His parents married in 1969. He was conceived in 1969. His maternal grandmother moved to Florida in 1969 and his mother rented the little house on Barberry.

1969. It had always been his favorite year, and he remembers, when he was in high school, and his history teacher told them to pick a year in the last two decades and get to know it through the reporter's questions—Who, what, where, why, when, how—there was no question what year to choose. 1969. It had always seemed to him a personal Eden, the time when his whole life lay ahead of him and his parents still faced a future together. Every detail he found about the year thrilled him—the first men on the moon, the Woodstock Festival, the start of Sesame Street and the Jackson 5. Except for Micky Mantle's retirement and Nixon's inauguration, he felt so happy with everything he discovered about 1969, which many had believed was the year the war would finally end. For years, when he was low or scared, he'd think, 1969...1969...and feel shored up. And here he was *leaning* on the year again, his back against the black stone, gathering the courage to move on.

Then quickly, efficiently, marine-like, he's moving ahead toward the columns of 1970. And then he's there at *his* section, and then staring at his name, chiseled in the black stone. Up and down the Wall are flowers, candles, photos, food, trinkets, but he hasn't planned on coming and so has brought nothing to lay before the name of his father.

Even in his ragged despair, he feels shy, and though everywhere people are calling to their dead, with strangers all around, he can't speak. Besides suddenly he's not sure what he came here to say. When he was little, and something troubled him and he wanted his father's comfort, but didn't know where to start, he'd write him letters, which dislodged the fears and doubts clinging to the bottom of his mind. He'd place the letters on his bed and run from the room, feeling instant relief, believing his father would read his every word and understand and later help him.

He finds his notebook and a pen in his backpack, and sits down, leaning against the Wall. He began most of those letters back then with the same words, and he writes them now.

*Daddy, I'm afraid,* he writes.

*The doctor says Homer's looking better, but I'm afraid he'll never get well.*

*And the baby. They say the hole in her heart is shrinking. But what if...?*

*Leo looks like shit and talks like a madman. What if he dies? What if he doesn't and does something crazy?*

*It's too late to be scared for Einstein. He was such a bud. Such a cool bud. Smart, honorable. He didn't have to die. Maybe I could have helped him. I'm afraid that's the truth.*

*The men on Homer's ward, and all the others all over who the brass are telling to shape up or ship out, I'm so scared for them.*

*I think I killed Roco when I let him sleep on my bed and I was sweating out all that desert shit. And maybe Ernie killed the cat. And that girl. Where is she? Mary?*

Can he say the rest? The thing he's most afraid of?

That he'd come down with the Rot?

And then Lily would catch it from him?

And if they had a baby, it could come out fucked up with eyes where it should have ears, and legs where arms should go, and vice versa? So many stories like that were going around on Homer's ward.

He couldn't let that happen.

*What should I do?* he writes.

"What should I do?" he whispers.

He sits against the Wall, waiting. When was the last time his father came to help him?

Steady, boy, steady. It's war and someone has to die, he'd said.

It was at the edge of the highway, he thinks now.

But not my son. I'm watching over you and all your buddies. You'll all get home. You'll all be fine.

How can you be sure? he asked his father. It looked like the world was ending.

His father said, Have I ever let you down? I won't ever let you down.

Now his father says nothing. He sees his name chiseled in the black marble with the names of the other dead. The dead don't hear, or read, or speak. He sees his own face in the black stone, shiny with tears, and he cradles it in his hands. When he can lift his head without crying, he crosses out his father's name and writes her name.

Everything else he's written he leaves for her to read to help her understand.

It's so clear suddenly what he has to do. So clear and so terrible.

*I've never felt sadder in my life, Lily. But I've never felt surer,* he writes.

*I'm doing it for you.*

*So that you get to live your life...all the way through.*

*With all the things you deserve. All the beautiful phases you deserve.*

*A long healthy life. Children. Healthy children.*

*I don't care what happens to me.*

*Midge, Associate, Fur, Pony, Pup....* He writes all the things he's called her. And then, *Lily, Goodbye.* He closes the notebook and writes her name on the cover. And then, *Please understand.*

The base of the wall is heaped with offerings, but between a strawberry shortcake and a Paddington bear, he manages to find a space to lean the notebook. When she read the note saying he'd gone to see his father, she'd come here and find the notebook with her name. And understand. And maybe forgive.

In the falling light, from fifty feet away, Lily makes him out. The way his chin rests on his chest, his fingers grasp the pen, his eyes devour the page signal across the evening sky, It's me, Tony, and no one else in the whole wide world. He lifts his eyes from the page and closes them tight, and his head begins to bob, which tells her that he has begun to cry. And her relief and joy swell even more. She had found him, safe and sound, doing what he needed to be doing. Tears were essential; without them you could never float to the far shore of acceptance.

What was he writing in the notebook? A letter to his father about that highway, the one he shouts about from his sleep some nights? Highway at the end of the war? Highway at the end of the world? He's told her nothing so it would be good if he shared it with someone. Or was he telling his dad about Homer and Ernie Polanco? All that they'd been through? That would be so valuable too. He looks so worried lately, and she wants all the toxic dread inside him washed out. Old wounds had to drain first before they closed up and gave you closure.

She wants to give him all the time he needs for his private time with Henry. She will wait till he's done writing to go up to him and give him a big, big hug and tell him how proud she is of him. She hates wasting time, and she searches for some paper in her bag to make some jottings. .

Things to do today. Tomorrow. Next week. There was so much she needed to get going. She'd make one for herself and one for him. She doesn't want to be pushy but she knows he needs her support and direction. She'd mark things *T* for teaching, *V* for her veterinarian future, *H* for helping with

Homer, Nancy, and baby, *W* for wedding, delayed perhaps, and far different than planned, but a wedding all the same. Two lives overlapping like doilies.

She can find no paper, which is actually just as well. This was no time to stop and jot. Driving home to the valley, the past in place behind them, they could strategize. Life was full of surprises. Which meant you had to revise your road map. But it did not mean give up. She'd share her perspective with him, and he'd feel better. He looked terrible when she poked her head out the door and saw him down the hall, talking with the crazy-looking Leo who'd handed her the note later on. Totally terrible—pale and tired and hopeless. He needed a transfusion of her energy and optimism. Come here, she'd say. She'd put her tongue way down him. There. All better, she'd say.

She looks up to see if he is done. But he's not where he was.

"Ton, Ton," she calls, walking up and down the length of the Wall, but there's no sign of him.

She races up to the street, but, except for a few sniffling strangers, it's empty. Down the longest block, the foggiest and longest block she's ever seen, and then around the windiest corner, she runs. They'd always planned on coming here together, and what a shame it would be if, after all these years, they ended up here alone, like they were lonely people with no one to share their closure on the past with or their opening of the future. He made sure she knew his plans so she doubts he wouldn't wait till she showed up, but it's true that by the time that wacko in the wheelchair gave her his message, a good half hour had passed and it was getting late, so he may have thought she wasn't coming at all and decided to go back to Mimi's and wait for her there.

She walks briskly, down another block and around another corner. Then another block and then another. Then there he is, leaning against the wall, his head in his hands.

"Ton, what are you doing," she calls, galloping toward

him. Sometimes he forgot where he parked the car, which upset him. "Don't be so hard on yourself."

He looks up. "Try to understand."

"Understand what?"

"Why I'm doing what I'm doing."

"What are you doing? Wait, tell me in the car. Let's go find the car together. You can't sweat the small things."

"The car's around the corner," he says. "Didn't you see the notebook? Didn't you read what I wrote?"

"I saw you writing in your notebook. I figured it was a letter to your father. And very private. So I wouldn't have read it even if I'd seen it up close, which I did not."

"I wrote *you* a letter. I told you...."

He hadn't intended to have to say it. And now face to face with her, he thinks he'll faint if he has to say it to her face.

"I told you why...because I could get sick and then...."

"You're not sick. You are so not sick....And you're not getting sick." No matter what happened in the Gulf, he was with her now, and she'd make sure that nothing harmed him. Not now. Not ever. "I'm sure of that." she says.

"You can't know that for sure. Maybe you're right, but maybe you're wrong," he says. "And if I got sick...and then made you sick...."

"You totally won't. Stop saying all these crazy things. Why are you saying these things?"

"I couldn't live with knowing I'd harmed you. When I had a choice....When there was something I could do to protect you...," he says. "When I could...go away," he whispers.

"Go away? To protect me? You want to protect me? Then stop talking. You can't leave. I don't want to live without you....End of story....And I'm not going to die till I'm old. And neither are you. I can put it in writing if that will make you feel better! I, Lily Dawn Engels, promise to live till the ripe old age of....one hundred and...fifteen and Anthony

Bravo will too...."

She's giggling, which always made him laugh. Today he can't, imagining life without her in it. A long, dark tunnel, without a speck of light or laughter. Where would he go? What would he do?

"I don't want to go away," he says.

"You don't have to, silly. You can't, actually. And not just because of me. You have to start teaching!"

He shakes his head. "They wrote me a letter....They rescinded the contract....They don't like my *perspective*...."

She clasps her arms around him and burrows into him, saying nothing, remembering the day she went to the school and pushed her way into the office. She hated that man so much. She'd misjudged him so bad. It was all her fault that Tony ended up in the clutches of that beast.

"Lily."

His voice is thick, from trying not to cry, she knows.

"Let's not cry," she says. "Let's not cry. Let's put our heads together."

Their heads *were* together—he'd lain his head on the top of her head, which she'd rested on his heart. She feels his tears dampening her hair.

"Don't cry, don't cry," she coos, looking up at him. "You'll see. A hundred schools will be glad to have Anthony Bravo's perspective. Anthony Bravo's war...and peace curriculum! You just have to get home ASAP to start sending out your resumé. You have to rest up and go round to schools....Practice for interviews. Oh my God, we have so much to do!"

"Lily," he says, "Listen."

"No, you listen. I know it's hard. But we've gotten through so much worse....Like real war," she says. "Not just teaching about war...or...not teaching. Losing one job when there are a million other teaching opportunities...."

"Listen," he says. "You have to listen....You're not listening....I have to do this....I don't want to but it's the only way I can be sure….By going….I'm going."

If she looked into his eyes, it would probably change his mind. "Look at me," she says. "Look at me." She tries to catch his gaze, but he's looking at the ground.

"I can't," he cries. "I can't stay. I can't…."

"Look at me," she tries again.

He turns away, studying the traffic light.

His face and body are stiff, tensing for action. When the light turns red, she knows, he will fly away.

"No, Tony. No, Tony!" she cries.

Each time she realized that someone she loved would or might soon be gone forever—her father, her mother, Homer that last day in the valley—she'd flung herself down on the ground, half hoping she'd crack her head and die. Now, she wants to hurl herself onto the pavement, or gutter, or the marble stairs beckoning across the street. She pushes him away and begins to run.

"Lily, where are you going? What are you doing?"

"You're not the only one who can go away forever. See how it feels when someone leaves *you* forever!"


For years, Mimi has wanted to come here with the children, but then one or both of them would get too scared. She wanted to come alone the first week she was in Washington, but when she found the time, she didn't have the energy. For just imagining the black wall, for even a moment, has always shaken her; actually seeing it, she knew, would knock her out for days. Now she feels like she's on steroids as she flies down the length of the Wall and back, mindless of the black stone or her dead husband, thinking only of the children. Where could they be?

She'd left Steven in his car on Constitution Avenue, stuck behind a truck, and she'd made it here on foot, following Lily's car as fast and as far as she could. And then she'd seen her car parked on E Street and then Tony's van parked on F.

They had probably run into each other and gone for coffee or a walk along the mall. Mobilizing for their visit here.

Alongside the date of his death, Henry's *address* here is etched in her mind. Maybe they were standing there all along and she just missed them. Quickly she finds his column. But no one's there.

She hadn't come here now for Henry, but seeing his row, and then his name, half way up the wall, she finds herself touching it, tracing the cold hollow of the chiseled letters. She braces herself for the pure pain she always expected to find here, a knife ripping her open, to chisel her heart.

Love you baby, love you darling! she wants to call to him, as she called to him that day up on the mountain when their son came back! But she's too worried to say a thing.

She turns and prowls the Wall again, then returns to Henry's spot. If she waited a few minutes, they'd probably appear. She is tired from racing around, and she sits, leaning on Henry's patch of wall. She has always imagined sitting here, when she finally came, leaning her head against the wall, just as she is now. And talking to him just as she used to. But again she can't speak.

Where were they? *I'm here. Can you see me?* She remembers her son's breathy child's whisper....*Can you see me in the dark, Daddy?* Night after night, on the other side of the wall, he'd sit in his bed, pouring out his heart to Henry. He was scared, his dad was brave, how did he get that way, did he think that one day if he tried really hard he could be just like him?

He didn't want to fight, darling, she told him once, when she heard him late one night, and found him marching around his room, his soup-pot helmet on his head, his broom-rifle in his arms. Your daddy didn't want to fight...or die, darling.

But he wasn't *afraid*, Tony cried, crumbling in her arms, then pushing her away.

She stands to scan the Wall one more time. It was too dark and too foggy to see anything. What if they can't see the traffic lights, or the curb…?

If anything happens, she thinks.

On their own, it seems, her hands pound the wall, and she calls to him, "If anything happens….If he gets sick too…I will never forgive you…."

A young man lying still on the ground, a woman and child lying beside him. The image grips her. Homer and Nancy and Abigail? Tony and Lily and *their* child?

"If anyone dies, I will kill you!" she shouts.

Soon her voice is too weak to yell, her hands too tired to pound. Her fingers are swelling, and she works off her wedding ring while she can. And then because she's chipped the turquoise heart embedded in the silver band and could never bear to look at it again, or at the Wall, or at his name, she bends to leave it on the ground.

She registers her name first, LILY DAWN ENGELS, and then the fact that it's written in her son's hasty schoolboy print, on the front of his green college notebook. Her keychain has a mini-light on it, and she finds it in her pocket and starts to read. Then flies up to the street.

Up and down the block, around the windiest corner, up and down the next block and the next, she runs, calling his name. Was Lily with him? Had she found him? Were they somewhere together?

"Tony…Lily," she calls.

When they were little, when she'd play hide and seek with them, neither of them ever finished the game. Afraid they'd never be found, they'd emerge from their hiding places, calling, Here I am, or, because they often hid together, Here we are…don't worry. She wishes they were still scared little kids, flying to her open arms. Not young adults doing God knows what!

Walking down the street, she tries to mask her rising panic as she calls to them in the dark. When they were young, but old enough for some independence, and late coming home from playing or school, dread would always seize her, but she'd try for a carefree call so as not to scare them off. For hearing panic, she knew, they would linger at the end of the street knowing that her anxious cries always morphed, at the sight of them, into furious shouts.

She sees Steven's car parked a few cars behind Lily's. Maybe Steven had found Sean on the street, and now they were both down at the Wall, expecting to find her and the kids. She hopes they come up soon to help her search. It's hard to see in the dark.

"Lily," Tony calls, and races across the street. "Please, Lily, stop."

She takes the marble steps two by two. Then turns around to assess the distance to the bottom. Hardly a minute before, across the street, nothing had made any sense to her except flying up the steps, then crashing onto the walkway below. But now he's down there, looking up at her. Does he mean to stay? Or just to talk his crazy talk some more, then go?

"Lily, please," he calls. "Stop."

"Why? Why should I? If you're sick, you're sick. But you're not and I'm not. Which doesn't matter anymore. You're leaving, aren't you? Go. I don't know who you are anymore."

"Don't say that. You know me better than anyone. All I want to do is make the right decision, for once in my life. To protect you. That's all I want. That's all I've ever wanted. Don't you know that?"

He darts across the street, shouting up at her. If he keeps talking, she'll listen. If he asks her questions, she'll have to answer. What was it they used to say to each other to prove they'd told the truth. Cross my heart and hope to die…. "Remember, Lily? Cross my heart?"

"All I remember is that you have no heart," she cries. "And you've broken mine."

"Don't say that!" he says. "You have my heart….You know that, don't you?"

He flies up the steps, and lifts her in his arms.

"Put me down. If you're only going to leave me, put me down this second."

She roars like a lion, but in his arms now, she feels smaller and lighter than ever. Like a doll or a puppy. Like Lemon, their cat that last day. Put her down. Lily had cried that—that day too! It's time to say goodbye. She's going to cat heaven....She's okay. Put her down. But he couldn't.

"Put me down!"

If he hadn't held her, maybe he could have explained things again. Then turned and left.

"I can't...," he says "I can't ...put you down.... I can't...."

"Can't *now*. But later you will? Tell me...tell me...tell me....Later, you'll put me down and leave me just like that?"

Why did she want him? "What can I give you?"

It's hard for her to form the words. For she's begun to weep, big yelps of fury and pain. *I me you*. That's what it sounds like when she says what she's never said to him—or anyone—before.

"I need you! I need you! I need you!"

Why did he make her say that? Couldn't he see that she felt so weighed down with worry. Abby was a miracle child with a magical future! She maintained that every waking hour—to help Nancy through her days and nights. But Mimi's eyes had made clear that the baby would need lots of care. And so would Homer! Even if all his symptoms lifted, he might never be who he'd been. Who was going to help Nancy if not her! Mimi was strong, but when she thought no one was looking, her face collapsed and she looked a hundred years old. And Steven. He did so much for them, but she'd seen how he had begun to need *them*, not for anything in particular, but to be nearby, making their friendly, family sounds and jokes.

"And you want to leave me! How could you leave me! Everyone needs you.... How could you...!"

"I can't. I won't," he says.

"Homcr. Einstcin…wc all nccd you."

"Einstein…died," he says. "Einstein died….That's why…."

He wants to tell her about the cat and the girl, but he can't.

"Something else?" she says. "Someone else…caught it?"

He shrugs. Maybe.

"If you got it, you got it. If I caught it, I caught it. But I refuse to believe anything bad's going to happen to us! I just refuse!"

From the marble landing, she makes out a slice of park wedged between this building and the next. She leads him down the steps and around a wall of evergreens.

"Come," she says. "Over there. Behind the trees." She needs to hold him.

"Lie down," she says. And when he does, she lies on top of him. The beat of his heart against her chest, the breeze of his breath on her neck comfort her. Like the first night he was back, when he told her about the war, the bombs, the dead, she licks his tears again and again till they almost stop.

His eyes begin to close. He could lie in her arms forever. Here, in this secret tent of green. Hidden from harm.

Below them, the lights from monuments and bridges pierce the dark, foggy night. There's no Washington, no Arlington, Lily thinks, no endless stretch of black leading to Monuten, but only this place. The bridges are glittering galaxies, and the columns of light are beams of a full silver moon. And in this spot at the edge of the world, there's only them.

Forever and ever.

Blood children.

Forever and ever.

She covers them with his old red baseball jacket. For suddenly it feels so cold.

Between twin Doric-columned buildings up ahead, Mimi sees a sliver of park with thick hedges. They used to hide behind the boxwood hedge in the backyard. It's hemlock, she sees as she comes closer, a thick wall of hemlock. Or maybe fir? It's too dark to tell. She lifts a branch to see to the other side. Does she just imagine two figures stretched on the ground? And a splash of dark red? Blood? she thinks, running to the end of the hedge and into the hidden garden.

It's a moonless night, but the lights from the monuments light the sky enough for Mimi to make out her blonde braid and her twig-thin legs. Lily, without a doubt. And the red puddle is not blood but a jacket, she can see, her son's scarlet satin baseball jacket. But where was her son?

She hears him, she thinks, his snore, or is it the rustling of leaves? She finds her little flashlight and in the second it takes for the light to come on and her eyes to adjust, she feels her fate hang. Alive or dead. Them and her. It was very simple. That spot in the river was not very far.

The small light reveals them both, her back, his chest, their entwined arms rising and falling with deep steady breaths, their nostrils floating misty plumes into the autumn air. She kneels beside them and bends to double-check, hearing their hearts beating like young hearts are supposed to.

She sits down beside them. How many nights had she sat in the dark beside them, the steady rhythm of their breath soothing her mind like the tide. Wake up, darlings, she knows she should say. But they look so pale and worn and a few minutes more couldn't hurt.

She remembers an old lullaby, a home-made favorite they concocted together in the dark, her beginning and the children finishing each line. The *Rest* Song, the children called it, hating even the word *sleep*.

Rest, darlings, rest…? Wasn't that how she began it?
*Rest, darlings, rest,* she'd sung….

*And we'll wake our very best,* one of them had added.

Then, *Sweet dreams to you...and I wish all our dreams come true.*

*Dream, darlings, dream...of fudge and ice cream.*

*Of days happy and bright...where no one would fight.*

*Dream of favorite friends and things...flying to us on glittery wings.*

*Favorite thoughts and favorite tales...like being strong...like my blue field.*

*Rest a while, dear boy and girl... rest then we'll wake up in a beautiful world.*

Wake up, darlings. In a minute she will whisper that in their ears, and tell them it's late and time to go back home. But just one minute more to watch their certain breaths, and their sealed eyes flutter with dreams.

*For more than a decade after the 1991 Gulf War, the U.S. government maintained that the symptoms exhibited by Gulf War veterans were not consistent with any physical illness that could be related to their military service. Though a third of Desert Storm veterans had reported disabling ailments ranging from memory loss to paralysis to cancer, and an estimated 11,000 had died, the Department of Defense insisted that stress alone could explain such a vast array of symptoms. In 2002, the Research Advisory Committee on Gulf War Illness, a congressionally mandated scientific panel, undertook review of the mounting scientific data, and in 2004 the Committee reported that many veterans of Desert Storm have long-term, multi-symptom illnesses consistent with exposures to wartime neurotoxins including sarin, PB, pesticides, and combinations of these. The impact of vaccines, depleted uranium dust, and oil fire smoke warranted continued attention, the Committee said, as did the illness of veterans' family members including children with birth defects. In November 2008, the Research Advisory Committee issued a new report that "leaves no doubt" of a causal connection between toxins and Gulf War Illness, presenting comprehensive and current findings.*

*The Committee's report does not lay to rest the matter of today's veterans and war-related illness. For every soldier who has died in the present war in Afghanistan and Iraq, eight have been evacuated for injury or illness. To date, over 300,000 veterans have been treated for wounds, loss of limbs, traumatic brain injury, and other illnesses including respiratory, neurological, urological, dermatological, and psychiatric conditions, ALS, and cancers. Forty-two percent of the veteran patients are diagnosed with a mental health disorder and twenty-two percent with PTSD; but the overlap of organic and psychiatric disorders has not yet been determined.*

*In the decade after the first Gulf War, the health of Iraqis deteriorated dramatically with birth defects increased three-fold, cancer rates five-fold, childhood cancers up seven-fold from the pre-war levels, and childhood deaths from war- and sanction-related illness estimated at half a million. Since the 2003 invasion, the situation has worsened, with more cases of malnutrition, malignancy, infant mortality, birth defects, and infectious disease. The full nature and scope of the environmental and health calamity in Iraq will take years to determine. A hundred novels could only begin to convey the losses and suffering of the Iraqi people from recent wars on their soil.*

Curbstone Press, Inc.
is a nonprofit publishing house dedicated to multicultural literature
that reflects a commitment to social awareness and change, with an
emphasis on contemporary writing from Latino, Latin American,
and Vietnamese cultures.

Curbstone's mission focuses on publishing creative writers whose work
promotes human rights and intercultural understanding, and on
bringing these writers and the issues they illuminate into the
community. Curbstone builds bridges between its writers and the
public—from inner-city to rural areas, colleges to cultural centers,
children to adults, with a particular interest in underfunded public
schools. This involves enriching school curricula, reaching out to
underserved audiences by donating books and conducting readings
and educational programs, and promoting discussion in the media.
It is only through these combined efforts that literature can truly
make a difference.

Curbstone Press, like all non-profit presses, relies heavily on the
support of individuals, foundations, and government agencies to bring
you, the reader, works of literary merit and social significance that
would likely not find a place in profit-driven publishing channels, and
to bring these authors and their books into communities across
the country.

If you wish to become a supporter of a specific book—one that is
already published or one that is about to be published—your
contribution will support not only the book's publication but also its
continuation through reprints.

We invite you to support Curbstone's efforts to present the diverse
voices and views that make our culture richer, and to bring these
writers into schools and public places across the country.
Tax-deductible donations can be made to:
Curbstone Press, 321 Jackson Street, Willimantic, CT 06226
phone: (860) 423-5110  fax: (860) 423-9242
www.curbstone.org